TERRY BROOKS

The TALISMANS of SHANNARA

Book Four of THE HERITAGE OF SHANNARA

www.orbitbooks.net

ORBIT

First published in the USA in 1993 by The Ballantine Publishing Group,
a division of Random House, Inc.
First published in Great Britain by Random House UK Limited 1993
Reprinted by Orbit 1998, 1999, 2000, 2001, 2002, 2003, 2005
This edition published in 2006 by Orbit
Reprinted 2009, 2011, 2013, 2014

A CIP catalogue record for this book
is available from the British Library.

ISBN 978-1-84149-554-5

Typeset by Hewer Text UK Ltd, Edinburgh
Printed and bound in Great Britain by
Clays Ltd, St Ives plc

Papers used by Orbit are from well-managed forests
and other responsible sources.

MIX
Paper from
responsible sources
FSC® C104740

Orbit
An imprint of
Little, Brown Book Group
100 Victoria Embankment
London EC4Y 0DY

An Hachette UK Company
www.hachette.co.uk

www.orbitbooks.net

A writer since high school, **Terry Brooks** published his first novel, *The Sword of Shannara*, in 1977. It became the first work of fiction ever to appear on *The New York Times* Trade paperback bestseller list, where it remained for more than five months. He has published numerous bestselling novels since.

A practising attorney for many years, Terry Brooks now writes full time and lives with his wife, Judine, in the Pacific Northwest and Hawaii. For more information go to www.terrybrooks.net

Find out more about Terry Brooks and other Orbit authors by registering for the free monthly newsletter at www.orbitbooks.net

By Terry Brooks

SHANNARA
First King of Shannara
The Sword of Shannara
The Elfstones of Shannara
The Wishsong of Shannara

Dark Wraith of Shannara

THE HERITAGE OF SHANNARA
The Scions of Shannara
The Druid of Shannara
The Elf Queen of Shannara
The Talismans of Shannara

DARK LEGACY OF SHANNARA
Wards of Faerie
Bloodfire Quest
Witch Wraith

DEFENDERS OF SHANNARA
The High Druid's Blade

THE MAGIC KINGDOM OF LANDOVER
Magic Kingdom for Sale – Sold!
The Black Unicorn
Wizard at Large
The Tangle Box
Witches' Brew

THE WORD AND THE VOID
Running with the Demon
A Knight of the Word
Angel Fire East

GENESIS OF SHANNARA
Armageddon's Children
The Elves of Cintra
The Gypsy Morph

LEGENDS OF SHANNARA
Bearers of the Black Staff
The Making of the Magic

OMNIBUS EDITIONS
The Sword of Shannara Trilogy
The Heritage of Shannara Omnibus
The Word and the Void Omnibus

For all my friends at Del Rey Books
Then and now
What a time we've had!

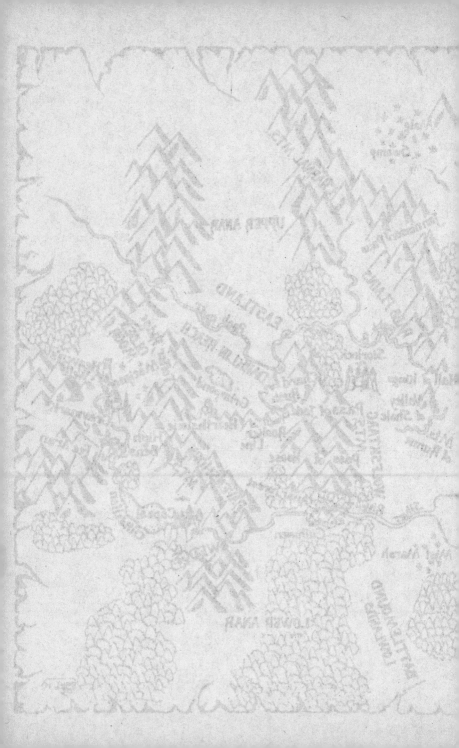

1

Dusk settled down about the Four Lands, a slow graying of light, a gradual lengthening of shadows. The swelter of the late summer's day began to fade as the sun's red fireball sank into the west and the hot, stale air cooled. The hush that comes with day's end stilled the earth, and leaves and grass shivered with expectation at the coming of night.

At the mouth of the Mermidon where it emptied into the Rainbow Lake, Southwatch rose blackly, impenetrable and voiceless. The wind brushed the waters of the lake and river, yet did not approach the obelisk, as if anxious to hurry on to some place more inviting. The air shimmered about the dark tower, heat radiating from its stone in waves, forming spectral images that darted and flew. A solitary hunter at the water's edge glanced up apprehensively as he passed and continued swiftly on.

Within, the Shadowen went about their tasks in ghostly silence, cowled and faceless and filled with purpose.

Rimmer Dall stood at a window looking out on the darkening countryside, watching the color fade from the earth as the night crept stealthily out of the east to gather in its own.

The night, our mother, our comfort.

He stood with his hands clasped behind his back, rigid

1

within his dark robes, cowl pulled back from his rawboned, red-bearded face. He looked hard and empty of feeling, and had he cared he would have been pleased. But it had been a long time since his appearance had mattered to the First Seeker – a long time since he had bothered even to wonder. His outside was of no consequence; he could be anything he chose. What burned within mattered. That gave him life.

His eyes glittered as he looked beyond what he was seeing to what one day would be.

To what was promised.

He shifted slightly, alone with his thoughts in the tower's silence. The others did not exist for him, wraiths without substance. Below, deep within the bowels of the tower, he could hear the sounds of the magic at work, the deep hum of its breathing, the rumble of its heart. He listened for it without thinking now, a habit that brought reassurance to his troubled mind. The power was theirs, brought from the ether into substance, given shape and form, lent purpose. It was the gift of the Shadowen, and it belonged to them alone.

Druids and others notwithstanding.

He tried a faint smile, but his mouth refused to put up with it and it disappeared in the tight line of his lips. His gloved left hand squirmed within the clasp of the bare fingers of his right. Power for power, strength for strength. On his breast, the silver wolf's-head insignia glittered.

Thrum, thrum, came the sound of the magic working down below.

Rimmer Dall turned back into the grayness of the room – a room that until recently had held Coll Ohmsford prisoner. Now the Valeman was gone – escaped, he believed; but let go in fact and made prisoner another way. Gone to find his brother, Par.

The one with the real magic.

The one who would be his.

The First Seeker moved away from the window and seated himself at the bare wooden table, the weight of his big frame causing the spindly chair to creak. His hands folded on the table before him and his craggy face lowered.

All the Ohmsfords were back in the Four Lands, all the scions of Shannara, returned from their quests. Walker Boh had come back from Eldwist despite Pe Ell, the Black Elfstone regained, its magic fathomed, Paranor brought back into the world of men, and Walker himself become the first of the new Druids. Wren Elessedil had come back from Morrowindl with Arborlon and the Elves, the magic of the Elfstones discovered anew, her own identity and heritage revealed. Two out of three of Allanon's charges fulfilled. Two out of three steps taken.

Par's was to be the last, of course. Find the Sword of Shannara. Find the Sword and it will reveal the truth.

Games played by old men and shades, Rimmer Dall mused. Charges and quests, searches for truth. Well, he knew the truth better than they, and the truth was that none of this mattered because in the end the magic was all and the magic belonged to the Shadowen.

It grated on him that despite his efforts to prevent it, both the Elves and Paranor were back. Those he had sent to keep the Shannara scions from succeeding had failed. The price of their failure had been death, but that did little to assuage his annoyance. Perhaps he should have been angry – perhaps even a little worried. But Rimmer Dall was confident in his power, certain of his control over events and time, assured that the future was still his to determine. Though Teel and Pe Ell had disappointed him, there were others who would not.

Thrum, thrum, the magic whispered.

And so . . .

Rimmer Dall's lips pursed. A little time was all that was needed. A little time to let events he had already set in motion follow their course, and then it would be too late for the Druid dead and their schemes. Keep the Dark Uncle and the girl apart. Don't let them share their knowledge. Don't let them join forces.

Don't let them find the Valemen.

What was needed was a distraction, something that would keep them otherwise occupied. Or better still, something that would put an end to them. Armies, of course, to grind down the Elves and the free-born alike, Federation soldiers and Shadowen Creepers and whatever else he could muster to sweep these fools from his life. But something more, something special for the Shannara children with all their magics and Druid charms.

He considered the matter for a long time, the gray twilight changing to night about him. The moon rose in the east, a scythe against the black, and the stars brightened into sharp pinpricks of silver. Their glow penetrated the darkness where the First Seeker sat and transformed his face into a skull.

Yes, he nodded finally.

The Dark Uncle was obsessed with his Druid heritage. Send him something to play against that weakness, something that would confuse and frustrate him. Send him the Four Horsemen.

And the girl. Wren Elessedil had lost her protector and adviser. Give her someone to fill that void. Give her one of his own choosing, one who would soothe and comfort her, who would ease her fears, then betray her and strip her of everything.

The others were no serious threat – not even the leader of the free-born and the Highlander. They could do nothing without the Ohmsford heirs. If the Dark Uncle was imprisoned in his Keep and the Elf Queen's brief reign ended, the Druid shade's carefully constructed plans would collapse about him. Allanon would sink back into the Hadeshorn with the rest of his ghost kin, consigned to the past where he belonged.

Yes, the others were insignificant.

But he would deal with them anyway.

And even if all his efforts failed, even if he could do nothing more than chase them about, harry them as a dog would its prey, still that would be sufficient if in the end Par Ohmsford's soul fell to him. He needed only that to put an end to all of the hopes of his enemies. Only that. It was a short walk to the precipice, and the Valeman was already moving toward it. His brother would be the staked goat that would bring him, that would draw him like a wolf at hunt. Coll Ohmsford was deep under the spell of the Mirrorshroud by now, a slave to the magic from which the cloak was formed. He had stolen it to disguise himself, never guessing that Rimmer Dall had intended as much, never suspecting that it was a deadly snare to turn him to the First Seeker's own grim purpose. Coll Ohmsford would hunt his brother down and force a confrontation. He would do so because the cloak would let him do nothing less, settling a madness within him that only his brother's death could assuage. Par would be forced to fight. And because he lacked the magic of the Sword of Shannara, because his conventional weapons would not be enough to stop the Shadowen-kind his brother had become, and because he would be terrified that this was yet another trick, he would use the wishsong's magic.

Perhaps he would kill his own brother, but this time kill him in truth, and then discover – when it was too late to change things back – what he had done.

And perhaps not. Perhaps he would let his brother escape – and be led to his doom.

The First Seeker shrugged. Either way, the result would be the same. Either way the Valeman was finished. Use of the magic and the series of shocks that would surely result from doing so would unbalance him. It would free the magic from his control and let him become Rimmer Dall's tool. Rimmer Dall was certain of it. He could be so because unlike the Shannara scions and their mentor he understood the Elven magic, his magic by blood and right. He understood what it was and how it worked. He knew what Par did not – what was happening to the wishsong, why it behaved as it did, how it had slipped its leash to become a wild thing that hunted as it chose.

Par was close. He was very close.

The danger of grappling with the beast is that you will become it.

He was almost one of them.

Soon it would happen.

There was, of course, the possibility that the Valeman would discover the truth about the Sword of Shannara before then. Was the weapon he carried, the one Rimmer Dall had given up so easily, the talisman he sought or a fake? Par Ohmsford still didn't know. It was a calculated risk that he would not find out. Yet even if he did, what good would it do him? Swords were two-edged and could cut either way. The truth might do Par more harm than good . . .

Rimmer Dall rose and walked again to the window, a shadow in the night's blackness, folded and wrapped against the light. The Druids didn't understand; they never had. Allanon was an anachronism before he had even become what Bremen intended him to be. Druids – they used the magic like fools played with fire: astounded at its possibilities, yet terrified of its risks. No wonder the flames had burned them so often. But that did not prevent them from refusing their mysterious gift. They were so quick to judge others who sought to wield the power – the Shadowen foremost – to see them as the enemy and destroy them.

As they had destroyed themselves.

But there was symmetry and meaning in the Shadowen vision of life, and the magic was no toy with which they played but the heart of who and what they were, embraced, protected, and worshipped. No half measures in which life's accessibility was denied or self-serving cautions issued to assure that none would share in the use. No admonitions or warnings. No games-playing. The Shadowen simply were what the magic would make them, and the magic when accepted so would make them anything.

The tree-tips of the forests and the cliffs of the Runne were dark humps against the flat, silver-laced surface of the Rainbow Lake. Rimmer Dall gazed out upon the world, and he saw what the Druids had never been able to see.

That it belonged to those strong enough to take it, hold it, and shape it. That it was meant to be used.

His eyes burned the color of blood.

It was ironic that the Ohmsfords had served the Druids for so long, carrying out their charges, going on their quests, following their visions to truths that never were. The stories were legend. Shea and Flick, Wil, Brin and Jair, and now Par. It had all been for nothing. But here is where it would end. For Par would serve the Shadowen and by doing so put an end forever to the Ohmsford-Druid ties.

'Par. Par. Par.'

Rimmer Dall whispered his name soothingly to the night. It was a litany that filled his mind with visions of power that nothing could withstand.

For a long time he stood at the window and allowed himself to dream of the future.

Then abruptly he wheeled away and went down into the tower's depths to feed.

2

The cellar beneath the gristmill was thick with shadows, the faint streamers of light let through by gaps in the floorboards disappearing rapidly into twilight. Chased from his safe hole through the empty catacombs, pinned finally against the blocked trapdoor through which he had thought to escape, Par Ohmsford crouched like an animal brought to bay, the Sword of Shannara clutched protectively before him as the intruder who had harried him to this end stopped abruptly and reached up to lower the cowl that hid his face.

'Lad,' a familiar voice whispered. 'It's me.'

The cloak's hood was down about the other's shoulders, and a dark head was laid bare. But still the shadows were too great . . .

The figure stepped forward tentatively, the hand with the long knife lowering. 'Par?'

The intruder's features were caught suddenly in a hazy wash of gray light, and Par exhaled sharply.

'Padishar!' he exclaimed in relief. 'Is it really you?'

The long knife disappeared back beneath the cloak, and the other's laugh was low and unexpected. 'In the flesh. Shades, I thought I'd never find you! I've been searching for days, the whole of Tyrsis end to end, every last hideaway, every burrow, and each time only Federation and Shadowen Seekers waiting!'

He came forward to the bottom of the stairs, smiling broadly, arms outstretched. 'Come here, lad. Let me see you.'

Par lowered the Sword of Shannara and came down the steps in weary gratitude. 'I thought you were . . . I was afraid . . .'

And then Padishar had his arms about him, embracing him, clapping him on the back, and then lifting him off the floor as if he were sackcloth.

'Par Ohmsford!' he greeted, setting the Valeman down finally, hands gripping his shoulders as he held him at arm's length to study him. The familiar smile was bright and careless. He laughed again. 'You look a wreck!'

Par grimaced. 'You don't look so well-kept yourself.' There were scars from battle wounds on the big man's face and neck, new since they had parted. Par shook his head, overwhelmed. 'I guess I knew you had escaped the Pit, but it's good seeing you here to prove it.'

'Hah, there's been a lot happen since then, Valeman, I can tell you that!' Padishar's lank hair was tousled, and the skin about his eyes was dark from lack of sleep. He glanced about. 'You're alone? I didn't expect that. Where's your brother? Where's Damson?'

Par's smile faded. 'Coll . . .' he began and couldn't finish. 'Padishar, I can't . . .' His hands tightened about the Sword of Shannara, as if by doing so he might retrieve the lifeline for which he suddenly found need. 'Damson went out this morning. She hasn't come back.'

Padishar's eyes narrowed. 'Out? Out where, lad?'

'Searching for a way to escape the city. Or in the absence of that, another hiding place. The Federation have found us everywhere. But you know. You've seen them yourself. Padishar, how long have you been looking for us? How did you manage to find this place?'

The big hands fell away. 'Luck, mostly. I tried all the places I thought you might be, the newer ones, the ones Damson had laid out for us during the previous year. This is an old one, five

9

years gone since it was prepared and not used in the last three. I only remembered it after I'd given up on everything else.'

He started suddenly. 'Lad!' he exclaimed, his eyes lighting on the Sword in Par's hands. 'Is that it? The Sword of Shannara? Have you found it, then? How did you get it out of the Pit? Where . . . ?'

But suddenly there was a scuffling of boots on wooden steps from the darkness behind, a clanking of weapons, and a raising of voices. Padishar whirled. The sounds were unmistakable. Armed men were descending the back stairs to the room Par had just vacated, come through the same door that had brought Padishar. Without slowing, they swept into the tunnels beyond, guided by torches that smoked and sputtered brightly in the near black.

Padishar wheeled back, grabbed Par's arm, and dragged him towards the trapdoor. 'Federation. I must have been followed. Or they were watching the mill.'

Par stumbled, trying to pull back. 'Padishar, the door – '

'Patience, lad,' the other cut him short, hauling him bodily to the top of the stairs. 'We'll be out before they reach us.'

He slammed into the door and staggered back, a look of disbelief on his rough face.

'I tried to warn you,' Par hissed, freeing himself, glancing back toward the pursuit. The Sword of Shannara lifted menacingly. 'Is there another way out?'

Padishar's answer was to throw himself against the trapdoor repeatedly, using all of his strength and size to batter through it. The door refused to budge, and while some of its boards cracked and splintered beneath the hammering they did not give way.

'Shades!' the outlaw leader spit.

Federation soldiers emptied out of the passageway into the room. A black-cloaked Seeker led them. They caught sight of Padishar and Par frozen on the trapdoor steps and came for them. Broadsword in one hand, long knife in the other, Padishar wheeled back down the steps to meet the rush.

The first few to reach him were cut down instantly. The rest slowed, turned wary, feinting and lunging cautiously, trying to cripple him from the side. Par stood at his back, thrusting at those who sought to do so. Slowly the two backed their way up the stairs and out of reach so that their attackers were forced to come at them head on.

It was a losing fight. There were twenty if there was one. One good rush and it would be all over.

Par's head bumped sharply against the trapdoor. He turned long enough to shove at it one final time. Still blocked. He felt a well of despair open up inside. They were trapped.

He knew he would have to use the wishsong.

Below, Padishar launched himself at their attackers and drove them back a dozen steps.

Par summoned the magic and felt the music rise to his lips, strangely dark and bitter-tasting. It hadn't been the same since his escape from the Pit. Nothing had. The Federation soldiers rallied in a counterattack that forced Padishar back up the stairs. Sweat gleamed on the outlaw's strong face.

Then abruptly something shifted above and the trapdoor flew open. Par cried out to Padishar, and heedless of anything else they rushed up the steps, through the opening, and into the mill.

Damson Rhee was there, red hair flying out from her cloaked form as she sped toward a gap in the sideboards of the mill wall, calling for them to follow. Dark forms appeared suddenly to block her way, yelling for others. Damson wheeled into them, quick as a cat. Fire sprang from her empty hand, scattering into shards that flew into her attackers' faces. She went spinning through them, the street magic flicking right and left, clearing a path. Par and Padishar raced to follow, howling like madmen. The soldiers tried in vain to regroup. None reached Par. Fighting as if possessed, Padishar killed them where they stood.

Then they were outside on the streets, breathing the humid night air, sweat streaking their faces, breath hissing like steam.

11

Darkness had fallen in a twilight haze of grit and dust that hung thickly in the narrow walled corridors. People ran screaming as Federation soldiers appeared from all directions, shouting and cursing, throwing aside any who stood in their way.

Without a word, Damson charged down an alleyway, leading Padishar and Par into a blackened tunnel stinking of garbage and excrement. Pursuit was instant, but cumbersome. Damson took them through a cross alley and into the side door of a tavern. They pushed through the dimly lit interior, past men hunched over tables and slumped in chairs, around kegs, and past a serving bar, then out the front door.

A shabby, slat-board porch with a low-hanging roof stretched away to either side. The street was deserted.

'Damson, what kept you?' Par hissed at her as they ran. 'That trapdoor . . .'

'My fault, Valeman,' she snapped angrily. 'I blocked the door with some machinery to hide it. I thought it would be safer for you. I was wrong. But I didn't bring the soldiers. They must have found the place on their own. Or followed Padishar.' The big man started to speak, but she cut him short. 'Quick, now. They're coming.'

And from out of the shadows in front and behind them, the dark forms of Federation soldiers poured into the street. Damson spun about, cut back toward the far row of buildings, and took them down an alleyway so tight it was a close squeeze just to pass through. Howls of rage chased after them.

'We have to get back to the Tyrsian Way!' she gasped breathlessly.

They burst through an entry to a market, skidding on food leavings, grappling with bins. A pair of high doors barred their way. Damson struggled futilely to free the latched crossbar, and finally Padishar shattered it completely with a powerful kick.

Soldiers met them as they burst free, swords drawn. Padishar swept into them and sent them flying. Two went down and did not move. The rest scattered.

Sudden movement to Par's left caused him to turn. A Seeker rose up out of the night, wolf's head gleaming on his dark cloak. Par sent the wishsong's magic into it in the form of a monstrous serpent, and the Seeker tumbled back, shrieking.

Down the street they ran, cutting crosswise to a second street and then a third. Par's stamina was being tested now, his breathing so ragged it threatened to choke him, his throat dry with dust and fear. He was still weak from his battle in the Pit, not yet fully recovered from the damage caused by the magic's use. He clutched the Sword of Shannara to his breast protectively, the weight of it growing with every step.

They rounded a corner and paused in the lee of a stable entry, listening to the tumult about them grow.

'They couldn't have followed me!' Padishar declared suddenly, spitting blood through cracked lips.

Damson shook her head. 'I don't understand it, Padishar. They've known all the safe holes, been there at each, waiting. Even this one.'

The outlaw chief's eyes gleamed suddenly with recognition. 'I should have seen it earlier. It was that Shadowen, the one who killed Hirehone, the one that pretended to be the Dwarf!' Par's head jerked up. 'Somehow he discovered our safe holes and gave them all away, just as he did the Jut!'

'Wait! What Dwarf?' Par demanded in confusion.

But Damson was moving again, drawing the other two after, charging down a walkway and through a square connecting half-a-dozen cross streets. They pushed wearily on through the heat and gloom, moving closer to the Tyrsian Way, to the city's main street. Par's mind whirled with questions as he staggered determinedly on. A Dwarf gave them away? Steff or Teel – or someone else? He tried to spit the dryness from his throat. What had happened at the Jut? And where, he wondered suddenly, was Morgan Leah?

A line of soldiers appeared suddenly to block the way ahead.

Damson quickly pushed Padishar and Par into the building shadows. Crowded against the darkened wall, she pulled their heads close.

'I found the Mole,' she whispered hurriedly, glancing right and left as new shouts rose. 'He waits at the leatherworks on Tyrsian Way to take us down into the tunnels and out of the city.'

'He escaped!' breathed Par.

'I told you he was resourceful.' Damson coughed and smiled. 'But we have to reach him if he's to do us any good – across the Tyrsian Way and down a short distance from those soldiers. If we get separated, don't stop. Keep going.'

Then before anyone could object, she was off again, darting from their cover into an alleyway between shuttered stores. Padishar managed a quick, angry objection, and then charged after her. Par followed. They emerged from the alleyway into the street beyond and turned toward the Tyrsian Way. Soldiers appeared before them, just a handful, searching the night. Padishar flew at them in fury, broadsword swinging with a glint of wicked silver light. Damson took Par left past the fighters. More soldiers appeared, and suddenly they were everywhere, surging from the dark in knots, milling about wildly. The moon had gone behind a cloud bank, and the streetlamps were unlit. It was so dark that it was impossible to tell friend from foe. Damson and Par struggled through the melee, twisting free of hands that sought to grab them, shoving away from bodies that blocked their path. They heard Padishar's battle cry, then a furious clash of blades.

Ahead, the night erupted suddenly in a brilliant orange flash as something exploded at the center of the Way.

'The Mole!' Damson hissed.

They charged toward the light, a pillar of fire that flared into the darkness with a *whoosh*. Bodies rushed past, going in every direction. Par was spun about, and suddenly he was separated from Damson. He turned back to find her and went down in a tangle of arms and legs as a fleeing soldier collided with him.

The Valeman struggled up, calling her name frantically. The Sword of Shannara reflected the orange fire as he turned first one way and then the other, crying out.

Then Padishar had him, appearing out of nowhere to lift him off his feet, sling him over one shoulder, and break for the safety of the darkened buildings. Swords cut at them, but Padishar was quick and strong, and no one was his match this night. The leader of the free-born launched himself through the last of the milling Federation soldiers and onto the walkway that ran the length of the buildings on the far side of the Way. Down the walk he charged, leaping bins and kegs, kicking aside benches, darting past the supporting posts of overhangs and the debris of the workday.

The leatherworks sat silent and empty-seeming ahead. Padishar reached it on a dead run and went through the door as if it weren't there, blunt shoulder lowering to hammer the portal completely off its hinges.

Inside, he swung Par down and wheeled about in fury.

There was no sign of Damson.

'Damson!' he howled.

Federation soldiers were closing on the leatherworks from every direction.

Padishar's face was streaked red and black with blood and dust. 'Mole!' he cried out in desperation.

A furry face poked out of the shadows at the rear of the factory. 'Over here,' the Mole's calm voice advised. 'Quickly, please.'

Par hesitated, still looking for Damson, but Padishar snatched hold of his tunic and dragged him away. 'No time, lad!'

The Mole's bright eyes gleamed as they reached him, and the inquisitive face lifted expectantly. 'Lovely Damson . . . ?' he began, but Padishar quickly shook his head. The Mole blinked, then swung away wordlessly. He took them through a door leading to a series of storage rooms, then down a stairway to a cellar. Along a wall that seemed sealed at every juncture,

15

he found a panel that released at a touch, and without a backward glance he took them through.

They found themselves on a landing joined to a stairway that ran down the city's sewers. The Mole was home again. He trundled down into the dank, cool catacombs, the light barely sufficient to enable Padishar and Par to follow. At the bottom of the stairs he passed a sooty blackened torch to the outlaw leader, who knelt wordlessly to light it.

'We should have gone back for her!' Par hissed at Padishar in fury.

The other's battle-scarred face rose from the shadows, looking as if it were chiseled from stone. The look he gave Par was terrifying. 'Be silent, Valeman, before I forget who you are.'

He sparked a flint and produced a small flame at the pitch-coated torch head, and the three started down into the sewer tunnels. The Mole scurried steadily ahead through the smoky gloom, picking his way with a practiced step, leading them deeper beneath the city and away from its walls. The shouts of pursuit had died completely, and Par supposed that even if the Federation soldiers had been able to find the hidden entry, they would have quickly lost their way in the tunnels. He realized suddenly that he was still holding the Sword of Shannara and after a moment's deliberation slipped it carefully back into its sheath.

The minutes passed, and with every step they took Par despaired of ever seeing Damson Rhee again. He was desperate to help her, but the look on Padishar's face had convinced him that for the moment at least he must hold his tongue. Certainly Padishar must be as anxious for her as he was.

They crossed a stone walkway that bridged a sluggish flow and passed into a tunnel whose ceiling was so low they were forced to crouch almost to hands and knees. At its end, the ceiling lifted again, and they navigated a confluence of tunnels to a door. The Mole touched something that released a heavy lock, and the door opened to admit them.

16

Inside they found a collection of ancient furniture and old discards that if not the same ones the Mole had been in danger of losing in his flight from the Federation a week ago were certainly duplicates. The stuffed animals sat in an orderly row on an old leather couch, button eyes staring blankly at them as they entered.

The Mole crossed at once, cooing softly, 'Brave Chalt, sweet Everlind, my Westra, and little Lida.' Other names were murmured, too low to catch. 'Hello, my children. Are you well?' He kissed them one after the other and rearranged them carefully. 'No, no, the black things won't find you here, I promise.'

Padishar passed the torch he was carrying to Par, crossed to a basin, and began splashing cold water on his sweat-encrusted face. When he was finished, he remained standing there. His hands braced on the table that held the basin, and his head hung wearily.

'Mole, we have to find out what happened to Damson.'

The Mole turned. 'Lovely Damson?'

'She was right next to me,' Par tried to explain, 'and then the soldiers got between us – '

'I know,' Padishar interrupted, glancing up. 'It wasn't your fault. Wasn't anybody's. Maybe she even got away, but there were so many . . .' He exhaled sharply. 'Mole, we have to know if they have her.'

The Mole blinked lazily and the sharp eyes gleamed. 'These tunnels go beneath the Federation prisons. Some go right into the walls. I can look. And listen.'

Padishar's gaze was steady. 'The Gatehouse to the Pit as well, Mole.'

There was a long silence. Par went cold all over. Not Damson. Not there.

'I want to go with him,' he offered quietly.

'No.' Padishar shook his head for emphasis. 'The Mole will travel quicker and more quietly.' His eyes were filled with despair as they found Par's own. 'I want to go as much as you do, lad. She is . . .'

He hesitated to continue, and Par nodded. 'She told me.'
They stared at each other in silence.

The Mole crossed the room on cat's feet, squinting in the
glare of the light from the torch Par still held. 'Wait here until
I come back,' he directed.

And then he was gone.

3

It had been a long and arduous journey that brought Par Ohmsford from his now long-ago meeting at the Hadeshorn with the shade of Allanon to this present place and time, and as he stood in the Mole's underground lair staring at the ruins and discards of other people's lives he could not help wondering how much it mirrored his own.

Damson.

He squeezed his eyes shut against the tears that threatened to come. He could not face what losing her would cost. He was only beginning to realize how much she meant to him.

'Par,' Padishar spoke his name gently. 'Come wash up, lad. You're exhausted.'

Par agreed. Physically, emotionally, and spiritually. He was beaten down in every way possible, the strength drained from him, the last of his hope shredded like paper under a knife.

He found candles set about and lit them off the torch before extinguishing it. Then he moved to the basin and began to wash, slowly, ritualistically, cleansing himself of grime and sweat as if by doing so he was erasing all the bad things that had befallen him in his search for the Sword of Shannara.

The Sword was still strapped to his back. He stopped halfway through his bathing and removed it, setting it against an old bureau with a cracked mirror. He stared at it as he might an enemy. The Sword of Shannara – or was it? He still didn't know. His charge from Allanon had been to find the Sword, and though once he had believed he had done so, now he was faced with the possibility that he had failed. His charge had been all but forgotten in the aftermath of Coll's death and the struggle to stay alive in the catacombs of Tyrsis. He wondered how many of Allanon's charges had been forgotten or ignored. He wondered if Walker or Wren had changed their minds.

He finished washing, dried himself, and turned to find Padishar seated at a three-legged table whose missing limb had been replaced by an upended crate. The leader of the free-born was eating bread and cheese and washing it down with ale. He beckoned Par to a place that had been set for him, to a waiting plate of food, and the Valeman walked over wordlessly, sat down, and began to eat.

He was hungrier than he had thought he would be and consumed the meal in minutes. All about him, the candles sputtered and flared in the near darkness like fireflies on a moonless night. The silence was broken by the distant sound of water dripping.

'How long have you known the Mole?' he asked Padishar, not liking the empty feeling the quiet fostered within him.

Padishar pursed his lips. His face was scratched and cut so badly that he looked like a badly formed puzzle. 'About a year. Damson took me to meet him one day in the park after nightfall. I don't know how she met him.' He glanced over at the stuffed animals. 'Peculiar fellow, but taken with her, sure enough.'

Par nodded wordlessly.

Padishar leaned back in his chair, causing it to creak. 'Tell me about the Sword, lad,' he urged, moving the ale cup in front of him, twisting it between his fingers. 'Is it the real thing?'

Par smiled in spite of himself. 'Good question, Padishar. I wish I knew.'

Then he told the leader of the free-born what had befallen him since they had struggled together to escape the Pit – how

Damson had found the Ohmsford brothers in the People's Park, how they had met the Mole, how they had determined to go back down into the Pit a final time to gain possession of the Sword, how he had encountered Rimmer Dall within the vault and been handed what was said to be the ancient talisman with no struggle at all, how Coll had been lost, and finally how Damson and he had been running and hiding throughout Tyrsis ever since.

What Par didn't tell Padishar was how Rimmer Dall had warned him that, like the First Seeker, Par, too, was a Shadowen. Because if it was the truth . . .

'I carry it, Padishar,' he finished, dismissing the prospect, gesturing instead toward the dusty blade where it leaned against the bureau, 'because I keep thinking that sooner or later I'll be able to figure out whether or not it is real.'

Padishar frowned darkly. 'There's a trick being played here somewhere. Rimmer Dall's no friend to anyone. Either the blade is a fake or he has good reason to believe that you can't make use of it.'

If I'm a Shadowen . . .

Par swallowed against his fear. 'I know. And so far I can't. I keep testing it, trying to invoke its magic, but nothing happens.' He paused. 'Only once, when I was in the Pit, after Coll . . . I picked up the Sword from where I had dropped it, and the touch of it burned me like live coals. Just for a minute.' He was thinking it through again, remembering. 'The wishsong's magic was still live. I was still holding that fire sword. Then the magic disappeared, and the Sword of Shannara became cool to the touch again.'

The big man nodded. 'That's it, then, lad. Something about the wishsong's magic interferes with use of the Sword of Shannara. It makes some sense, doesn't it? Why not a clash of magics? If it's so, Rimmer Dall could give you the Sword and never have to worry one whit.'

Par shook his head. 'But how would he know it would work that way?' He was thinking now that it was more likely the

21

First Seeker knew the Sword was useless to a Shadowen. 'And what about Allanon? Wouldn't he know as well? Why would he send me in search of the Sword if I can't use it?'

Padishar had no answers to any of these questions, of course, so for a moment the two simply stared at each other. Then the big man said, 'I'm sorry about your brother.'

Par looked away momentarily, then back again. 'It was Damson who kept me from . . .' He caught his breath sharply. 'Who helped me get past the pain when I thought it was too much to bear.' He smiled faintly, sadly at the other. 'I love her, Padishar. We have to get her back.'

Padishar nodded. 'If she's lost, lad. We don't know anything for sure.' His voice sounded uncertain, and his eyes were worried and distant.

'Losing Coll is as much as I can stand.' Par would not let his gaze drop.

'I know. We'll see her safely back, I promise.'

Padishar reached for the ale jug, poured a healthy measure into his own cup, and, as an afterthought, added a small amount to Par's. He drank deeply and set the cup down carefully. Par saw that he had said as much as he wanted to on the matter.

'Tell me of Morgan,' Par asked quietly.

'Ah, the Highlander.' Padishar brightened immediately. 'Saved my life in the Pit after you and your brother escaped. Saved it again – along with everyone else's – at the Jut. Bad business, that.'

And he proceeded to relate what had happened – how the Sword of Leah had been shattered in their escape from the Pit and its Shadowen, how the Federation had tracked them to the Jut and laid siege, how the Creepers had come, how Morgan had divined that Teel was a Shadowen, how the Highlander, Steff, and he had tracked Teel deep into the caves behind the Jut where Morgan had faced Teel alone and found just enough of his broken Sword's magic to destroy her, how the free-born had slipped away from the Federation trap, and how Morgan had left them then to go back to Culhaven and the Dwarves so that he might keep his promise to the dying Steff.

'I gave him my promise that I would go in search of you,' Padishar concluded. 'But I was forced to lie quiet at Firerim Reach first while my broken arm mended. Six weeks. Still tender, though I don't show it. We were supposed to meet Axhind and his Rock Trolls at the Jannisson two weeks past, but I got word to them to make it eight.' He sighed. 'So much time lost and so little of it to lose. It's one step forward and two back. Anyway, I finally healed enough to keep my end of the bargain and come find you.' He laughed wryly. 'It wasn't easy. Everywhere I looked the Federation was waiting.'

'Teel, then, you think?' Par asked.

The other nodded. 'Had to be, lad. Killed Hirehone after stealing his identity and his secrets. Hirehone was trusted; he knew the safe holes. Teel – the Shadowen – must have gotten that information from him, drained it from his mind.' He spat. 'Black things! And Rimmer Dall would pretend to be your friend! What lies!'

Or worse, the truth, Par thought, but didn't say it. Par feared that his affinity with the First Seeker, whatever its nature, let Rimmer Dall glean the secrets he would otherwise keep hidden – even those he was not immediately privy to, those kept by his friends and companions.

It was a wild thought. Too wild to be believed. But then much of what he had encountered these past few weeks was of the same sort, wasn't it?

Better to believe that it was all Teel, he told himself.

'Anyway,' Padishar was saying, 'I've set guards to watch the Reach ever since we settled there, because Hirehone knew of it as well, and that means the Shadowen may know too. But so far all's been quiet. A week hence we keep the meeting with the Trolls, and if they agree to join we have an army to be reckoned with, the beginning of a true resistance, the core of a fire that will burn right through the Federation and set us free at last.'

'At the Jannisson still?' Par asked, thinking of other things.

'We leave as soon as I return with you. And Damson,' he added quickly, firmly. 'A week is time enough to do it all.' He didn't sound entirely sure.

'But Morgan's not come back yet?' Par pressed.

Padishar shook his head slowly. 'Don't worry about your friend, lad. He's tough as leather and swift as light. And determined. Wherever he is, whatever he's doing, he'll be fine. We'll see him one day soon.'

Oddly enough, Par was inclined to agree. If ever there was someone who could find a way out of any mess, it was Morgan Leah. He pictured his friend's clever eyes, his ready smile, the hint of mischief in his voice, and found that he missed him very much. Another of his journey's casualties, lost somewhere along the way, stripped from him like excess baggage. Except the analogy was wrong – his friends and his brother had given their lives to keep him safe. All of them, at one time or another. And what had he given them in return? What had he done to justify such sacrifice?

What good had he accomplished?

His eyes fell once more upon the Sword of Shannara, tracing the lines of the upraised hand with its burning torch. Truth. The Sword of Shannara was a talisman for truth. And the truth he most needed to discover just now was whether this blade for which so much had been given up was real.

How could he do that?

Across from him Padishar stretched and yawned. 'Time to get some rest, Par Ohmsford,' he advised, rising. 'We need our strength for what lies ahead.'

He moved to the couch on which the stuffed animals were seated, gathered them up perfunctorily, and plopped them down on a nearby chair. Turning back to the couch, he settled himself comfortably on the worn leather cushions, boots hanging off one end, head cradled in the crook of one arm. In moments he was snoring.

Par stayed awake for a time watching him, letting the dark

24

thoughts settle in his mind, keeping his resolve from scattering like leaves in a wind storm. He was afraid, but the fear was nothing new. It was the eroding of hope that unsettled him most, the crumbling of his certainty that whatever happened he would find a way to deal with it. He was beginning to wonder if that was so anymore.

He rose finally and went to the chair where Padishar had dumped the stuffed animals. Carefully he gathered them up – Chalt, Lida, Westra, Everlind and the others – and carried them to where the Sword of Shannara leaned up against the bureau. One by one, he arranged them about the Sword, placing them at watch – as if by doing so they might aid him in keeping the demons from his sleep.

When he was finished, he walked to the back of the Mole's lair, found some discarded cushions and old blankets, made himself a pallet in a corner dominated by a collection of old paintings, and lay down.

He was still listening to the sound of water dripping when he finally drifted off to sleep.

When he woke again, he was alone. The couch where Padishar had been sleeping was empty and the Mole's chambers were silent. All of the candles were extinguished save for one. Par blinked against the sharp pinprick of light, then peered about into the gloom, wondering where Padishar had gone. He rose, stretched, walked to the candle, used it to light the others, and watched the darkness shrink to scattered shadows.

He had no idea how long he had slept; time lost all meaning within these catacombs. He was hungry again, so he made himself a meal from some bread, cheese, fruit, and ale, and consumed it at the three-legged table. As he ate, he stared fixedly across the room at the Sword of Shannara, propped in the corner, surrounded by the Mole's children.

Speak to me, he thought. Why won't you speak to me?

He finished eating, shoving the food in his mouth without tasting it, drinking the ale without interest, his eyes and his mind focused on the Sword. He pushed back from the table, walked over to the blade, lifted it away from its resting place, and carried it back to his chair. He balanced it on his knees for a time, staring down at it. Then finally he pulled it free of its scabbard and held it up before him, turning it this way and that, letting the candlelight reflect off its polished surface.

His eyes glittered with frustration.

Talisman or trickster – which are you?

If the former, something was decidedly wrong between them. He was the descendant of Shea Ohmsford and his Elven blood was as good as that of his famous ancestor; he should have been able to call up the power of the Sword with ease. If it was the Sword in truth, of course. Otherwise . . . He shook his head angrily. No, this was the Sword of Shannara. It was. He could feel it in his bones. Everything he knew of the Sword, everything he had learned of it, all the songs he had sung of it over the years, told him that this was it. Rimmer Dall would not have given him an imitation; the First Seeker was too eager that Par accept his guidance in the matter of his magic to risk alienating him with a lie that would eventually be discovered. Whatever else Rimmer Dall might be, he was clever – far too clever to play such a simple game . . .

Par left the thought unfinished, not as certain as he wanted to be that he was right. Still, it felt right, his reasoning sound, his sense of things balanced. Rimmer Dall wanted him to accept that he was a Shadowen. A Shadowen could not use the Elven magic of the blade because . . .

Because why?

The truth would destroy him, perhaps, and his own magic would not allow it?

But when the Sword of Shannara had burned him in the Pit after he had destroyed Coll and the Shadowen with him, hadn't it been the *blade*'s magic that had reacted to his rather than the other way around? Which magic was resisting which?

He gritted his teeth, his hands clenching tightly about the Sword's carved handle. The raised hand with its torch pressed against his palm, the lines sharp and clear. What was the problem between them? Why couldn't he find the answer?

He shoved the blade back into its scabbard and sat unmoving in the candle-lit silence, thinking. Allanon had given him the charge to find the Sword of Shannara. Him, not Wren or Walker, and they had Elven Shannara blood as well, didn't they? Allanon had sent him. Familiar questions repeated themselves in his mind. Wouldn't the Druid have known if such a charge was pointless? Even as a shade, wouldn't he have been able to sense that Par's magic was a danger, that Par himself was the enemy?

Unless Rimmer Dall was right and the Shadowen weren't the enemy – the Druids were. Or perhaps they were all enemies of a sort, combatants for control of the magic, Shadowen and Druid, both fighting to fill that void that had been created at Allanon's death, that vacuum left by the fading of the last real magic.

Was that possible?

Par's brow furrowed. He ran his fingers along the Sword's pommel and down the bindings of the scabbard.

Why was the truth so difficult to discover?

He found himself wondering what had become of all the others who had started out on the journey to the Hadeshorn. Steff and Teel were dead. Morgan was missing. Where was Cogline? What had become of him after the meeting with Allanon and the giving of the charges? Par found himself wishing suddenly that he could speak with the old man about the Sword. Surely Cogline would be able to make some sense of all this. And what of Wren and that giant Rover? What of Walker Boh? Had they changed their minds and gone on to fulfill their charges as he had?

As he thought he had.

His eyes, staring into the space before him, lowered again to the Sword. There was one thing more. Now that he had possession of the blade – perhaps – what was he supposed to do with it? Giving Allanon the benefit of the doubt on who was good and who was bad and whether Par was doing the right thing, what purpose was the Sword of Shannara supposed to serve?

What truth was it supposed to reveal?

He was sick of questions without answers, of secrets being kept from him, of lies and twisted half-truths that circled him like scavengers waiting to feast. If he could break just a single link of this chain of uncertainty and confusion that bound him, if he could sever but a single tie . . .

The door slipped open across the room, and Padishar appeared through the opening. 'There you are,' he announced cheerfully. 'Rested, I hope?'

Par nodded, the Sword still balanced on his knees. Padishar glanced down at it as he crossed the room. Par let his grip loosen. 'What time is it?' he asked.

'Midday. The Mole hasn't come back. I went out because I thought I might be able to learn something about Damson on my own. Ask a few questions. Poke my nose in a few holes.' He shook his head. 'It was a waste of time. If the Federation has her, they're keeping it quiet.'

He slumped down on the sofa, looking worn and discouraged. 'If he isn't back by nightfall, I'll go out again.'

Par leaned forward. 'Not without me.'

Padishar glanced at him and grunted. 'I suppose not. Well, Valeman, perhaps we can at least avoid another trip down into the Pit . . .'

He stopped, aware suddenly of what that implied, then looked away uncomfortably. Par lifted the Sword of Shannara from his knees and placed it next to him on the floor. 'She told me that you were her father, Padishar.'

The big man stared at him wordlessly for a moment, then smiled faintly. 'Love seems to cause all sorts of foolish talk.'

He rose and walked to the table. 'I'll have something to eat now, I think.' He wheeled about abruptly, and his voice was as hard as stone. 'Don't ever repeat what you just said. Not to anyone. Ever.'

He waited until Par nodded, then turned his attention to putting together a meal. He ate from the same scraps of food as the Valeman, adding a bit of dried beef he scavenged from a food locker. Par watched him without comment, wondering how long father and daughter had kept their secret, thinking how hard it must have been for both of them. Padishar's chiseled features lowered into shadow as he ate, but his eyes glittered like bits of white fire.

When he was finished, he faced Par once more. 'She promised – she swore – never to tell anyone.'

Par looked down at his clasped hands. 'She told me because we both needed to have some reason to trust the other. We were sharing secrets to gain that trust. It was right before we went down into the Pit that last time.'

Padishar sighed. 'If they find out who she is – '

'No,' Par interrupted quickly. 'We'll have her back before then.' He met the other's penetrating gaze. 'We will, Padishar.'

Padishar Creel nodded. 'We will, indeed, Par Ohmsford. We will, indeed.'

It was several hours later when the Mole appeared soundlessly through the entryway, sliding out of the dark like one of its shadows, eyes blinking against the candlelight. His fur stood on end, bristling from his worn clothes and giving him the look of a prickly scrub. Wordlessly he moved to extinguish several of the lights, leaving the larger part of his chambers shrouded once more in the darkness with which he was comfortable. He scooted past to where his children sat clustered on the floor, cooed softly to them for a moment, gathered them up tenderly, and carried them back to the sofa.

He was still arranging them when Padishar's patience ran out.

'What did you find out?' the big man demanded heatedly. 'Tell us, if you think you can spare the time!'

The Mole shifted without turning. 'She is a prisoner.'

Par felt the blood drain from his face. He glanced quickly at Padishar and found the big man on his feet, hands clenched.

'Where?' Padishar whispered.

The Mole took a moment to finish settling Chalt against a cushion and then turned. 'In the old Legion barracks at the back of the inner wall. Lovely Damson is kept in the south watch-tower, all alone.' He shuffled his feet. 'It took me a long time to find her.'

Padishar came forward and knelt so that they were at eye level. The scratches on his face were as red as fire. 'Have they . . .' He groped for the words. 'Is she all right?'

The Mole shook his head. 'I could not reach her.'

Par came forward as well. 'You didn't see her?'

'No.' The Mole blinked. 'But she is there. I climbed through the tower walls. She was just on the other side. I could hear her breathe through the stone. She was sleeping.'

The Valeman and the leader of the free-born exchanged a quick glance. 'How closely is she watched?' Padishar pressed.

The Mole brought his hands to his eyes and rubbed gently with his knuckles. 'Soldiers stand watch at her door, at the foot of the stairs leading up, at the gate leading in. They patrol the halls and walkways. There are many.' He blinked. 'There are Shadowen as well.'

Padishar sagged back. 'They know,' he whispered harshly.

'No,' Par disagreed. 'Not yet.' He waited for Padishar's eyes to meet his own. 'If they did, they wouldn't let her sleep. They're not sure. They'll wait for Rimmer Dall – just as they did before.'

Padishar stared at him wordlessly for a moment, a glimmer of hope showing on his rough features. 'You might be right. So we have to get her out before that happens.'

'You and me,' Par said quietly. 'We both go.'

The leader of the free-born nodded, and an understanding passed between them that was more profound than anything words could have expressed. Padishar rose and they faced each other in the gloom of the Mole's shabby chambers, resolve hardening them against what most certainly lay ahead. Par pushed aside the unanswered questions and the confusion over the Sword of Shannara. He buried his doubts over the use of his own magic. Where Damson was concerned, he would do whatever it took to get her free. Nothing else mattered.

'We will need to get close to her,' Padishar declared softly, looking down at the Mole. 'As close as we can without being seen.'

The Mole nodded solemnly. 'I know a way.'

The big man reached out to touch his shoulder. 'You will have to come with us.'

'Lovely Damson is my best friend,' the Mole said.

Padishar nodded and took his hand away. He turned to Par. 'We'll go after her now.'

4

The man in the high castle was Walker Boh, and he walked its parapets and battlements, its towers and keeps, all of the corridors and walkways that defined its boundaries like the wraith he had been and the outcast he felt. Paranor, the castle of the Druids, was returned, come back into the world of men, brought alive by Walker and the magic of the Black Elfstone. Paranor stood as it had three hundred years before, lifting out of the dark forest where wolves prowled and thorns the size of lance-points bristled protectively. It rose out of the earth, set upon a bluff where it could be seen across the whole of the valley it dominated, from the Kennon to the Jannisson, from one ridgeline of the Dragon's Teeth to the other, spires and walls and gates. As solid as the stone from which it had been built more than a thousand years earlier, it was the Keep of legends and folk tales made whole once more.

But shades, Walker Boh thought in his despair, what it had cost!

'It was waiting for me down in the tower well, the essence of the Druid magic he had set at watch,' Walker explained to Cogline that first night, the night he had emerged from the Keep with Allanon's presence at haunt within. 'All those years it had been waiting, his spirit or some part of that spirit, concealed in the serpentine mist that had destroyed the Mord

Wraiths and their allies and sent Paranor out of the land of men to wait for the time it would be summoned back again. Allanon's shade had been waiting as well, it seems, there within the waters of the Hadeshorn, knowing that the need for the Keep and its Druids would one day prove inexorable, that the magic and the lore they wielded must be kept at hand against the possibility that history's evolution would take a different path than the one he had prophesied.'

Cogline listened and did not speak. He was still in awe of what had happened, of whom Walker Boh had become. He was afraid. For Walker was Walker still, but something more as well. Allanon was there, become a part of him in the transformation from man to Druid, in the rite of passage that had taken place in the Keep's dark hold.

Cogline had ventured, in his spirit form, just long enough to pull Walker back from the madness that threatened to engulf him before he could come to grips with the change that was taking place. In those few seconds Cogline had felt the beginnings of Walker's change – and he had fled in horror.

'The Black Elfstone drew the mist into itself and thereby into me,' Walker whispered, the words a familiar repetition by now, as if saying them would make them better understood. His stark visage lowered into the cowl of his robe, a mask still changing. 'It brought Allanon within. It brought all of the Druids within – their history and lore and magic, their knowledge, their secrets, all that they were. It spun them through me like threads on a loom that weaves a new cloth, and I could feel myself invaded and helpless to prevent it.'

The face within the cowl swung slightly toward the old man. 'I have all of them inside me, Cogline. They have made a home within me, determined that I should have their knowledge and their power and that I should use it as they did. It was Allanon's plan from the beginning – a descendant of Brin to carry forth the Druid lineage, one that would be chosen when the need arose, one who would serve and obey.'

Iron fingers fastened suddenly on Cogline's shoulder and

made him wince. 'Obey, old man! That is what they intend of me, but not what they shall have!' Walker Boh's words were edged with bitterness. 'I can feel them working about inside, living things! I can sense their presence as they whisper their words and try to make me heed. But I am stronger than they are, made so by the very process that they used to change me. I survived the trial they set for me, and I will be what I choose, be they living within my body and mind, be they shades or memories of the past, be they what they will! If I must be this . . . this *thing* they have made of me, I shall at least give it my voice and my heart!'

So they walked, Cogline as cold as death listening to the tormented Walker Boh, Walker as hot as the fires that had begun to burn anew within the furnaces below Paranor's stone walls, his fury made over into the strength that sustained him against what was happening.

For the change continued even now as they walked the castle corridors, the old man and the becoming Druid, shadowed by the silent presence of Rumor the moor cat, as black-browed as his masters. The change swirled through Walker like smoke in the wind, stirred by the hands of the Druids gone, their spirits alive within the one who would permit the magic to live again. It came as knowledge revealed in bits and pieces and sometimes in sharp bursts, knowledge gained and preserved through the years, all that the Druids had discovered and shaped in their order, the whole of what had sustained them through the years of the Warlock Lord and the Skull Bearers, through the Demons within the Forbidding, through the Ildatch and the Mord Wraiths, through all the trials of dark evil set to challenge humankind. The magic revealed itself little by little, peeking forth from the jumble of hands and eyes and whispered words that roiled in Walker Boh's mind and gave him no peace.

He did not sleep at all for three days. He tried, exhausted to the point of despair, but when he endeavored to let himself go, to slip away into the comfort of the rest he so desperately needed, some new facet of the change lurched alive and brought him upright as if he were a puppet on strings, making him aware of its need, of its presence, of its determination to be heard. Each time he would fight it, not to prevent it from being, for there was no sense in that, but to assure that it was not accepted without question, that the knowledge was perused and studied, that he recognized its face and was cautioned thereby against blind use. The Druids were not his maker, he reminded himself over and over again. The Druids had not given him his life and should not be allowed to dictate his destiny. *He* would do that. *He* would decide the nature of his life, power of magic or no, and in doing so would be accountable only to himself.

Cogline and Rumor stayed with him, as exhausted as he was, but frightened for him and determined that he would not be left alone to face what was happening. Cogline's was the voice that Walker needed to hear now and again in response to his own, a caution and reassurance to blunt his lamentations of disgust. Rumor was the shaggy dark certainty that some things did not change, a presence as solid and dependable as the coming of day after night, the promise that there could be a waking from even the worst of nightmares. Together they sustained him in ways he could not begin to describe and that they in turn could not begin to understand. It was enough that they sensed that the bond was there.

Three days passed, then, before the change finally ran its course and the transformation was made complete. All at once the hands stopped molding, the eyes disappeared, and the whispers faded. Within Walker Boh, everything suddenly went still. He slept then and did not dream, and when he woke he knew that while he was changed in ways he was only beginning to discover, still he was in the deepest part of himself the same person he had always been. He had preserved the heart of the man who mistrusted the Druids and their magics, and while the Druids now lived within him and would have their voice in the way he conducted his life, nevertheless they would be ruled by beliefs that had preceded their coming and would survive their stay. Walker rose in the solitude of his sleeping chamber, alone in the darkness that the windowless room provided, at peace with himself for the first time he could remember, the long, terrible journey to fulfill the charge he had been given ended, the ordeal of the transformation set for him finished at last. Much had come undone and more than a little had been lost, but what mattered above all else was that he had survived.

He went out then to Cogline and found him sitting close-by with the moor cat curled at his feet, worry lines etched in his aging face, uncertainty reflected in his eyes. He came up to the old man and raised him to his feet as if he were a child – grown impossibly strong with the change, made over by the hands and eyes and voices until he was as ten men. He put his good arm about the frail old body and held his mentor gently.

'I am well again,' he whispered. 'It is over and I am safe.'

And the old man gripped him back and cried into his shoulder.

They talked then as they had of old, two men who had experienced more than their share of surprises in life, joined by the common bond of the Druid magic and by the fates that had brought them to this time and place. They spoke of Walker's change, of the feelings it had generated, of the knowledge it had brought, and of the needs it might fulfill. They were whole again, flesh-and-blood men, and Paranor was returned. It was the beginning of a new era in the world of the Four Lands, and they were at the first moment in time that would determine how that era evolved. Walker Boh was uncertain even now how he was to wield the Druid magic – or even that he should. There was the Shadowen threat to consider, but the nature and extent of that threat remained a mystery. Walker had been given the Druid lore, but not an insight into what he was expected to do with it – especially as regarded the Shadowen.

'My transformation has left me with certain insights that weren't there before,' Walker confided. 'One is that the use of Druid magic will prove necessary if the Shadowen threat is to be ended. But whose insight is it – mine or Allanon's? Can I trust it, I wonder? Is it a truth or a fiction?'

The old man shook his head. 'I think you must discover that for yourself. I think Allanon wants it that way. Hasn't it always been left to the Ohmsfords to discover the truth of things on their own? Gamesplaying, you once called it. But isn't it really much more than that? Isn't it the nature of life? Experience comes from doing, not from being told. Experiment and discover. Seek and find. It is not the machinations of the Druids that compel us to do so; it is our need to know. It is, in the end, the way we learn. I think it must be your way as well, Walker.'

What should be done first, they decided, was to find out what had become of the other scions of Shannara – Par, Coll, and Wren. Had they fulfilled the charges they had been given? Where were they and what secrets had they uncovered in the weeks that had passed since their meeting at the Hadeshorn?

'Par will have found the Sword of Shannara or be searching for it,' Walker declared. They sat within the Druid study, the Histories spread out before them, perused this time for particulars that Walker remembered from his previous readings and now understood differently with the knowledge his transformation had wrought. 'Par was driven in his quest. He was all iron and determination. Whatever the rest of us chose to do, he would not have given up.'

'Nor Wren either, I think,' the old man offered thoughtfully. 'There was as much iron in her, though it was not so apparent.' He met Walker's gaze boldly. 'Allanon's shade sensed what would drive each of you, and I think no one ever really stood a chance of being able to walk away.'

Walker leaned back in the chair that cushioned him, lean face shadowed by lank dark hair and beard, the eyes so penetrating it seemed that nothing could hide from them.

'From the time of Shea Ohmsford, the Druids have made us their own, haven't they?' he mused, cool and distant. 'They found in us something that could be shackled, and they have held us prisoner ever since. We are servants to their needs – and paladins to the races.'

Cogline felt the air in the room stir, a palpable response to the flow of magic that rose from Walker's voice. He had sensed it more than once since Walker had come out of the Keep, a measure of the power bestowed on him. More Druid than man, he was a manifestation of the dark arts and lore that once, long ago, the old man had studied and rejected in favor of forms of the old-world sciences. Opportunity lost, he thought. But sanity gained. He wondered if Walker would find peace in his own evolution.

'We are just men,' he said cautiously.

And Walker replied, smiling, 'We are just fools.'

They talked late into the night, but Walker remained undecided on a course of action. Find the others of his family, yes – but where to begin and how to go about it? Use of his newfound magic was an obvious choice, but would that use reveal him to the Shadowen? Did his enemies know what had happened yet – that he had become a Druid and that Paranor had been brought back? How strong was the Shadowen magic? How far could it reach? He should not be too quick to test it, he kept repeating. He was still learning about his own. He was still discovering. He should not be hasty about what he chose to do.

The debate wore on, and as it did so it began to dawn on Walker that something was different between Cogline and himself. He thought at first that his reluctance to commit to a course of action was simply indecision – even though that was very unlike him. He soon realized it was something else altogether. While they talked as they had of old, there was a distance between them that had never been there before, not even when he had been angry with and mistrustful of the old man. The relationship between them had changed. Walker was no longer the student and Cogline the teacher. Walker's transformation had left him with knowledge and power far superior to Cogline's. Walker was no longer the Dark Uncle hiding out in Darklin Reach. The days of living apart from the races and forswearing his birthright were gone forever. Walker Boh was committed to whom and what he had become – a Druid, the only Druid, perhaps the single most powerful individual alive. What he did could affect the lives of everyone. Walker knew that. Knowing, he accepted that his decisions must be his own and the making of them could never again be shared, because no one, not even Cogline, should have to bear the weight of such a terrible responsibility.

When they parted finally to sleep, exhausted anew from their efforts, Walker found himself besieged by a mix of feelings. He had grown so far beyond the man he had been that in many ways he was barely recognizable. He was conscious of the old man staring after him as he retreated down the hall to his sleeping room and could not shake the sense that they were drawing apart in more ways than one.

Cogline. The Druid-who-never-was made companion to the Druid-who-would-be – what must he be feeling?

Walker didn't know. But he accepted reluctantly that from this night forward things would never be the same between them again.

He slept then, and his dreams were tenuous and filled with faces and voices he could not recognize. It was nearing dawn when he woke, an urgency gripping him, whispering insidiously at him, bringing him out of his sleep like a swimmer out of water, thrusting to the surface and drawing in huge gulps of air. For a moment he was paralyzed by the suddenness of his waking, frozen with uncertainty as his heart pounded within his chest and his eyes and ears struggled to make sense of the darkness surrounding him. At last he was able to move, swinging his legs down off the bed, steadied by the feeling of the solid stone beneath his feet. He rose, aware that he was still wearing the dark robes in which he had fallen asleep, the clothing he had been too tired to remove.

Something stirred just outside his door, a soft padding, a rubbing against the ancient wood.

Rumor.

He went to the door and opened it. The big cat stood just without, staring up at him. It circled away anxiously and came back again, big head swinging up, eyes gleaming.

It wants me to follow, Walker thought. Something is wrong.

He wrapped himself in a heavy cloak and went out from his sleeping chamber into the tomblike silence of the castle. Stone walls muffled the sound of his feet as he hurried down the ancient corridors. Rumor went on ahead, sleek and dark in the gloom, padding soundlessly through the shadows. Without slowing, they passed the room in which Cogline slept. The trouble did not lie there. The night faded about them as they went, dawn rising out of the east in a shimmer of silver that seeped through the castle windows in wintry, clouded light. Walker barely noticed, his eyes fixed on the movement of the moor cat as it slid through the overlapping shadows. His ears strained to hear something, to catch a hint of what was waiting. But the silence persisted, unbroken.

They climbed from the main hall to the battlement doors and went out into the open air. The dawn was chill and empty-feeling. Mist lay over the whole of the valley, climbing the wall of the Dragon's Teeth east and stretching west to the Streleheim in a blanket that shrouded everything between. Paranor lay wrapped within its upper folds, its high towers islands thrusting out of a misty sea. The mist swirled and spun, stirred by winds that came down off the mountains, and in the weak light of the early dawn strange shapes and forms came alive.

Rumor padded down the walkway, sniffing the air as he went, tail switching uneasily. Walker followed. They circled the south parapet west without slowing, seeing nothing, hearing nothing. They passed open stairwells and tower entry-ways, ghosts at haunt.

On the west battlement, Rumor slowed suddenly. The hair on the moor cat's neck bristled, and his dark muzzle wrinkled in a snarl. Walker moved up beside him and quickly placed a reassuring hand on the coarse hair of his back. Rumor was facing out now into the gloom. They stood just above the castle's west gate.

Walker peered into the mist. He could sense it, too.

Something was out there.

The seconds slipped away, and nothing showed. Walker began to grow impatient. Perhaps he should go out for a look.

Then suddenly the mist drew back, seemed to pull away as if in revulsion, and the riders appeared. There were four of them, gaunt and spectral in the faint light. They came slowly, purposefully, as gray as the gloom that had hidden their approach. Four riders atop their mounts, but none was human, and the animals they rode were loathsome parodies, all scales and claws and teeth. Four riders, each markedly different from the other, each with a mount that was a mirror of itself.

Walker Boh knew at once that they were Shadowen. He knew as well that they had come for him.

Coolly, dispassionately, he studied them.

The first was tall and lean and cadaverous. Bones pressed out against skin shrunk tight against it, the skeletal frame hunched forward like a cat at hunt. The face was a skull in which the jaw hung open slackly and the eyes stared out, too wide and too blank to be seeing. It wore no clothes, and its naked body was neither that of a man nor of a woman, but something in between. Its breath clouded the air before it, a vile green mist.

The second lacked any semblance of identity. It was human-shaped, but had no skin or bones. It was instead a raging cloud of darkness, buzzing and shrieking within its form. The cloud had the look of flies or mosquitoes trapped behind glass, gathered so thick that they shut out the light. The wicked sounds that issued from this rider seemed to warn that it hid within its spectral form an evil too dreadful to imagine.

The third was more immediately recognizable. Armored head to foot, it bristled with spikes and cutting edges and weapons. It wore maces and knives, swords and battle-axes, and carried a huge pike strung with skulls and finger bones laced together in a chain. A helmet hid its face, but the eyes that peered out through the visor slit were as red as fire.

The last rider was cloaked and hooded and as invisible as the night. No face could be seen within the concealing cowl. No hands showed to grip the reins of its sinewy mount. It rode hunched forward like a very old man, all bent and gnarled, a creature crippled by age and time. But there was no sense of weakness about it, nothing to suggest that it was anything of what it appeared. This rider rode steady and sure, and what crippled it was neither time nor age but the weight of the burden it bore for the lives it had taken.

Slung across its back was a scythe.

Walker Boh went cold with recognition. Far back in the Druid Histories, recorded from the old world of Men, there was mention of these four. He knew who they were, whom they had been created to be. Now Shadowen had taken on their guises, assumed the identities of the dark things of old.

His chest tightened. Four riders. The Four Horsemen of the legends, the slayers of mortal men come out of a time so distant it had been all but forgotten. But he had read the tales, he repeated to himself, and he knew what they were.

Famine. Pestilence. War. Death.

Walker's hand lifted away from Rumor, and the cat began to growl deep in his chest. Shadowen, Walker thought in a mix of awe and fear, created to be something that never was, that was only a manifestation of abstracts, of killing ways, come now to destroy me.

He wondered anew at who and what the Shadowen were, at the source of power that would let them be anything they

42

chose. His transformation had given him no insight into this. He was as ignorant of their origins now as he had been at the start of things. Yes, they were as dark as the shade of Allanon had forewarned. Yes, they were an evil that used magic as a weapon to destroy. But who were they? Where had they come from? How could they be destroyed?

Where could he find the answers to his questions?

He watched the Four Horsemen advance, settled atop their lurching, writhing mounts, things that vaguely resembled horses but were intended to be much more. Breath steamed on the morning air like poisonous vapor. Claws scraped and crunched on the rock. Heads lifted and muzzles drew back to show hooked, yellowed teeth. Steadily, the Horsemen came on.

When they reached the gates, they stopped. They made no move to pass through. They showed no interest in advancing. In a line they faced the gate and waited.

Walker waited with them. The minutes passed and the light brightened slowly, the gloom taking on a whiteness as the dawn neared.

Then at last the sun crested the mountains east, a faint glimmer above the dark peaks, and at the gates below, the rider Famine suddenly advanced. When it was next to the barrier, it lifted its skeletal hand and knocked. The sound was a dimly heard, echoing, hollow thud – the shudder that life makes as it departs the body for the final time. Walker cringed in spite of himself, revolted by how it made him feel.

Famine backed away then, and one by one the Four Horsemen turned right, spreading out in a thin line to circle the castle walls. Around they went, passing beneath Walker one by one as he watched them return and disappear again, keeping carefully apart in their movement so that there was always one at each wall, one at each corner of the compass.

A siege, Walker realized. The knock was a challenge, and if he did not come out to answer it, they intended to keep him trapped within. Rimmer Dall and the Shadowen had discovered that Paranor was back and that Walker had accepted the mantle of Allanon. The Horsemen had been sent in response.

Walker folded his arms within his cloak. *We'll see who traps whom*, he thought darkly.

He stood looking down for a while longer on the apparitions below, then went to wake Cogline.

5

The sewers beneath Tyrsis were dank and chill in a twilight dark that seeped along gutters and down grates like spilled ink. Daylight had gone west, and the night hovered in shadows that lengthened from buildings and walls, a ghost come to life. Footsteps and voices faded homeward, and the weariness of day's end was a sigh echoed by the hot summer wind as it settled into pockets of still, suffocating heat in the runnels of the city's streets and byways, an airless blanket laid over the catacombs below.

Padishar Creel, Par Ohmsford, and the Mole groped their way slowly and steadily through those catacombs, three of the shadows that grew out of night's coming, as silent as the dust stirred by the boots passing in the streets above. They breathed through their mouths, the sewer smells oppressive and rank within the twisting conduits, the city's waste a sluggish flow at the edges of their feet. At times they climbed iron ladders and stone steps, at times they crawled through narrow tunnels, all the while working their way outward from the city's center toward its walls and the bluff face, the watchtower where Damson Rhee was held prisoner, and the confrontation that waited.

'We will not return without her,' Padishar had declared. 'Whatever proves necessary to free her, we will do. Once we have her, we will not give her up again.

'Mole,' he had whispered, kneeling before the strange little fellow. 'You will guide us in and, if possible, out again. But you will not fight, do you understand? Keep yourself clear and safe. Because, Mole, once we have freed Damson' – there was no suggestion, Par noted, that they would not – 'you alone will know how to see her safely away again. Agreed?' And the Mole had nodded solemnly.

'Par, yours is a harder task still,' the leader of the free-born had continued, turning next to the Valeman. 'If we encounter the Shadowen, you must use your magic to keep them from us. The Highlander was able to do so with his sword when we were trapped in the Pit. This time it will be up to you. I lack any means to defend against these monsters. If we encounter them, lad, don't hesitate.'

Par had already decided that use of the wishsong in this endeavor was a foregone conclusion, so he was quick to give Padishar his promise. What he could not promise – and what he did not tell the other – was that he was no longer certain he could control the magic. It had already proved unreliable, already shown that it could take on a life of its own, unleashing power that might well consume him. But such fears as recognition of this danger generated paled against his feelings for Damson Rhee. Buried by the struggle they had shared to escape the city and its hunters, and by the fact that he had felt her safe with him, his feelings had surfaced instantly with the report of her taking, and now they raged within him like a fire unchecked. He loved her. Perhaps he had loved her from the first, but certainly since she had held him together after Coll's death. She was as much a part of him as anything separate could possibly be, and he could not stand the thought of losing her. He would give anything to see her safe again. He would give everything. If it meant risking the fury of a magic that could change him irrevocably, that could even destroy him, then so be it. If Rimmer Dall was right about who and what he was, then there was nothing he could do to save himself in any case. He would not shy from the dangers of the magic where Damson's safety was at stake. He would do what he must.

So they had set out, each determined that Damson was worth losing everything, knowing the risk was such that everything could well be lost. Now the sewers stretched away in narrow, winding tunnels before them, the darkness closing fast about the little light that remained. Soon they would be forced to use torchlight to see, and that would be especially dangerous as they neared the city's walls. For there the dark things would likely be at watch below ground as well as above, and torchlight would be seen coming from a long way off.

They hurried on, the Mole's sharp eyes and steady senses choosing their way unerringly, sorting out which paths were safe, avoiding the ones that might impede them. As they went, they could hear the sounds of the city above drifting down in trickles and snatches, bits and pieces of a life as disconnected from their own as the living from the dead. Par's thoughts drifted. It felt somehow as if they were entombed within the stone of the bluff on which Tyrsis had been built, specters at haunt just out of sight of the people they had once been. It seemed to the Valeman, on reflection, that he was indeed more ghost than human, that in his flight from the Shadowen and the other dangers encountered on this journey he had become transformed in a way that he did not entirely understand and as a result had been stripped of substance and left ethereal. He moved now in a shadow existence, increasingly bereft of friends and family, left trapped in a tangle of magics that were causing him to disintegrate. There should have been a way to save himself, he knew, but somehow he could not seem to discover what it was.

They reached a broad confluence of pipes and slowed behind the Mole's cautious signal. Huddled close at the bottom of a well from which a stone stairway climbed, they held their last council.

'The stairway leads to a cellar within the inner wall,' whispered the Mole. His nose was damp and gleaming. 'From there we must climb to a hall, follow it to an entryway that leads outside again, cross to another door, enter, and follow a second hall to a hidden passageway that will take us up through the watchtower to where Damson waits.'

He looked from Padishar to Par and back again, intent.

The big man nodded. 'Federation guards?'

The Mole blinked. 'Everywhere.'

'Shadowen?'

'In the tower, somewhere.'

Padishar gave Par a wry smile. 'Somewhere. Very incisive.' He hunched his big shoulders. 'All right. Remember what I said, the both of you. Remember what you are to do – and not to do.' He glanced at Par. 'If I fall, you go on – if you can. If not, get to Firerim Reach and find help there. Promise me.'

Par nodded, thinking as he did that the promise was a lie, that he would never turn back, not until Damson was safe, no matter what.

Padishar reached back over his shoulder and tightened the straps that secured the broadsword to his back, then checked the long knives and short sword strapped about his waist. The handle of yet another long knife protruded from one boot. All were carefully sheathed and wrapped in cloth to keep the metal from rattling or reflecting light. Par wore only the Sword of Shannara. The Mole carried no weapons at all.

Padishar looked up again. 'All right, then. Let's go in.'

In single file they climbed the stairs, crouching low against the stone, easing their way toward the faint light that shone above. A grate came into view, bars of iron that cast a web of shadows down the steps and onto their bodies. There was silence above, an empty, hollow nothingness.

On reaching the grate, the Mole paused to listen, his head cocked in the manner of an animal at hunt – or at risk – then reached up and with surprising strength lifted the grate away almost soundlessly. Stepping from the well, he carried the grate overhead as the other two climbed swiftly free, then set it carefully back in place.

They stood in a cellar that was one in a series of interconnected rooms, all in a line that ran away to either side as far as the eye could see. Stores were stacked everywhere, crates of weapons, tools, clothes, and sundry goods, all carefully labeled and piled back against the thick stone walls on wooden pallets. Barrels were housed in an adjoining chamber, and barely visible through the gloom the rusting frames of old beds formed a maze of metal bones. High on the walls, just below the cellar ceiling and just above the ground without, a row of narrow, barred windows let in thin streamers of dusk's fading light.

The Mole took them ahead through the maze of cellar rooms, past the stacks of stores, and around the tangle of crates to where a second set of stairs climbed to a heavy wooden door. They went up the stairs cautiously, and Par felt the hairs on the back of his neck prickle with the possibility that unseen eyes watched their every move. He peered left and right, overhead and all about, but saw nothing.

At the door they stopped again while the Mole used a small metal implement to spring the lock. In seconds they were through, moving swiftly into the hallway beyond. They were inside the citadel's inner wall now, the second line of defense to the city and the location of the barracks that housed most of the Federation garrison. The corridor was straight and narrow, and riddled with doors and windows that might give them away to anyone. But no one appeared in the moments it took them to reach the entry the Mole sought, and they were through another door almost before Par had time to take a steadying breath.

Now they stood in a shadowed alcove that looked out across the courtyard that lay between the inner and outer walls of the city. Federation soldiers stood watch at gates and on ramparts, dim shapes in the growing dark. Lights flickered from the windows of the sleeping quarters and guardhouses and off the battlements and gates. Booted feet scraped in the stillness. Voices rose in low murmurs. Somewhere, a whetstone was sharpening metal. Par felt his stomach tighten. The sounds of activity were all about.

They clung to the shadows of the alcove for long minutes, listening and watching, waiting before trying to go on. Par could hear Padishar's breathing as the big man hunched next to him against the wall. His own breathing punctuated the rapid beating of his heart. Stirrings of the wishsong's magic rose out of the depths of his chest, down deep where emotions have their beginnings, and he fought to keep it under control. He found himself thinking again about what would happen when he tried to use the magic. It was there, and he would use it – of that he was certain. But whether it would obey him was another matter entirely, and it occurred to him suddenly that if it should indeed overwhelm him and cause him to become the thing that Rimmer Dall had warned he must be, what was to prevent him from turning on his friends?

Damson, he decided. Damson and what she meant to him would keep the magic in hand.

Then the Mole was moving again, sliding away from the darkened entry along the roughened stone of the great wall. Padishar followed instantly, and Par found himself hurrying to keep up almost before he knew what he was doing. They inched swiftly through the blackness, shying when light from the torches brightened their path in soft pools, trying to blend into the stone, to think of themselves as invisible so that they would in fact become so. Federation soldiers continued to move all about, impossibly loud, uncomfortably close, and each moment it seemed certain to Par that they must be discovered.

But seconds later they were before another door, this one unlocked, and then through it to the light beyond . . .

A startled Federation soldier stood before them, pike held casually in his hands as he prepared to go out on watch. His mouth gaped open, and for a second he froze. His hesitation cost him his life. Padishar was on him instantly. One hand came up to cover his mouth. The blade of a long knife flashed in the other and then disappeared. Par saw the soldier's eyes widen in surprise. He saw the pain and then the emptiness. The soldier slumped into Padishar's arms like a rag doll. The pike fell away, and the quick hands of the Mole caught it before it could strike the floor. In a hall of stone and old wood lit by fire that flickered at the ends of pitch-coated torches fixed in the mortared walls, the intruders stood breathless and unmoving with the dead soldier clutched between them and listened to the silence.

Then Padishar lifted the body in his arms, carried it back into the shadows of a niche, and shoved it from view. Par watched it happen as if from a great distance, removed somehow from the event, as cold as the stone about him. He tried not to look. He could still hear the sound the soldier made when he died. He could still see the look in his eyes.

They went down the passageway swiftly, wary of other soldiers who might appear, listening for the silence to be disturbed. But they met no one else, and almost before Par realized it they were through a small, iron-bound door that was barely visible even from within the shadowed niche in which it was set.

The door closed behind them, and they stood in a blackness as complete as moonless night. Par could smell wood and dust and feel the roughness of boards beneath his feet. There was a moment's pause as the Mole rummaged about. Then a flint struck – once, twice – and a candle's thin flame cast its small glow. They were in a closet of some sort, barely six feet square, crammed with odd supplies and debris. The Mole moved things carefully aside, freeing a space at the back of the cubicle, and then pushed against the wall. A section of it that had been invisible to the naked eye came away in the form of a small door swinging inward.

Quickly they moved through. A narrow space opened between walls of stone and wood shoring, so low-ceilinged that Padishar was forced to crouch to avoid bumping his head. One big hand came up guardedly. Par saw blood on the hand and felt suddenly the nearness of his own death, as if it were something the dead soldier's eyes had foretold.

The Mole slid past him and began to lead them down through the walls, edging past stone projections, iron nails, and jagged wood splinters. Cobwebs brushed at their faces and small rodents ran squeaking through the dark ahead. The candle's flame was a dim glow against the black.

They began to climb, finding rungs hammered into the shoring and steps cut in the rock, a mix of ladders and ramps that wound up through the walls. They were in the tower now, working their way toward its apex and Damson's prison. From time to time they would hear voices, muffled and faint. It grew steadily warmer and more airless, and Par began to sweat. Their passageway became smaller and more difficult to navigate, and Padishar was having trouble squeezing through.

Then abruptly the Mole stopped, frozen in place. The leader of the free-born and the Valeman went still as well, crouched in the near blackness, listening. There was only the silence to be heard, but Par sensed something nevertheless – the feel of something alive and moving, just through the walls, just on the other side. Within him, the magic of the wishsong stirred like a hungry cat, and its fire purred anxiously. Par closed his eyes and concentrated on muting its sound.

What he sensed beyond the wall was one of the Shadowen.

He felt his breath catch in his throat as an image formed in his mind of the black thing, a vision brought to life by his magic. It stole along a corridor within the tower, hooded and cloaked, fingers testing the air like tentacles in search of prey. Could it sense them as well? Did it know they were there? The magic rustled like a snake inside Par Ohmsford, coiling, tensing, gathering force. Par muffled it and would not let go. Too soon! It was too soon!

The air whispered in his ear as if it were alive. He gritted his teeth and held on.

Then the Shadowen was gone, fading like a momentary thought, dark and evil and full of hate. The wishsong's magic cooled, easing down once again. Par felt some of the tautness let go, and the muscles in his chest and stomach relaxed. He was aware of Padishar looking at him, of the uneasiness mirrored on the other's face. Padishar reached back to grip his shoulder questioningly. Par felt the iron in the other's fingers, and stole some of its strength. He managed a quick, reassuring nod.

They continued on, climbing still, edging ahead through the gloom. Everywhere it was still, the small sounds of Federation voices and boots gone completely. The night was a blanket of silence in which every living thing seemed to have drifted off to sleep. Deceptive, Par thought as he labored on. Dangerous.

A moment later they stopped again, this time at a stretch of mortared stone wall framed by heavy timbers that buttressed one end of a floor overhead. The Mole handed the candle to Padishar and began to explore the stone with his fingers. Something clicked beneath his careful touch, and a section of the wall gave way. A seam of light appeared, faint and smoky.

The Mole turned back to Padishar. His voice was hushed. 'They keep her one flight down through the second door somewhere.' He hesitated. 'I could show you.'

'No,' Padishar said at once. 'Wait here. Wait for us to come back.'

The Mole studied him a moment and then nodded reluctantly. 'Second door,' he repeated.

With both hands braced against it, he pushed the portal in the wall all the way open. Padishar and Par Ohmsford stepped cautiously through.

They stood on a landing in a stairwell where the steps both climbed and descended. A door across from them was closed and barred, the metal thick with rust. Torches rested in iron brackets hammered into the stone, their glow tracing the line of the worn steps, their acrid smoke rising into the tower's gloom.

Everything was silent.

Behind them, the hidden door swung closed again.

Par glanced at Padishar. The big man was looking about guardedly. There was renewed uneasiness in his eyes. He shook his head at something unseen.

They began the descent, backs against the wall, ears straining to catch any threatening sounds. The stairs curled in serpentine fashion along the wall, the patches of torchlight just barely meeting at the turns. A hint of night sky was visible now and again through the slits in the stone, high and beyond reach from where they passed. Par's stomach was churning. He thought he heard something on the steps above, a small scraping of boots, a rustle of clothing. He blinked and wiped the sweat from his face. There was only silence.

They reached the next landing. There was a single door, unguarded, unlocked. They opened it and passed through easily. Par didn't like it. If this was where Damson was being kept, there should have been guards. He glanced again at Padishar, but the big man was looking ahead, down a dimly lit corridor that ran to the promised second door. They moved to it swiftly, and as they did Par felt the magic of the wishsong again stir suddenly to life. He gasped at the swiftness of its coming, almost doubling over with the heat it generated, like a furnace door being opened.

Something was wrong.

He grasped Padishar's arm. The big man turned, startled. Par jerked about, sensing movement behind, a dark presence . . . The Shadowen! They were –

And the door behind them flew open with a crash. Three black-cloaked Seekers surged through, Shadowen forms hunched and twisted within the concealing garb, weapons glinting in the torchlight. Padishar's broadsword scraped free of its scabbard. Par reached back for the Sword of Shannara, then jerked his hands away as if from live coals. He would be burned if he touched it! Burned, he knew!

'Padishar!' he gasped.

The big man wheeled toward the door behind them, but it,

too, swung wide, and two more of the black-cloaked monsters appeared. Both ends of the corridor were blocked now, and Par Ohmsford and Padishar Creel were trapped.

'The Mole!' Padishar swore, certain they had been betrayed.

But Par did not hear him. The Seekers rushed to seize them, and the magic of the wishsong exploded in the sound of his warning cry, filling the tower with fury. It enveloped him like a whirlwind, pressing him back against an astonished Padishar. He fought to contain it, but it overpowered him effortlessly. Then it broke away in shards of white-hot fire that flew at the Shadowen. The black figures threw up their arms, but the wishsong's magic tore through them and they were turned to ash. Par screamed, unable to help himself, and the wishsong broke through the walls like a flood through a dam, shattering mortared seams and blowing holes through the stone. Padishar flinched away, then grabbed at Par in desperation and hauled him bodily through the second door, slamming it shut behind them.

Par dropped to his knees, the wishsong silent once more.

'I . . . I can't breathe!' he gasped.

Padishar yanked him to his feet. 'Par! Shades, lad! What's happening to you? What's wrong?'

Par shook his head in despair. The magic's evolution continued unchecked within him. Substantive again, not imaginary. Brin's magic, not Jair's. A fire he could not control, smoldering, waiting . . .

His hands clasped the other's arms and his breath returned, a cooling within that stilled the madness. 'Find Damson!' he hissed. 'Maybe she's here, Padishar! Find her!'

There were shouts all about, the cries of Federation soldiers rushing along the ramparts and into the watchtower. Padishar grasped Par's tunic and dragged the Valeman after him as he hurried along a hall studded with heavy wooden doors, all locked and barred.

'Damson!' the big man called frantically.

Behind them, beyond the door through which they had fled, Par thought he heard the whisper of Shadowen robes.

'They're coming!' he warned, feeling the heat of the wishsong's magic beginning to build again.

'Damson!' Padishar Creel howled.

There was a muffled reply from behind one of the doors. Releasing Par, the leader of the free-born rushed on, calling out his daughter's name. The reply came again, and he skidded to a stop. The broadsword rose and fell, hacking at one of the doors. Shouts rose from a stairwell at the far end of the corridor. Padishar hammered at the door with several jarring strokes, then threw himself at what remained, his shoulder lowered. The door flew off its hinges and Padishar disappeared inside.

Par rushed to the opening and stopped. Padishar was back on his feet, bloodied and dazed, and Damson Rhee was hugging him, red hair dusty and tangled, her pale face smudged with dirt. Her eyes were all fire as they swept up to find the Valeman.

'Par,' she breathed softly, and rushed to hold him.

The hallway behind was filled with the sound of armed men. Par turned to meet the attack, but Padishar Creel was past him in an instant and into the corridor. There was a chilling clash of weapons.

'Par!' the big man called. 'Take her and run!'

Without thinking, Par grabbed Damson's arm and pulled her after him through the door. Padishar stood toe to toe with a knot of Federation soldiers. More appeared in the stairwell beyond. The leader of the free-born threw back the foremost by sheer strength alone and spun about in fury.

'Drat you, boy – run! Now! Remember our agreement!'

Then the soldiers were on him again, and he was fighting for his life. Two went down, then another, but there were more to take their place. Too many, Par thought. Too many to stand against. He felt his chest tighten. He must help his friend. But that would mean using the wishsong's magic, the fire he could not control. It would mean seeing those men ripped to pieces. It would mean chancing that Padishar would be ripped to pieces as well.

And he had given the big man his promise.

'Padishar,' he heard Damson breathe in his ear and felt her start toward the big man.

Instantly he had hold of her and was dragging her back the way they had come, away from the fighting. He had made his choice. 'Par!' she screamed in anger, but he shook his head no. They reached the closed door. Were there Shadowen behind it? Par could not hear them; he could not hear anything above the sounds of the battle behind him.

'We can't leave him!' Damson was screaming.

He pulled her close. 'We have to.' Before him, the wooden door loomed, hiding what lay behind, forbidding and silent. He braced himself, summoning the wishsong's magic because this time there was no choice. The magic stirred, anxious.

Please, he thought, *let me keep control of it just this once*!

He flung open the door, ready to send the magic careening down the corridor beyond, white-hot and deadly. Silence greeted him. Moonlight flooded down through cracks in the shattered stone. Debris littered the floor. The passage was empty.

He cast a final look back at the embattled Padishar Creel, a solitary barrier against the flood of Federation soldiers seeking to break past. There was no hope for Padishar, he knew. It had been a trap from the beginning. And the trap was about to close.

Yet there was still time to save Damson.

As they had agreed they would, whatever the cost.

With Damson still clinging to his arm, he charged ahead into the empty corridor, leaving Padishar Creel behind.

6

They were through the stairwell door and back out on the landing in seconds. A haze of sound and fury rose from the corridor behind them, where Padishar held the Federation soldiers at bay.

Par wheeled back and kicked the tower door shut.

Which way?

From below, he could hear the thudding of boots and the shouts of men as they ascended the stairs. They could not go down.

'Let go of me!' Damson cried furiously, and yanked free of him. Her green eyes were bright with tears and anger. 'You left him!'

Par was barely listening. They had to go up, back the way they had come, back to where the Mole waited. Unless Padishar had been right and the Mole had indeed betrayed them. It was possible. The Mole might have been taken days ago when the Federation had first found them in his lair. But, no, if he had been taken then, he would not have helped them escape when they had fled the gristmill; he would have let the Federation have them and been done with the matter. But what if he had been caught when he had gone in search of Damson this last time – taken and subverted, made over into a Shadowen?

Damson was tearing at him. 'We have to go back, Par! He

58

needs us! He's my father!' Her teeth bared. 'He came back for you!'

Par wheeled on her, grasped her arms, and dragged her so close that he could feel the heat of her breath on his face. 'I'll only say this once. I gave him my promise. Whatever else happened, you were to be gotten safely away. He's given himself up for you, Damson, and it is not going to be for nothing! Now, run!'

He spun her about and shoved her up the stairwell. They raced up the steps, listening to the sounds of pursuit grow closer. Par's face was grim with purpose. If the Mole had betrayed them, they were finished whichever way they ran. If he had not, then their only chance was to find him.

They reached the next landing, and Par cast about in vain for the hidden door. He could not remember where it was; he hadn't paid that much attention when he had come through. Now everything looked the same.

'Mole!' he shouted in desperation.

Immediately the wall split apart to his left, and the Mole's furry face peered out. 'Here! Here, lovely Damson!' he called frantically.

They hurried through the opening, and the Mole pushed the wall closed behind them. 'Padishar?' he inquired anxiously, and the way he spoke and the look that came into his damp eyes suggested to Par for reasons he would never be able to explain that no betrayal had taken place.

'They have him,' the Valeman answered, forcing himself to look directly at Damson. She turned aside instantly.

'Come away, then,' the Mole urged, the candle in his hand as he scurried ahead of them. 'Hurry.'

They went back down into the tower walls, winding and twisting their way through the gloom, listening to the cries of soldiers filter through the stone in a muffled cacophony. They reached the closet and passed quickly into the hallway beyond. Outside, soldiers ran past the barracks windows, headed for the watchtower and the gates.

Torchlight sparked and flared as it was brought to bear against the darkness, and the sound of bolts being thrown and crossbars being dropped into their metal fitting was deafening. Pressed against the wall in a pool of darkness, the Mole held his charges in place for a moment, then beckoned them ahead. They ran in a crouch through the empty corridor to the door that had brought them and pushed through to the courtyard without.

Darkness had fallen, and the moon and stars were hidden by clouds that hung low and sullen across the bluff. Fire cast its smoky light through the gloom with little effect. Figures charged about everywhere, but it was impossible to make out their faces.

'This way!' the Mole whispered hoarsely.

They moved left along the wall, hurrying because everyone else was hurrying as well. They slipped through the dark, just three more bodies in the confusion, another three for which no one had time or interest.

They were almost to the door leading back to the city's underground when they were challenged. A shout brought them about, and a dark figure came striding out of the gloom. For an instant Par thought it was Padishar, miraculously escaped, but then he saw the markings of a Federation captain on a dark uniform. All three froze at his approach, uncertain what to do. The captain reached them, his dark bearded face coming into the light.

Then Damson stepped forward, smooth and relaxed, smiling at him. A confused look appeared on his face. She gave him an instant more, then hit him three times across the face with the blade of her hand, the blows so quick that Par could barely see them. She stepped into him, drew his arm across her shoulder, and threw him down. He wheezed and tried to cry out, but a final blow to the throat silenced him for good.

Damson rose and pushed past Par to where the Mole was already disappearing through the door. Par remembered in that instant how easily she had overcome him that night in the

60

People's Park when he had believed her responsible for the Federation trap that had ensnared Padishar and the others. She might have done so again in the watchtower, he realized. She could have forced him to go back if she had wished. Why hadn't she?

They were inside the inner wall again, hurrying back down to the cellars that had brought them. The sounds without were fading now, muffled behind the layers of stone block. They reached the trapdoor and passed through, descending the steps to the tunnels below. From there, they moved swiftly through the gloom, away from the city's walls and back toward its center. Soon they were deep within the sewers and everything was silent.

'Let's . . . let's just rest a moment,' Par suggested finally, out of breath from running, needing to think, to decide what to do next.

'Here,' the Mole offered, directing them to a platform that served as a base for a ladder climbing to the streets at a confluence of tunnels and pipes. Overhead, light shone dimly through a grate. The streets were still and empty of life. 'I will go back and make certain we are not followed.'

He disappeared into the dark, leaving them the candle. The Valeman and the girl watched him go, then settled themselves gingerly in place, backs to the wall, side by side with the candle before them. Par felt drained. He stared at the darkness beyond the candle's flame, exhaustion spreading through him. He could hear Damson breathing, could feel the heat of her body.

'You know what they'll do to him,' she said finally. He didn't respond, looking straight ahead. 'They'll make him one of them. They'll use him.'

If they manage to take him alive, Par thought. And maybe not even then. Rimmer Dall is unpredictable.

'Why didn't you make me go back for him?' he asked her.

There was a long silence before she spoke. 'I would never do that to you.'

He didn't say anything for a moment, letting the import of the words sink in. 'I'm sorry about Padishar,' he said finally. 'I didn't want to leave him either.'

'I know,' she said quietly.

She said it in such a matter-of-fact way that he looked over at her to make certain he had heard her correctly. Her eyes met his. 'I know,' she repeated. The pain in her voice was palpable. 'It wasn't your fault. Padishar made you promise to save me first. He would have made me promise as well if our positions had been reversed.' She looked away again. 'I was just angry when I saw . . .' She shook her head.

'Are you all right?'

She nodded wordlessly, and her eyes closed.

'Do they know who you are?'

She glanced over again. 'No. Why would they?'

He took a deep breath. 'The Mole. That was a trap back there, Damson. They were waiting for us. They had some reason to believe we would come for you. What better reason than if they knew that you were Padishar Creel's daughter? Padishar thinks the Mole gave us away.'

There was new anger in her eyes. 'Par, the Mole saved us! Saved you, anyway. I was just unlucky. The Federation recognized me from the streets, and they knew I had helped you escape the gristmill.' She hesitated. 'That was a trap as well, wasn't it? They knew . . .' She paused again, uncertain of where she was going.

'It could have been the Mole,' Par pressed. 'He could have been taken when he came to look for you. Or sometimes before.'

'And helped us escape anyway?' she asked incredulously. 'Why? What would be the point? The Federation would have had us all if he hadn't gotten us out of the watchtower.'

'I know. I was thinking that, too.' He shook his head. 'But they keep finding us, Damson. How do they do that? The Shadowen seem to have an ear to every wall. It's insidious. Sometimes it seems as if there isn't anyone left to trust.'

Her smile was bitter. 'There isn't, Par. Not anyone. Didn't you realize that? There's only you and me. And can we even trust each other?'

He stared at her in shock. A sadness came into her eyes, and she reached out quickly, put her arms about him, and drew him close.

'I'm sorry,' she said, and he could feel her crying.

'I thought I might have lost you for good,' he whispered into her hair. He felt her nod slightly. 'I'm so tired of all this. I just want it to end.'

They clung to each other in silence, and Par let himself drift with the feel of her, closing his eyes, letting the weariness seep away. He wished suddenly that he were back in the Vale, returned home again to his family and his old life, that Coll were alive, and that none of this had ever happened. He wished he had it all to do over again. He would not be so eager to go in search of Allanon. He would not be so quick to undertake his search for the Sword of Shannara.

And he would not be tricked into believing that his magic was a gift.

He thought then of how much a part of him the wishsong had once been and how alien it seemed now. It had broken free of his control again when he had called upon it in the watchtower. Despite his preparations, despite his efforts. Could he even say, in fact, that he had summoned it – or had it simply come on its own when it sensed those Shadowen? Surely it had done as it chose in any case, lancing out like knives to cut them apart. Par felt himself shudder at the memory. He would never have wished for that. The magic had destroyed the black things without thought, without compunction. His brow furrowed. No, not the magic. Him. He had destroyed them. He had not wanted to, perhaps, but he had done so nevertheless. Par didn't like what that suggested. The Shadowen were what they were, and perhaps it was true that they would not hesitate the span of a breath to kill him. But that did not change who and what he was. He could still see the eyes of that soldier

Padishar had killed. He could see the life fade from them in an instant's time. It made him want to cry. He hated the fact that it was necessary and that he was a part of it. Understanding the reasons for it did not make it any more palatable. Yet what sort of hypocrite was he, despairing for a single life one moment and putting an end to half-a-dozen the next?

He didn't want to know the answer to that question. He didn't think he could bear it. What he recognized was that the magic of the wishsong had changed somehow within him and in so doing had changed him as well. It made him think more closely of Rimmer Dall's claim that he, too, was a Shadowen. After all, what was the difference between them?

'Damson?'

The Mole's tentative voice whispered from out of the black and parted her from him as she looked up. Funny, he thought, how the Mole only speaks to her.

The little fellow slipped into the light, blinking and squinting. 'They do not follow. The tunnels are empty.'

Damson looked back at Par. 'What do we do now, Elf-boy?' she whispered, reaching up to brush back his hair. 'Where do we go?'

Par smiled and took the hand in his own. 'I love you, Damson Rhee,' he told her quietly, his words so soft they were lost in the rustle of his clothing.

He rose. 'We get out of his city. We try to find help. From Morgan or the free-born or someone. We can't continue on alone.' He looked down at the hunched form of the Mole. 'Mole, can you help us get away?'

The Mole glanced at Damson. 'There are tunnels beneath the city that will take you to the plain beyond. I can show you.'

Par turned back to Damson. For a moment she did not speak. Her green eyes were filled with unspoken thoughts. 'All right, Par, I'll go,' she said at last. 'I know we can't stay. Time and luck are running out for us here in Tyrsis.' She stepped close. 'But now you must give me your promise – just as you

gave it to Padishar. Promise that we will come back for him –
that we won't leave him to die.'

*She does not give a moment's consideration to the possibility
that he might already be dead. She believes him stronger than
that. And so do I, I guess.*

'I promise,' he whispered.

She leaned close and kissed him on the mouth, hard. 'I love
you, too, Par Ohmsford,' she said. 'I'll love you to the end.'

It took them the remainder of the night to navigate the maze of
tunnels that lay beneath Tyrsis, the ancient passageways that
had served long ago as bolt holes for the city's defenders and
now served as their escape. The tunnels crisscrossed over and
back again, sometimes broad and high enough for wagons to
pass through, sometimes barely large enough for the Mole and
his charges. At places the rock was dry and dusty and smelled
of old earth and disuse; at times it was damp and chill and
stank of sewage. Rats squealed at their coming and disappeared into the walls. Insects skittered away like dry leaves
blown across stone. The sound of their boots and their breathing echoed hollowly down the passageways, and it seemed that
they could not possibly go undetected. But the Mole chose
their path carefully, frequently taking them away from the
most direct route, choosing on the basis of things that he alone
sensed and knew. He did not speak to them; he guided them
ahead through his silent netherworld like the specter at haunt
he had become. Now and again he would pause to look back at
them or to study something he found on the tunnel floors or to
consider the gloom that pressed in about them, distracted and
distant in his musings. Par and Damson would stop with him,
waiting, watching, and wondering what he was thinking. They
never asked. Par wanted to, but if Damson thought it wise to
keep silent he was persuaded to do so as well.

At last they reached a place where the darkness ahead was
broken by a hazy silver glow. They stumbled toward it

through a curtain of old webbing and dust, scrambling up a rocky slide that narrowed as it went until they were bent double. Bushes blocked the way forward, so thick that the Mole was forced to cut a path for them using a long knife he had somehow managed to conceal within his fur. Pushing aside the severed branches, the three crawled through the last of the concealing foliage and emerged into the light.

They came to their feet then and looked about. The mountains sheltering the bluff on which Tyrsis was settled rose behind them, a jagged black wall against the light of the dawn breaking east, the shadow of its peaks stretching away north and west across the plains like a dark stain until it disappeared into the trees of the forests beyond. The air was warm and smelled of grasses dried by the summer sun. Birdsong rose from the concealment of the trees, and dragonflies darted over small pools of weed-grown water formed by streams that ran down out of the rocks behind them.

Par looked over at Damson and smiled. 'We're out,' he said softly, and she smiled back.

He turned to the Mole, who blinked uncertainly in the unfamiliar light. Impulsively, he reached down. 'Thank you, Mole,' he said. 'Thank you for everything.'

The Mole's face furrowed, and the blinking grew more rapid. A hand came up tentatively, touched Par's, and withdrew. 'You are welcome,' was the soft reply.

Damson came over, knelt before the Mole, and put her arms about him. 'Good-bye for now,' she whispered. 'Go somewhere safe, Mole. Stay well away from the black things. Keep hidden until we return.'

The Mole's arms lifted and his wrinkled hands stroked the girl's slim shoulders. 'Always, lovely Damson. Always, for you.'

She released him then, and the Mole's fingers brushed her face gently. Par thought he saw tears at the corners of the little fellow's bright eyes. Then the Mole turned from them and disappeared back into the gloom.

They stared after him for a moment, then looked at each other.

'Which way?' Par asked.

She laughed. 'That's right. You don't know where Firerim Reach is, do you? I forget sometimes, you seem so much a part of things.'

He smiled. 'Hard to remember when you didn't have me to look after, isn't it?'

She gave him a questioning look. 'I'm not complaining. Are you?'

He moved over to her and held her for a moment. He didn't say anything; he simply stood with his arms about her, his cheek against her auburn hair, and his eyes closed. He thought about all they had come through, how many times their lives had been at risk, and how dangerous their journey had been. So little distance traveled to come so far, he mused. So little time to have discovered so much.

Still holding her, he stroked her back in small circles and said, 'I'll tell you something. It sometimes seems as if I'm frightened all the time. Ever since Coll and I first left Varfleet, all those weeks ago, I've been afraid. Everything that happens seems to cost something. I never know what I'm going to lose next, and I hate it. But what frightens me most, Damson Rhee, is the possibility that I might lose you.'

He tightened his arms about her, pressing her close. 'What do you think about that?' he whispered.

Her response was to tighten her arms back.

They walked through the early morning without saying much after that, leaving behind the city of Tyrsis, moving north across the plains to the forested threshold of the Dragon's Teeth. The day warmed quickly, crystals of night's dew faded with the sun's rise, and dampness dried away into stirrings of dust. They saw no one for a long time, and then only peddlers and families coming in from their farms to market in the city. Par found himself thinking of home again, of his parents and Coll, but it all seemed to be something that had happened a long time ago. He might wish that things were as they had been and that all that had happened since his encounter with Cogline had not – but he knew he might as well wish the day become night and the sun the moon. He looked at Damson walking beside him, at the soft strong lines of her face and the movement of her body, and let what might have been slide quickly away.

At midday they crossed the Mermidon into the forests beyond and stopped to eat. They foraged for fresh water, berries, roots, and vegetables, and made do. It was cool and silent within the trees while the day's heat suffocated the surrounding land in an airless, sweltering blanket. After eating, they decided to sleep for a time, weary from their night's efforts and anxious to take advantage of their refuge. It was only several hours further to the Kennon Pass, Damson advised, where they would cross through the Dragon's Teeth into the valley that had once been Paranor's home. From there they would travel north and east to the Jannisson Pass and Firerim Reach. In another two days, she promised, they should reach the free-born.

But they slept longer than they had planned, lulled by the coolness and the soothing sound of the wind in the trees, and it was nearing sunset when they came awake again. They rose and set out at once, anxious to make up as much time as they could. If the moon was out, they could navigate the pass at night. Otherwise, they would have to wait until morning. In either case, they wanted to reach the Kennon by nightfall.

So they traveled swiftly, unhindered by heavy stands of scrub or grasses in woods that were well traveled and spacious, feeling rested and fit after their sleep. The sun drifted west, edging down into the trees until it was a bright flare of gold and crimson through the screen of the leaves and branches. The moon appeared in skies that were clear and blue, and the day birds began to grow silent in response to the coming of night. Par felt at ease for the first time in days, at peace with himself. He was relieved to be out of Tyrsis, clear of her sewers and cellars, free of the confinement of her walls, safe from the things that had hunted him there. He looked over at Damson often and smiled when he did. He thought of Padishar and tried to keep from being sad. His thoughts scattered through the trees and across the carpet of the earthen floor like small creatures at play. He let them wander where they chose, content to let them go.

Not once did it occur to him that it might be wise to hide his trail.

Sunset burned like fire across the plains below Tyrsis as day inched toward night and the heat began to dissipate. Shadows lengthened and grew, taking on strange and suggestive shapes, coming alive with the dark. They rose out of gullies and ravines, from forests and solitary groves, stretching this way and that as if to flex their limbs on waking from the sleep that prepared them for going abroad to hunt.

One of those shadows moved with insidious purpose along the empty stretches running north to the Mermidon, a faint darkness hidden within the long grasses through which it passed. As the light failed it grew bolder, rising up now and again to sniff the air before lowering back to the earth to keep the scent it followed fresh. It ate as it went, sustaining itself with whatever it found, roots and berries, insects and small animals, anything it came across that was unable to escape. For the most part its attention was focused on the trail it followed, on the smell of the one it hunted so diligently, the one that was the source of its madness.

At the Mermidon it lifted to its hindquarters, a hunched-over, gnarled form wrapped in a shining black cloak that somehow resisted the dust and grime that coated its wearer. Hands skinned and scraped so badly they bled clutched at the cloak so that it would not wash free as it forded that river at a shallows. The cloak never left it, not for a moment. The cloak sustained it in some way, it knew. The cloak was what protected it.

Yet it seemed a source of the madness as well. Some part of the creature's mind whispered that this was so. It whispered it to the creature in warning, over and over again.

But most of what worked in the creature's thoughts assured it that the cloak was good and necessary to its survival, and that the madness was caused instead by the one it tracked. By him. (My brother?) The name would not come. Only the face. The madness buzzed within its head, through its ears, and out its mouth like a swarm of gnats, itching and biting and consuming its reason until it could think of nothing else.

Earlier that day, in the shadow of late afternoon, come abroad in the hated light because the madness drove it from its den with increasing frequency, it had found at last the scent of the one it hunted. (His name? What was his name?) Prowling the base of the bluff night after night for more than a week now, it had grown increasingly desperate, needing to find him, to search him out so that relief would come, so that the madness would end.

But how? How would it end?

It didn't know. Somehow it would happen. When it found the cause. When it . . . hurt him like he was hurting it . . .

The thought drifted before its eyes, unclear. But there was pleasure in the thought, in the taste and feel of it.

Teeth and eyes gleamed in the brightening moonlight.

On the far side of the river, the creature picked up the trail easily and again began to track. Fresh it was. As clear as the stench of something dead and left to rot in the sun. Not far it was. Another few hours, perhaps less . . .

A shudder passed through the creature. Anticipation. Need. The seeds of the madness in flower.

Coll Ohmsford put his nose to the ground like the animal he had become and disappeared into the trees.

7

Dusk was edging into night by the time Par and Damson reached the base of the Dragon's Teeth and the trail that wound upward through the cliffs to the Kennon. Moonlight flooded down from the north, and the skies were clear and bright with stars. The day's heat had cooled, and there was a breeze blowing out of the mountains.

Somewhere in the trees of the forest behind, an owl hooted softly and was still.

Because there was light enough to navigate the trail and they were well rested, the Valeman and the girl pushed on. The night was well suited for travel, even in the mountains, and they made good time climbing from the lower slopes into the pass. As they went, night descended and the silence deepened, the forest and its inhabitants falling away behind them in a pool of black, the rocks closing about and becoming silhouettes that rose jagged and stark against the sky. Their boots scraped and crunched on the loose stone and their breathing grew labored, but beyond those immediate sounds the world was still and empty-feeling.

Time passed, and midnight approached. They were well into the pass now, approaching its apex, the point where the trail would start down again into the valley beyond. The light ahead seemed brighter than the light behind, a phenomenon for which neither the Valeman nor the girl could account, and they exchanged more than one questioning glance. It was not until they had reached the top of the pass, deep within the mountain peaks, the way forward a long, broad corridor through the rock, that they realized that what they were seeing was not the light of moon or stars, but the blaze of watch fires burning directly ahead.

Now the glance they exchanged was a wary one. Why were there watch fires burning here? Who had set them?

They proceeded more cautiously than before, keeping well into the shadows on the dark side of the pass, stopping frequently to listen for what might be waiting ahead. Even so, they almost missed seeing the guards posted on a rise several hundred yards further on, positioned so as to give them a clear view of anyone trying to slip past. The guards were soldiers, and they wore Federation uniforms. Par and Damson melted instantly into the shadows and out of view.

'What are they doing here?' the girl whispered in Par's ear.

The Valeman shook his head. There was no reason for them to be here that he could figure out. The free-born were nowhere near the Kennon. Firerim Reach was far to the east. There was only the valley beyond, and there was nothing in the valley, hadn't been anything there for that matter since . . .

His mind froze and his eyes went wide.

Since Paranor had disappeared.

He took a deep breath and held it, remembering Allanon's charge to Walker Boh. Was it possible that Walker had . . . ?

He did not finish the thought. He would not let himself. He knew he was jumping to conclusions, that the presence of the soldiers in the pass could be for any number of reasons.

Yet something inside whispered that he was right. The soldiers were there because Paranor was back.

He bent hurriedly to Damson. She stared at him in surprise, seeing the excitement in his eyes. 'Damson.' He breathed her name. 'We have to get past those guards. Or at least . . .' His mind raced. 'At least we have to get far enough into the rocks to see what's beyond, what's down in the valley. Can we do that? Is there a way? Another way?'

He was speaking so fast that his words were tumbling over one another. Walker Boh, he was thinking. The Dark Uncle. He had almost forgotten about Walker – had all but given up on him since their separation at the Hadeshorn. But Walker was unpredictable. And Allanon had believed in him, enough so that he had determined that the charge to find Paranor should be his.

Shades! His heart was pumping so fast it seemed to jump inside his chest. What if . . . ?

Damson's hand on his arm startled him. 'Come with me.'

They retraced their steps through the pass to a cut in the rocks where a narrow trail led upward. Slowly, they began to climb. The trail twisted and wound about, sometimes doubling back on itself, sometimes angling so steeply that they were forced to proceed on hands and knees, pulling themselves upward by gripping rocks and bits of scrub. The minutes slipped by and still they climbed, sweating freely now, breathing through their mouths, their muscles beginning to ache. Par did not question where they were going. These mountains had been the stronghold of the free-born for years. No one knew them better. Damson would know what she was about.

At last the trail flattened again and angled forward toward the glow from the watch fires. They were high in the peaks now, well above the pass. The air blew chilly and sharp here, and sound was muffled. They went forward in a crouch as the rocks to either side gave way to a narrow bluff. The wind whipped against them violently, and the light of the fires spread against the screen of the night sky like a misted autumn sunset.

The trail ended at a drop that fell away hundreds of feet along a cliff face. Below and halfway up lay the north entrance to the Kennon Pass. It was there that the watch fires burned, dozens of them, steady and bright within the shelter of the rocks. Sleeping forms lay all about, wrapped in blankets.

Horses were tethered on a picket line. Sentries patrolled at every juncture. The Federation had blocked the pass completely.

Almost afraid of what he would find – or wouldn't find – Par lifted his gaze beyond the Federation encampment to the valley beyond. For a moment he couldn't see anything, his vision weakened from staring at the fires, the blackness into which he peered a sweeping curtain that shrouded the whole of the horizon. He waited for his eyes to adjust, keeping them focused on the dark. Slowly the valley began to take shape. In the softer light of moon and stars, the silhouettes of mountains and forests etched themselves against the skyline; lakes and rivers glimmered in dull flashes of silver, and the fuzzy deep gray of nighttime meadows and grassy hills were a patchwork against the black.

'Par!' Damson whispered suddenly, and her fingers tightened on his arm. Leaning into him with excitement, her hand lifted hurriedly to point.

And there was Paranor.

She had seen it first – far out in the valley, washed in moonlight and centered on a great rise. Par caught his breath and leaned forward, stretching out as far as he could from the edge of the drop to make certain that he was not deceived, that he was not mistaken . . .

No. There was no mistake. It was indeed the Druid's Keep, come back out of time and history, come back from dreams of what might once have been into the world of men. Par still couldn't believe it. No one living had ever seen Paranor. Par himself had only sung about it, envisioning it from the stories he had heard, from the tales of generations of Ohmsfords now long dead. Gone for all those years, gone for so long that it was only legend to most, and suddenly here it was, returned to the Four Lands – here, as real as life, walls and ramparts, towers and parapets, rising up out of the earth phoenixlike amid the dark girdle of the forests that encircled it protectively below.

74

Paranor. Somehow Walker Boh had found a way to bring it back.

Par's smile stretched ear to ear as he reached for Damson and hugged her until he feared she would break in two. She hugged him back as fiercely, laughing softly as she did. Then they broke apart, stared downward a final time at the dark bulk of the castle, and wormed their way back along the bluff into the shelter of the rocks.

'Did you see it?' Par exclaimed when they were safely away again. He hugged her once more. 'Walker did it! He brought back Paranor! Damson, it's happening! The charges Allanon gave us are coming to pass! If I really do have the Sword of Shannara and if Wren has found the Elves . . . !' He caught himself. 'I wonder what's happened to Wren? I wish I knew something more, confound it! And where's Walker? Do you think he's down there, inside the castle? Is that why the Federation has blocked the pass – to keep him there?' His hands gestured excitedly against her back. 'And what about the Druids? What do you think, Damson? Has he found them?'

She shook her head, grinning at him. 'We won't know for a while, I'm afraid. We're still stuck on the wrong side of the pass.' The smile faded, and she loosened his arms gently. 'There's no way around those soldiers, Par. Not unless you want to use your magic to disguise us. What do you think? Do you want to do that? Could you?'

Cold blossomed in the pit of his stomach. The wishsong again. There was no escape from it. He could feel its magic stir inside him in anticipation of the possibility that it might be needed again, that it might be given a new release . . .

Damson saw the change that came into his face and pulled him quickly to his feet. 'No, you won't use the magic. Not if you don't have to, and you don't. We can go another way – east below the mountains and then north across the Rabb. A little longer journey perhaps, but just as sure.'

He nodded, relief washing through him. Her instincts were

right. He was frightened of using the magic. He didn't trust it anymore. 'All right,' he agreed, forcing a smile. 'That's what we'll do.'

'Come on, then.' She pulled at his hand. 'Let's go back the way we came. We can sleep a few hours and then start out again.' Her smile was brilliant. 'Think of it, Par. Paranor!'

They retraced their steps along the narrow pathway, easing down out of the rocks to the main pass, and then began the trek south. They traveled swiftly, excited by what they had found, anxious to convey the news to others. But after the first rush of euphoria had passed, Par found himself having second thoughts. Perhaps he was being premature in celebrating the return of Paranor. Allanon's shade had never explained what purpose would be served in fulfilling the charges he had given. Paranor was back, but what difference did it make? Were the Druids back as well? If so, would they help in the battle against the Shadowen?

Or would they, as Rimmer Dall had suggested, prove to be the real enemy of the races?

As they twisted and wound their way along the trail toward the dark belt of the forests below, Par's mood darkened steadily. Walker had been wary of Allanon's motives. He had been the first to warn against the Druids. What had happened then to make him change his mind? Why had he agreed to bring back Paranor? Par wished he could speak with him, just for a moment. He wished he could talk to almost anyone from the original company who had come with him to the Hadeshorn. He was tired of feeling alone and abandoned in this. He was weary of having questions with no answers.

They reached the base of the Dragon's Teeth two hours later and moved back into the shelter of the trees. Behind them, the glow of the Federation watch fires had long since faded into the rocks, and the excitement of discovering Paranor had turned to insistent doubt. Par kept his thoughts to himself, but Damson's occasional glance suggested she was not fooled by his silence. It seemed to Par that they were so close and knew each other so well by now that words weren't necessary for communication. Damson could read his thoughts. She knew what he was thinking; he could see it in her eyes.

She took the lead as they entered the trees, turning them east along the base of the mountains, guiding them through heavier undergrowth to where the trees spread apart and there were grassy clearings and small streams in which to set camp. The night was filled with small, delicate sounds, a balance of contentment that no predator disturbed. The wind had died away, and the air before them turned frosty with their breath as they walked. The moon had disappeared below the horizon, and they were left with starlight to show them the way.

They did not go far, no more than a mile, before Damson settled on a glade beside a small spring for their resting place. A few hours, she advised; they would start out again before daybreak. They wrapped themselves in blankets that had been provided by the Mole from one of his underground caches and lay close to each other in the dark, staring up into the trees. Par cradled the Sword of Shannara in the crook of one arm, its length resting against his body, wondering again what purpose his talisman was meant to serve, wondering how he was ever supposed to find out.

Wondering still, at the very back of his mind, if it was really what he believed it to be.

'I think it is a good thing,' Damson whispered just before he fell asleep. 'I don't think you should worry.'

He wasn't sure what she was talking about, and although he was tempted he didn't ask.

He woke while it was still dark, the sunrise a faint glimmering of silver far east, barely visible through the tops of the trees. It was the silence that woke him, the sudden absence of all sound – the birds and insects gone still, the animals frozen to ice, the whole of the immediate world turned empty and dead. He sat up with a start, as if waking from a bad dream. But it was the silence that had interrupted his slumber, and he was struck with the thought that no dream could ever be as terrifying.

Shadows cloaked the glade, deep and melting pools of damp. Gloom hung across the air like smoke, and there was a faint hint of mist through the trees. Par's hands were on the Sword of Shannara, the blade clutched before him as if to ward off his fear. He glanced about hurriedly, saw nothing, looked about some more, then came to his feet warily. Damson was awake as well now, sleepy-eyed as she lifted from her blanket, stifling a yawn.

Still as death, Par thought. His eyes shifted anxiously.

What was wrong? Why was it so quiet?

Then something moved in the deepest of the glade's shadows, a shifting of blackness barely discernible to the naked eye, the kind of motion that comes when clouds drift across the face of the moon. Except that there were no clouds or moon, nothing but the night sky and its fading stars.

Damson stood up beside him. 'Par?' she whispered questioningly.

He did not avert his eyes from the movement. It began to take shape, an insidious coalescence that lent definition to what moments before had been nothing but the night.

A figure appeared, stunted and crouched, all black and faceless beneath a concealing cloak and hood.

Par stared. There was something about this intruder that was familiar, something he could almost put a name to. It was in the way it moved, or held itself, or breathed. But how could that be?

The figure approached, not walking as a man or animal would, but slouching like something that was neither and still both. It hunched its way out of the deep gloom and came toward them, the sound of its breathing suddenly audible. *Huff, huff,* a rasping cough, a hiss. Black-cloaked and hooded, it stayed hidden in its silky covering of night until all at once its

78

head lifted and the light caught the faint glimmer of its crimson eyes.

Par felt Damson's fingers close on his arms.

It was Shadowen.

A weary and futile acceptance came with the Valeman's recognition of his enemy. He must fight again after all. He must call upon the wishsong once more. There was no end to it, he thought dully. Wherever he went, they found him. Each time he thought he had used the magic for the last time, he was required to use it one time more. And one time after that. Forever.

The Shadowen advanced, a humping of black cloth and a dragging of limbs. The thing seemed barely able to make itself move, and it clung to its cloak as if it could not bear to let go. The cloak, too, was an odd thing – all shiny black and as clean as new cloth despite the ragged, soiled appearance of the thing that wore it. Par felt the wishsong's magic begin building within him, unbidden, rising up on its own, the core of a fire that would not stay quenched. He let it come, knowing the futility of trying to stop it, realizing that there was no other choice. He did not even try to look for a way to escape the glade. Running, after all, was pointless. The Shadowen would simply track them. It would keep coming until it was stopped.

Until he killed it.

He winced at the words and thought, *Not again!* – seeing the face of that soldier in the watchtower, seeing all their faces, all the dead from all the encounters . . .

The creature stopped. Within the cloak, its head shook violently, as if it were beset by demons that only it could see. It made a sound; it might have been crying.

Then its face lifted into the light, and Par Ohmsford felt the world fall away beneath him.

He was looking at Coll.

Ravaged, twisted, bruised, and dirtied, the face before him was still Coll's.

For a moment, he thought he was going mad. He heard

Damson's gasp of disbelief, felt himself take an involuntary step backward, and watched his brother's lips part in a twisted effort to speak.

'Par?' came the plea.

He gave a low, despairing cry, cut it short immediately, and with a supreme effort steadied himself. No. No, this had been tried once, tried and failed. This was not Coll. This was just a Shadowen pretending to be his brother, a trick to deceive him . . .

Why?

He groped for an answer. To drive him mad, of course. To make him . . . to force him to . . .

He clenched his teeth. Coll was dead! He had seen him die, destroyed in the fire of the wishsong's magic – Coll, who had become one of them, a Shadowen, like this one . . .

Something whispered at the back of his mind, a warning that took no discernible form, words that lacked meaning beyond their intent. *Caution, Valeman! Beware!*

His hands still clenched the Sword of Shannara. Without thinking, still lost in the horror of what he was seeing, he brought the blade and scabbard up before him like a shield.

Instantly, the Shadowen was on him, closing the distance between them in the blink of an eye, moving far more swiftly than should have been possible for such a twisted body. It sprang into him, giving forth an anguished shriek, and Coll's face rose up, large and terrifying, until it was right against his own and he could smell the stench of it. Gnarled hands closed about the handle of the Sword of Shannara and tried to wrench it free. Down the Valeman and the Shadowen went in a tangle of arms and legs. Par heard Damson cry out, and then he was rolling away from her, fighting for possession of the Sword. His hands shifted from the scabbard to the pommel, trying to gain leverage, to twist the blade free. He was face to face with his adversary as he fought. He could see into the depth of his brother's eyes . . .

No! No, it wasn't possible!

They tumbled into the trees, into grasses that whipped and sawed at their hands and faces. The scabbard to the Sword slid free, and now there was only the razor-sharp metal of the blade between them, jerking back and forth like a deadly pendulum as they struggled. Par became tangled in the folds of the strange, glimmering cloak, and the feel of it against his skin was repulsive, like the touch of something living. Thrashing wildly, he flung the trailing cloth away. He kicked out, and the Shadowen grunted as Par's knee jammed into its body. But it would not let go, hands clasped about the blade in a death grip. Par was furious. The Shadowen seemed to have no purpose other than to hang onto the Sword. Its eyes were fixed on the blade. Its face was slack and empty. Par's hands shifted to grasp what remained of the handle, coming tight against those of his adversary, feeling the rough, sweating skin. Their fingers intertwined as each sought to break the other's grip, their bodies thrashing and twisting . . .

Par gasped. A tingling sensation entered his fingers and spread into his hands and arms. He jerked backward in surprise – felt the Shadowen jerk as well. A flush of warmth surged through him, an odd pulse of heat that was centered in the palms of his hands.

His eyes snapped down.

The blade of the Sword of Shannara had begun to give off a faint blue glow.

Par's eyes widened. What was happening? Shades! Was it the magic? The magic of the Sword of –

The talisman flared sharply, and the blue light turned to white fire that blazed as bright as the midday sun. In its terrifying glow, he saw the face of the Shadowen change, the slackness disappearing as the features tightened in shock. Par wrenched wildly at the blade, but the Shadowen hung on.

From what seemed like a long way off, he heard Damson call his name once.

Then the Sword's light was surging through him, the white fire flaring like blood down the limbs of his body, cool but

81

insistent as it took possession. It surrounded him and then drew him away, outward from himself into the blade and then into the body of the Shadowen. He fought to resist the abduction, but found himself powerless. He entered the dark-cloaked figure, feeling the other shudder at the intrusion. Par tried to cry out and could not. He tried to break free and failed. Down into the Shadowen he went, raging and despairing all at once. The Shadowen was all around him, was there before him, eyes and mouth wide with disbelief, features contorted into something . . .

Someone . . .

Coll! Oh, it was Coll!

He might have whispered the words. He might have shrieked them aloud. He could not tell. There, in the dark center of his adversary's soul, the lies fell away before the power of the Sword of Shannara and became the truth. This was no Shadowen he fought, no dark demon with his brother's face, but his brother in fact. Coll, come back from the dead, come back to life, as real as the talisman they both clasped. Par saw the other shudder with some recognition of his own, realizing in the next instant that it was a recognition of what he had become. He saw his brother's tears, heard his wail of despair, and saw him convulse as if stricken with poison. His brother's mind shut down, too devastated by the revelation of what he had become to witness anything more. But Par saw the rest of it, all that his brother could not. He saw the truth of the cloak that wrapped Coll, a thing called the Mirrorshroud, Shadowen-made, stolen by his brother so that he could escape his imprisonment at Southwatch. He saw Rimmer Dall smile darkly, looming above them both from within a vortex of images. But most terrible of all, he saw the madness that engulfed his brother, that drove him in search of Par, in search of the perceived cause of his pain, determined to put an end to both . . .

Then Coll thrashed uncontrollably and tore free, his hands releasing their grip on the Sword of Shannara. The images ceased instantly, the white fire dying. Par tumbled backward, his head striking the base of a tree with stunning force. Through a spinning dark haze he watched his brother, Shadowen-consumed, still wrapped within the hateful cloak, rise up like a netherworld specter. For an instant he crouched there, hands pressed against his hooded head as if to crush the images still locked within, shrieking against his madness. In the next he was gone, fled into the trees, crying as he went until the cries were just an echo in his horrified brother's mind.

Damson was there then, helping Par to his feet, holding him up until she was sure he could stand alone. Her eyes were anxious and frightened, and he was conscious of the way she moved her body to shelter him. Soft streaks of morning light dappled their faces as they clung to each other. Together they stared out into the forest gloom, as if somehow they might catch a final glimpse of the creature who fled from them.

'It was Coll.' Par breathed the words as if they were anathema. 'Damson, it was Coll!'

She stared at him in disbelief, not daring a reply.

'And this!' He brought up the Sword of Shannara, still clasped in his scraped, raw hands. 'This is the Sword.'

'I know,' she whispered, more certain of this second declaration. 'I saw.'

He shook his head, still trying to comprehend. 'I don't know what happened. Something triggered the magic. I don't know what. But something. It was there, buried inside the Sword.' He wheeled to face her. 'I couldn't bring it out alone, but when both of us held the blade, when we struggled . . .' His fingers tightened on her arms. 'I saw him, Damson – as clearly as I see you. It was Coll.'

Damson held herself rigid. 'Par, Coll is dead.'

'No.' The Valeman shook his head adamantly. 'No, he is not dead. That was what I was supposed to think. But that wasn't Coll I killed in the Pit. It was someone or something else.

That' – he gestured toward the trees – ' was Coll. The Sword showed me, Damson. It showed me the truth. Coll was imprisoned at Southwatch and escaped. But he's been changed by that cloak he wears. There is some sort of malevolent magic in it, something that subverts you if you wear it. It's Coll, but he's turning into a Shadowen!'

'Par, I saw his face, too. And it looked a little like Coll, but not enough that – '

'You didn't see everything,' he cut her short. 'I did, because I was holding the Sword, and the Sword of Shannara reveals the truth! Remember the legends?' He was so excited he was shouting. 'Damson, this is the Sword of Shannara! It is! And that was Coll!'

'All right, all right.' She nodded quickly, trying to calm him. 'It was Coll. But why was he chasing us? Why did he attack you? What was he trying to do?'

Par's lips tightened. 'I don't know. I didn't have time to find out. And Coll doesn't know what's happening either. I could see what he was thinking for a moment – as if I was inside his mind. He realized what had been done to him, but he didn't know what to do about it. That was why he ran, Damson. He was horrified at what he had become.'

She stared at him. 'Did he know who you were?'

'I don't know.'

'Or how to help himself? Did he know enough to take off the cloak?'

Par took a deep breath. 'I don't think so. I'm not even sure he can.' His face was stricken. 'He looked so lost, Damson.'

She put her arms around him then, and he held her as if she were a rock without which the sea of his uncertainty might wash him away. All about them darkness was fading as sunrise brightened the skies east. Birds were coming awake with cheerful calls, and a faint scattering of dampness sparkled on the grass.

'I have to go after him,' Par said into her shoulder, feeling her stiffen at the words. 'I have to try to help him.' He shook

84

his head despairingly. 'I know it means breaking my promise to go back for Padishar. But Coll's my brother.'

She moved so that she could see his face. Her eyes searched his and did not look away. 'You've made up your mind about this, haven't you?' She looked terrified. 'This is probably a trap, you know.'

His smile was bitter. 'I know.'

She blinked rapidly. 'And I can't come with you.'

'I know that, too. You have to continue on to Firerim Reach and get help for your father. I understand.'

There were tears in her eyes. 'I don't want to leave you.'

'I don't want to leave you either.'

'Are you sure it was Coll? Absolutely sure?'

'As sure as I am that I love you, Damson.'

She brought her arms about him again. She didn't speak, but buried her face in his shoulder. He could feel her crying. He could feel himself breaking apart inside. The euphoria of finding Paranor was gone, the discovery itself all but forgotten. The sense of peace and contentment he had experienced so briefly on getting free of Tyrsis was buried in his past.

He pulled away again. 'I'll come back to you,' he said quietly. 'Wherever you are, I'll find you.'

She bit at her lower lip, nodding. Then she fumbled through her clothing, reaching down the front of her tunic. A moment later she pulled forth a thin, flat metal disk with a hole in it through which a leather cord had been threaded and then tied about her neck. She looked at the disk a moment, then at him.

'This is called a Skree,' she said. 'It is a kind of magic, a street magic. It was given to me a long time ago.' There was fire in the look she gave him. 'It can only be used once.'

Then she took the disk in both hands and snapped it in two as easily as she might a brittle stick. She handed the loose half to him. 'Take it and bind it about your neck. Wear it always. The halves will seek each other out. When the metal glows, it will tell us we are close. The brighter it becomes, the closer we will be.'

She pressed the broken half of the disk into his hands. 'That is how I will find you again, Par. And I will never stop looking.'

He closed his fingers about the disk. He felt as if a pit had opened beneath him and was about to swallow him up. 'I'm sorry, Damson,' he whispered. 'I don't want to do this. I would keep my promise if I could. But Coll's alive, and I can't – '

'No.' She put her fingers against his lips to silence him. 'Don't say anything more. I understand. I love you.'

He kissed her and held her against him, memorizing the touch and feel of her until he was certain the memory was burned into him. Then he released her, retrieved the scabbard for the Sword, picked up his blanket, rolled it up, and slung it over his shoulder.

'I'll come back to you,' he repeated. 'I promise I will.'

She nodded without speaking and would not look away, so he turned from her instead and hurried off into the trees.

8

It was nearing midafternoon of the day following the separation of Par and Damson when Morgan Leah at last came in sight of the borderland city of Varfleet. The summer was drifting toward autumn now, and the days were long and slow and filled with heat that arrived with the sun and lingered on until well after dark. The Highlander stood on a rise north of the city and looked down at the jumble of buildings and crooked streets and thought that nothing would ever be the same for him again.

It had been more than two weeks since he had parted company with Walker Boh – the Dark Uncle gone in search of Paranor, the Black Elfstone his key to the gates of time and distance that locked away the castle of the Druids, and the Highlander come looking for Padishar Creel and the Ohmsford brothers.

Two weeks. Morgan sighed. He should have reached Varfleet in two days, even afoot. But then nothing much seemed to work out the way he expected it these days.

What had befallen him was ironic considering what he had survived during the weeks immediately preceding. On leaving Walker, he had followed the Dragon's Teeth south along the western edge of the Rabb. He reached the lower branch of its namesake river by sunset of his second day out and made camp close-by, intent on crossing at sunrise and completing his journey the next day. The plains were sweltering and dusty, and there were pockets of the same sickness that marked the Four Lands everywhere, patches of blight where everything was poisoned. He thought that he had avoided these, that he had kept well clear in his passing. But when he woke at dawn on that third morning he was hot and feverish and so dizzy that he could barely walk. He drank some water and lay down again, hoping the sickness would pass. But by midday he was barely able to sit up. He forced himself to his feet, recognizing then how sick he was, knowing it was necessary that he find help immediately. His stomach was cramping so badly he could not straighten up, and his throat was on fire. He did not feel strong enough to cross the river, so instead he wandered upstream onto the plains. He was hallucinating when he came upon a farmhouse settled in a shady grove of elm. He staggered to the door, barely able to move or even speak, and collapsed when it opened.

For seven days he slept, drifting in and out of consciousness just long enough to eat and drink the small portions of food and water he was offered by whoever it was who had taken him in. He did not see any faces, and the voices he heard were indistinct. He was delirious at times, thrashing and crying out, reliving the horrors of Eldwist and Uhl Belk, seeing over and over again the stricken face of Quickening as she lay dying, feeling again the anguish he had experienced as he stood helplessly by. Sometimes he saw Par and Coll Ohmsford as they called to him from a great distance, and always he found that try as he might he could not reach them. There were dark things in his dreams as well, faceless shadows that came at him unexpectedly and from behind, presences without names, unmistakable nevertheless for who and what they were. He ran from them, hid from them, tried desperately to fight back against them – but always they stayed just out of his reach, threatening in ways he could not identify but could only imagine.

His fever broke at the end of the first week. When at last he was able to open his eyes and focus on the young couple who had cared for him, he saw in their faces an obvious relief and realized how close he had come to not waking at all. His sickness had left him drained of strength, and for several days after he had to be fed by hand. He managed to stay awake for short periods and to speak a little when he did. The young wife with the straw-blond hair and the pale blue eyes looked after him while her husband worked in the fields, and she smiled with concern when she told him that his dreams must have been bad ones. She gave him soup and bread with water and a small ration of ale. He accepted it gratefully and thanked her repeatedly for looking after him. Sometimes her husband would appear, standing next to her and looking down at him, bluff and red-faced from the sun, with kind eyes and a broad smile. He mentioned once that Morgan's sword was safely put aside, that it had not been lost. Apparently that had been part of the nightmares as well.

At the end of the two weeks Morgan was taking his meals with them at their dinner table, growing stronger daily, close to returning to normal. His memories lingered, however – the feeling of pain and nausea, the sense of helplessness, the fear that the sickness was the door to the darkness that would come at the end of his life. The memories stayed, for Morgan had come close to dying too often in the past few weeks to be able to put them aside easily. He was marked by what he had experienced and endured as surely as if scarred in battle, and even the farmer and his wife could see in his eyes and face what had been done to him. They never asked for an explanation, but they could see.

He offered to pay them for their care and predictably they refused. When he said good-bye to them seventeen days later, he slipped half of what money remained to him into the pocket of the wife's worn apron when she wasn't looking. They watched after him as parents might a child until he was out of sight.

And so not only was his arrival at Varfleet and his search for

Padishar and Par and Coll considerably delayed, but he was left as well with a renewed sense of his own mortality. Morgan Leah had come down out of Eldwist and the Charnals still grappling with Quickening's death, devastated by the loss he felt with her passing, in awe of her strength in carrying out her father's wish that she give up her own life in order that the land should be restored. An elemental that had become more human than her father had anticipated, she remained for Morgan an enigma for which he did not believe he would ever find a resolution. Coupled with this realization was the undeniable pride and strength he had found in helping to defeat Uhl Belk and in regaining anew the magic of the Sword of Leah. When the Sword had been made whole again, somehow so had he. Quickening had given him that. In the loss of Quickening, Morgan realized, he had somehow found himself. The contradictions between what had been lost and gained had warred within him as he traveled south with Walker and Horner Dees, a conflict that would never be entirely settled, and it was not until the sickness had overtaken him that their raging was forced to give way to the more basic need of finding a way to stay alive.

Now, staring down at the city, come back out of several nightmare worlds, out of the lives he had expended in those worlds, so distant that they might have been lived by someone else, Morgan reflected that he stood at the beginning of yet another life. He found himself wondering if those who had known him in the old life would ever recognize now who he was.

He entered Varfleet as just another traveler come down out of the north, a Southlander weathered and seasoned from troubles that were his own business, and he was pretty much ignored by the people of the city, who, after all, had troubles of their own to worry about. He passed through the poorer sections where families lived in makeshift shelters and children begged in the streets, conscious again of how little the ill-named Federation Protectorate had done to help anyone in

Callahorn. He passed into the city proper, where the smells of cooking and sewage mingled unpleasantly, the merchants hawked their wares in strident voices from carts and shopfronts, and the tradesmen serviced the needs of those who could afford the price. Federation soldiers patrolled the streets, a threatening presence wherever they went, looking as uncomfortable as the people they were charged with policing. If you stripped away the weapons and uniforms, the Highlander thought darkly, it would be hard to tell who was who.

He found a clothing shop and used most of his remaining money to buy pants, a tunic, a well-made forest cloak, and some new boots. His own clothing was frayed and soiled and worn beyond help, and he left it all behind in the shop when he departed, taking only his weapons. He asked for directions to the Whistledown, not certain even now what it was, and was told by the shopkeeper that it was a tavern that could be found at the center of the city on Wyvern Split.

Making his way through the crowds and the midday heat, Morgan recalled anew the instructions that Padishar Creel had given him weeks ago. He was to go to the Whistledown and show the hawk ring to a woman named Matty Roh. She would know how to find Padishar. Morgan fingered the hawk ring where it was buried in his pocket, safely tucked away for the time he would need it. He mused on how often he had doubted that such a time would come. The rough outline of the hawk emblem pressed against his skin as he twisted it about, bringing back memories of the outlaw chief. He wondered if Padishar Creel had been forced to come back from the dead as often as he had these past few weeks. The possibility brought a bitter smile to his lips.

He found Wyvern Split and turned down its length toward a square ringed by taverns, inns, and pleasure houses. Not a very attractive part of the city, but a busy one. He shifted the Sword of Leah from where it was draped across his back, adjusting the straps, feeling sad and weary and at the same time buoyed – an odd mix, but somehow a proper one. Sickness and loss had worn him down, but surviving both had strengthened his resolve. There was not much out there, he believed, that he could not get through. He needed that conviction. For weeks he had watched his friends and companions slip away, some lost to fortune, some to the machinations of others. He had seen his own plans repeatedly altered, his course turned aside time and again to serve a higher – or at least a different – purpose. He had done what he had believed right in each case, and he had no reason to second-guess himself. But he was tired of having his life rearranged like furniture in a room where each time he turned to look everything was in a different place. He had honored Steff's dying wish and gone back to Culhaven to rescue Granny Elise and Auntie Jilt. He had given himself then to Quickening and her journey to Eldwist. Now it was time to do what he had been promising himself he would do since escaping Tyrsis and the Pit.

It was time to find Par and Coll, to give them what protection he could, to see to it that he stayed with them until . . .

He gave a mental shrug. Well, until they no longer needed him, he guessed – whenever that might be.

And where were they now? he wondered for what must have been the hundredth time. What had become of them since their own escape?

Thinking of them made him uneasy. It always did. Too much time had passed since he had left them. The danger of the Shadowen was too great for the Valemen to have been left out there alone. He hoped Padishar had found them by now. He hoped that they'd had an easier time of things than he had.

But he wouldn't have cared to place a bet on it.

He arrived at the square and saw the Whistledown off to the left in the far corner. A weather-beaten wooden sign carved with a flute and a foaming tankard over the name announced its location. It was a slat-boarded building like all the others clustered about it, sharing a common wall with the ones on either side, looming three stories against the skyline, with curtained windows on the second and third floors where there were either living quarters for the owners and their families or sleeping rooms for hire. The square was thronged with people coming and going from this place to that, more than a few meandering from tavern to tavern, some so drunk they could hardly stand. Morgan avoided them, moving aside to let those he encountered pass, smelling the sweat and dirt of their bodies and the stench of the streets. Wyvern Split, he thought, was a cesspool.

He reached the Whistledown's open doors, stepped through, and was surprised to find that the inside of the ale house bore an entirely different look. Although it was plain and sparsely furnished, the floors were scrubbed clean, the wood trim on the serving bar was polished to a high sheen, the tables and chairs and stools were neatly arranged, and the smell of cedar chips and lacquer was everywhere. Ale casks gleamed in their racks against the wall behind the serving counter, and there were glass doors and metal trim on the tankard cupboard. A pair of heavy swinging doors at the end of the serving counter hung closed. A massive stone fireplace dominated the wall to the left of the counter, and a narrow staircase leading to the upper floors took up most of the wall to the right. Serving bowls and cleaning cloths were stacked on the counter itself.

But it was something else that caught Morgan's eye and held it, something so obviously out of place that he had to take a second look to be certain he was not mistaken about what he was seeing.

There were bunches of wildflowers arranged in large vases on shelves bracketing the ale casks and tankard cupboard.

Flowers – here, of all places! He shook his head.

The swinging doors opened and a boy with a broom pushed through. He was tall and lean with short-cropped black hair and fine, almost delicate features. He moved with fluid grace as he swept down the length of the serving counter, almost as if dancing, working the broom in front of him, lost in thought. He whistled softly, unaware yet of Morgan.

Morgan shifted his stance enough to announce that he was there, and the boy looked up at once.

'We're closed,' he said. Cobalt eyes fixed on the Highlander, a frank, almost challenging stare. 'We open at dusk.'

Morgan stared back. The boy's face was smooth and hairless, and his hands were long and thin. The clothes he wore were loose and shapeless, hanging on him as if on sticks, belted at his narrow waist and tied at his ankles. He wore shoes instead of boots, low-cut, stitched leather things that molded to his feet.

'Is this the Whistledown?' Morgan asked, deciding he had better make sure.

The boy nodded. 'Come back later. Go take a bath first.'

Morgan blinked. Take a bath? 'I'm looking for someone,' he said, beginning to feel uncomfortable under the other's steady gaze.

The boy shrugged. 'I can't help you. There's no one here but me. Try across the street.'

'Thanks, but I'm not looking for just anyone . . .' Morgan began.

But the boy was already turning away, working the broom back up the floor against the counter. 'We're closed,' he repeated, as if that settled the matter.

Morgan started forward, a hint of irritation creeping into his voice. 'Wait a minute.' He reached for the other's shoulder. 'Hold on a minute. Did you say you were the only one . . . ?'

The boy wheeled about smoothly as Morgan touched him, the broom came up, and the blunt end jabbed the Highlander hard below the rib cage. Morgan doubled over, paralyzed, then dropped to one knee, gasping.

The boy came up beside him and bent close. 'We're closed, I told you. You should pay better attention.' He helped Morgan to his feet, surprisingly strong for being so lean, and guided him to the door. 'Come back later when we open.'

And the next thing Morgan knew he was back outside on the street, leaning against the slat-board wall of the building, arms clasped about his body as if he were in danger of falling apart – which was not too far off the mark in terms of how he felt. He took several deep breaths and waited for the ache in his chest to subside.

This is ridiculous, he thought angrily. A boy!

He managed to straighten finally, rubbed at his chest, adjusted the shoulder straps of his sword where they had begun to chafe, and walked back through the Whistledown's doors.

The boy, who was sweeping behind the counter now, did not look pleased to see him. 'What seems to be your problem?' he asked Morgan pointedly.

The Highlander walked to the counter and glared. 'What seems to be my problem? I didn't have a problem until I came in here. Don't you think you were a little quick with that broom?'

The boy shrugged. 'I asked you to leave and you didn't. What do you expect?'

'How about a little help? I told you I was looking for someone.'

The boy sighed wearily. 'Everyone is looking for someone – especially the people who come in here.' His voice was low and smooth, an odd mix. 'They come in here to drink and to feel better. They come in here to find company. Fine. But they have to do it when we're open. And we're not open. Is that plain enough for you?'

Morgan felt his temper begin to slip. He shook his head. 'I'll tell you what's plain to me. What's plain to me is that you don't have any manners. Someone ought to box your ears.'

The boy set the broom down and put his slim hands on the counter. 'Well, it won't be you who does it. Now turn around and go back out that door. And forget what I said before. Don't come back later. Don't come back at all.'

For a moment Morgan considered reaching over the counter, taking hold of the boy by the scruff of his neck, and pulling him across. But the memory of that broom handle was too recent to encourage precipitous action, and besides, the boy didn't look the least bit afraid of him.

Keeping his anger in check, he folded his arms across his chest and held his ground. 'Is there anyone else here that I can talk to besides you?' he asked.

The boy shook his head.

'The owner, maybe?'

The boy shook his head.

'No?' Morgan decided to take a chance. 'Is the owner's name Matty Roh?'

There was a flicker of recognition in the cobalt eyes, there for an instant and then gone. 'No.'

Morgan nodded slowly. 'But you know who Matty Roh is, don't you?' He made it a statement of fact.

The boy's gaze was steady. 'I'm tired of talking to you.'

Morgan ignored him. 'Matty Roh. That's who I came here to find. And I came a long way. Which is why I need a bath, as you so rudely pointed out. Matty Roh. Not some nameless companion for some unmentionable purpose, thanks just the same.' His voice was taking on a sharper edge. 'Matty Roh. You know the name; you know who she is. So if you want to be rid of me, just tell me how to find her and I'll be on my way.'

He waited, arms folded, feet planted. The boy's expression never changed; his gaze never moved off Morgan. But his hands slipped down behind the serving counter and came up again holding a thin-bladed sword. The way they held it suggested a certain familiarity.

'Now, what's this?' Morgan asked quietly. 'Am I really that unwelcome?'

The boy was as still as stone. 'Who are you? What do you want with Matty Roh?'

Morgan shook his head. 'That's between her and me.' Then

he added, 'I'll tell you this much. I'm not here to cause trouble. I just need to speak with her.'

The boy studied him for a long time, gaze level and fixed, body still. He stood behind the serving counter like a statue, and Morgan had the uneasy feeling that he was poised between fleeing and attacking. Morgan watched the eyes and the hands for a hint of which way the boy would go, but there was no movement at all. From outside, the sounds of the street drifted in through the open doors and hung shrill and intrusive in the silence.

'I'm Matty Roh,' the boy said.

Morgan Leah stared. He almost laughed aloud, almost said something about how ridiculous that was. But something in the boy's voice stopped him. He took a closer look at the other – the fine, delicate features, the slim hands, the lean body concealed beneath the loose-fitting clothing, the way he held himself. He remembered how the boy had moved. None of it seemed quite right for a boy. But for a girl . . .

He nodded slowly. 'Matty Roh,' he said, his surprise still evident. 'I thought you were a . . . that you were . . .'

The girl nodded. 'That's what you were supposed to think.' Her hand did not move off the sword. 'What do you want with me?'

For a moment Morgan did not respond, still grappling with the idea that he had mistaken a girl for a boy. Worse, that he had let her make him look like such a fool. But you mustered the defenses available to you when you lived in a place like Wyvern Split. The girl was clever. He had to admit her disguise was a good one.

He reached into his tunic pocket and drew forth the ring with the hawk emblem and held it out. 'Recognize this?'

She took a quick look at the ring, and her hand tightened on the sword. 'Who are you?' she asked.

'Morgan Leah,' he said. 'We both know who gave me the ring. He told me to come to you when I needed to find him.'

'I know who you are,' she declared. Her gaze stayed level, appraising. 'Do you still carry a broken sword, Morgan Leah?'

An image of Quickening as she lay dying flashed in his mind. 'No,' he said quietly. 'It was made whole again.' He pushed back the pain the memory brought and forced himself to reach over his shoulder and touch the sword's hilt. 'Do you want to have a look?'

She shook her head no. 'I'm sorry I gave you such a bad time. But it's difficult to know who to trust. The Federation has spies everywhere – Seekers more often than not.'

She picked up her own sword and slipped it back under the counter. For a moment she didn't appear to know what to do next. Then she said, 'Would you like something to eat?'

He said he would, and she took him through the swinging doors in back into a kitchen where she seated him at a small table, scooped some stew into a serving bowl from a kettle hung over a cooking fire in the hearth, cut off several slices of bread, poured ale into a mug, and brought it all over to where he waited. He ate and drank eagerly, hungrier than he had been in days. There were wildflowers in a vase on the table, and he touched them experimentally. She watched him in silence, the same serious expression on her face, studying him with that frank, curious gaze. The kitchen was surprisingly cool, with a breeze blowing in through the open back door and venting up the chimney of the fireplace. Sounds from the streets continued to drift in, but the Highlander and the girl ignored them.

'It took you a long time to get here,' she said when he had finished his meal. She carried his dishes to a sink and began to wash them. 'He expected you sooner than this.'

'Where is he now?' Morgan asked. They were taking great pains to avoid saying Padishar Creel's name – as if mention of it might alert the Federation spies set at watch.

'Where did he say he would be?' she countered.

Still testing, Morgan. thought. 'At Firerim Reach. Tell me something. You're being pretty careful about me. How am I supposed to know I can trust you? How do I know you really are Matty Roh?'

She finished with the dishes, set them to dry on the counter, and turned to face him. 'You don't. But you came looking for me. I didn't come looking for you. So you have to take your chances.'

He rose. 'That's not very reassuring.'

She shrugged. 'It isn't meant to be. It isn't my job to reassure you. It's my job to make sure you're who you say you are.'

'And are you sure?'

She stared at him. 'More or less.'

Her stare was impenetrable. He shook his head. 'When do you think you might know?'

'Soon.'

'And what if you decide I'm lying? What if you decide I'm someone else?'

She came forward until she was directly across the table from him, until the blue of her eyes was so brilliant that it seemed to swallow all the light.

'Let's hope you don't have to find out the answer to that question,' she said. She held his gaze challengingly. 'The Whistledown stays open until midnight. When it closes, we'll talk about what happens next.'

As she turned away, he could have sworn she almost smiled.

9

Morgan spent the rest of the day in the kitchen with an old woman who came in to do the cooking but devoted most of her time to sipping ale from a metal flask and stealing food from the pots. The old woman barely gave him a glance and then only long enough to mutter something undecipherable about strange men, so he was left pretty much to himself. He took a bath in an old tub in one of the back rooms (because he wanted to and not because Matty Roh had suggested it, he told himself), carrying steaming water in buckets heated over the fire until he had enough to submerse himself. He languished in the tub for some time, letting more than just the dirt and grit soak away, staying long after the water had cooled.

After the Whistledown had opened for business he left the kitchen and went out into the main room to have a look around. He stood at the serving counter and watched the citizens of Varfleet come and go. The crowd was a well-dressed one, men and women both, and it was immediately clear that the Whistledown was not a workingman's tavern. Several of the tables were occupied by Federation officers, some with their wives or consorts. Talk and laughter was restrained, and no one was particularly boisterous. Once or twice soldiers from Federation patrols paused long enough for a quick glance inside, but then passed on. A strapping fellow with curly dark hair drew ale from the casks, and a serving girl carried trays of the foaming brew to the tables.

Matty Roh worked, too, although it was not immediately apparent to Morgan what her job was. At times she swept the floor, at times she cleared tables, and occasionally she simply went about straightening things up. He watched her for some time before he was able to figure out that what she was really doing was listening in on the conversations of the tavern patrons. She was always busy and never seemed to stand about or to be in any one place for more than a moment, a very unobtrusive presence. Morgan couldn't tell if anyone knew she was a girl or not, but in any case they paid almost no attention to her.

After a time she came up to the counter carrying a tray full of empty glasses and stood next to him. As she reached back for a fresh cleaning rag she said, 'You're too obvious standing here. Go back into the kitchen.' And then she turned back to the crowd.

Irritated, he nevertheless did as he was told.

At midnight the Whistledown closed. Morgan helped clean up, and then the old cook and the counterman said good-night and went out the back door. Matty Roh blew out the lamps in the front room, checked the locks on the doors, and came back into the kitchen. Morgan was waiting at the little table for her, and she came over and sat down across from him.

'So what did you learn tonight?' he asked, half joking. 'Anything useful?'

She gave him a cool stare. 'I've decided to trust you,' she announced.

His smile faded. 'Thanks.'

'Because if you're not who you say you are, then you are the worst Federation spy I've ever seen.'

He folded his arms defensively. 'Forget the thanks. I take it back.'

'There is a rumor,' she said, 'that the Federation have captured Padishar at Tyrsis.' Morgan went still. The cobalt

101

eyes stayed fastened on him. 'It had something to do with a prison break. I overheard a Federation commander talking about it. They claim to have him.'

Morgan thought about it a moment. 'Padishar's hard to trap. Maybe a rumor is all it is.'

She nodded. 'Maybe. It wasn't so long ago that they claimed to have killed him at the Jut. They said the Movement was finished.' She paused. 'In any case, we'll learn the truth at Firerim Reach.'

'We're going?' Morgan asked quickly.

'We're going.' She rose. 'Help me pack some food. I'll get us some blankets. We'll slip away before it gets light. It will be better if we aren't seen leaving.'

He stood up with her and moved over to the pantry. 'What about the tavern?' he asked. 'Doesn't someone have to look after it?'

'The tavern will stay closed until I return.'

He glanced up from stuffing a loaf of bread into a sack. 'You lied to me, didn't you? You are the owner.'

She met his gaze and held it. 'Try not to be so stupid, Highlander. I didn't lie to you. I'm the manager, not the owner. The owner is Padishar Creel.'

They finished putting together supplies and sleeping gear, strapped everything across their backs, and went out the back door into the night. The air was warm and filled with the smells of the city as they hurried down empty streets and alleyways, keeping close watch for Federation patrols. The girl was as silent as a ghost, a knife-lean figure cutting smoothly through the building shadows. Morgan noticed that she wore the sword she'd kept hidden beneath the counter, the narrow blade strapped across her back beneath her other gear. He wondered, rather unkindly, if she'd brought her broom. At least her odd shoes were gone, replaced by more serviceable boots.

They passed from the city into the land beyond and marched north to the Mermidon where they crossed at a shallows and turned east. They followed the line of the Dragon's Teeth, and by daybreak they were traveling north again across the Rabb. They walked steadily until sunset, pausing long enough at midday to eat and to wait out the worst of the afternoon heat. The plains were dusty and dry and empty of life, and the journey was uneventful. The girl spoke little, and Morgan was content to leave things that way.

At sunset they made camp close against the Dragon's Teeth beside a tributary of the Rabb, settling themselves in a grove of ash that climbed into the rocks like soldiers on the march. They ate their evening meal as the sun disappeared behind the mountains, its hazy mix of red and gold melting across the plains and sky. When they were finished, they sat watching the dusk deepen and the river's waters turn silver in the light of the moon and stars.

'Padishar told me you saved his life,' the girl said after a time.

She hadn't spoken a word all through dinner. Morgan looked over, surprised by the suddenness of the declaration. She was watching him, her strange blue eyes deathless.

'I saved my own in the bargain,' he replied, 'so it wasn't an entirely selfless act.'

She folded her arms. 'He said to keep watch for you and to take good care of you. He said I'd know you when I saw you.'

Her expression never changed. Morgan grinned in spite of himself. 'Well, he makes mistakes like everyone else.' He waited for a response and, when there was none, said, a bit huffy, 'You may not believe this but I can take pretty good care of myself.'

She looked away, shifting to a more comfortable position. Her eyes gleamed in the starlight. 'What is it like where you come from?'

He hesitated, confused. 'What do you mean?'

'The Highlands, what are they like?'

He thought for a moment she was teasing him, then decided she wasn't. He took a deep breath and stretched out, remembering. 'It is the most beautiful country in the Four Lands,' he said, and proceeded to describe it in detail – the hills with their carpets of blue, lavender, and yellow grasses and flowers, the streams that turned frosty at dawn and blood-red at dusk, the mist that came and went with the changing seasons, the forests and the meadows, the sense of peace and timelessness. The Highlands were his passion, the more so since his departure weeks earlier. It reminded him again how much home meant to him, even a home that was really no longer his now that the Federation occupied it – though in truth, he thought, it was still more his than theirs because he kept the feel of it with him in his mind and its history was in his blood and that would never be true for them.

She was silent for a time when he finished, then said, 'I like how you describe your home. I like how you feel about it. If I lived there, I think I would feel the same.'

'You would,' he assured her, studying the profile of her face as she stared out across the Rabb, distracted. 'But I guess everyone feels that way about their home.'

'I don't,' she said.

He straightened up again. 'Why not?'

Her forehead furrowed. It produced only a slight marring of her smooth features but gave her an entirely different look, one at once both introspective and distant. 'I suppose it's because I have no good memories of home. I was born on a small farm south of Varfleet, one of several families that occupied a valley. I lived there with my parents and my brothers and one sister. I was the youngest. We raised milk cows and grain. In summer, the fields would be as gold as the sun. In fall, the earth would be all black after it was plowed.' She shrugged. 'I don't remember much other than that. Just the sickness. It seems a long time ago, but I guess it wasn't. The land went bad first, then the stock, and finally my family. Everything began to die. Everyone. My sister first, then my mother, my brothers, and my father. It was the same with the people who lived on the other farms. It happened all at once. Everyone was dead in a few months. One of the women on the other farms found me and took me to Varfleet to live with her. We were the last. I was six years old.'

She made it all sound as if it were nothing out of the ordinary. There was no emotion in her voice. She finished and looked away. 'I think there might be some rain on the way,' she said.

They slept until dawn, ate a breakfast of bread, fruit, and cheese, and began their trek north again. The skies were clouding when they woke, and a short time after they crossed the Rabb it began to rain. Thunderheads built up, and lightning streaked the blackness. When the rain began to come down in torrents, they took shelter in the lee of an old maple set back against a rocky rise. Brushing water from their faces and clothes, they settled back to wait out the storm. The air cooled slightly, and the plains shimmered with the damp.

Shoulder to shoulder, they sat with their backs against the maple, staring out into the haze, listening to the sound of the rain.

'How did you meet Padishar?' Morgan asked her after they had been quiet for a time.

She brought her knees up and wrapped her arms about them. Water beaded on her skin and glistened in her black hair. 'I apprenticed to Hirehone when I was old enough to work. He taught me to forge iron and to fight. After a while I was better than he was at both. So he brought me into the Movement, and that's how I met Padishar.'

Memories of Hirehone crowded Morgan's mind. He let them linger a moment and then banished them. 'How long have you been looking after the Whistledown?'

'A couple of years. It offers an opportunity to learn things that can help the free-born. It's a place to be for now.'

He glanced over. 'But not where you want to end up, is that what you're saying?'

She gave him a flicker of a smile. 'It's not for me.'

'What is?'

'I don't know yet. Do you?'

He thought about it. 'I guess I don't. I haven't let myself think beyond what's been happening these past few weeks. I've been running so fast I haven't had time to stop and think.'

She leaned back. 'I haven't been running. I've been standing in place, waiting for something to happen.'

He shifted to face her. 'I was like that before I came north. I spent all of my time thinking of ways to make life miserable for the Federation occupiers – all those officers and soldiers living in the home that had belonged to my family, pretending it was theirs. I thought I was doing something, but I was really just standing in place.'

She gave him a curious glance. 'So now you're running instead. Is that any better?'

He smiled and shrugged. 'At least I'm seeing more of the country.'

The rains slowed, the skies began to clear, and they resumed their journey. Morgan found himself sneaking glances at Matty Roh, studying the expression on her face, the lines of her body, and the way she moved. He thought her intriguing, suggestive of so much more than what she allowed to show. On the surface she was cool and purposeful, a carefully fixed mask that hid stronger and deeper emotions beneath. He believed, for reasons he could not explain, that she was capable of almost anything.

It was nearing midday when she turned him into the rocks and they began to follow a trail that ran upward into the hills fronting the Dragon's Teeth. They entered a screen of trees that hid the mountains ahead and the plains behind, and when they emerged they were at the foot of the peaks. The trail disappeared with the trees, and they were soon climbing more rugged slopes, picking their way over the rocks as best they could. Morgan found himself wondering, rather uncharitably, if Matty Roh knew where she was going. After a while they reached a pass and followed it through a split in the rocks into a deep defile. The cliff walls closed about until there was only a narrow ribbon of clouded blue sky visible overhead. Birds took flight from their craggy perches and disappeared into the sun. Wind whistled in sudden gusts down the canyon's length, a shrill and empty sound.

When they stopped for a drink from the water skin, Morgan glanced at the girl to see how she was holding up. There was a sheen of sweat on her smooth face, but she was breathing easily. She caught him looking, and he turned quickly away.

Somewhere deep in the split Matty Roh took them into a cluster of massive boulders that appeared to be part of an old slide. Behind the concealing rocks they found a passageway that tunneled into the cliff wall. They entered and began to climb a spiraling corridor that opened out again onto a ledge about halfway up. Morgan peered down cautiously. It was a straight drop. A narrow trail angled upward from where they stood, the cut invisible from below, and they followed the pathway to the summit of the cliff and along the rim to another split, this one barely more than a crack in the rocks, so narrow that only one person at a time could pass through.

Matty Roh stopped at the opening. 'They'll come for us in a moment,' she announced, slipping the water skin from her shoulder and passing it to him so that he could drink.

He declined the offering. If she didn't need a drink, neither did he. 'How will they know we're here?' he asked.

That flicker of a smile came and went. 'They've been watching us for the past hour. Didn't you see them?'

He hadn't, of course, and she knew it, so he just shrugged his indifference and let the matter drop.

Shortly afterward a pair of figures emerged from the shadows of the split, bearded, hard-faced men with longbows and knives. They greeted Matty Roh and Morgan perfunctorily, then beckoned for them to follow. Single file, they entered the split and passed along a trail that wound upward into a jumble of rocks that shut away any view of what lay ahead. Morgan climbed dutifully, unable to avoid noticing that Matty Roh continued to look as if she were out for a midday stroll.

Finally they reached a plateau that stretched away north, south, and west and offered the most breathtaking views of the Dragon's Teeth and the lands beyond that Morgan had ever seen. Sunset was approaching, and the skies were turning a brilliant crimson through the screen of mist that clung to the mountain peaks. Hence the name Firerim Reach, thought Morgan. East, the plateau backed up against a ridge grown thick with spruce and cedar. It was here that the outlaws were encamped, their roofed shelters crowded into the trees, their cooking fires smoldering in stone-lined pits. There were no walled fortifications as there had been at the Jut, for the plateau dropped away into a mass of jagged fissures and deep canyons, its sheer walls unscalable by one man let alone any sort of sizable force. At least, that was the way it appeared from where Morgan stood, and he assumed it was the same on all sides of the quarter-mile or so stretch of plain. The only way in appeared to be the way they had come. Still, the Highlander knew Padishar Creel well enough to bet there was at least one other.

He turned as a familiar burly figure lumbered up to meet them, black-bearded and ferocious-looking with his missing eye and ear and his scarred face. Chandos embraced Matty Roh warmly, nearly swallowing her up in his embrace, and then reached out for Morgan.

'Highlander,' he greeted, taking Morgan's hand in his own and crushing it. 'It's good to have you back with us.'

'It's good to be back.' Morgan extracted his hand painfully. 'How are you, Chandos?'

The big man shook his head. 'Well enough, given everything that's happened.' There was an angry, frustrated look in his dark eyes. His jaw tightened. 'Come with me where we can talk.'

He took Morgan and Matty Roh from the rim of the cliffs across the bluff. The guards who had brought them in disappeared back the way they had come. Chandos moved deliberately away from the encampment and the other outlaws. Morgan glanced questioningly at Matty Roh, but the girl's face was unreadable.

When they were safely out of earshot, she said immediately to Chandos, 'They have him, don't they?'

'Padishar?' Chandos nodded. 'They took him two nights earlier at Tyrsis.' He turned and faced Morgan. 'The Valeman was with him, the smaller one, the one Padishar liked so well – Par Ohmsford. Apparently the two of them went into the Federation prisons to rescue Damson Rhee. They got her out, but Padishar was captured in the attempt. Damson's here now. She arrived yesterday with the news.'

'What happened to Par?' Morgan asked, wondering at the same time why there had been no mention of Coll.

'Damson said he went off in search of his brother – something about the Shadowen.' Chandos brushed the question aside. 'What matters at the moment is Padishar.' His scarred face furrowed. 'I haven't told the others yet.' He shook his head. 'I don't know if I should or not. We're supposed to meet with Axhind and his Trolls at the Jannisson at the end of the week. Five days. If we don't have Padishar with us, I don't think they'll join up. I think they'll just turn around and go right back the way they came. Five thousand strong!' His face flushed, and he took a steadying breath. 'We need them if we're to have any kind of chance against the Federation. Especially after losing the Jut.'

He looked at them hopefully. 'I was never much at making plans. So if you've any ideas at all . . .'

Matty Roh shook her head. 'If the Federation has Padishar, he won't stay alive very long.'

Chandos scowled. 'Maybe longer than he'd like, if the Seekers get their hands on him.'

Morgan recalled the Pit and its inhabitants momentarily and quickly forced the thought away. Something about all this didn't make sense. Padishar had gone looking for Par and Coll weeks ago. Why had it taken him so long to find them? Why had the Ohmsford brothers remained in Tyrsis all that time?

And when Par and Padishar had gone into the prisons to rescue Damson Rhee, where was Coll? Did the Shadowen have Coll as well?

It seemed to Morgan that there was an awful lot unaccounted for.

'I want to speak with Damson Rhee,' he announced abruptly. He had wondered about her at the beginning, and suddenly he was beginning to wonder about her all over again.

Chandos shrugged. 'She's sleeping. Walked all night to get here.'

Images of Teel danced in Morgan's head, whispering insidiously. 'Then let's wake her.'

Chandos gave him a hard stare. 'All right, Highlander. If you think it's important. But it will be your doing, not mine.'

They crossed to the encampment and passed through the cooking fires and the free-born at work about them. The sun had dropped further in the west, and it was nearing dinnertime. There was food in the cooking kettles, and the smells wafted on the summer air. Morgan scarcely noticed, his mind at work on other matters. Shadows crept out of the trees, lengthening as dusk approached. Morgan was thinking about Par and Coll, still in Tyrsis after all this time. They had escaped the Pit weeks ago. Why had they stayed there? he kept wondering. Why for so long?

As the questions pressed in about him, he kept seeing Teel's face – and the Shadowen that had hidden beneath.

They reached a small hut set well back in the trees, and Chandos stopped. 'She's in there. You wake her if you want. Come have dinner with me when you're finished, the both of you.'

Morgan nodded. He turned to Matty Roh. 'Do you want to come with me?'

She gave him an appraising look. 'No. I think you should do this on your own.'

It seemed for a moment as if she might say more, but then she turned and walked off into the trees after Chandos. She knew something she wasn't telling, Morgan decided. He watched her go, thinking once again that Matty Roh was a good deal more complex than what she revealed.

He looked back at the hut, momentarily undecided as to how he should go about bracing Damson Rhee. Suspicions and fears shouldn't be allowed to get in the way of common sense. But he couldn't shake the image of Teel as a Shadowen. It could easily be the same with this girl. The trick was in finding out.

He reached back over his shoulder to make certain that the Sword of Leah would slide free easily, took a deep breath, then walked up to the door and knocked. It opened almost immediately, and a girl with flaming red hair and emerald eyes stood looking out at him. She was flushed, as if she had just awakened, and her dark clothing was disheveled. She was tall, though not as tall as Matty, and very pretty.

'I'm Morgan Leah,' he said.

She blinked, then nodded. 'Par's friend, the Highlander. Yes, hello. I'm Damson Rhee. I'm sorry, I've been sleeping. What time is it?' She peered up at the sky through the trees. 'Almost dusk, isn't it? I've slept too long.'

She stepped back as if to go inside, then stopped and turned to face him again. 'You've heard about Padishar, I suppose. Did you just get here?'

He nodded, watching her face. 'I wanted to hear what happened from you.'

'All right.' She did not seem surprised. She glanced over her shoulder, then came out into the light. 'Let's talk out here. I'm tired of being shut away. Tired of being inside where there's no light. How much did Chandos tell you?'

She moved away from the hut into the trees, a very determined stride, and he was swept along in her wake. 'He told me that Padishar had been taken by the Federation when he and Par came to rescue you. He said Par had left you to go find Coll – that it had something to do with the Shadowen.'

111

'Everything has something to do with the Shadowen, doesn't it?' she whispered, her head lowering wearily.

She walked over to one end of a crumbling log and sat down. Morgan hesitated, still guarded, then sat with her. She turned slightly so that she was facing him. 'I have a very long story to tell you, Morgan Leah,' she advised.

She began with finding Par and Coll after they had escaped the Pit in Tyrsis. She told of how they had decided to go back down into the Shadowen breeding ground one final time, how they had enlisted the help of the Mole and found their way through the tunnels beneath the city to the old palace. From there the brothers had gone off together in search of the Sword of Shannara. Par had come back alone, carrying with him what he believed to be the talisman, half-mad with grief and horror because he had killed his brother. She had nursed him for weeks in the Mole's underground home, slowly bringing him back to himself, carefully bringing him out of his dark nightmare. From there they had fled from safe house to safe house, the Sword of Shannara in tow, hiding from the Seekers and the Federation, looking for a way to escape the city. Finally Padishar had found them, but in the process of yet another escape from the Federation, Damson herself had been taken. Padishar and Par had come back to rescue her, and that in turn had led to Padishar's capture. Fleeing the city completely, because at last there was a way to do so and there was nothing they could do for Padishar without help, they had come north through the Kennon.

She touched his arm impulsively. 'And what we saw, Morgan Leah, from high in the pass, far off in the distance beyond the Federation watch fires, but as clear as I see you, was Paranor. It is back, Highlander, returned out of the past. Par was certain of it. He said it meant that Walker Boh had succeeded!'

Then, growing subdued again, she described their journey back out of the pass and their fateful encounter with Coll – or the thing Coll had become, wrapped in that strange, shimmer-

112

ing cloak, hunched and twisted as if his bones had been rearranged. In the struggle that followed the power of the Sword of Shanara had somehow been invoked, revealing what Par now thought to be the truth about the brother he believed dead.

'He went after Coll, of course,' she finished. 'What else could he do? I did not want him to go, not without me – but I did not have the right to stop him.' She searched Morgan's eyes. 'I am not as certain as he that it is Coll he tracks, but I realize that he must find out one way or the other if he is ever to be at peace.'

Morgan nodded. He was thinking that Damson Rhee had given up an awful lot of herself to help Par Ohmsford, that she had risked more than he would have expected anyone to risk besides himself and Coll. He was thinking as well that the story she had told him had a feeling of truth to it, that it seemed right in the balance of things. The doubts he had brought with him coming in began to fade away. Certainly Par's persistence in going after the Sword of Shannara was in character, as was this new search to find his brother. The problem now was that Par was more alone than ever, and Morgan was reminded once again of his failure to watch out for his friend.

He realized Damson was studying him, a hard, probing look, and without warning his suspicions flared anew.

Damson Rhee – was she the friend that Par believed or the enemy he sought so desperately to escape? Certainly she could have been the reason he'd had so many narrow escapes, the reason the Shadowen had almost trapped him so many times. But then, too, wasn't she also the reason he had escaped?

'You're not certain of me, are you?' she asked quietly.

'No,' he admitted. 'I'm not.'

She nodded. 'I don't know what I can do to convince you, Morgan. I don't know that I even want to try. I have to spend whatever energy is left me finding a way to free Padishar. Then I will go in search of Par.'

He looked away into the trees, thinking of the dark suspicions that the Shadowen bred in all of them, wishing it could be otherwise. 'When I was at the Jut with Padishar,' he said, 'I was forced to kill a girl who was really a Shadowen.' He looked back at her. 'Her name was Teel. My friend Steff was in love with her, and it cost him his life.'

He told her then of Teel's betrayals and the eventual confrontation deep within the catacombs of the mountains behind the Jut where he had killed the Shadowen who had been Teel and saved Padishar Creel's life.

'What frightens me,' he said, 'is that you could be another Teel and Par could end up like Steff.'

She did not respond, her gaze distant and lost. She might have been looking right through him. There were tears in her eyes.

He reached back suddenly and drew out the Sword of Leah. Damson watched him without moving, her green eyes fixing on the gleaming blade as he placed it point downward in the earth between them, his hands fastened on the pommel.

'Put your hands on the flat of the blade, Damson,' he said softly.

She looked at him without answering, and for a long time she did not move. He waited, listening to the distant sounds of the free-born as they gathered for dinner, listening to the silence closer at hand. The light was fading rapidly now, and there were shadows all about. He felt oddly removed from everything about him, as if he were frozen in time with Damson Rhee.

Not this girl, he found himself praying. *Not again.*

At last she reached out and touched the Sword of Leah, her palms tight against the metal. Then she deliberately closed her fingers about the edge. Morgan watched in horror as the blade cut deep into her flesh, and her blood began to trickle down its length.

'A Shadowen couldn't do that, could it?' she whispered.

He reached down quickly and pried her fingers away. 'No,'

he said. 'Not without triggering the magic.' He lay the talisman aside, tore strips of cloth from his cloak, and began to bind her hands. 'You didn't have to do that,' he reproached her.

Her smile was faint and wistful. 'Didn't I? Would you have been sure of me otherwise, Morgan Leah? I don't think so. And if you're not sure of me, how can we be of help to each other? There has to be trust between us.' She fixed him with her gentle eyes. 'Is there now?'

He nodded quickly. 'Yes. I'm sorry, Damson.'

Her bound hands reached up to clasp his own. 'Let me tell you something.' The tears were back in her eyes. 'You said that your friend Steff was in love with Teel? Well, Highlander, I am in love with Par Ohmsford.'

He saw it all then, the reason she had stayed with Par, had given herself so completely to him, following him even into the Pit, watching over him, protecting him. It was what he would have done – had tried to do – for Quickening. Damson Rhee had made a commitment that only death would release.

'I'm sorry,' he said again, thinking how inadequate it sounded.

Her hands tightened on his and did not let go. They faced each other in the dusk without speaking for a long time. As he held her hands, Morgan was reminded of Quickening, of the way she had felt, of the feelings she had invoked in him. He found that he missed her desperately and would have given anything to have her back again.

'Enough testing,' Damson whispered. 'Let's talk instead. I'll tell you everything that's happened to me. You do the same about yourself. Par and Padishar need us. Maybe together we can come up with a way to help.'

She squeezed his hands as if there were no pain in her own and gave him an encouraging smile. He bent to retrieve the Sword of Leah, then started back with her through the trees toward the glow of the cooking fires. His mind was spinning, working through what she had told him, sorting out impressions from facts, trying to glean something useful. Damson was right. The Valeman and the leader of the free-born needed them. Morgan was determined not to let either down.

But what could he do?

The smell of food from the cooking fire reached out to him enticingly. For the first time since he had arrived, he was hungry.

Par and Padishar.

Padishar first, he thought.

Chandos had said five days.

If the Seekers didn't reach him first . . .

It came to him in a rush, the picture so clear in his mind he almost cried out. He reached over impulsively and put his arm around Damson's shoulders.

'I think I know how to free Padishar,' he said.

10

Five days the Four Horsemen circled the walls of Paranor, and five days Walker Boh stood on the castle battlements and watched. Each dawn they assembled at the west gates, shadows come from the gloom of fading night. One would approach, a different one each time, and strike the gates once in challenge. When Walker failed to appear they would resume their grim vigil, spreading out so that there was one at each compass point, one at each of the main walls, riding in slow, ceaseless cadence, circling like birds of prey. Day and night they rode, specters of gray mist and dark imaginings, silent as thought and certain as time.

'Incarnations of man's greatest enemies,' Cogline mused when he saw them for the first time. 'Manifestations of our worst fears, the slayers of so many, given shape and form and sent to destroy us.' He shook his head. 'Can it be that Rimmer Dall has a sense of humor?'

Walker didn't think so. He found nothing amusing about any of it. The Shadowen appeared to possess boundless raw power, the kind of power that would let them become anything. It was neither subtle nor intricate; it was as straightforward and relentless as a flood. It seemed able to build on itself and to sweep aside anything that it found in its path. Walker did not know how powerful the Horsemen were, but he was willing to bet that they were more than a match for him.

Rimmer Dall would have sent nothing less to deal with a Druid – even one newly come to the position, uncertain of his own strength, of the extent of his magic, and of the ways it might be made to serve him. At least one of Allanon's charges to the Ohmsfords had been carried out, and it posed a threat that the Shadowen could not afford to ignore.

Yet the purpose of the charges remained a mystery that Walker could not solve. Standing atop Paranor's walls, watching the Four Horsemen circle below, he pondered endlessly why the charges had been given. What was it that the Sword of Shannara was supposed to accomplish? What purpose would it serve to have the Elves brought back into the world of men? What was the reason for returning Paranor and the Druids? Or one Druid at least, he mused darkly. One Druid, made over out of bits and pieces of others. He was an amalgam of those who had come and gone, of their memories, of their strengths and weaknesses, of their lore and history, of their magic's secrets. He was an infant in his life as a Druid, and he did not yet know how he was supposed to act. Each day he opened new doors on what others before him had known and passed on, knowledge that revealed itself in unexpected glimpses, light coming from the darkened corners of his mind as if let in through shuttered windows thrown wide. He did not understand it all, sometimes doubted it, often questioned its worth. But the flow was relentless, and he was forced to measure and weigh each new revelation, knowing it must have had worth once, accepting that it might again.

But what role was he supposed to play in the struggle to put an end to the Shadowen? He had become the Druid that Allanon had sought, and he had made himself master of Paranor. Yet what was he supposed to do with this? Surely he had magic now that might be used against the Shadowen – just as the Druids had used magic before to give aid to the Races. He possessed knowledge as well, perhaps more knowledge than any man alive, and the Druids had used this as a weapon, too. But it seemed to Walker that his newfound power

lacked any discernible focus, that he needed first to understand the nature of his enemy before he could settle on a way to
defeat it.

Meanwhile, here he was, trapped within his tower fortress
where he could not help anyone.

'They do not try to enter,' Cogline observed at one point
after three days of vigilance atop the castle walls. 'Why do you
think that is?'

Walker shook his head. 'Perhaps they do not need to. As
long as we remain locked within, their purpose is served.'

The old man rubbed his whiskered chin. He had grown
older since his release from the half life to which the magic of
the Druid Histories had consigned him. He was lined and
wrinkled anew, more stooped than before, slower in his walk
and speech, frail beyond what his years allowed. Walker did
not like what he saw, but said nothing. The old man had given
much for him, and what he had given had clearly taken its toll.
But he did not complain or choose to talk of it, so there was no
reason for Walker to do so either.

'It may be that they are afraid of the Druid magic,' Walker
continued after a moment, his good hand lifting to rest on the
battlement stone. 'Paranor has always been protected from
those that would enter uninvited. The Shadowen may know of
this and choose to stay without because of it.'

'Or perhaps they wait until they have tested the nature and
extent of that magic,' Cogline said softly. 'They wait to discover how dangerous you are.' He looked at Walker without
seeing him, eyes focused somewhere beyond. 'Or until they
simply grow tired of waiting,' he whispered.

Walker considered ways in which he might defeat these
Shadowen, turning those ways over and over in his mind like
artifacts hiding clues to the past. The Black Elfstone was an
obvious choice, secreted now in a vault deep within the
catacombs of the Keep. But the Elfstone would exact its
own price if called upon, and it was not a price that Walker
was willing to pay. There was no reason to think that the

Elfstone would not work against the Four Horsemen, draining their magic away until nothing remained but ashes. But the nature of the Elfstone required that the stolen magic be transferred into the holder, and Walker had no wish to have the Shadowen magic made part of him.

There was also the Stiehl, the strange killing blade taken from the assassin Pe Ell at Eldwist, the weapon that could kill anything. But Walker did not relish the prospect of using an assassin's weapon, especially one with the history of the Stiehl, and thought that if weapons were required, there were plenty at hand that could be used against the Shadowen.

What he needed most, he knew, was a plan. He had three choices. He could remain safely within Paranor's walls, hoping to wait the Shadowen out; he could go out and face them; or he could try to slip past them without being seen. The first offered only the faintest possibility of success, and besides, time was not something of which he had an abundance in any case. The second seemed incontestably foolhardy.

That left the third.

Five days after the Four Horsemen laid siege to Paranor, Walker Boh decided to attempt an escape.

Underground.

He told Cogline of his plan at dinner that night – a dinner comprising some few small stores left over from three centuries gone and frozen in time with the castle, sorely depleted stores that reinforced the importance of breaking the siege. There were tunnels beneath the castle that opened into the forests beyond, concealments known only to Druids past and now to him. He would slip through such a tunnel that night and emerge behind where the Horsemen patrolled the walls. He would be clear of them and gone before they knew he had escaped.

Cogline frowned and looked doubtful. It seemed entirely too easy to him. Surely the Shadowen would have thought of such a possibility.

But Walker had made up his mind. Five days of standing about was long enough. Something had to be tried, and this was the best he could come up with. Cogline and Rumor would remain within the Keep. If the Horsemen attempted an assault before Walker returned, they should slip out the same way he had gone. Cogline reluctantly agreed, bothered by something he refused to discuss, so agitated that Walker came close to pressing for an explanation. But the old man's enigmatic behavior was nothing new, so in the end Walker let the matter drop.

He waited for midnight, watching from the walls until late to make certain that the Shadowen kept to their rounds. They did, spectral shapes in the dark below, circling ceaselessly. The fog that had blanketed the valley for the better part of four days had lifted that dawn, and now with the coming of night Walker Boh saw something new in the valley. Far west, where the Dragon's Teeth turned north into the Streleheim, there were watch fires at the mouth of the Kennon Pass. An army was camped there, blocking all passage. The Federation, Walker thought, staring out across the trees of the forest below, across the hills beyond, to the light. Perhaps their presence in the pass was unrelated to that of the Shadowen at Paranor, but Walker didn't think so. Knowingly or not, the Federation served the Shadowen cause – a tool for Rimmer Dall and others in the Coalition Council hierarchy – and it was safe to assume that the soldiers in the Kennon had something to do with the Four Horsemen.

Not that it mattered. Walker Boh wasn't worried for a moment that Federation soldiers would prove any hindrance to him.

When midnight came, he left the castle walls and went down through the Keep. He wore clothes as black as night, loose-fitting and serviceable, and carried no weapons. He left Cogline and Rumor peering after him as he entered the fire pit. His memories were Allanon's and those of Druids gone before, and he found he knew his way as well as if the Keep had always been his home. Doors hidden within the castle stone opened at his touch, and passageways were as familiar as the haunts of Hearthstone in the days before the dreams of Allanon. He found the tunnels that ran beneath the rock on which Paranor rested and worked his way down into the earth. All about him he could hear the steady thrum of the fires contained in the furnaces beneath the Keep, throbbing steadily within their core of rock deep below the castle walls, the only sound within the darkness and silence.

It took him over an hour to make his way through. There were numerous passageways beneath the castle, all intertwined and leading from a single door that only he could open. He chose the one that led west, seeking to exit within the sheltering trees of the forests that lay between the Horsemen and the Kennon Pass, certain that once free of the Shadowen he could slip past the Federation soldiers easily. When he reached the concealed opening, he paused to listen. There was no sound above him. There was no movement. Still, he felt uneasy, as if sensing that despite appearances all was not well.

He went out from the tunnel into the black of the forest, rising from the earth like a shadow within a covering of brush and rocks. Through gaps in the canopy of limbs overhead he could see the stars and a hint of the waning moon. It was silent within the trees, as if nothing lived there. He searched for a hint of the presence of the gray wolves and did not find it. He listened for the small sounds of insects and birds, and they were missing. He sniffed the air and smelled an odd mustiness.

He breathed deeply and stepped out into the open.

He heard, rather than saw, the sweep of the scythe arcing toward him, and flung himself aside just before it struck. Death grunted with the effort of the swing, a cloaked black shape to one side. Walker rolled to his feet, seeing another shape materialize to his right. War, all in armor, blade edges and spikes glinting wickedly, hurled a mace that thudded into the tree next to him and caused the trunk to split apart. Walker whirled away, careening wildly past the skeletal arms of

Famine, white bones reaching, clutching. They were all there, all of them, he realized in despair. Somehow they had found him out.

He darted away, hearing the buzz and hiss of Pestilence, feeling dry heat and smelling sickness close beside. He leaped a small ravine, his fear giving him unexpected strength, a fiery determination building within him. The Horsemen came after, dismounted now in their effort to trap him, bits of night broken free like the edges of a shattered blade. He heard their movement as he might the rustle of leaves in a slight wind, small whispers. There was nothing else – no footsteps, no breathing, no scrape of weapons or bone.

Walker raced through the trees, no longer sure in which direction he was running, seeking only to elude his pursuers. He was suddenly lost in the darkness of the forest corridors, fleeing to no purpose but to escape, any advantage of surprise lost. The Shadowen came on, a swift and certain pursuit. He was aware of their movements out of the corner of his eye. They had him flushed now, and they were hunting him as dogs would a fox.

No!

He whirled then and brought his magic to bear, throwing up a wall of fire between himself and his pursuers, sending the flames back into their faces like white-hot spikes. War and Pestilence shrank away, slowed, but Famine and Death came on, unaffected. Of course, Walker thought as he ran anew. Famine and Death. Fire would not harm them.

He crossed a stream and swerved right toward the rise of Paranor, towers and walls sharp-edged against the night. He had been running that way without knowing it, and now saw it as his only chance of escape. If he could gain the castle before they caught him . . .

Cogline! Was the old man watching?

Something rose out of the night before him, serpentine and slick with moisture. Claws reached for him and teeth gleamed. It was one of the Shadowen mounts, set there to cut him off.

He slipped beneath its grasp, a bit of night that could not be held, the magic making him as swift and ephemeral as the wind. The serpent thing hissed and slashed wildly, sending gouts of earth flying. Walker Boh was behind it by then, racing away with the quickness of thought. Ahead the castle of the Druids loomed – his sanctuary, his haven from these things –

A black motion to his left sent him skidding away as Famine lashed out with a sword carved of bone, a dull white gleaming that tore at the edges of his clothing. Walker lost his footing and went down, tumbling along a slope, rolling wildly through brush and long grass and into a slick of standing water. Something rushed past, just missing him with a click of jaws. Another of the serpents. Walker came to his feet, flinging fire and sound in all directions in a desperate effort to shield himself. He had the satisfaction of hearing something shriek in pain, of hearing something else grunt as if clubbed, and then he was moving again. Trees rose off to one side, and he disappeared into them, searching out the concealment of the deep shadows. His breathing was ragged and uneven, and his body ached. To his dismay, he found himself moving away from the castle again, turned aside from the safety he had hoped to gain.

A shadow flitted off to his left, swift and silent, a black cloak and a glint of an iron blade. *Death.* Walker was tiring, worn from his flight, from being forced to change direction so often. The Shadowen had hemmed him in and were closing. He did not think he could reach the castle before they caught up to him. He sought to change directions back again, but saw movement between himself and the Keep and heard a hiss of anticipation and the sudden rustle of scales through the grasses and brush. Walker could barely keep his panic in check, feeling it as a growing tightness in his throat. He had been too quick to assume, too sure of himself. He should have known it would not be this easy. He should have anticipated better.

Branches slapped at his face and arms as he forced his way

into a stretch of deep woods. Behind, the serpent closed. It seemed as if he could feel its breath on his neck, the touch of claws and teeth on his body. He increased his pace, broke free of the underbrush into a clearing, and found Death waiting, cloaked and hooded, scythe lifted. The Shadowen struck at him, missed as he veered sideways, swung a second time, and Walker caught hold of the scythe to deflect it. Instantly a cold numbed his hand and arm, hollow and bone-chilling, and he jerked away in pain, thrusting the scythe and its wielder aside as he did so. Something else moved in from the right, but he was running again, throwing himself back into the forest, slipping past rows of dark trunks as if turned substanceless, all the while feeling the numbness settle deeper.

So cold!

His strength was failing now, and he was no closer to safety than before. Think, he admonished himself furiously. *Think!* Shadows moved all about, the skeletal shape of Famine, the hideous buzz of Pestilence, the rumble of War in his unbreachable armor, the silent rush of Death, and with them the serpents they commanded.

Then suddenly a memory triggered, and Walker Boh grasped for the thread of hope it offered. There was a trapdoor hidden in the earth just ahead and beneath it a tunnel leading back into Paranor. The trapdoor was Allanon's memory, come alive in the terror and anguish of the moment, recalled just in time. *There, left!* Walker swerved, lurching ahead, hand and arm feeling as dead as the one he had lost. *Don't think about it!* He threw himself into a covering of brush, whipping past leafy barriers, down a ravine, and across a narrows.

There!

His hand dropped to the earth, clawing for the hidden door with nerveless fingers. It was here, he thought, here in this patch of ground. Sounds approached from behind, closing. He found an iron ring, grasped it, and heaved upward. The door came away with a thud, falling back. Walker tumbled through the opening and down the stairs beyond, then scrambled back to his feet. There were shadows at the entry, coming through. He raised his damaged hand and arm, fighting through the numbness and chill, and called for the magic. Fire exploded up the stairs and filled the opening. The shadows disappeared in a ball of light. There was a rending of earth and stone, and the entire entrance collapsed.

Walker lurched away into the tunnel, choking and coughing from the dust and smoke. Twice he glanced back to make certain that nothing followed.

But he was alone.

He was besieged by doubts and fears as he made his way back to the Keep through the tunnels, assailed by demons that bore the faces of his enemies. It seemed as if he could hear his Shadowen pursuers even here, come down into the earth to finish what they had started. Death, War, Pestilence, and Famine – what was rock and earth to them? Could they not penetrate anywhere? What was to keep them out?

But they did not come, for, notwithstanding the forms and identities they had assumed, they were not invincible and not truly the incarnations they pretended to be. He had heard them cry out in pain; he had felt their substance. The numbness in his hand and arm was beginning to recede, and he welcomed the tingling gratefully, feeling anew the pain of loss of his other limb, wishing he could live that part of his life over again.

He wondered how much more of himself he would be forced to cede before this struggle was over. Wasn't he lucky just to be alive? How narrow his escape from the Shadowen had been this time!

And then suddenly it occurred to him that perhaps he hadn't really escaped anything. Perhaps he had been *allowed* to escape. Perhaps the Horsemen had only been toying with him. Hadn't they had enough chances to kill him if they wanted to? It seemed on reflection that they might have been trying to scare him rather than kill him, to instill enough fear in him that he would be unable to function at all once he was back within the Druid's Keep.

But he discarded the idea almost immediately. It was ridiculous to think that they wouldn't have killed him if they could. They had simply tried and failed. He had possessed enough skill and magic to save himself even in the confusion of an ambush, and he would take what comfort he could from that.

Aching and worn, he reentered Paranor's walls and made his way back into the Keep. Cogline would be waiting. He would have to confess his failure to the old man. The thought troubled him, and he was aware that it was his preconception of the invincibility of the Druids that stood in the way of acceptance. But he could not afford pride. He was a novice still. He was just beginning to learn.

Slowly the fears and doubts dropped away, and the demons disappeared. There would be another day, he promised – another time and place in which to deal with the Horsemen.

When it came, he would be ready.

11

Morgan Leah explained his plan to rescue Padishar Creel to Damson Rhee and Chandos during dinner. He pulled them aside where they would not be overheard, huddling on the open bluff about their food and drink, listening to the night sounds and watching the stars brighten in the darkening sky while they talked. He first had Damson relate again the particulars of her own escape from the city, letting her tell the story as she chose, glancing back and forth between the girl and the fierce-looking freeborn. When she had finished, he set his empty plate aside – he had consumed everything while she talked – and leaned forward intently.

'They will expect a rescue attempt,' he advised softly, glancing at each in turn. 'They know we won't just give up on him. They know how important he is to us. But they will not expect us to come at them the same way. They will expect a different approach this time – a major effort involving a large number of men maybe, a diversion of some sort perhaps leading to an allout assault. They will expect us to try to catch them off guard. So we have to give them something other than what they're looking for before they realize what it is they're seeing.'

Chandos snorted. 'Are you making any sense, Highlander?'

Morgan permitted himself a quick grin. 'Above all else, we

have to get in and out again quick. The longer this takes, the more dangerous it becomes. Bear with me, Chandos. I just want you to understand the reasoning behind what I'm about to suggest. We have to think the way they do in order to anticipate their plan to trap us and find a way to avoid it.'

'You're sure there will be a trap, then?' the big man asked, rubbing his bearded chin. 'Why won't they just dispose of Padishar and be done with it? Or why not do to him what they did to Hirehone?' He glanced quickly at Damson, who was tight-lipped.

Morgan clasped a hand on the other's broad shoulder. 'I can't be sure of anything. But think about it for a moment. If they dispose of Padishar, they lose any chance of getting their hands on the rest of us. And they want us all, Chandos. They want the free-born wiped out.' He faced Damson. 'Eventually, they will use Padishar the same way they used Hirehone. But they won't do that right away. First of all, they know we will be looking for it. If Padishar comes back, what's the first thing we'll ask ourselves? Is it really Padishar – or is it another of the Shadowen? Second, they know we found a way to discover the truth about Teel. And they know we might do it again with Padishar. Third, and most important, we have the use of magic and they want it. Rimmer Dall has been chasing Par Ohmsford from the beginning and it must have something to do with his magic. Same with Walker Boh. And the same with me.'

He leaned forward. 'They'll try to use Padishar to bring us to them because they know we won't attempt a rescue without bringing the magic along, that we won't challenge theirs without being able to call on ours. They want that magic – just like they want all the magic – and this is their best chance to get it.'

Chandos frowned. 'So you figure it's the Shadowen that we'll really be up against?'

Morgan nodded. 'It's been the Shadowen right from the beginning. Teel, Hirehone, the Creepers, Rimmer Dall, the

Gnawl, that little girl Par encountered on Toffer Ridge – everywhere we've gone, the Shadowen have been there waiting. They control the Federation and the Coalition Council as well; they have to. Of course it's the Shadowen we'll be up against.'

'Tell us your plan,' Damson urged quietly.

Morgan leaned back again, folding his arms comfortably. 'We go back into Tyrsis through the tunnels – the same way Damson escaped. We dress ourselves in Federation uniforms, just as Padishar did at the Pit. We go up into the city, to the watchtower or prisons or wherever they have Padishar. We enter in broad daylight and set him free. We go in one way and out another. We do it all in a matter of a few minutes.'

Chandos and Damson both stared at him. 'That's it? That's the whole plan?' Chandos demanded.

'Wait a minute,' Damson interrupted. 'Morgan, how do we get back into the tunnels? I can't remember the way.'

'No, you can't,' Morgan agreed. 'But the Mole can.' He took a deep breath. 'This plan depends mostly on him. And you persuading him to help.' He paused, studying her green eyes. 'You will have to go back into the city and find him, then come down through the catacombs to lead us in. You will have to find out where Padishar is being held so that we can go right to him. The Mole knows all the secret passageways, all the tunnels that lie beneath the city of Tyrsis. He can find a way for us to go. If we just appear at their door, they won't have time to stop us. It's the best chance we have – do what they expect us to do, but not in the way they're anticipating.'

Chandos shook his head. 'I don't know, Highlander. They know about Damson; they'll be looking for her.'

Morgan nodded. 'But she's the only one the Mole will trust. She has to go in first, through the gates. I'll go with her.' He looked at her. 'What do you think, Damson Rhee?'

'I think I can do it,' she declared quietly. 'And the Mole will help – if they haven't caught up with him yet.' She frowned doubtfully. 'They have to be hunting for him down in those same tunnels we'll be coming through.'

'But he knows them better than the soldiers do,' Morgan said. 'They've been trying to catch him for weeks now and haven't been able to do so. We just need another few days.' He looked at the girl and the big man in turn. 'It is the best chance we're going to get. We have to try.'

Chandos shook his head once more. 'How many of us will this take?'

'Two dozen, no more.'

Chandos stared at him, wide-eyed. 'Two dozen! Highlander, there's five thousand Federation soldiers quartered in Tyrsis, and who knows how many Shadowen! Two dozen men won't stand a chance!'

'We'll stand a better chance than two hundred — or two thousand, if we had that many to muster, which we don't, do we?' The big man's jaw tightened defensively.

'Chandos, the smaller the company, the better the chance of hiding it. They'll be looking for something larger; they'll expect it. But two dozen men? We can be on top of them before they know who we are. We can disguise two dozen among five thousand a lot more easily than two hundred. Two dozen is all we need if we get close enough.'

'He's right,' Damson said suddenly. 'A large force would be heard in the tunnels. There would be nowhere for them to hide in the city. We can slip two dozen in and hide them until the attempt.' She looked directly at Morgan. 'What I don't know is whether two dozen will be enough to free Padishar when the time comes.'

Morgan met her gaze. 'Because of the Shadowen?'

'Yes, because of the Shadowen. We don't have Par with us this time to keep them at bay.'

'No,' Morgan agreed, 'you have me instead.' He reached back over his shoulder, drew out the Sword of Leah, brought it around in front of him, and jammed it dramatically into the earth. It rested there, quivering slightly, polished surface smooth and silver in the starlight. He looked at them. 'And I have this.'

'Your talisman,' Chandos muttered in surprise. 'I thought it was broken.'

'It was healed when I went north,' Morgan replied softly, seeing Quickening's face appear and then fade in his mind. 'I have the magic back again. It will be enough to withstand the Shadowen.'

Damson glanced from one face to the other, confused. Perhaps Par hadn't told her about the Sword of Leah. Perhaps he hadn't had time in the struggle to escape Tyrsis and reach the free-born. And no one knew about Quickening save for Walker Boh.

Morgan did not care to explain, and he did not try. 'Can you find the men?' he asked Chandos instead.

The black eyes fixed him. 'I can, Highlander. Twenty times that for Padishar Creel.' He paused. 'But you're asking them to place a lot of faith in you.'

Morgan jerked his sword free of the earth and slid it back into its sheath. In the distance, along the bluff edge, free-born patrolled in the darkness. Behind, back against the trees, cooking fires burned low, and the clank and rattle of cookware was beginning to diminish as the meal ended and thoughts turned to sleep. Pipes were lit, small bits of light against the black, fireflies that wavered in the concealment of the trees. The sound of voices was low and easy.

Morgan looked at the big man. 'If there were a better choice, Chandos, I would take it gladly.' He held the other's dark gaze. 'What's it to be, yes or no?'

Chandos looked at Damson, his gold earring a small glitter as his head turned. 'What do you say?'

The girl brushed back her fiery hair, the look in her eyes a determined one, edged with flashes of anger and hope. 'I say we have to try something or Padishar is lost.' Her face tightened. 'If it was us instead of him, wouldn't he come?'

Chandos rubbed at the scarred remains of his ear. 'In your

case, he already did, didn't he?' He shook his head. 'Fools to the end, we are,' he muttered to no one in particular. 'All of us.' He looked back at Morgan. 'All right, Highlander. Two dozen men, myself included. I'll pick them tonight.'

He rose abruptly. 'You'll want to leave right away, I expect. First light, or as soon thereafter as we can put together supplies for the trip.' He gave Morgan a wry look. 'We don't have to live off the land by any chance, do we, Highlander?'

Morgan and Damson stood up with him. Morgan extended his hand to the free-born. 'Thank you, Chandos.'

The big man laughed. 'For what? For agreeing to a madman's scheme?' He clasped Morgan's hand nevertheless. 'Tell you what. If this works, it'll be me thanking you a dozen times over.'

Muttering, he trudged off toward the cooking fires, carrying his empty plate, shaggy head lowered into his barrel chest. Morgan watched him go, thinking momentarily of times gone by and of places and companions left behind. The thoughts were haunting and filled with regrets for what might have been, and they left him feeling empty and alone.

He felt Damson's shoulder brush up against his arm and turned to face her. The emerald eyes were thoughtful. 'He may be right about you,' she observed quietly. 'You may be a madman.'

He shrugged. 'You backed me up.'

'I want Padishar free. You seem to be the only one with a plan.' She arched one eyebrow. 'Tell me the truth – is there any more to this scheme than what you've revealed?'

He smiled. 'Not much. I hope to be able to improvise as I go along.'

She didn't say anything, just studied him a moment, then took his arm and steered him out along the bluff face. They walked without saying anything for a long time, crossing from the edge of the trees to the cliffs and back again, breathing the scent of wildflowers and grasses on the wind that skipped down off the ridges of the peaks beyond. The wind was warm and soothing, like silk against Morgan's skin. He lifted his face to it. It made him want to close his eyes and disappear into it.

'Tell me about your sword,' she said suddenly, her voice very quiet. Her gaze was steady despite the sudden shifting of his eyes away from her. 'Tell me how it was healed – and why you hurt so much, Morgan. Because you do in some way, don't you? I can see it in your eyes. Tell me. I want to hear.'

He believed her, and he discovered all at once that he did want to talk about it after all. He let himself be pulled down onto a flat-surfaced rock. Sitting next to her in the darkness, both of them facing out toward the cliffs, he began to speak.

'There was a girl named Quickening,' he said, the words thick and unwieldy sounding as he spoke them. He paused and took a deep, steadying breath. 'I loved her very much.'

He hoped she didn't see the tears that came to his eyes.

He spent the night rolled into a blanket at the edge of the trees, body wedged within the roots of an ancient elm, head cradled by his rolled-up travel cloak. The makeshift bedding proved less than satisfactory, and he woke stiff and sore. As he shook the leaves and dust out of the cloak he realized that he had not seen Matty Roh since the night before, that he hadn't actually seen her even at dinner, although he had been pretty pre-occupied with his plan for rescuing Padishar – his great and wonderful plan that on reflection in the pale first light of dawn appeared pretty makeshift and decidedly lacking in common sense. Last night it had seemed pretty good. This morning it just looked desperate.

But he was committed to it now. Chandos would have already begun preparations for the journey back to Tyrsis. There was nothing to be gained by second-guessing.

He stretched and headed for the little stream that ran down out of the rocks behind him some distance back in the trees. The cold water would help to unclog his brain, chase the sleep from his eyes. He had talked with Damson Rhee until well after midnight. He had told her everything about Quickening and the journey north to Eldwist. She had listened without saying much, and somehow it had brought them closer together. He found himself liking her more, found himself trusting her. The suspicions that had been there earlier had faded. He began to understand why Par Ohmsford and Padishar Creel had gone back for her after the Federation had taken her prisoner. He thought that he would have done the same.

Nevertheless, there was something she wasn't telling him about her relationship with the Valeman and the leader of the free-born. It was neither a deception nor a lie; it was simply an omission. She had been quick enough to acknowledge that she was in love with Par, but there was something else, something that predated her feelings for the Valeman, that formed the backbone for everything that had led to her own involvement in trying to recover the Sword of Shannara from the Pit. Morgan wasn't sure what it was, but it was there in the fabric of her tale, in the way she spoke of the two men, in the strength of her conviction that she must help them. Once or twice Morgan had almost been able to put his finger on what it was that she was keeping to herself, but each time the truth skittered just out of reach.

In any case, he felt better for having told someone about Quickening, for having given some release to the feelings he had kept bottled up inside since his return. He'd slept well after that, a dreamless rest cradled in the crook of that old tree, able to let go a little of the pain that had dogged him for so many weeks.

He heard the sound of the stream ahead, a small rippling against the silence. He crossed a clearing, pushed through a screen of brush, and found himself staring at Matty Roh.

She sat across from him at the edge of the stream, her pants rolled up and her bare feet dangling in the water. The moment he appeared she jerked away, reaching for her boots. Her feet came out of the water in a flash of white skin, disappearing into the shadow of her body almost immediately. But for just an instant he had a clear view of them, hideously scarred, the toes missing or so badly deformed that they were almost unrecognizable. Her black hair shivered in the light with the urgency of her movements as she turned her face away from him.

'Don't look at me,' she whispered harshly.

Embarrassed, he turned away at once. 'I'm sorry,' he apologized. 'I didn't know you were here.'

He hesitated, then started away, following the stream toward the rocks, the picture of her feet uncomfortably clear in his mind.

'You don't have to leave,' she called after him, and he stopped. 'I . . . I just need a minute.'

He waited, looking out into the trees, hearing voices now from just beyond where he stood, a snatch of laughter here, a quick murmur there.

'All right,' she said, and he turned back again. She was standing by the stream with her pants rolled down and her boots on. 'I'm sorry I snapped at you like that.'

He shrugged and walked over to her. 'Well, I didn't mean to surprise you. I'm still a little bit asleep, I guess.'

'It wasn't your fault.' She looked embarrassed as well.

He knelt by the stream and splashed water on his face and hands, used soap to wash himself, and rubbed himself dry again on a soft cloth. He could have used a bath, but didn't want to take the time. He was conscious of the girl watching him as he worked, a silent shadow at his side.

He finished and rocked back on his heels, breathing deeply the morning air. He could smell wildflowers and grasses.

'You're leaving for Tyrsis to rescue Padishar,' she said suddenly. 'I want to go with you.'

He looked up at her in surprise. 'How did you know about the rescue?'

She shrugged. 'Doing what I've trained myself to do – keeping my eyes and ears open. Can I come?'

He stood up and faced her. Her eyes were level with his. He

was surprised all over again at how tall she was. 'Why would you want to do that?'

'Because I'm tired of standing about, of doing nothing more than listening in on other people's conversations.' Her gaze was steady and determined. 'Remember our conversation on the trail? I said I was waiting for something to happen? Well, it has. I want to go with you.'

She stepped back a pace, measuring him. 'I would hate to think that you were stupid enough to be worried about me,' she said bluntly. 'The fact of the matter is I can take care of myself a lot better than you can. I've been doing it for a much longer time. You might remember how things went back at the Whistledown when you tried to grab me.'

'That doesn't count!' he snapped defensively. 'I wasn't ready – '

'No, you weren't,' she cut him short. 'And that is the difference between us, Highlander. You aren't trained to be ready, and I am.' She stepped close again. 'I'll tell you something else. I'm a better swordsman than anyone this side of Padishar Creel – and maybe as good as he is. If you don't believe me, ask Chandos.'

He stared at her, at the piercing cobalt eyes, at the thin line of her lips, at the slender shoulders squared and set, everything thrust forward combatively, daring him to challenge her.

'I believe you,' he said, and meant it.

'Besides,' she said, not relaxing herself an inch, 'you need me to make your plan work.'

'How do you know about – '

'You're the wrong one to go into Tyrsis with Damson,' she interrupted, ignoring his unfinished question. 'It should be me.'

'. . . the plan?' he finished, trailing off. He put his hands on his hips, frustrated. 'Why should it be you?'

'Because I won't be noticed and you will. You're too obvious, Highlander. You look exactly like what you are! Anyway, your face is known to the Federation and mine isn't.

And if anything goes wrong, you don't know your way around Tyrsis, and I do. I've been there many times. Most important of all, they won't be looking for two women. We'll walk right past them, and they won't give us a second glance.'

She squared up to him again. 'Tell me I'm wrong,' she challenged.

He smiled in spite of himself. 'I guess I can't do that.' He looked away into the trees, hoping the answer to her demand lay there. It didn't. He looked back again. 'Why don't you ask Chandos? He's in charge, not me.'

Her expression did not change. 'I don't think so. At least not in this case.' She paused, waiting. 'Well? Can I go?'

He sighed, suddenly weary. Maybe she was right. Maybe having her along would be a good idea. She certainly gave a convincing argument. Besides, hadn't he just finished telling himself that his plan needed help? Perhaps Matty Roh was a little of what was needed.

'All right,' he agreed. 'You can come.'

'Thanks.' She turned away and started back toward the camp, her cloak slung over one shoulder.

'But Chandos has to agree, too!' he called after her, still looking for a way out.

'He already has!' she shouted back in reply. 'He said to ask you.'

She gave him a quick smile over her shoulder as she disappeared into the trees.

Chandos was terse and withdrawn at breakfast, and Morgan left him alone, choosing to sit instead with Damson Rhee. The long table they occupied was crowded and the men were boisterous, so the Highlander and the girl didn't say much to each other, concentrating on their food and the conversation around them. Matty Roh appeared briefly, passing next to Morgan without looking at him, on her way to someplace else. She paused long enough to say something to Chandos, which caused him to scowl deeply. Morgan didn't hear what she said but had no trouble imagining what it might be.

When the meal was concluded Chandos pushed to his feet, bellowed at everyone still seated to get to work, and called Damson and Morgan aside. He took them out of the trees and onto the open bluff once more, waiting until they were out of earshot to speak. Dark-visaged and gruff, he announced that during the night word had arrived through the free-born network that the Elves had returned to the Westland. This news was several days old and not entirely reliable, and he wanted to know what Morgan and the girl thought.

'I think it's possible,' Morgan said at once. 'Returning the Elves to the Westland was one of the charges given to the Ohmsfords.'

'If Paranor is back, the Elves could be back as well,' agreed Damson.

'And that would mean that all the charges have been fulfilled,' Morgan added, growing excited now. 'Chandos, we have to know if it's true.'

The big man's scowl returned. 'You'll want another expedition, I suppose – as if one wasn't enough!' He sighed wearily. 'All right, I'll send someone to check it out, a messenger to let them know they have friends in Callahorn. If they're there, we'll find them.'

He went on to add that he had chosen the men for the journey to Tyrsis and that supplies and weapons were being assembled as they spoke. Everything should be in place by mid-morning, and as soon as it was they would depart.

As he turned to leave, Morgan asked impulsively, 'Chandos, what's your opinion of Matty Roh?'

'My opinion?' The big man laughed. 'I think she gets pretty much anything she wants.' He started away again, then called back, 'I also think you'd better watch your step with her, Highlander.'

He went on, disappearing into the trees, yelling orders as he went.

Damson looked at Morgan. 'What was that all about?'

Morgan told her about his meeting with Matty at Varfleet and their journey to Firerim Reach. He told her about the girl's insistence that she be included in their effort to rescue Padishar. He asked Damson if she knew anything about Matty Roh. Damson did not. She had never met her before.

'But Matty's right about two women attracting less attention,' she declared. 'And if she was able to persuade both you and Chandos that she should go on this journey, I'd say you'd both better watch out for her.'

Morgan left to put together his pack for the trek south, strapped on his weapons, and went back out on the bluff. Within an hour the company that Chandos had chosen was assembled and ready to leave. It was a hard and capable-looking bunch, some of them men who had fought side by side with Padishar against the Creeper at the Jut. A few recognized Morgan and nodded companionably. Sending one man on ahead to scout for any trouble, Chandos led the rest, Morgan and Damson and Matty Roh with them, down off Firerim Reach toward the plains beyond.

They walked all day, descending out of the Dragon's Teeth to the Rabb, then turning south to cross the river and continue on toward Varfleet. They traveled quickly, steadily through the heat, the sky clear and cloudless, the sun burning down in a steady glare, causing the air above the dusty grasslands to shimmer like water. They rested at midday and ate, rested again at midafternoon, and by nightfall had reached the flats that led up into the Valley of Shale. A watch was set, dinner was eaten, and the company retired to sleep. Morgan had walked with Damson during the day, and bedded down close to her that night. While she probably neither needed nor wanted it, he had assumed a protective attitude toward her, determined that if he could not do anything for Par or Coll just at the moment, at least he could look after her.

Matty Roh had kept to herself most of the day, walking apart from everyone, eating alone when they rested, choosing

140

to keep her own company. No one seemed all that surprised that she was along; no one seemed to question why she was there. Several times Morgan thought to speak with her, but each time he saw the set of her face and the deliberate distance she created between herself and others, and decided not to.

At midnight, restless from dreams and the anticipation of what lay ahead, he awoke and walked down to the edge of the grove of trees in which they had sheltered to look up at the sky and out across the plains. She appeared suddenly at his elbow. Silent as a ghost, she stood next to him as if she might have been expected all along. Together, they stared out across the empty stretch of the Rabb, studying the outline of the land in the pale starlight, breathing the lingering swelter of the day in the cooling night.

'The country I was born in looked like this,' she said after a time, her voice distant. 'Flat, empty grasslands. A little water, a lot of heat. Seasons that could be harsh and beautiful at the same time.' She shook her head. 'Not like the Highlands, I expect.'

He didn't say anything, just nodded. A stray bit of wind ruffled her black hair. Somewhere in the distance, a wolf howled, its cry fading unanswered into silence.

'You don't know what to make of me, do you?'

He shrugged. 'I suppose I don't. You're a pretty confusing person.'

Her smile in response was there and gone in an instant. Her delicate features were shadowed and gave her a gaunt look in the dim light. She seemed to be working something through.

'When I was five years old,' she said after a moment, 'just before I reached my sixth birthday, not long after my sister died, I was out playing in a field near the house with my older brother. It was a pasture, left fallow that year. There were milk cows in it, grazing. I remember seeing one of the cows lying on its side down in a depression. It had a funny look about it, and I walked down to see what was wrong. The cow was looking at me, its eyes wide and staring, very frightened. It didn't seem to be able to cry out. It was dying, half in and half out of some sort of muddy sinkhole that I had never seen there before. Its body was being eaten away.'

She folded her arms across her chest as if she was cold. 'I don't know why, but I wanted a closer look. I walked right up to it, didn't stop until I was no more than several yards away. I should have called for my brother, but I was little and I didn't think to do so. I looked at the cow, wondering what had happened. And suddenly I felt this burning on the soles of my feet. I looked down and saw that I was standing in some of the same mud that the cow had gotten into. The mud was streaked with greenish lines and bubbling. It had eaten right through my shoes. I turned and ran, crying now, calling out for help. I ran as fast as I could, but the pain was faster. It went all through my feet. I remember looking down and seeing that some of my toes were gone.'

She shivered at the memory. 'My mother washed me as best she could, but it was too late. Half my toes were gone, and my feet were scarred and burned as if they had been set on fire. I developed a fever. I was in bed for two weeks. They thought I was going to die. But I didn't; I lived. They died instead. All of them.'

Her smile was bitter and ironic. 'I just thought you should know after this morning. I don't like people to see what happened to me.' She looked at him briefly, then turned away again. 'But I wanted you to understand.'

She stood with him a moment longer, then said good-night and disappeared back into the trees. He stared after her for a long time, thinking about what she had said. When he returned to the campsite and rolled himself back into his blanket, he could not sleep. He could not stop thinking about Matty Roh.

They set out again at dawn, shadows in the faint gray light that seeped out of the east. The day was overcast, and by midday it had begun to rain. The company trudged on through the forested hill country north of Varfleet and the Mermidon, following the line of the Dragon's Teeth west. Twice the scout came back to warn of Federation patrols and they were forced to take cover until the patrols had passed. The land was gray and shone damply through the rain, and they encountered no one else. Morgan walked with Matty Roh, moving up next to her unbidden, staying with her through the day. She said nothing to discourage him and did not move away. She spoke little, but she seemed comfortable with his presence. When they stopped to eat lunch, she shared with him the small bit of fruit she was carrying.

By nightfall, they had crossed the Mermidon and come in sight of Tyrsis. The city glowed bleakly from the bluff heights as they stared up at it from across the approaching plains. Rain continued to fall, steady and unrelenting, turning the dusty earth to mud. Damson and Matty Roh would not attempt to enter the city until morning, when they could mingle with the usual tradesmen come up for the day from the surrounding villages. Chandos sent the scout on ahead to see if he could learn anything useful from travelers departing the city. The rest of the company bedded down in a grove of old maples, finding to their displeasure that dry spaces were few and far between.

It was nearing midnight when the scout returned. Morgan was still awake, huddled with Chandos and Matty Roh, all of them listening as Damson described what she knew of the tunnels beneath Tyrsis and the Federation prisons. The scout bent to whisper something to Chandos, furtive and quick. Chandos turned ashen. He dismissed the scout and turned to the Highlander and the girls.

The Federation had announced its intention to execute Padishar Creel. The execution would be public. It would take place at noon on the day after tomorrow.

Chandos got up and walked away, shaking his head. Morgan sat with Damson and Matty Roh in stunned silence. He had guessed wrong. The Federation had decided to rid itself of

143

Padishar once and for all. The leader of the free-born had less than two days to live.

Morgan's eyes met Damson's, then Matty's. They were all thinking the same thing. Whatever rescue plan they tried, they had better get it right the first time.

12

Wind blew across Wren Elessedil's face, cooling it against the heat of the midday sun. Her short cropped hair whipped from side to side with its passing, and the whistling rush past her ears drowned out all other sounds. There was a cadence to it that lulled and soothed despite its thrust, that wrapped about in the manner of a warm cloak on a cold night. She smiled at the feeling, closed her eyes, and gave herself over to its embrace.

Wren was seated astride the giant Roc Spirit, flying high over the Westland forests south and east of Arborlon, approaching the Mermidon where it brushed the vast swamp they called the Shroudslip and edged down into the plains of the Tirfing. Tiger Ty sat in front of her, straddling Spirit's neck where it joined the shoulders, just forward of the great wings. Both Wing Rider and Elf Queen were strapped tightly to the bird's harness, securely fastened against the possibility of a fall. The sky was bright and cloudless, the sun's light bathing the land from horizon to horizon in melted gold. Below, where the earth stretched away in a patchwork maze of green and brown, it was hot and humid in the long, slow days of late summer, and everything seemed to stand still. But here, high above the heat, where the wind blew steady and cool, Wren soared through space and time unchecked, and there was within her that sense of escape that flight inevitably generated.

Her eyes opened and there was bitterness in her smile. Certainly she had spent enough time seeking escape in one form or another to recognize the feeling, she thought.

It was ten days now since her return to the Four Lands. The nightmare of Morrowindl was behind her and beginning to fade into the recesses of her memory. Her sleep was still haunted by dreams of what had been – by the monsters that had pursued the little company down Killeshan's ruptured mountain slopes to the beaches, by the faces of those who had died in the attempt, by the fear and anguish she had felt, and by the terrible sense of loss that she did not think would ever leave her. She still woke from those dreams, shaking and cold in spite of the summer heat, leaving her bed to walk alone through the palace halls, a driven spirit. Even now Morrowindl, gone back into the ocean in that fiery conflagration, whispered to her from out of the past, from out of its watery grave, its voice a constant reminder of how she had gotten to where she was and what it had cost her.

But there was little time to dwell on what had been, for the demands of the present overshadowed everything. She was Queen of the Elves, entrusted with the safety and welfare of her people. It was the charge that Ellenroh had given her; it was the charge she had accepted. But not all those for whom she had been given responsibility believed in her. It was not easy convincing the Elves that she was the one who should lead them. After the first rush of euphoria over finding themselves free of Morrowindl and returned once again to the Westland faded, they began to question. Who was this barely grown girl who had declared herself their queen – this girl who was not even a pure-blooded Elf, but a mix of Elf and Man? Who had decided that she should lead them, should govern them, should make decisions that would affect their lives? It was claimed that she was the granddaughter of Ellenroh, the daughter of Alleyne, a child of the Elessedils and the last of them left to rule. But she was a stranger, too, come out of nowhere, unknown and untested. Who was she, that she should be queen?

Eton Shart and Barsimmon Oridio were among those who continued to doubt – her first minister and the general of her armies, men she could not afford to lose. They did not say so to her face or even publicly, but their aloofness was obvious. They had served Ellenroh long and faithfully, and they had not expected to lose her. Worse, they had not expected to find someone they barely knew assuming her place. Certainly not an outsider, and a girl at that. Wren understood their reticence; she also understood that she could not permit it to continue unresolved.

Triss and the Home Guard were her real support. Triss had come with her out of Morrowindl, had seen her struggle with the power of the Elfstones, with the demons that pursued them, and with the responsibility she had been given. He accepted her as queen because he had been there when Ellenroh had named her and had exacted his pledge of loyalty. Triss had declared her queen to the High Council, to the army, and especially to the Home Guard, who were charged with her protection. The Home Guard, unlike the other branches of the Elven government, had accepted her instantly and without reservation. Having lost Ellenroh, they were now fiercely committed to her. Nothing would harm this queen, they swore. This queen would have their full protection. It was the kind of support she desperately needed, and Triss, as captain of the Home Guard, made certain that she had it.

Still, Home Guard support alone would not be enough in the long run. She needed to win over both the High Council and the army if she was to be accepted as queen. That meant she needed to win over Eton Shart and Barsimmon Oridio, and she did not know how to do that. Despite her efforts to convince them of the merits of accepting her, they remained distant and aloof, polite but decidedly cool. Time was running out. Ten days the Elves had been back in the Westland, and by now the Federation and the Shadowen knew. For more than a century the Federation had claimed that the Elves were the source of the land's sickening, and here at last was an opportunity to put things right. No matter that it was the wrong set of Elves, she mused; the Federation was hardly likely to worry about making any distinction between good and bad. Eradicate them all and the problem was solved.

Which was why she was flying south with Tiger Ty. The effort to begin that eradication was already under way.

Tiger Ty touched Spirit lightly along the neck, and the Roc responded by swinging downward toward a bluff that faced out across the river. The bird descended easily, gracefully, and in moments they were settled on a grassy bank at the edge of a forest of broad-leaved trees. Wren disengaged herself from the straps and climbed down, stretching her cramped muscles. She was still not used to riding the giant Rocs, though she had done so several times now since her return. The Wing Riders had begun to come back into the Westland as well, resettling themselves in the old Wing Hove south of the Irrybis. Wren had gone to speak to them, asking for their support, telling them of the danger they all faced if the Shadowen weren't stopped. Tiger Ty, a respected member of the community, had spoken in her behalf, adding his own rough assessment of her character. A girl who's got more sand than a dozen of us, he'd said. A girl with sharp edges, but quick-thinking and smart. A girl who's got use of the magic, but uses it with caution and respect. The Land Elves – and the Wing Riders – could do worse.

She smiled at the memory. The Wing Riders had agreed to help. Almost thirty of them were already settled at Arborlon, made a part of her personal command.

'Something to eat?' Tiger Ty asked, strolling up to her in that rolling gait he used, bowlegged and spindly. He was as grizzled and nut-brown as ever, but no longer as gruff. When he spoke to her these days there was something new in his voice – something that almost suggested deference.

She nodded, then seated herself on the grass across from

him. She accepted a hunk of cheese, an apple, and a cup of ale poured from a stoppered skin. She crossed her legs and was taking a bite of the cheese when she felt a stirring against her breast. A furry face poked out of her tunic, and Faun appeared, sniffing the air tentatively.

'Ha! The Squeak doesn't miss a thing, does she?' Tiger Ty laughed, cut off a bite of his cheese, and passed it to the little creature. Faun took it from him cautiously, slipped clear of Wren's clothing, plopped down on the grass, and began to eat.

'She likes you,' Wren observed.

Tiger Ty snorted. 'Shows you Tree Squeaks don't have the sense of tree stumps!'

They ate in silence, finished, and sat back contentedly, staring out from the bluff across the river to where the plains of the Tirfing stretched away in an unbroken wave of dusty grasses.

'How much farther?' Wren asked after a moment.

Tiger Ty shrugged. 'Another hour at most. They were traveling pretty fast when I spotted them.'

A Federation army, sighted by the patrolling Wing Rider, had brought Wren out of Arborlon in spite of the objections of Triss and the Home Guard. It was necessary, she felt, to have a close look at the enemy before she brought her plan of action before the High Council and its skeptics.

She took a final drink from her cup, finishing the last of the ale. If things had been difficult up to now, she had a feeling that they were about to get a whole lot worse.

They climbed back aboard Spirit, fastened themselves in place, and lifted off into the dazzling blue. Faun was inside her tunic, snuggled down comfortably against her body. Spirit gained height, then settled into a flat glide that swept them down the snaking length of the Mermidon to where it bypassed the Shroudslip. There they left the river and began to follow the line of the Irrybis where it bordered the Tirfing east. Time slipped quickly past, and it seemed only moments later that Tiger Ty lifted one arm to point south.

A huge column of dust rose into the swelter of summer heat that hung over the plains. Tiger Ty glanced back at her and she nodded.

The Federation army.

They continued due south, following a line parallel to the army, keeping in the shadow of the cliffs. Tiger Ty would circle back around and come in from behind the army with the sun at his back. That way they would not be seen. As yet, no one knew anything about the Wing Riders. Wren had decided it would be better if things remained that way.

Swiftly they sped south, and when the column of dust was well behind them they banked left across the plains. They continued to circle until the sun was directly behind them, then swung back toward the dust. They rose higher than before, trying to place as much glare as possible at their backs in case anyone was scanning the sky.

Minutes later, the Federation army came in sight.

It was a huge, sprawling, dark stain against the sun-scorched grasslands, three companies deep, column after column of black-and-red-garbed soldiers and horsemen, great iron-and-wood fighting machines, siege equipment, wagons and supplies. The army seemed to stretch on forever, the dust of its wake obscuring everything for miles. Wren felt her heart sink at the size of the enemy. The Elves could barely muster a tenth of the fighting men the Federation had assembled, and it was reported that there were another five thousand soldiers garrisoned in Tyrsis. If they were forced to confront this army head on, the Elves would be annihilated.

Which was the general idea, of course, she thought disconsolately.

She counted lines and columns and companies carefully as Tiger Ty took Spirit close to the back of the army and then banked the Roc sharply away again, heading south once more, still within the protective glare of the sun. There had been no shouts or pointed arms from below. Apparently they had not been seen.

It took them most of the remainder of the day to make the return flight, and Wren used the time to think about what she would say to the High Council that night. She found herself thinking that it would be nice if she could just keep on flying, traveling to a place so far away that the Federation would never find her. But there was no such place, of course. For even if the Federation couldn't reach her, the Shadowen could. They had proved that on Morrowindl. The Shadowen sickness was everywhere, and no one would be safe again until a cure was found.

It was nearing sunset when Arborlon, the home city of the Elves, came in sight again, a shading of wood colors, metal stays, and spots of bright clothing amid the green. Spirit swung wide above the Rill Song, the river's blue waters turned diamond tipped in the fading light, and settled gently down onto the grassy bluffs of the Carolan. Wren was barely out of her restraining straps and on the ground again before the Home Guard, Triss in the lead, were hurrying down from the city proper to make certain she was safe. She gave them a reassuring wave and a welcoming smile, then bent quickly to Tiger Ty.

'Not a word of what we saw,' she whispered. 'Not yet.'

The Wing Rider's fierce black eyes locked on her. 'Until you meet with the High Council?'

She nodded. 'Until.'

'They won't like what you have to tell them – not that that's anything new. Wooden-headed mules!'

She smiled, quick and furtive. 'You know me. I just keep chipping away.'

The rough face grimaced. 'Do you meet with them tonight?'

'Probably within the hour.'

'Mind if I sit in? Help do a little of that chipping? I pride myself on my woodcutting.'

The look she gave him was filled with gratitude. 'Thanks, Tiger Ty. The Wing Riders should be represented in this, too. You can most certainly sit in.'

151

She turned away then as Triss and the others of the Home Guard reached her, relief reflected in their hard faces.

'My lady, you are well?' Triss asked quietly, his usual greeting. He was still scraped and bruised from their battle with the Wisteron on Morrowindl. His broken left arm was splinted and cradled in a cloth sling. But there was strength again in his lean face, and confidence and determination mirrored in his eyes. He had managed to put Morrowindl's ordeal behind him better than she.

'Fine,' she answered, her usual reply. 'I want you to call together the members of the High Council, Triss. All of them, within the hour.'

'Yes, my lady,' he acknowledged, and turned away, disappearing across the bluff.

Wren gave a short wave to Tiger Ty, then started after Triss, angling toward the Gardens of Life and the Elessedil palace. Lights were coming on in the treelanes and streets of the city as the shadows deepened, and the air was filled with the tantalizing aroma of cooking. She reached inside her tunic and brought Faun out to sit on her shoulder as she walked. She breathed the forest air, reaching out beyond the food smells for the tree and grass scents that lay beyond. A breeze wafted up from the river, cool and soothing in the dying heat of the day.

Home Guard fanned out around her. They would stay with her now everywhere she went, disappearing completely with the darkness, invisible protectors against any threat. She smiled. They worried so for her safety, and yet she was better able than they to protect against danger, better trained and better equipped. They thought themselves necessary, and she did not do anything to discourage that belief. But she always knew where they were, could always sense them out there watching over her, even in the deepest night. She had been trained to be aware of such things since she was a child. Her teacher had been the best.

Garth. The memories rushed through her, and she forced them away. Garth was gone.

She reached the entrance to the Gardens of Life. The Black Watch stood at attention as she approached, protectors of the Ellcrys, the tree of the Forbidding. Their eyes followed her as she passed, though she did not acknowledge them. She went into the Gardens, into their seclusion, listening to the chirps and clicks of insects come awake in the growing darkness, smelling the flowers and grasses more strongly here, the rich scent of black earth. She climbed the hill to where the Ellcrys stood and stopped in front of her. She did this every night, a ritual of sorts. At times she would do nothing but stand there, looking and thinking. At times she would reach out and touch the tree, as if to let it know that she was there. Coming to the Ellcrys seemed to renew her own strength, to give her a fresh determination to carry through with her life. The kinship she felt with the tree, with the woman it had been, with the strength of commitment embodied in the tale of how it had come into being, was sustaining. *From flesh and blood to leaves and limbs, from woman to tree, from mortal life to life everlasting.*

On her shoulder Faun rubbed against her neck as if to reassure her that everything was all right.

A cure for the Races, she mused, changing subjects if not moods, thinking again of the army that approached, of the Shadowen threat she must find a way to end. It would take more than the Elves to accomplish this, she knew. Allanon had told the Ohmsfords as much when he had sent them to fulfill their separate charges – Par to find the Sword of Shannara, Walker Boh to find the Druids and Paranor, and Wren to find the Elves. Had Par and Walker succeeded as she had? Were all the charges now fulfilled? She knew that she had to find out. Somehow she had to make contact with the others who had gathered at the Hadeshorn. On the one hand she must discover what had become of them and on the other apprise them of what had happened to her. They must be told the truth of the Shadowen, that the Shadowen were Elves who had recovered the old magic of faerie and become subverted by it in the same way as the Warlock Lord and his Skull Bearers nearly five hundred years earlier. How they had recovered this magic and how it sustained them remained a mystery. But the knowledge she held must be passed on to the others. She felt it instinctively. Until that was done, any cure for the Shadowen sickness would remain out of reach.

What to do? Already some among the Elves had gone out from Arborlon into the far reaches of the Westland to establish new homes. Farmers had begun to settle in the Sarandanon, the fertile valley that had served as the breadbasket of the Elven nation for centuries. Trappers and hunters had begun ranging north to the Breakline and south to the Rock Spur. Craftsmen were anxious to open new markets for their wares. Everywhere, there was a push to reclaim old homesteads and towns. Most important of all, Healers and their acolytes had gone forth to seek out those places in which the Westland's sickness was worst in an attempt to stem its spread – carrying on an Elven tradition that had lasted since the beginning of time. For the Elves had always been healers, a people who believed that they were one with the earth into which they were born, the purveyors of the philosophy that something must be given back to the world that sustained them. As with the Gnome Healers at Storlock, who cared for the earth's people, the Elven Healers were committed in turn to the people's earth.

But they and the farmers, trappers, hunters, traders, and others were at risk in the Westland unless the Elven army protected them against the threat mounting from without. If the Queen of the Elves could not find a way to keep the Federation at bay long enough to put an end to the Shadowen . . .

She left the thought hanging, turning away from the Ellcrys in disgust. So much was needed, and try as she might she could not provide it alone.

The sky was streaked scarlet above the trees west, a vivid smear against the mountainous horizon that had the look of blood. Or at least that was the image that flashed in Wren Elessedil's mind.

Your memories never leave you, she thought – even those you wish would, even those you wish had never been.

She walked down out of the Gardens, eyes on the ground in front of her. She wondered about Stresa. It had been days since she had seen the Splinterscat. Unlike Faun, Stresa was more comfortable in the wild and preferred the woods to the city. He had made his home somewhere close to Arborlon and would appear unexpectedly from time to time, but consistently refused to think about living with her in the Elessedil family home. Stresa was content with his new country, happy in his solitary life, and he had promised more than once that he would be there if she ever needed him. The trouble was that she needed him more than she cared to admit. But Stresa had gone through a lot for her already and was happy now; she did not have the right to place fresh demands on him just to assuage her own insecurity.

Still, she missed him greatly. Stresa, that strange and unpredictable creature from the world that had cost the Elves so much, would always be her friend.

It was dark now, the sun disappeared entirely beneath the horizon west, the stars a scattering of pinprick lights, the moon a fading crescent east above the treetops, the night's sounds gentle and soothing and filled with the promise of sleep. Would that it were so for her, she thought. Sleep would come hard this night, harder than most, for she must meet with the High Council and determine the fate of the Elves. And of herself, perhaps, as well.

She walked from the Gardens, passing the Black Watch once more, listening to the barely discernible sounds of the Home Guard shadowing her. Sometimes she found herself wishing she were a Rover girl again and nothing more, her life made simple anew, all of the constraints of her stewardship lifted, her freedom restored. She would give up being queen. She would give up the Elfstones, those three blue talismans that nestled within the leather bag hung about her neck, the symbol of the magic that had been bequeathed to her by her mother, of the power she had been given to wield. She would shed her life as if it were a season's skin grown old, and she would become . . .

What? What would she become, she wondered?

In truth, she no longer knew – maybe because it no longer mattered.

When she walked into the chambers of the High Council barely a quarter of an hour later, those she had summoned were waiting, seated about the council table at which the queen presided. She entered with Tiger Ty trailing (he had remained outside until now, uncertain of his welcome in her absence) and walked directly to her seat at the head of the table. Everyone rose in deference, but she perfunctorily waved them back into their seats.

The room was cavernous. High walls of stone and wood supported a star-shaped ceiling formed of massive oak beams. The High Council was dominated at the far end by a dais which supported the throne of the Elven Kings and Queens and which was flanked by the standards of the ruling Elven houses and at its center by the ancient twenty-one-chair round table. Benches forming gallery seats for public viewing when the full Council was in session ran the length of either wall.

There were six members present this night besides herself, the full complement of the High Council's inner circle. Triss was there, as Captain of the Home Guard; Eton Shart as First Minister; Barsimmon Oridio as General of the Elven Armies; Perek Arundel as Minister of Trade; Jalen Ruhl as Minister of Home Defense; and Fruaren Laurel as Minister of Healing. Only Laurel was new, appointed on the Council's recommendation when Wren told them she wanted a minister responsible for overseeing efforts to heal the Elven Westland. Laurel was cooperative and hardworking, a woman in her middle years with a steady, likeable disposition; but like Wren she was unproven. She held a secondary position in the eyes of the remainder of the Council. Wren liked her but wasn't sure she could be counted on in a fight.

She would find out tonight.

She stood in front of her chair and faced the High Council. 'I asked Wing Rider Tiger Ty to sit in on this session of the Council since the subject matter directly concerns his people.' She made it a statement of fact and did not ask approval. She beckoned the gnarled Wing Rider forward from where he stood by the door. 'Sit there, please,' she said, indicating a vacant seat by Fruaren Laurel.

Tiger Ty sat. The chamber went very still as those assembled waited for Wren to speak. The doors leading in were closed, sealed by the Home Guard on Wren's orders until such time as she permitted them to be opened again. Torches burned in brackets affixed to the stone of the walls and in free-standing stanchions at the front and back of the room. Smoke rose toward the ceiling and dispersed through air loops high overhead. The smoke left a faint coppery taste to the chamber air.

Wren straightened. She had not bothered to change her clothes, deciding she would not make the concession to the dictates of formality. They would have to accept her as she was. She had left Faun in her chambers. She would have wished for Cogline or Walker Boh or any of those who had stood with her once and were now dead or scattered, but wishing for help from any quarter was pointless. If she was to succeed this night in what she intended to do, she would have to do it on her own.

'Ministers, Council Members, my friends,' she began, looking from face to face, her voice measured and calm. 'We have all come a very long way from where we were only weeks ago. We have seen a great many changes take place in the life of the Elven people. None of us could have foreseen what would happen; maybe some of us wish things had turned out differently. But here we are, and there is no going back. Morrowindl is behind us forever, and the Four Lands are before us. When we agreed to come back, we knew what would be waiting for us – a struggle with the Federation, with the Shadowen, with Elven magic hideously subverted, with our past brought forward to become our future. We knew what would be waiting, and now we must face it.'

She paused, her gaze steady. 'Yesterday the Wing Riders spotted a Federation army coming up from the deep Southland. Today, with Tiger Ty, I flew south to have a look for myself. We found the army within the Tirfing, a day's march above the Myrian. The army is ten times ours and travels with siege and war machines and supplies to sustain it well into another month. It comes north and west. It comes in search of us. If I were to guess, I would say it would reach us in another ten days.'

She stopped, waiting for a response. Her eyes traveled from face to face.

'Ten times ours?' Barsimmon Oridio repeated doubtfully. 'How accurate is your estimation, my lady?'

Wren had been anticipating this. She gave him a count, column by column, company by company, machines and wagons, foot soldiers and horsemen, leaving nothing out. When she was finished, the general of her armies was pale.

'An army of that size will wipe us out,' said Eton Shart quietly. As always, he was composed, his hands folded on the table before him, his expression unreadable.

'If we engage it,' Jalen Ruhl amended. The minister of defense was slight and stoop-shouldered, his voice a deep rumble in his narrow chest. 'The Westland is a big place.'

'Are you suggesting we hide?' Barsimmon Oridio demanded incredulously.

'Hiding won't work,' Eton Shart interjected shortly. 'We can't leave the city or we give up the Ellcrys. If the Ellcrys is destroyed, the Forbidding comes down. Better we all perish than that happen.'

There was a long pause as the ministers glanced at each other doubtfully.

'A concession of some sort, perhaps?' Perek Arundel suggested, ever the compromiser. He was handsome in a soft way, rather vain, but shrewd and quick-thinking. He looked about. 'There must be a way to make peace with the Coalition Council.'

Again Eton Shart shook his head. 'It was tried before. The Coalition Council is a puppet of the Shadowen. Any compromise will involve occupation of the Westland and agreement to serve the Federation. I don't think we came all the way back from Morrowindl to embrace a lifetime of that.'

He looked at Wren. 'What are your thoughts, my lady? I am certain you have assessed the situation on your own.'

Again she was ready. 'It seems our choices are these. Either we fortify Arborlon and await the Federation army here or we take our army out to meet them.'

'Go out to meet them?' Barsimmon Oridio was aghast. His heavy frame shifted combatively, and his aged face furrowed. 'You have said yourself they have ten times our strength. What point would there be in forcing a battle?'

'It would give us the advantage of not letting them dictate time and place and circumstance,' she replied. She was still standing, keeping her vantage point so that she could continue to look down at them and they up at her. 'And I said nothing about forcing a battle.'

Again there was silence. Barsimmon Oridio flushed. 'But you said that – '

'She said we could go out and meet them,' Eton Shart interrupted. He was sitting forward now, interested. 'She did not say anything about fighting them.' His gaze stayed on Wren. 'But what would we do once we were out there, my lady?'

'Harass them. Draw them off. Hit and run. Whatever it takes to delay them. Fight them if we get a chance to hurt them badly, but avoid a direct confrontation where we would lose.'

'Delay them,' the first minister repeated thoughtfully. 'But sooner or later they will catch up to us – or reach Arborlon. Then what?'

'We would be better off spending the time setting traps, fortifying the city, and gathering in supplies,' Perek Arundel offered. 'We withstood the demons when the Ellcrys failed two hundred years ago. We can withstand the Federation as well.'

Barsimmon Oridio grunted and shook his head. 'Study your history, Perek. The gates to the city were taken and we were overrun. If the young girl Chosen hadn't transformed into the Ellcrys anew, it would have been over for us.' He swung his heavy head away. 'Besides, we had allies in that fight – not many, but a few, some Dwarves and the Legion Free Corps.'

'Perhaps we shall have allies again,' Wren declared suddenly, bringing all eyes back to her. 'There are free-born in the mountains north of Callahorn, a sizable number, the Dwarf Resistance in the Eastland, and the Troll nations north. Some of them might be persuaded to help us.'

'Not likely,' the general of her armies said gruffly, incisively, declaring the matter at an end. 'Why should they?'

Wren had brought the discussion to where she wanted it; she had the Council listening to her, looking for an answer to what seemed an unsolvable dilemma.

She straightened. 'Because we'll give them a reason, Bar.' She used his nickname easily, familiarly, the way Ellenroh had. 'Because we'll give them something they didn't have before. Unity. The Races united against their enemies in a common cause. A chance to destroy the Shadowen.'

Eton Shart smiled faintly. 'Words, my lady. What do they mean?'

She faced him. He was her biggest hurdle in this business. She had to have his support. 'I'll tell you what they mean, Eton. They mean that for the first time in three centuries we have a chance to win.' She paused for emphasis. 'Do you remember what brought me in search of the Elves, First Minister? Let me tell the story once again.'

And she did, all of it, from the journey to the Hadeshorn and the Shade of Allanon to the search for Morrowindl and Arborlon. She repeated Allanon's charges to the Ohmsfords.

160

She had shown no one the Elfstones save Triss, but she brought them out now as she finished her tale, dumped them in her hand, and held them out to be seen.

'This is my legacy,' she said, shifting the hand with the Elfstones from face to face. 'I did not want it, did not ask for it, and more than once have wished it gone. But I promised my grandmother I would use it on behalf of the Elves and I will. Magic to combat magic. The Shadowen must deal with me and with the others the shade of Allanon has called upon – my kindred in some instances, but whoever is destined to wield the Sword of Shannara and the Druid power. I think all the talismans have been brought back, not just the Elfstones – all the magics that the Shadowen fear. If we can combine their power and unite the men and women of the free-born and the Resistance and perhaps even the Trolls of the Northland, we have the chance we need to win this fight.'

Eton Shart shook his head. 'There are a great many conditions attached to all of this, my lady.'

'Life is filled with conditions, First Minister,' she replied. 'Nothing is guaranteed. Nothing is assured. Especially for us. But remember this. The Shadowen come from us, and their magic is ours. We created them. We gave them life through our misguided efforts to recapture something that was best left in the past. Like it or not, they are our responsibility. Ellenroh knew this when she decided we must come back into the Four Lands. We are here, First Minister, to set things right. We are here to put an end to what we started.'

'And you will lead us in this, of course?'

He put just enough emphasis on the question to convey his own doubts that she possessed the strength and ability to do so. Wren fought down her anger.

'I am Queen,' she pointed out quietly.

Eton Shart nodded. 'But you are very young, my lady. And you have not ruled long. You must expect some hesitation from those of us who have helped govern longer.'

'What I expect is your support, First Minister.'

'Unconditional support for anyone would be foolish.'

'A reluctance to acknowledge that there may be wisdom in youth would be foolish as well. Get to the point.'

Eton Shart's bland face tightened. There was an uncomfortable shifting about the table. No one was looking at him. He was as alone in this as Wren.

'I am not questioning you . . .' he began.

'Yes, you are, First Minister,' she snapped.

'You must remember that I was not there when you were named Queen, my lady, and I – '

'Stop right there!' She was furious now, and she did not bother to hide it. 'You are right, Eton Shart. You were not there. You were not there to see Ellenroh Elessedil die. Or Gavilan. Or the Owl. Or Eowen Cerise. You were not there to see Garth give his life for ours in our fight against the Wisteron. You did not have to help him die, First Minister, as I did, because to let him live would have condemned him to become one of the Shadowen!'

She steadied herself with an effort. 'I gave up everything to save the Elves – my past, my freedom, my friends, everything. I do not begrudge that. I did it because my grandmother asked it of me, and I loved her. I did it because the Elves are my people, and while I have been gone from them a long time I am still one of them. One of you, First Minister. I am finished explaining myself. I have nothing to answer for to you or anyone. Either I am Queen or I am not. Ellenroh believed me so. That was enough for me; it ought to be enough for you. This debate ends here.'

She let her gaze rest heavily on Eton Shart. 'We must be friends and allies, First Minister, if we are to have any chance against the Federation and the Shadowen. There must be trust between us, not doubt. It will not always be easy, but we must work to understand each other. We must support and encourage, not belittle and deride. There is no room in our lives for anything less. Though we might wish it otherwise, we must accept what fate has decreed for us.'

She took a deep breath, looking away to the others. 'As Ellenroh once did, I ask for your support. I think we must go out to meet the Federation army and deal with it as we determine best. I think we shall discover that there are others who will help us. Hiding will gain us nothing. Isolating ourselves is exactly what the Federation hopes for. We must not give them the satisfaction of finding us frightened and alone. We are the oldest people on the earth, and we must act the part. We must provide leadership for the people of the other, younger Races. We must give them hope.'

She looked at them. 'Who stands with me?'

Triss rose at once. Tiger Ty rose with him, looking decidedly awkward. Then, to her pleasant surprise, Fruaren Laurel, who had not said a word the entire time, stood up as well.

She waited. Four stood, four remained seated. Of the four who stood, only three were members of the High Council. Tiger Ty was only an emissary of his people. If nothing changed, Wren lacked the support she needed.

She turned her gaze on Eton Shart, then held out her hand to him, a gesture at once conciliatory and challenging. He stared at her in surprise, eyes questioning. He hesitated momentarily, undecided, then reached out to accept her hand and rose. 'My lady,' he acknowledged, and bowed. 'As you say, we must stand together.'

Barsimmon Oridio rose, too. 'Better a gamecock than a plucked chicken,' he grumbled. He shook his head, then looked at Wren with something akin to admiration in his aging eyes. 'Your grandmother would have advised us in the same way, my lady.'

Jalen Ruhl and Perek Arundel stood up reluctantly, casting helpless glances at each other as they did so. They were not persuaded, but they did not care to stand alone against her. Wren gave them a gracious nod. She would take what she could get.

'Thank you,' she said quietly. She squeezed Eton Shart's hand and released it. 'Thank you all. Let us remember in the days that come what we have committed to this night. Let us remember to let our belief and trust in each other sustain us.'

She looked about the table, at each face, at the way their eyes were fixed on her. For that moment, at least, she had bound them to her, and she was indeed their queen.

13

Walker Boh deliberated for two days before he again tried to escape the Shadowen siege of Paranor.

Perhaps he wouldn't have gone even then, but he found himself slipping into a dangerous state of mind. The more he thought about various ways of breaking free, the more it seemed he needed to consider further. Each plan had its flaws, and each flaw became magnified as it was held up this way and that for examination. Nothing he conceived seemed exactly right, and the harder he worked at discovering a foolproof method of gaining his escape, the more he began to doubt himself. Finally it became apparent that if he allowed himself to go on, he would lose all confidence and in the end be unable to act at all.

It was all part of a game that the Shadowen were playing with him, he was afraid.

His first encounter with the Four Horsemen had left him physically battered, but those injuries were not the ones that troubled him. It was the psychological damage that refused to mend, that lingered within like a fever. Walker Boh had always been in control of his life, able to manipulate events around him and to keep intrusions at bay. He had accomplished this mostly by isolating himself within the familiar confines of Darklin Reach, where the dangers to be faced and problems to be solved were familiar and within the purview of his enormous capabilities. He had command of magic, intelligence coupled with extraordinary insight, and other assorted abilities that ranged from the intuitive to the acquired – all of which were far superior to those of anyone against whom he chose to direct them.

But that was changed. He had crossed out of Darklin Reach and come into the outside world. This was his home now, the cottage at Hearthstone reduced to ashes, the life he had known gone into another time. He had traveled a road that had altered his existence as surely as dying. He had taken up Allanon's charge and followed it through to its conclusion. He had recovered the Black Elfstone and brought back Paranor. He had become the first of the new Druids. He was someone entirely different than the person he had been only weeks ago. That change had given him new insight, strength, knowledge, and power. But it had also exposed him to new responsibilities, expectations, challenges, and enemies. It remained to be decided if the former would be sufficient to overcome the latter. For the moment at least, the matter was unresolved. Walker Boh might fall and be lost forever – or he might find a way to climb back to safety. He was a man hanging from a precipice.

The Shadowen knew this. They had come for him as soon as they had discovered that Paranor was returned. Walker was still a child in his role as Druid, and now was the time when he would be most vulnerable. Besiege him, frustrate him, distract his development, kill him if possible, but cripple him at all costs – that was the plan.

And the plan was working. Walker had come back into Paranor, after his first aborted attempt at escape, aware of several very unpleasant truths. First, he did not possess sufficient power to break free in a head-to-head confrontation. The Four Horsemen were his equal and more, their magic a match for his own. Second, he could not slip past them undetected. Third, and worst of all, their experience was superior to his own – and they did not fear him. They had

166

come looking for him. They had done so openly, without subterfuge. They had challenged him, daring him to come out and fight them. They circled Paranor in open disdain of what he might do. He was a prisoner in his own castle, reduced to trying to come up with a plan that would let him be free, and the Four Horsemen were betting he couldn't do it. It was possible, he was forced to admit, that they were right.

'You are working too hard at this,' Cogline advised him finally, finding him back on the walls, staring down at the wraiths circling below. He looked gaunt and pale, ragged and worn. 'Look at you, Walker. You barely sleep. You take no notice of your appearance – you have not bathed since your return. You do not eat.'

A frail hand rubbed at the whiskers of the old man's chin. 'Think, Walker. This is what they want. They are afraid of you! If they weren't, they would simply force the gates and finish this business. But that won't be necessary if you can be made to doubt yourself, to panic, to forgo the caution and resolve that got you this far. If that happens, they will have won. Sooner or later, they think, you will do something foolish, and then they will have you.'

It was the most that Cogline had said to him since his return. Walker stared at him, at the ancient, weather-beaten face, at the stick-thin body, at the arms and legs jutting from his robes like poles. Cogline had welcomed him back with reassurances, but mostly he had seemed removed and distant – just as he had for those few days before Walker had first tried to go out. Something was happening with Cogline, some secret conflict, but Walker had been too preoccupied with his own problems then, as he was now, to take time to decipher what it was.

Nevertheless, he let the old man lead him down from the parapets to the inner shell of the castle and a hot meal. He ate without enthusiasm, drank a little ale, and decided that a bath was a good idea after all. He sat in the steaming water, letting it cleanse him inside and out, feeling the heat soothe and relax his body and mind. Rumor kept him company, curled up against the side of the tub as if to share its warmth. While Walker dried himself and dressed again, he pondered the enormous calm of the moor cat, the facade that all cats assumed as they regarded the world about them, considering it in their own impenetrable way. A little of that calm would be useful, he thought.

Then his thoughts shifted abruptly.

What was wrong with Cogline?

He left his own troubles behind with the bathwater and went out to find the old man. He came on him in the library, reading once more the Druid Histories. Cogline looked up as he entered, startled by his appearance or by something it suggested – Walker could not tell which.

Walker sat beside him on a carved, cushioned bench. 'Old man, what is it that bothers you?' he asked quietly. He reached out to place a reassuring hand on the other's thin shoulder. 'I see the worry in your eyes. Tell me.'

Cogline shrugged in an exaggerated manner. 'I worry for you, Walker. I know how strange everything seems to you since . . . well, since all this began. It cannot be easy. I keep thinking there must be something I can do to help.'

Walker looked away. *Since the Black Elfstone*, he thought. *Since Allanon made himself a part of me, come in through the magic left to keep Paranor safe until the Druids' return. Strange is hardly the word for it.*

'You need not worry for me,' he replied, his smile ironic. *At least not about that.* The warring within of the past and the present had faded as the two assimilated, and the lives and knowledge of the Druids had become his own. He thought of the way the magic had churned through him, burning away defenses until there had been nothing left for him to do but to accept it as his own.

'Walker.' Cogline was staring at him, focused now. 'I do not think Allanon would have put you through this if he did not believe that it would leave you with sufficient power to stand against the Shadowen.'

'You have more faith than I.'

Cogline nodded solemnly. 'I always have, Walker. Didn't you know that? But my faith will be yours as well one day. It simply takes time. I have been given that time and used it to learn. I have been alive a long time now, Walker. A long time. Faith is a part of what gives me the strength to go on.'

Walker took his hand away. 'I had faith in myself. I had it when I knew who and what I was. But that has changed, old man. I am someone and something else entirely, and I am being asked to place my faith in a stranger. It is hard for me to do that.'

'Yes,' Cogline agreed. 'But it will happen – if you give it time.'

'If I have the time to give,' Walker Boh finished.

He went out again. Rumor trailed, a black shadow slipping from lamplight to lamplight in the gloom, head swaying rhythmically, tail switching. Walker was aware of him without thinking of him, his thoughts turned again to the Shadowen without.

There must be a way . . .

Strength alone was not enough. The power of the Druid magic was impressive, but it had never been enough by itself even for those Druids come and gone. Knowledge was necessary as well. Cleverness. Resolve. Unpredictability. This last most of all, perhaps – an intangible that was the special province of survivors. Did he have it? he wondered suddenly. What did he have besides what the Druid magic had given him that he could call upon? He had made much out of the fact that nothing done to him by the Druids would change who he was. But was that so? If so, then what part of himself could he call upon now to enable him to believe in himself once again?

And wasn't that the key to everything? That he believe in himself enough that he should not despair?

He went back up to the battlements, Rumor trailing. The night was clear and bright with stars, and the air smelled clean and fresh. He breathed it deeply as he walked atop the walls, not looking down at what waited there, letting his thoughts slip free as he went, unburdened. He found himself thinking about Quickening, the daughter of the King of the Silver River, the elemental who had given everything to restore life to a land of stone, to give the earth a chance to heal. He pictured her face and listened in his memory to her voice. He felt the slight weight of her that last time as he carried her to the edge of Eldwist, the sense of sureness that had emanated from her, the sense of power. Dying, she was fulfilling her promise. It was what she had wanted. But she had bequeathed some part of her life to him, a sense of purpose and need, a resolve that he would do in life what she could only do in death.

He stopped, staring out at the night. How far he had traveled, he thought in genuine amazement. How long a journey it had been. All to reach this point, to arrive at this place and time.

He paused in his meandering, faced inward to the castle spires, to the walls and towers that loomed over him, rising darkly into the night. Was this where his life was supposed to end? he wondered suddenly. Was this where the journey finally stopped?

It had been a pointless struggle if that was so.

He turned and looked down over the wall. One of the Horsemen was passing directly below, a faint luminescence against the dark. Death, he thought, but it was hard to tell. It made no difference in any case. Names notwithstanding, identities assumed aside, they were all Death in one form or another. Shadowen killers lacking use and purpose beyond their ability to destroy. Why had they allowed themselves to become so? What choice had made them thus?

He watched that rider fade and waited for the next. All night they would patrol and at dawn assemble once more before the gates to issue their challenge anew . . .

He caught himself. All together, before the gates.

A glimmer of hope flickered in his mind. What if he were to answer that challenge?

170

His face grim-set, he wheeled from the wall and went down the battlements in search of Cogline.

Dawn arrived with a silvering of the eastern skies that hinted of mist and heat. The air was still and sultry even this early, a remnant of yesterday's swelter, a promise that this summer did not intend to give way easily to autumn. Birds sounded their calls in snappish, weary tones, as if unwilling to herald the morning's start.

The Four Horsemen were assembled before the gates, lined up in the grayness on their nightmare mounts. The serpents clawed distractedly at the earth as their riders sat mutely before Paranor's high walls, specters without voice, lives without balance. As the light crested the tips of the Dragon's Teeth, War urged his monstrous carrier forward, lifted his armored hand, and struck the gate with a hollow thud. The sound lingered in the silence that followed, an echo that disappeared into the trees and the gloom. The gate shuddered and went still.

War started to turn away.

Walker Boh was waiting. He was already outside the walls, come through a hidden door in a tower barely fifty feet away. He was cloaked by his magic in a spell of invisibility, shrouded in the touch and look and smell of ancient stone so that he appeared just another part of Paranor. They had not been looking for him. Even if they had, he believed he would not have been discovered.

He brought up his good arm, the magic already summoned, gathered within until it was white-hot, and he sent it hurtling toward the Shadowen.

The magic exploded into War and cut the unsuspecting wraith entirely in half. The serpent mount bolted, War's legs and lower torso still clinging to it, and disappeared.

Walker struck again. The magic hammered into the remaining three, catching them bunched tightly together and entirely unprepared. Fire exploded everywhere, engulfing them. The serpents reared and clawed in fury, wheeling about in an effort to escape. Walker sent the fire in front of their eyes so that they could not see and into their nostrils so that they could not smell, so that it clogged their senses and drove them mad. The Shadowen slammed up against one another, blinded and confused.

I've got them! Walker thought in elation.

His strength was draining from him fast, but he did not relent. He dropped the spell of invisibility, saving as much of himself as he could, and pressed the attack further, willing the magic into fire, willing the fire to consume. One of the Horsemen broke free, steaming and spitting like embers kicked by a boot. It was Pestilence, the strange body come apart into a buzzing swarm of darkness, all of its shape and definition lost. Famine had gone down, horse and rider writhing on the earth in a desperate effort to extinguish the flames that were consuming them. Death spun out of control, wheeling in a frenzy.

Then the impossible happened. Through smoke and flame, come back from where it had fled stricken and ruined, War reappeared atop its serpent mount.

But War had become whole again.

Walker stared in disbelief. He had severed the Horseman at the midpoint of its body, seen the top half fall away, and now War was back together, looking as if nothing had been done to it at all.

It charged Walker, closing the distance between them, armored body leaning forward eagerly, metal gleaming in the faint dawn light. Walker could hear the thunder of the clawed feet, the rasp of breathing, the shriek of armor, and the whistle of air giving way before its coming.

It wasn't possible!

Instinctively Walker shifted the magic to meet the attack, gathering it in one final burst. It caught the Horseman and its mount in a whirlwind of fire and spun them away, sweeping them off the pathway circling the castle and down into the trees where they disappeared with a crash.

But there was no time to follow up the attack. The remaining Horsemen had recovered themselves. Death pivoted toward him, gray-cloaked and hooded, gleaming scythe lowered. Pestilence followed, hissing like a sackful of snakes, its body taking shape as it came. Walker cut Death's serpent's legs from beneath it and sent both tumbling in a heap. By then Pestilence was almost on top of him. He jumped aside, cat quick. But the Horseman's outstretched fingers grazed him as it passed.

Instantly a wave of nausea swept through Walker. He dropped to his knees, weakened and dazed. *Just a touch had been all!* He swung about to track Pestilence and sent a new lance of fire into the Shadowen's dark back. Pestilence broke apart in a swarm of black flies.

Everything seemed to slow down for Walker Boh. He watched Famine approach in a heavy, sluggish, lurching rush. He tried to respond, but his strength seemed to have deserted him. He was aware of the day beginning, of new light brightening the eastern horizon, diffusing in thick, syrupy streamers across the trailing robes of departing night. He could feel the air, could taste and smell it, the scents of fresh leaves and grasses mingling with dust and heat. Paranor was a monstrous stone shadow at his elbow, close enough to touch and yet impossibly far.

He should not have dropped his cloak of invisibility. He had lost any advantage he had possessed.

He sent fire lancing into Famine and turned its attack aside, the Horseman's skeletal body hunching and breaking apart from the blow.

Dead, but not really, Walker thought, feeling himself turning feverish and hot.

The horsemen swarmed back from all directions, serpents rising up and converging on him. Why wouldn't they die? How could they keep coming? The questions rolled thickly off his tongue, and he was aware suddenly that he was speaking them aloud, that a sort of delirium was settling in. He was impossibly weak as he stumbled back toward the wall, mustering his strength to face the renewed rush. His plan was falling apart. He had misjudged something. What was it?

He lifted his arm and sent the fire sweeping in all directions, scattering it into his attackers in a desperate effort to keep them at bay. But his strength was depleted now, expended in his initial attack, siphoned away by Pestilence. The magic barely slowed the Shadowen, who broke through its screen and came on. War threw a jagged-edged mace at him, and he watched it hurtle toward him, unable to act. At the last moment he summoned magic enough to deflect it, but still the iron struck him a glancing blow, spinning him backward into Paranor's stone with such force that the breath was knocked from him.

The blow saved his life.

As he clawed at the stone of Paranor's wall to keep himself from falling, he found the seam of the hidden door. For an instant his head cleared, and he remembered that he had left himself a way to escape if things went wrong. He had forgotten it in the rage of battle, in the grip of the fever and delirium. He still had a chance. The Four Horsemen were bearing down on him, closing impossibly fast. The fingers of his hand raced along the hidden door's seam, numb and bloodied. If only he had two hands, two arms! If only he was whole! The thought was there and gone in an instant, the despair that summoned it banished by his fury.

There was a shriek of metal and claws.

His fingers closed on the release.

The door swung inward, carrying him with it, a shapeless bundle of robes. As it did, he threw back into the space it left shards of fire as sharp as razors. He heard them tear into his pursuers, thought that perhaps he heard the Shadowen scream somewhere inside his mind.

174

Then he was in musty, cool darkness, the sound and fury shut away with the closing of the door, the battle over.

Cogline found him in the passageway beneath the castle's ramparts, curled in a ball, so exhausted he could not bring himself to move. With considerable effort, the old man brought Walker to his bed and laid him in it. He undressed him, sponged him with cool, clean water, gave him medicines, and wrapped him in blankets to sleep. He spoke words to Walker, but Walker could not seem to decipher them. Walker replied, but what he said was unclear.

He knew that he was alive, that he had survived to fight another day, and that was all that mattered.

Shivering, aching, bone-weary from his struggle, he let himself be settled in and left in darkness to rest. He was conscious of Rumor curling up beside him, keeping watch against whatever might threaten, ready to summon Cogline if need required it. He swallowed against the dryness in his throat, thinking that the sickness would pass, that he would be well again when he woke. Determined that he would be.

His eyes closed, but as they did so his mind locked tightly on a final, healing thought.

The battle had been lost this day. The Four Horsemen had broken him again. But he had learned something from his defeat – something that ultimately would prove their undoing.

He took a long slow breath and let it out again. Sleep swept through his body in warm, relaxing waves.

The next time he faced the Shadowen, he promised himself before drifting off, sheathing his oath in layers of iron resolve, he would put an end to them.

14

While Walker Boh was fighting to break free of the Four Horsemen at Paranor, Wren Elessedil was convincing the Elven High Council to engage the Federation army marching north to destroy them, and Morgan Leah was leading Damson and a small company of freeborn to rescue Padishar Creel at Tyrsis, Par Ohmsford was tracking his brother, Coll.

It was an arduous, painstaking effort. When Damson and he had separated, he had begun his search immediately, aware that Coll was only minutes ahead of him, thinking that if he was quick enough, he would surely catch up to him. Sunrise had broken, the darkness that might have hampered his efforts fading to scattered shadows and patches of mist that lingered in the trees. Coll was fleeing in mindless disregard of everything but the vision shown him by the Sword of Shannara. He was confused and terrified, his pain had been palpable. In such a state, how much effort would he make to conceal his flight? How far could he run before exhaustion overtook him?

The answer was not the one Par had anticipated. Although he was able to follow his brother's tracks easily enough, the trail clear amid a wreckage of brush and grasses, he found himself unable to gain ground. Despite everything – or perhaps because of it – Coll seemed to have discovered within himself unexpected strength. He was running from Par, not just hastening away, and he was not pausing to rest. Nor was he running in a straight line. He was charging all over the place, starting out in one direction and then within moments reversing himself, not for any discernible reason, but seemingly out of whim. It was as if he had gone mad, as if demons pursued him, shut inside his head so that he could not determine from where they came.

And, indeed, Par thought as he followed after, it must seem so to Coll.

By nightfall, he was exhausted. His face and arms were streaked with dust and sweat, his hair was matted in clumps, and his clothes were filthy. Having discarded everything else to lighten his load and give him more speed, he was carrying only the Sword of Shannara, a blanket, and a water skin. Nevertheless, he could still barely walk. He wondered how Coll had managed to stay ahead of him. His fear should have exhausted him hours ago. The Mirrorshroud and its Shadowen magic must be driving his brother like a whip would an animal. The thought made Par despair. If Coll did not slow, if he did not regain even some small measure of his judgment, the exertion would kill him. Or if the exertion didn't, then some mistake brought on by careless disregard for personal safety would. There were dangers in this country that could kill a man even when he was employing a healthy measure of caution and common sense. At the moment, it seemed, Coll Ohmsford was possessed of neither.

When he stopped finally, Par found himself just west of where the Mermidon divided, one tributary running east toward the Rabb, the other turning south toward Varfleet and the Runne. Follow the second branch far enough and you would reach the Rainbow Lake. You would also reach Southwatch. That was the direction that Coll had been traveling when it had grown too dark to follow his trail farther. The more Par considered the matter, the more it seemed that his brother had been following that path all along – albeit in a meandering way. Back to Southwatch and the Shadowen. It made sense, if the magic of the cloak was subverting Coll.

Par wrapped up in his blanket and propped himself against the rough surface of an old shagbark hickory to think things through. The Sword of Shannara lay on the ground next to him, and his fingers traced the outline of the carved hilt with its raised hand and burning torch. If the Shadowen magic was controlling his brother, Coll might not have any idea at all what he was doing. He might have come looking for Par without knowing why; he might be fleeing now in the same condition. Except that the Sword had shown Coll the same vision it had shown Par, so that meant Coll had seen the truth about himself. Par had felt a bonding in those moments; Coll had been joined to him long enough for both to see. Had that changed things in any way? Having seen the truth about himself, was he trying to shake free of the Shadowen magic?

Par closed his eyes tightly against the strain of his weariness. He needed to sleep but was unwilling to do so until he had figured out what was happening. Damson had warned him that the pursuit was probably some sort of trap. Coll did not just happen on them. He had been sent by the Shadowen. Why? To hurt him or to kill him? Par wasn't sure. How had Coll managed to find him? How long had he been searching? The questions buzzed through his mind like angry hornets, intrusive and demanding, stingers poised. *Think!* Perhaps the magic of the cloak had let Coll find him – had driven Coll to find him. The magic had infected his brother, had turned him into the Shadowen thing, all the while Coll believing it was helping him escape his captors, fooled into donning it so that it could begin its work, tricked . . .

Par took a deep breath. He could barely breathe at all, picturing Coll as one of them, one of the things in the Pit, the things that were living even when they were already dead.

He drank some water because water was all he had. How long had it been since he had eaten? he wondered. Tomorrow he would have to forage or hunt. He needed to regain his strength. No food and little rest would eventually catch up to him. He could not afford to be foolish if he was to be of any use to his brother.

He forced his thoughts back to Coll, wrapping the blanket closer in the gathering night. It was cool in the trees by the river, the summer heat banished to other realms. If Coll had not come to kill him, why had he come? Not for any good reason surely. Coll was not Coll now.

Par blinked. To steal the Sword of Shannara perhaps?

The idea was intriguing, but it made no sense. Why would Rimmer Dall hand the Sword over to Par only to dispatch Coll later to steal it back? Unless Coll was someone else's tool. But that made even less sense. There was only one enemy here, despite all of the First Seeker's protestations. Rimmer Dall had gone to a great deal of trouble to make Par think he had killed his brother. The Shadowen had sent Coll for a reason, but it was not to steal back the Sword of Shannara.

Par let himself consider for a moment how odd it was that the Sword had finally revealed itself to him. He had tried everything to trigger the magic, and until then nothing had worked. He had always believed that it really was the talisman, that it was not a fake, even though Rimmer Dall had given it to him willingly. He had sensed its power, even when it did not respond to him. But the doubts had persisted and more than once he had despaired. Now suddenly, unexpectedly, the magic had been brought to life, all because of his struggle with Coll.

And Par didn't have a clue as to why.

He slid down the tree trunk until he was resting on his back, staring up through the leafy boughs of the hickory at the clear, starlit sky. He just needed to get comfortable, he told himself. Just needed to ease a little of the aching of his body. He could think better if he did that. He knew he could.

He fell asleep telling himself so.

*   *   *

When he woke it was dawn, and Coll was staring down at him. His brother was crouched atop a mound of rocks not twenty feet off, twisted and hunched like a scavenger. He was wrapped in the Mirrorshroud, the folds glimmering wickedly in the faint silver light as if dew were woven through the fabric. Coll's face was haggard and drawn, and his eyes, always so calm and steady, were darting about with fear and loathing.

Par was so startled that he couldn't bring himself to move. It had never occurred to him that his brother might circle back – would even have the presence of mind to do so. Why had he come? To attack him anew, to try to kill him perhaps? He stared at Coll, into his stricken face and sunken eyes. No, Coll was there for something else. He looked as if he wished to approach, as if he wanted to speak, as if he was seeking something from Par. And maybe he is, Par thought suddenly. The Sword of Shannara had given Coll his first glimpse of truth since he had donned the Mirrorshroud. Perhaps he wanted more.

He lifted slowly and started to hold out his hand.

Instantly Coll was gone, leaping from the rock into the shadows beyond and bounding away into the trees.

'Coll!' Par screamed after him. The echo faded and died. The sound of Coll's running disappeared into silence, lost as the distance between them widened anew.

Par foraged for berries and roots, convinced as he ate a meager breakfast that if he didn't find real food by nightfall he would be in serious trouble. He ate quickly, thinking of Coll all the while. There had been such terror in his brother's eyes – and such fury. At Par, at himself, at the truth? There was no way to know. But Coll was aware of him still, was actively seeking him out, and there was still a chance to catch up with him.

What would he do, though, when he did? Par hadn't thought that far ahead. Use the Sword of Shannara again, he answered himself, almost without thinking. The Sword was

180

Coll's best hope for getting free of the Mirrorshroud. If Coll could be made to see the nature of the magic that possessed him, perhaps a way could be found to throw the cloak and its magic off. Perhaps Par could manage to tear it off him if nothing else. But the Sword was the key. Coll hadn't recognized anything until the Sword's magic engaged him, but the truth had shown in his eyes then. Par would use the talisman again, he told himself. And this time he wouldn't stop until Coll was free.

He picked up his blanket and set out again. The day was sultry and still, the heat growing quickly to a sticky swelter that left Par's clothing damp with sweat. He picked up Coll's trail and followed it to the Mermidon and across, heading north, then back again south. This time his brother continued in a direct line for several hours, traveling the east bank into the Runne Mountains. He passed Varfleet across the river, seeing trawlers and ferries maneuvering sluggishly on the broad expanse, thinking that it would be good to have a boat, thinking a second later that a boat was useless while he was tracking prints on dry land. He remembered when Coll and he had fled Varfleet weeks earlier and come south down the Mermidon, the beginning of everything. He remembered how close they had been then, despite their arguments over the direction of their lives and the purpose of Par's magic. It all seemed to have happened a very long time ago.

Toward midafternoon he came upon a small landing with a fishing dock and trading post several miles downriver of Varfleet. The post was ramshackle and cluttered, its tenants a taciturn, recalcitrant bunch with scarred, callused working hands and sun-browned faces. He was able to trade his ring for fishing line and hooks, flint, bread, cheese, and smoked fish. He carried everything just beyond sight of the landing, plopped down, and ate half of the foodstuffs without stopping for breath. When he was finished, he resumed his trek south, feeling decidedly better about himself. The line and hooks would allow him to fish, and the flint would give him a fire. He was beginning to realize that catching up to Coll could take a lot longer than he had expected.

He found himself thinking again about why Coll had come in search of him – or more accurately, why he had been sent. If it wasn't to kill him or to steal the Sword, that didn't leave much. Perhaps Coll's coming was intended to provoke some sort of response from him. Damson's warning whispered once again – the chase was probably a Shadowen trap. But how could the Shadowen know their meeting would trigger the magic of the Sword of Shannara and reveal the truth about who Coll was, that Par would be able to see him as anything but a Shadowen? Coll might have been sent as a lure to draw Par after – that certainly seemed like Rimmer Dall – but again, how could the Shadowen know that Par would discover his brother's identity?

Unless he wasn't supposed to find out . . .

Par stopped abruptly. He was passing beneath a huge old oak. It was shady there and cool. He could feel a breeze waft in off the Mermidon. He could hear the sound of the river's sluggish flow. He could smell the water and the woods.

. . . until it was too late.

He felt his throat tighten. What if he had this whole business backward? What if Coll wasn't supposed to kill him? What if he was supposed to kill Coll?

Why?

Because . . .

He struggled with the answer. It was almost there, just on the edge of his reasoning. A whisper of words, straining to be recognized, to be understood.

He could not quite reach them.

He started off again, frustrated. He was on the right track, even if he didn't have all the particulars straight yet. It was Coll out there, leading him on, fleeing without knowing why, coming back at night to make certain Par was following. It was the Sword of Shannara Par carried, and its magic that had told him the truth. It was the Shadowen who had orchestrated this whole business, who were playing with them as if they were children set at a game, made to perform for the enjoyment of others.

It has to do with the magic of the wishsong, Par thought suddenly. It has to do with that.

It would come to him, he knew. He just needed to keep thinking about it. He just needed to keep reasoning it through.

He had not found Coll by sunset of the second day, and he made camp in a rock-sheltered niche that protected his back while allowing him to see whatever approached from the front. He did not build a fire. A fire would obscure his night vision when it grew dark. He ate a little more of his provisions, wrapped himself in his blanket, and settled back against the rocks to wait.

The night deepened and the stars came out. Par watched the shadows define and take shape in the pale light. He listened to the sluggish flow of the river against the rocks and the cries of the night birds circling its waters. He breathed the cooling, damp air, and allowed himself to wonder for the first time in two days about Damson Rhee. It was strange being without her after the time they hid together in Tyrsis, the two of them fighting to stay free. He worried for her, but reassured himself by deciding that she was probably better off than he was. By now she would have reached the freeborn and be engaged in an effort to rescue Padishar. By now she was safe.

Or as safe as either of them could be until this business was finished.

Thoughts of Damson, Padishar, Morgan Leah, Wren, and Walker Boh crowded into his mind, fragments of his memories of those who had been lost along the way. It sometimes seemed to him that he was destined to lose everyone. So much effort expended and so little gained – the weight of it bore down on him.

He drew his knees up to his chest protectively, tightening

himself into a ball. The Sword of Shannara pressed against his back; he had forgotten to unstrap it. The Sword, his charge from Allanon, his chance for life, his sole hope for someday getting free of the Shadowen – a lot had been given up for it. He wondered anew what purpose the talisman was supposed to serve. Surely something wondrous, for magic like this was created for nothing less. But how was he supposed to discover that purpose – especially here, lost somewhere in the Runne, chasing after poor Coll? He should be searching for Walker Boh and for Wren, the others who had been given charges by Allanon.

But that was wrong, of course. He should be doing exactly what he was; he should be searching for his brother so that he could help him. If he lost Coll, who had stood by him through so much, who had given up everything, lost him after losing him once already, after having found him again . . .

He shook his head. He would not lose Coll. He would not allow that to happen.

The minutes slipped away, and Par Ohmsford continued to wait. Coll would come. He was certain of it. He would come as he had the night before. Perhaps he would only sit and stare at Par, but at least he would be there, nearby.

He reached into his tunic and brought out the broken half of Skree that Damson had given to him. He had wrapped it tight with a leather cord and hung it about his neck. If Damson was close, the Skree was supposed to brighten. He inspected it thoughtfully. The metal reflected dully in the pale starlight, but did not glow. Damson was far away.

He looked at the Skree a moment longer, then slipped it back into his tunic. Another bit of magic to keep him safe, he thought ruefully. The wishsong, the Sword of Shannara, and the Skree. He was well equipped with talismans. He was awash in them.

But his bitterness served no purpose, so he tried to brush it away. He took off the Sword and set it on the ground beside him. Somewhere out on the Mermidon a fish splashed. From

184

the trees behind him came the low hoot of an owl, sudden and compelling.

A heritage of magic, he thought, unable to help himself, the darkness of his mood inexorable, *and all it does is make me wonder if Rimmer Dall is right – if I am indeed a Shadowen.*

The thought lingered as he stared out into the night.

The thing that was a mix of Shadowen and Coll Ohmsford stared out from its concealment in the trees some fifty feet from where the one who tracked it sat waiting for it to appear.

But I will not, no, it thought to itself. *I will stay here, safe within the dark, where I belong, where the shadows protect me from . . .*

What? It could not remember. This other creature? The strange weapon it carried? No, something else. The cloak it wore? It fingered the material uncertainly, feeling something unpleasant stir at the tips of its fingers as it did so, aware again of the vision it had witnessed when it had struggled with the other, the one who was . . . who was . . . It could not remember. Someone it had known. Once, long ago. Confusion beset it; the confusion never left, it seemed.

The Shadowen/Coll thing shifted silently, eyes never leaving the figure wedged into the rocks.

It thinks it can see me from there, but it is wrong. It can see nothing I do not wish it to see – not while I wear the cloak, not while I have the magic. I come to it when I wish, and I go away when I choose. It cannot see me. It cannot catch me. It hunts me, but I take it where I wish. I take it south, south to, to . . .

But it wasn't sure, the confusion clouding its thoughts again, distracting it. It could think better if it took off the cloak, it sometimes seemed. But no, that would be foolish. The cloak protected it, the Mirrorshroud, given to it by – no, stolen, taken from – no, tricked away by someone . . . dangerous . . .

The thoughts came and went, fragmented and fleeting.

They spun like eddies in a river, touching down against silt and rock for just an instant before moving on.

Tears of frustration came to its eyes, and it brought one soiled hand up to brush them away. Sometimes it remembered things from before, from when it did not wear the cloak, from when it was someone else. The memories made it sad, and it seemed that something bad had been done to it to cause the memories to make it feel that way.

I saw, for a moment, in the light in my mind, in that vision, I saw something about myself, about who I was, am, could be. I want to see it again!

It fled now from the thing it had hunted once, frightened of it without knowing why. The cloak reassured, but even the cloak did not seem enough to protect it against this other. And flight from its pursuer always seemed to bring it back around to where that pursuer waited, a circle of running it could not understand. If it ran from its pursuer, why did the running bring it back again? Sometimes the cloak soothed and sheltered against the pursuer and the memories, but sometimes it felt as if the cloak were fire against its skin, burning away its identity, making it into something terrible.

Take off the cloak!

No, foolish, foolish! The cloak protects!

And so the battle raged within the tormented thing that was both Coll and Shadowen, driving it this way and that, wearing it down and building it up again, pulling and pushing both at once until there was nothing of reason and peace left within it.

Help me, it pleaded silently. *Please, help me.*

But it did not know who it was asking for help or what form that help should take. It stared down through the darkness at the one who tracked it, thinking that its hunter would sleep soon. What should it do then? Should it go down there, creeping, creeping, silent as clouds drifting in the sky, and touch it, touch . . .

The thought would not complete. The cloak seemed to fold more tightly about it, distracting it. Yes, creep down perhaps, show its hunter that it was not afraid (but it was!), that it could do as it wished in the night, in its cloak, in the safety of the magic . . .

Help me.

It chocked on the words, trying to shriek them aloud, unable to do so. It closed its eyes against the pain and forced itself to think.

Take something from it, something it needs, that it treasures. Take something that will make it . . . hurt as I do. Reason jarred loose a familiar memory. *I know this one, know from when, when we were, we were . . . brothers! This one can help, can find a way . . .*

But the Coll/Shadowen thing was not certain of this, and the thought faded away with the others, lost in the teeming fragments that jostled and fought for consideration in the confused mind. It was both drawn to and repelled by the one it watched, and the conflict would not resolve itself no matter how much effort was expended.

Tears came again, unbidden, unwanted. The soiled, scraped hands knotted and tightened. The ravaged face fought to shape itself into something recognizable. For a second Coll was back, recovered out of the web of dark magic that imprisoned him.

Need to act, to do something that will let the other know!
Need to take something away!
I must!

Par was asleep when he felt the tearing at his neck. He jerked and thrashed wildly in an effort to stop it, not knowing what it was or who was causing it. Something was choking him, closing off his throat so that he could not breathe. There was a weight atop him, climbing on him, wrapping about.

A Shadowen!

Yet the wishsong had not warned him, so it could not be

that. He summoned the magic now, desperate to save himself. He felt it build with agonizing slowness. Something was breathing on his face and neck. There was a flash of teeth, and he felt coarse hair rub against his skin. His hand reached out to brace himself so that he might shove upward against his attacker. His hand brushed the handle of the Sword of Shannara, and the metal burned him like fire.

Then the pressure on his throat abruptly released, the weight on his body lifted, and through a haze of colored light and gloom he saw a crumpled, hunched form race away into the night.

Coll! It had been Coll!

He came to his feet, bewildered and frightened, fighting for air and balance. What was going on? Had Coll been sent to kill him after all? Had he tried to choke him to death? He watched the dark form disappear into the shadows, lost in the rocks and trees almost instantly. There was no mistake. It had been Coll. He was certain of it.

But what was his brother trying to do?

He thought suddenly of the Sword, glanced hurriedly down, and found it lying untouched next to where he stood. Not the Sword, he thought. What then?

He groped at his neck, aware suddenly of new pain. His hand came away wet with blood. He felt again. He found a collar of bruised, torn flesh. He touched it gingerly, questioningly.

And then he realized that the Skree was gone.

His brother had stolen it. He must have seen Par hold it up while he was hiding out there in the dark. He must have come down after Par had fallen asleep, crept up on him, pinned him to the ground, yanked at the leather cord about his neck so that he choked, bitten it through when nothing else worked, and carried off Damson's talisman.

Why?

So that Par would follow him, of course. So that Par would have to give chase.

188

The Valeman stood staring after his brother, after the thing his brother had become, stunned. In the silence of his mind it seemed he could hear the other cry out to him.

Help me, Coll was saying.

Help me.

15

When it grew light enough to see, Par went after his brother. Sunrise was early, the day clear and bright, and the trail Coll left easy to follow once again. Par redoubled his efforts, pushing himself harder than before, determined that this time Coll would not get away. They were deep within the Runne Mountains by now, hemmed in by canyon walls as they followed the Mermidon south, and there was little room for deviation. Nevertheless, Coll continued to wander away from the riverbank as if searching for a way out. Sometimes he would get almost half a mile before the mountains blocked his path. Once he was able to climb to a low ridge and follow it south for several miles before it dead-ended at another cliff face and turned him aside. Each time Par was forced to follow so as not to lose the trail, afraid that if he simply kept to the riverbank Coll would double back. The effort of the pursuit drained him of his strength, and the muggy, windless air made him light-headed. The day passed, sunset came, and still he had not found Coll.

He fished for his dinner that night, using the hook and line from the trading center, cooked and ate his catch, and left what remained – a more than generous portion – on a flat rock several dozen feet off from where he slept. He was awake most of the night, hearing and seeing things that weren't there, dozing infrequently and fitfully. He did not see Coll once.

190

When he woke, he found the fish gone – but it might have been eaten by wild animals. He didn't think so, but there was no way to be sure.

For the next three days he continued his pursuit, working his way downriver, edging steadily closer to the Rainbow Lake and Southwatch. He began to worry that he was not going to catch up to Coll until it was too late. Somehow his brother was managing to keep just ahead of him, even with his diminished capacity to reason, even in his half-Shadowen state. Coll was not thinking clearly, not choosing the easiest or quickest paths, not bothering to hide his tracks, not doing anything but somehow managing to keep just out of reach. It was frustrating and troubling at once. It seemed inevitable that he would find Coll too late to help him – or perhaps even to help himself, if the Shadowen discovered them. If Rimmer Dall found Coll first, what was Par supposed to do then? Use the Sword of Shannara? He had tried that once to no avail. Use the magic of the wishsong? He had tried that as well and found it dangerously unpredictable. Still, he might have no choice. He would have to use the wishsong if that was the only way he could free his brother. The price he would have to pay was not a consideration.

He thought often now of how the wishsong had evolved and what it seemed to be doing to him when he summoned it. He tried to think what he might do to protect himself, to keep the magic under control, to prevent it from getting away from him entirely. The power was building in a manner he could not comprehend, evolving just as it had with Wil Ohmsford years ago, manifesting itself in new and frightening ways that suggested something fundamental was changing inside Par as well. When he considered the extent of that evolution, he was terrified. At one time it had been the magic of Jair Ohmsford, a wishsong that could form images out of air, images that seemed real but were only imaginings imprinted on the minds of those who listened. Now it seemed more the magic of Jair's sister, Brin, magic that could change things in

191

truth, that could alter them irrevocably. But with Par it could create as well. It could make things out of nothing, like that fire sword in the Pit, or the shards of metal and wind in the watchtower at Tyrsis. Where had power like that come from? What could have made the magic change so drastically?

What frightened him most, of course, was that the answer to all of his questions about the source of his magic was the same, a faint and insidiously confident whisper in his mind, the words spoken to him by Rimmer Dall when he had faced the First Seeker in the vault that had housed the Sword of Shannara.

You are a Shadowen, Par Ohmsford. You belong with us.

Six days into his pursuit, four after the theft of the Skree, the afternoon heat so intense it seemed to color the air and burn the lungs, Coll's trail turned sharply into the river and disappeared.

Par stopped at the water's edge, scanned the ground in disbelief, backtracked to make certain he had not been deceived, and then sat down in a patch of shade beneath a spreading poplar to gather his thoughts.

Coll had gone into the river.

He stared out across its waters, over the sluggish, broad surface to the tree-lined bank beyond. The Mermidon turned out of the Runne where they were now, closing on the Rainbow Lake. The mountains continued south along the east bank, but the west flattened out into hilly grasslands and scattered groves of hardwoods. If Coll had been thinking clearly, he might have chosen to cross where travel was easier. But Coll was in the thrall of the Mirrorshroud. Par decided he couldn't be sure of anything. In any event, if Coll had crossed, he must cross as well.

He stripped off his clothing, used the fishing line and some deadwood to create a makeshift raft, lashed his clothing, blanket, pack, and the Sword of Shannara in place, and slipped into the river. The water was cold and soothing. He pushed off into the current, swimming with it at an angle toward the far shore. He took his time and was across about a mile down. He climbed out, dried himself, dressed, lashed the Sword and his gear to his back, and set off to find Coll's trail again.

But the trail was nowhere to be found.

He searched upriver and down until it was dark and discovered nothing. Coll had disappeared. Par sat in the dark staring out at the river's flat, glittery surface and wondered if his brother had drowned. Coll was a good swimmer under normal circumstances, but maybe his strength had finally given out. Par forced himself to eat, drank from his water skin, rolled himself into his blanket, and tried to sleep. Sleep would not come. Thoughts of Coll tugged and twisted at him, memories of the past, the weight of all that had come about since the beginning of the dreams. Par was assailed by conflicting emotions. What was he supposed to do now? What if Coll was really gone?

Sunrise was a deep red glow out of the east shadowed by a gathering of clouds west. The clouds rolled across the horizon, coming into Callahorn like a wall. Daylight was pale and thin, and the air turned dead still. Par rose and started out again, heading south along the river, still searching for his brother. He was tired and discouraged, and on the verge of quitting. He kept wondering what he was doing, chasing after a ghost, chasing after a Shadowen thing, being led on like a dumb animal. How did he know it was really Coll? Maybe Damson had been right. Couldn't the Shadowen have fooled him in some way? What if Rimmer Dall had tampered with the Sword, or changed its magic so that it deceived? Suppose this was all some sort of elaborate trap. Was there any way to tell?

He quit thinking altogether after a while because there were no possibilities left that he hadn't considered and he was wearing himself out to no good purpose. He simply kept walking, following the river as it meandered south through the hill country, scanning the ground mechanically, everything inside beginning to shut down into a black silence.

To the west, the clouds began to darken as they neared, and a sudden wind gusted ahead of them in warning. Birds flew screaming into the mountains east, flashes of white disappearing into the shadows.

Ahead, only miles down river, Southwatch appeared, its black obelisk etched against the skyline. Par watched it grow steadily larger as he approached, a fortress standing firm in the path of the coming storm. Par's eyes swept its walls and towers as he edged closer to stands of trees and rocks to gain cover. Nothing showed itself. Nothing moved.

Then suddenly, unexpectedly, he came upon Coll's trail again. He found it at the river's edge where his brother had emerged after having been carried south for what must have been at least seven or eight miles. He was certain it was Coll, even before he found a bootprint that confirmed it. The trail set off west into the hills and the coming storm.

But the trail was hours old. Coll had come ashore yesterday and set out at once. Par was at least a day behind.

Nevertheless, he began to track, grateful to have found any trail at all, relieved to know that his brother was still alive. He trudged inland from the river, the light failing rapidly now as the storm neared, the air turning slick and damp, and the grasses whipping wildly against his legs. Clouds roiled and tumbled overhead, filling the skies to overflowing. Par glanced back to where he had last seen Southwatch, but the Shadowen tower had disappeared into the gloom.

Rain began to fall in scattered drops, cool on his heated skin, then stinging as the wind gusted sharply and blew them into his face.

Moments later he crested a rise and saw Coll.

His brother was sprawled motionless on a stretch of dusty grass, facedown beneath a leafless, storm-ravaged oak that rose out of the center of a shallow vale. At first glance he appeared to be dead. Par started forward hurriedly, his heart sinking. *No*, was all he could think. *No*. Then he saw Coll stir, saw his arm move slightly, rearranging itself. A leg followed, drawing up, then relaxing again. Coll wasn't dead; he was simply exhausted. He had finally run himself out.

Par came down off the rise into the teeth of a wind that howled and bucked as it swept out of the enveloping black. The sound of his approach was lost in its shriek. He bent his head and pushed forward. Coll had gone still again. He did not hear Par. Par would reach him before Coll knew he was there.

And then what? he wondered suddenly. What would he do then?

He reached back over his shoulder deliberately and pulled out the Sword of Shannara. Somehow he would find a way to call forth the talisman's magic once more, to hold his brother fast while it worked its way through him, forcing him to see the truth, shredding the Shadowen cloak, freeing him for good.

At least, that's what he hoped would happen. He breathed in the smell and taste of the storm. Well, he would have his chance. Coll would not be as strong now as he was before. And Par would not be the one caught off guard.

As he closed on Coll, coming underneath the ruined oak's skeletal limbs, thunder – the storm's first – rumbled out of the black. Coll started at the sound, rolled onto his back, and stared upward at his brother ten feet away.

Par stopped, uncertain. Coll looked at him from within the shadows of the Mirrorshroud's velvet-black hood, his eyes blank and uncomprehending. A hand lifted weakly to pull the cloak closer about his hunched body. He whimpered and drew his knees up.

Par held his breath and started forward again, a step, another, the wind thrusting at him, billowing his clothes out from his body, whipping his hair from side to side. He kept the Sword of Shannara as still as he could against his body, unable to hide it now, hoping to keep it from becoming Coll's point of focus.

A jagged streak of lightning darted across the sky followed by a deafening peal of thunder that reverberated from horizon to horizon.

Coll came to his knees, eyes wide and frightened. For a second his hands relaxed their grip on the cloak, letting it fall away, and his face gained back a measure of its old look. Coll Ohmsford was there again in that moment's time, staring out at his brother as if he had never gone away. There was recognition in his face, a stunned, grateful relief that smoothed away pain and despair. Par felt a surge of hope. He wanted to call out to his brother, to assure him everything would be all right, to tell him he was safe now.

But in the next instant Coll was gone. His face disappeared back into the Shadowen thing that the Mirrorshroud had made, and a twisted, cunning visage took its place. Teeth bared, and his brother went into a crouch, snarling.

He's going to flee again! Par thought in anguish.

But instead Coll rushed him, bounding to his feet and closing the distance between them almost before Par could bring up the Sword of Shannara in defense. Coll's hands closed over Par's, grappling with the handle of the talisman, twisting at it to wrest it free. Par hung on, lurching forward and back as he fought with his brother for control of the blade. Rain poured down on them, a torrent of such ferocity that Par was left almost blinded. Coll was right up against him, pressed so close he could feel his brother's heartbeat. Their hands were locked above their heads as they wrenched at the Sword, swinging it this way and that, the metal glistening wetly.

Lightning struck north, a flash of intense light followed by a huge clap of thunder. The ground shook.

Par tried to summon the magic of the Sword but couldn't. It had come easily enough before – why wouldn't it come now? He tried to fight past his brother's madness, past the fury of his attack. He tried to block out his fear that nothing would help, that the power was somehow lost again. Across the slick, windswept grasses the Ohmsford brothers struggled, fighting for possession of the Sword of Shannara, grunts and shouts lost in the sound of the storm. Over and over Par sought unsuccessfully to summon the magic. Despair washed through him. He was losing this battle, too. Coll was bigger than he was, and his size and weight were wearing Par down. Worse, his brother seemed to be growing stronger as his own strength failed. Coll was all over him, kicking and clawing, fighting as if he had gone completely mad.

But Par would not give up. He clung desperately to the Sword, determined not to lose it. He let his brother shove him back, muscle him about, thrust him this way and that, hoping the efforts would tire Coll, slow him down, weaken him enough that Par could find a way to knock him unconscious. If he could manage that, he might have a chance.

Lightning flashed again, quick and startling. In its momentary glare Par caught a glimpse of shadowy forms gathering on the rise above the vale, dozens of them, twisted and gnarled and stooped, the gleam of their eyes like blood.

Then they were gone again, swallowed in the black storm night. Distracted, Par blinked away the rain that ran into his eyes, trying to peer past Coll's struggling form. What had he just seen out there? Again the lightning flashed, just as Coll thrust out wildly and toppled him to the sodden grass. He saw nothing this time, fighting to keep the breath in his lungs as he struck the ground. Coll threw himself on Par, howling. But Par let his brother's momentum work against him, tumbling the other over his head and twisting himself free.

He came to his feet, dazed and searching. The gloom was so thick he could barely see the ravaged oak. The rise was invisible.

Coll came at him again, but this time Par was ready. Breaking through the other's guard, he struck Coll sharply on the head with the hilt of the Sword. Coll dropped to his knees, stunned. He groped at the air in front of him, as if grasping for something that only he could see. A trickle of red ran down his face from where the blow had broken the skin, blood diffusing and turning pink as it mingled with the rain. His features began to change, losing their Shadowen cast, turning human again. Par started to strike, trembling in despair and exhaustion, then stopped as he saw the other's eyes fix on him in wonder.

It was his brother looking at him. It was Coll.

He dropped to his knees in the slick grass and mud, facing Coll. His brother's lips were moving, the words he was speaking lost in the howl of the wind and rain. He was shivering with cold and something more. He began shaking his head slowly beneath the glistening cover of the Mirrorshroud, twisting within the dark folds as if it were the hardest thing he had ever had to do. *Coll*. Par mouthed his name. Coll's hands came up to grasp the folds of the Shadowen cloak, shook violently, and then dropped away. *Coll*.

Desperate to help his brother before the chance was gone, Par impulsively jammed the Sword of Shannara into the earth before him and reached past it to take hold of Coll's hands. Coll did not resist, his eyes empty and dull. Par guided Coll's hands to the pommel of the Sword and fastened the chill, shaking fingers in place, holding them there with his own. *Please, Coll. Please stay with me*. Coll was staring at him, seeing him now and at the same time seeing right through him. The Sword of Shannara bound them, held them fast, fingers intertwined, pressed against the raised torch carved into the handle and against each other.

Par saw the distorted reflection of his face in the rain-streaked surface of the blade. 'Coll!' he screamed.

His brother's eyes snapped up. *Please let the magic come*, Par begged. *Please!*

Coll's eyes were fixed on him, searching for more.

'Coll, listen to me! It's Par! It's your brother!'

Coll blinked. There was a hint of recognition. There was a glint of light. Beneath his own hands, Par could feel Coll's tighten on the Sword's hilt.

Coll!

Light flared down the length of the Sword's smooth blade, quick and blinding, a white fury that engulfed everything in a moment's time. Fire followed, cool and brilliant as it burned outward from the Sword and into Par's body. He felt it extend and weave, drawing him out of himself and into the talisman, there to find Coll waiting, there to join them as one. He felt himself twist through the metal and out again to somewhere far beyond. The world from which he had been drawn disappeared – the damp and the mud, the dark and the sound. There was whiteness and there was silence. There was nothing else.

Just Coll and himself. Just the two of them.

Then he was aware of the shimmering black length of the Mirrorshroud wrapping about his brother's head and body, writhing like a snake. The cloak was alive, working itself this way and that, twisting violently against the pull of something invisible, something that was threatening to tear it apart.

Par could hear it hiss.

The Sword of Shannara. The magic of the Sword.

He let his thoughts flow deep into his brother's mind, down into the darkness that had settled there and was now fighting hard to remain. *Listen to me, Coll. Listen to the truth.* He forced his brother's mind to open, casting aside the Shadowen magic he found waiting there, heedless of his own safety, oblivious to everything but the need to set his brother free. The magic of the sword armored and sustained him. *Listen to me.* His voice cracked like a whip in his brother's mind. He assembled his words and gave them shape and form, images that matched the intensity of the wishsong when it told the tales of three hundred years gone. The truth of who and what Coll had become released in a rush that could not be slowed or turned aside, flooding inward. Coll saw how he had been subverted. He saw what the cloak had done to him. He saw the way in which he had been turned against his brother, sent to fulfill some dark intent of which neither of them was aware. He saw everything that had been so carefully hidden by the Shadowen magic.

He saw as well what was needed in order that he should be free of it.

The pain of those revelations was intense and penetrating.

Par could feel it reverberate through his brother, the waves washing back upon himself. His brother's life was laid bare before him, a stark and unrelenting series of truths that cut to the bone. Par fought his panic and the pain and faced them unflinching, steady because his brother needed him to be so. He could hear Coll's silent scream of anguish at what he was being shown. He could see that anguish reflected in Coll's eyes, deep and harsh. He did not turn away. He did not soften. The truth was the Sword of Shannara's white fire, burning and cleansing, and it was their only hope.

Coll reared back and screamed then, the sound bringing them out of the white silence and back into the black, howling fury of the storm, kneeling together in the mud and wet grasses beneath that ancient oak, beneath the dark, roiling clouds. There was swirling, misty gloom all about, as if the last of the daylight had been stripped away. Rain blew into their faces, blinding them to everything but a shimmer of each other grasping as one the glittering length of the Sword. Lightning struck, brilliant and searing, and then thunder sounded in a tremendous blast.

Coll Ohmsford's hands wrenched free of the Sword, tearing loose Par's as well. Coll rose, a stricken look on his face. But it was *his* face Par saw, his *brother's* face, and nothing of the Shadowen horror that had sought to claim it. Coll reached back in a frenzy and tore loose the Mirrorshroud. He ripped it away and threw it to the earth. The Mirrorshroud landed in a heap amid the dampness and muck and at once began to steam. It shuddered and twisted, then began to bubble. Green flames sprang from its shimmering folds, burning wildly. The fire spread, inexorable, consuming, and in seconds the Mirrorshroud was turned to ash.

Par came wearily to his feet and faced his brother, seeing in Coll's eyes what he had been searching for. Coll had come back to him. The Sword of Shannara had shown him the truth about the Mirrorshroud – that it was Shadowen-sworn, that it had been created to subvert him, that the only way he could ever be free was to take off the cloak and throw it away. Coll had done so. The Sword had given him the strength.

But even in that moment of supreme elation, when the struggle had been won and Coll had been returned to him, Par felt something uneasy stir within. There should have been more, a voice whispered. The magic should have done something more. Remember the tales of five hundred years gone? Remember the first Ohmsford? Remember Shea? The magic had done something different for Shea when he had summoned it. It had shown him the truth about himself, revealed first all that he had sought to hide away, to disguise, to forget, to pretend did not exist. It had shown to Shea Ohmsford the truth about himself, the harshest truth of all, in order that he might be able to bear after any other truth that was required of him.

Why had nothing of this truth been shown to him? Why had everything been of Coll alone?

Lightning flashed again, and Par's thoughts disintegrated in the movement of the dark forms on the rise surrounding them, forms so clearly revealed this time that there could be no mistaking what they were. Par turned, seeing them crouched and waiting everywhere, twisted and dark, red eyes gleaming. He felt Coll edge close, felt his brother take up a protective stance at his back. Coll was seeing them now as well.

A strange mix of despair and fury washed through Par Ohmsford. The Shadowen had found them.

Then Rimmer Dall descended from the ranks, the raw, harsh features lifted into the rain, the eyes as hard as stone and as red as blood. A dozen steps from them, he stopped. Without saying a word, he lifted his gloved hand and beckoned. The gesture said everything. They must come with him. They belonged to him. They were his now.

Par heard the First Seeker's voice in his mind, heard it as surely as if the other had spoken. He shook his head once. He would not come. Neither he nor Coll. Not ever again.

'Par,' he heard his brother speak his name softly. 'I'm with you.'

There was a sudden rasp of the Sword of Shannara's blade against the pull of the earth as Coll slowly drew it free. Par turned slightly. Coll was holding the talisman in both hands, facing out at the Shadowen.

Fiercely determined that nothing would separate them again, Par Ohmsford summoned the magic of the wishsong. It responded instantly, anxious for its release, eager for its use. There was something terrifying about the voracious intensity of its coming. Par shuddered at the feelings it sent through him, at the hunger it unleashed inside. He must control it, he warned himself, and despaired that he could do so.

Across the darkness that separated them, Par could see Rimmer Dall smile. All about the crest of the rise, he could see the Shadowen begin to edge down, the rasp of claws and teeth sliding through the wind's quick howl, the glint of red eyes turning the rain to steam. How many were there? Par wondered. Too many. Too many even for the wishsong's volatile magic. He cast about desperately, looking for a place to break through. They would have to run at some point. They would have to try to reach the river or the woods, someplace they would have a chance to hide.

As if such a place existed. As if there were any chance for them at all.

The magic gathered at his fingertips in a white glow that seethed with fury. Par felt Coll press up against him, and they stood back to back against the closing circle.

Lightning flashed and thunder rolled across the blackness, booming into the wind's rush. In the distance, trees swayed, and leaves torn from their limbs scattered like frightened thoughts. Run, Par thought. Run now, while you can.

And then a light flared at the base of the ancient oak, a brightness sure and steady, seeming to grow out of the air. It came forward into the gloom, swaying gently, barely more than a candle's flicker through the curtain of the rain. The movement of the Shadowen froze into stillness. The wind faded to a dull rush. Par saw the smile on Rimmer Dall's face disappear. His cold eyes shifted to where the light approached, easing out of the murk to reveal the small, slender form that directed it.

It was a boy carrying a lamp.

The boy came toward Par and Coll without slowing, the lamp held forth to guide his way, eyes dark and intense, hair damp against his forehead, features smooth and even and calm. Par felt the magic of the wishsong begin to fade. He did not feel threatened by this boy. He did not feel afraid. He glanced hurriedly at Coll and saw wonder mirrored in his brother's dark eyes.

The boy reached them and stopped. He did not spare even the slightest glance for the monsters that snarled balefully in the gloom beyond the fringes of his lamp. His eyes remained fixed on the brothers.

'You must come with me now, if you are to be made safe,' he said quietly.

Rimmer Dall rose up like a dark spirit, throwing off the protection of his robes so that his arms were left free, the one with the dark glove stretching out as if to tear away the light. 'You don't belong here!' he hissed in his stark, whispery voice. 'You have no power here!'

The boy turned slightly. 'I have power wherever I choose. I am the bearer of the light of the Word, now and always.'

Rimmer Dall's eyes were on fire. 'Your magic is old and used up! Get away while you can!'

Par stared from one face to the other. What was going on? Who was this boy?

'Par!' he heard Coll gasp.

And he saw the boy begin to change suddenly into an old man, frail and bent with age, the lamp held away from him as if to hold it closer would burn.

'And your magic,' the old man whispered to Rimmer Dall, 'is stolen, and in the end it will betray you.'

He shifted again toward Par and Coll. 'Come away now. Don't be frightened. There are small things that I can still do

203

for you, and this is one.' The seamed face regarded them. 'Not frightened, are you? Of an old man? Of an old friend of so many of your family? Do you know me? You do, don't you? Of course. Of course you do.' One hand reached out and brushed theirs. It was the feel of old paper or dried leaves. Something sparked within as he did so. 'Speak my name,' he said.

And abruptly they knew. 'You are the King of the Silver River,' they whispered together, and the lamplight reached out to gather them in.

Instantly the Shadowen attacked. They came down off the slope in a black tide, their shrieks and howls shattering the odd calm that the King of the Silver River had brought with him. They came in a gnashing of teeth and a tearing of claws, rending the air and earth in fury. Before them came Rimmer Dall, transformed into something indescribable, a shadow so swift that it cut through the space separating him from the Ohmsfords in an instant's time. Iron bands wrapped about Par's throat and Coll's chest, tightening and suffocating. There was a feeling of being swallowed whole into the blackness it caused, of falling away into a pit that was too deep to measure. For an instant they were lost, and then the voice of the King of the Silver River reached out to gather them in, cradling them like the hands of a mother holding her child, freeing them from the iron bands and carrying them up from the darkness.

Rimmer Dall's voice was the grate of iron on stone, and the voice of the King of the Silver River disappeared. Again the blackness closed and the bands took hold. Par struggled desperately to get free. He could feel the terrible sway of magics wielded by the combatants, the strengths of the First Seeker and the ancient spirit as they fought for control of Coll's life and his. His brother had become separated from him somehow; he could no longer feel him pressing close. For a moment he could see Coll, could make out the other's familiar features, and then even that was gone.

'Par, I have to tell you – ' he heard his brother call out.

Inside, the magic of the wishsong was building, and his brother's words disappeared in its rush.

The lamp of the King of the Silver River cut against the Shadowen dark, forcing it away. Par reached toward the light, stretching out his hands. But the darkness surged back again, a shriek of desperation and anger. It scythed across the light and shut Par away.

In terror Par released his magic. It roared out of him like floodwaters in a spring storm, a torrent that could not be slowed. Par felt the magic explode everywhere, white-hot and fierce, burning everything. It swept about him in a fury, and Par could do nothing to stop it.

He felt himself change, felt himself shift away from his body, turn his face aside and mask who and what he was. The change was terrifying and real; it was as if his skin was being shed.

He saw the lamp of the King of the Silver River disappear. He saw the darkness close about.

Then his strength gave out, consciousness left him completely, and he saw nothing at all.

16

When Barsimmon Oridio advised Wren, following the High Council's decision to engage the approaching Federation force rather than wait for it in Arborlon, that it would take at least a week to assemble and provision the whole of their army, she determined to set forth with as many men as he could have ready in two days to act as a vanguard. Predictably, the old warrior balked, challenging the sense of taking a small force against so many, questioning what would happen if it was trapped and forced to fight. She listened patiently, then explained that the purpose of the vanguard was not to engage the enemy, but to monitor it and perhaps to slow it by letting it discover the presence of another army in the field. There was no reason to worry, she assured. Bar could select the commander of the vanguard, and she would be bond by his decisions. Bar fussed and fumed, but in the end he gave in, satisfying himself with her promise that she would wait until he arrived with the bulk of the army before attempting any sort of offensive engagement.

Word went out to the Elves who had settled the surrounding countryside of the approach of the Federation army and of the danger that it posed. Those who wished could come to Arborlon, which would serve as a defense for the Elven people. Those who chose to remain where they were should be prepared to flee if the Federation broke through. Wing Riders were dispatched to the farthest points and to the Wing Hove. Runners were used elsewhere. Families from the settlements nearest the city began to drift in almost immediately. Wren settled them in camps scattered across the bluff and away from the defenses that were being built. There could be no closing away of the city behind walls this time. The Elfitch had been destroyed in the demon attack in Elventine Elessedil's time, and the Keel had been left behind on Morrowindl. Bulwarks would be constructed, but they would be neither tall nor high nor unbroken. The cliffs of the Carolan and waters of the Rill Song offered some natural protection against an attack from the west, and there were high mountains north and south, but the Federation was most likely to come at them from the east through the Valley of Rhenn. Whatever defenses were to be employed would have to be settled there.

Wren spoke with her ministers and the commanders of her army at length about what form those defenses might take. There were heavy woods all the way east from the city to the plains, much of them impassable for a force the size of the one that approached. It was agreed that the Federation army would seek to use its size to crush the Elves, and scattering itself through the trees would not seem an attractive alternative to its commanders. Therefore it would come through the Rhenn and follow the main road west to the city, there to deploy. But even that approach would not be easy. It had been many years since the road had been used regularly – barely at all since the Elves had disappeared from the Westland. Much of it had been reclaimed by the forest. It was more trail than road these days. It was narrow and winding and filled with places where a small force could hold out for a time against a much larger one. Fortifications would be built at as many of these places as time allowed, using pitfalls and traps to hinder any advance. Meanwhile, the main Elven army would attempt to slow the Federation forces on the grasslands east, relying on its cavalry, bowmen, and Wing Riders to offset the superior numbers of Southland infantry. If that failed, a last stand would be made at the Rhenn.

One team of builders was dispatched to begin work on the defenses for the approach east while a second set about fortifying the Carolan. An attack from the west was unlikely, but there was no point in leaving anything to chance.

Meanwhile, the enormous job of outfitting and provisioning the Elven army commenced under the direction of Barsimmon Oridio. Wren stayed out of the old soldier's way, content to have him busily engaged in something besides questioning her. Out of everyone's hearing she quietly advised Triss that she wanted a large contingent of Home Guard to go on her expedition as well and Tiger Ty that she wanted a dozen Wing Riders. Both forces would be under her personal command. It was fine to leave battlefield tactics to men like Bar, but a major confrontation was the last thing she wanted. She had thought the matter through very carefully. Harass, harry, and delay, she had told the Council – that was what the Elves could reasonably hope to accomplish. Garth had taught her everything there was to know about that kind of fighting. She had not said anything to the Council, but the week required to assemble the Elven army might prove too long a delay. The vanguard, in truth, was simply a screen that would allow her to act more quickly. The Federation army needed to be disrupted now, at once. Unconventional tactics were called for, and the Home Guard and Wing Riders were perfect for the job.

On the morning of the third day, she set out with a force that consisted of a little more than a thousand men – eight hundred infantry made up essentially of bowmen, three hundred cavalry, a hundred of the Home Guard under the command of Triss, and the dozen Wing Riders she had requested of Tiger Ty. The Wing Riders were directed by a seasoned veteran named Erring Rift, but Tiger Ty was there was well, insisting that no one but he should take the queen skyward should she wish to do any further scouting. Barsimmon Oridio had appointed a lean, hard-faced veteran named Desidio, to lead the expedition. Wren knew him to be reliable, tough, and smart. It was a good choice. Desidio was experienced enough to do what was needed and to not do anything more. That was fine with Wren. The Home Guard were hers, and the Wing Riders were independent and could follow who they chose. It would make for a good balance.

That she was going at all was a point of some debate among the ministers, but she had made it clear from the first night that a Queen of the Elves must always lead if she expects anyone to follow. She had intended from the beginning to go out with the army, she reminded them, and there was no point in waiting about to do it. She had spent a lifetime learning to survive, and she possessed the power of the Elfstones to protect her. She had less reason than most to worry. She did not intend to make excuses.

In the end she got her way because no one was prepared to go up against her on the matter. Some, she thought rather uncharitably, seeing the black looks on the faces of Jalen Ruhl and Perek Arundel, might be hoping her rash insistence would come back to haunt her.

She left Eton Shart in charge of the Council and the city. The ministers would not cross him, and the Elves knew and respected him. He would be able to guide them in whatever way was necessary, and she had confidence that he would know what to do. Her first minister might not yet be convinced that she was the queen her people needed, but he had given his pledge of support and she believed he would not break it. Of the others she was less certain, though Fruaren Laurel seemed committed to her now. But they would all toe the line for Eton Shart.

Barsimmon Oridio was there to see her off, declaring that he would follow within a few days, reminding her of her promise to wait for him. She smiled and winked, and that unnerved him enough that he stalked away. She was aware of Triss on one side, stone-faced, and Desidio, eyeing her covertly from the other. Tiger Ty had already set out, flying Spirit away at day-break to scout the Federation's progress. The remainder of the Wing Riders would leave at sunset to link up with them at their campsite near the Rhenn. The Elven Hunters marched out to the waves and cheers of the people of the city, young and old come down to see them off, waving banners and ribbons and calling out their wishes for success. Wren glanced about doubtfully. It all felt very strange. Their departure was festive and gay, and it forecast nothing of the injury and death that was certain to follow.

They traveled swiftly that first day, strung out along the narrow roadway to avoid clogging, scouts dispersed into the trees at regular intervals to warn of impending danger. They were in their own country and so paid less heed to the precautions they might otherwise have observed. Wren rode with Triss and the Home Guard, screened front and back by Hunters, carefully protected against anything that might threaten. It made her smile to think how different things were from when she was a simple Rover girl. Now and again she had to suppress an urge to leap down off her horse and race away into the cool green stillness of the trees, returning to the life from which she had come, returning to its peace.

Faun had been left at home, closed within Wren's room on the second floor of the Elessedil home. The Streleheim was no place for a forest creature, she had reasoned. But the Tree Squeak had a mind of its own and was not always persuaded by what Wren believed was best. So by the time the vanguard stopped to rest and water the horses at midday, there was Faun, streaking from the foliage in a dark blur to throw herself on her startled mistress. In seconds the little creature had burrowed down into the folds of Wren's riding cloak and was comfortably settled. Wren shrugged obligingly and accepted what she could obviously not change.

The late summer heat was sticky and damp, and by day's end men and horses alike were sweating freely. They camped in a canopied stretch of oak and hickory several miles from the Rhenn, close by a stream and pool so that they could wash and drink, but back within the shade and concealment of the forest. Desidio sent a patrol of horsemen ahead into the pass to make certain that all was well, then sat down with Wren and Triss to discuss how they would proceed. Tiger Ty would bring news of the Federation army's location when he returned, and presuming the army was still proceeding northward through the Tirfing, the Elves might then travel south across the open plains, relying on scouts to prevent them from running into an ambush, or might keep within the fringe of the trees where they would not be so easily seen. Wren listened patiently, glanced at Triss, then said she preferred that they travel in the open so as to make better time. Once they had made contact with the Federation, they could then use the forest in which to hide while they decided what to do next. Desidio gave her a sharp look at the words 'decide what to do next,' but then nodded his agreement, rose, and walked away.

They had just finished eating dinner when Tiger Ty winged down through the trees, dusty and hot and tired. He settled Spirit a short distance down the trail, where the giant Roc was less likely to disturb the horses, then strode determinedly back toward the camp. Wren and Triss walked out to greet him and were joined by Desidio. The Wing Rider was brief and to the point. The Federation army had reached the Mermidon and begun crossing. By tomorrow sometime, they would have completed the task and be on their way north. They were making very good time.

Wren accepted the news with a frown. She had hoped to catch up to them on the far side of the river and keep them there. That had been wishful thinking, it seemed. Events were moving more quickly than she wanted them to.

She thanked Tiger Ty for the report and sent him off to get something to eat.

'You are thinking that the Elven army is too far away,' Desidio said quietly, his lean face pinched with thought.

She nodded. 'They are still the best part of a week even from here.' Her green eyes fixed him. 'I don't think we can allow the Federation to get that close to Arborlon before we try to stop them.'

They stared at each other. 'You heard the general,' Desidio said. 'We're to wait for the main army.' His face showed nothing.

She shrugged. 'I heard. But General Oridio isn't here. And you are.'

The dark eyebrows lifted inquiringly. 'You have something in mind, my lady?'

She held his gaze. 'I might. Would you be willing to listen, when it's time?'

Desidio rose. 'You are the queen. I must always listen.'

When he had departed, she gave Triss a doubtful smile. 'He knows what I am up to, don't you think?'

Triss eased his splinted arm away from his body and then let it settle back again. In another day the splint would be gone. Triss was impatient for that to happen. He considered her question and shook his head. 'I don't think anyone knows what you are up to, my lady,' he said softly. 'That's why they are frightened of you.'

She accepted the observation without comment. Triss could tell her anything. What they had shared coming out of Morrowindl allowed for that. She looked off into the trees. Dusk was spreading shadows in dark pools that ate up the light. Sometimes, since Garth had died, she found herself wondering if they might be trying to swallow her as well.

Moments later the sound of horses' hoofs drew her attention back toward the camp. The scouts dispatched to the Rhenn had returned, and they had brought someone with them. They thundered to a stop, sawing on the reins of their snorting, lathered mounts. The horses had been ridden hard. Triss rose quickly, and Wren came up with him. The riders and their charge – one man – had dismounted and were making their way through a cluster of Elven Hunters to where Desidio waited, a gaunt shadow against the firelight. There was an exchange of words, and then Desidio and the unidentified man turned and came toward her.

She got a closer look as the pair neared and saw that it wasn't a man with Desidio after all. It was a boy.

'My lady,' her commander said as he approached. 'A messenger from the free-born.'

The boy came into the light. He was blond and blue-eyed and very fair-skinned beneath the browning from sun and wind. He was small and quick-looking, compact without being heavily muscled. He smiled and bowed rather awkwardly.

'I am Tib Arne,' he announced. 'I have been sent by Padishar Creel and the free-born to give greetings to the Elven people and to offer support in the struggle against the Federation.' His speech sounded very rehearsed.

'I am Wren Elessedil,' she replied, and offered her hand. He took it, held it uncertainly for a moment, and released it. 'How did you find us, Tib?'

He laughed. 'You found me. I came west out of Callahorn in search of the Elves, but you made my job easy. Your scouts were waiting at the mouth of the valley when I entered.' He glanced about. 'It seems I have arrived just in time for something.'

'What sort of help do the free-born offer?' she asked, ignoring his observation. He was too quick by half.

'Me, for starters. I am to be your ready and willing servant, your link to the others until they arrive. The free-born assemble in the Dragon's Teeth for a march west. They should be here within the week. Five thousand or more with their allies, my queen.'

Wren saw Triss lift his eyebrows. 'Five thousand strong?' she repeated.

Tib shrugged. 'So I was told. I'm just a messenger.'

'And a rather young one at that,' she observed.

His smile was quick and reassuring. 'Oh, not so young as I look. And I do not travel alone. I have Gloon for protection.'

Wren smiled back. 'Gloon.'

He nodded, then stuck his fingers in the corners of his mouth and gave a shrill whistle that silenced everything about them. Up came his right arm, and now Wren saw that he wore a thick leather glove that ran to his elbow.

Then down out of the darkness hurtled a shadow that was darker still, a whistle of sound and fury that sliced through the air like black lightning. It landed on the boy's glove with an audible thud, wings spread and cocked, feathers jutting out like spikes. In spite of herself, Wren shrank away. It was a bird, but a bird like no other she had ever seen. It was big, larger than a hawk or even an owl, its feathers slate gray with red brows and a crest that bristled menacingly. Its beak was yellow and sharply hooked. Its claws were two sizes too large for the rest of its body, and its body was squat and blocky, all sinew and muscle beneath its feathers. It hunched its head down into its shoulders like a fighter and stared at Wren through hard, wicked eyes.

'What is that?' she asked the boy, wondering suddenly where Faun was hiding – hoping she was hiding well.

'Gloon? He's a war shrike, a breed of hunting bird that comes out of the Troll country. I found him as a baby and raised him. Trained him to hunt.' Tib seemed quite proud. 'He makes sure nothing happens to me.'

Wren believed it. She didn't like the look of the bird one bit. She forced her eyes away from it and fixed on the boy. 'You must eat and rest here for tonight, Tib,' she offered. 'But shouldn't you go back in the morning and let the free-born know where we are? We need them to get here as quickly as they can.'

He shook his head. 'They come already and nothing I can do will move them along any quicker. When they get closer, they will send a message – another bird. Then I will send Gloon.' He smiled. 'They will find us, don't worry. But I am to stay with you, my queen. I am to serve you here.'

214

'You might serve best by going back,' the implacable Desidio observed.

Tib blinked and looked confused. 'But . . . but I don't want to go back!' he blurted out impulsively. He suddenly seemed as young as he looked. 'I want to stay here. Something is going to happen, isn't it? I want to be part of it.' He glanced quickly at Wren. 'You're Elves, my queen, and no one has seen Elves before, ever! I . . . I wasn't the first choice for this journey. I had to argue a long time to win the job. Don't make me leave right away. I can help in some way, I know I can. Please, my queen? I've come a long way to find you. Let me stay awhile.'

'And Gloon as well, I suppose?' She smiled.

He smiled back instantaneously. 'Oh, Gloon will stay hidden until he is called.' He threw up his hand, and the war shrike streaked upward and disappeared. Tib watched him go, saying, 'He looks after himself, mostly.'

Wren glanced at Desidio, who shook his head doubtfully. Tib didn't seem to see, his eyes still directed skyward.

'Tib, why don't you get something to eat and then go to bed,' Wren advised. 'We'll talk about the rest of it in the morning.'

The boy looked at her, blinked, stifled a yawn, nodded, and trotted off dutifully behind Desidio. Tiger Ty passed them coming up from the cooking fire with a plate of food and cast a sharp glance back at the boy on reaching Wren.

'Was that a war shrike I saw?' he growled. 'Nasty bird, those. Hard to believe that boy could train one. Most of them would as soon take your head off as look at you.'

'That dangerous?' Wren asked, interested.

'Killers,' the Wing Rider answered. 'Hunt anything, even a moor cat. Don't know how to quit once they've started something. It's rumored that in the old days they were used to hunt men – sent out like assassins. Smart and cruel.' He shook his head. 'Nasty, like I said.'

She glanced at Triss. 'Maybe we don't want it around, then.'

Tiger Ty started away. 'I wouldn't.' He stretched. 'Time for sleep. The others flew in an hour ago, in case you didn't see. We'll scout things out again tomorrow morning. Night.'

He ambled off into the dark, gnarled, bowlegged, rocking from side to side like some old piece of furniture that had been jostled in passing. Wren and Triss watched him go without comment. When he was gone, they looked at each other.

'I'm sending Tib back,' she said.

Triss nodded. Neither of them spoke after that.

Wren slept, curled into her light woolen blanket at the edge of the firelight, dreaming of things that were forgotten as quickly as they were gone. Twice she woke to the sounds of the night, tiny chirpings and buzzings, small movements in the brush, and the rustle of things unseen far overhead in the branches of the trees. It was warm and the air was still, and the combination did not make for a sound sleep. Home Guard slept around her; Triss was less than a dozen feet away. At the edges of her vision she saw others on patrol, vague shadows against the darkness. Curled in the crook of her arm, Faun stirred fitfully. The night edged away in a crawl, and she swam listlessly through sleep and waking.

She was just settling in for yet another try, the deepest part of the night reached, when a prickly face poked into view directly in front of her. She jumped in fright.

'Hssst! Easy, Wren Elessedil!' said a familiar voice.

Hurriedly she pushed herself up on one elbow. 'Stresa!'

Faun squeaked in recognition, and the Splinterscat hissed it into silence. Lumbering close, it sat back on its haunches and regarded her with those strange blue eyes. 'It didn't seem phhttt a good idea to let you go off on your own.'

She smiled in spite of herself. 'You nearly scared me to death! How did you get past the guards?'

The Splinterscat's tongue licked out, and she could have sworn that it smiled. 'Really, now, Elf girl. They are only men. Sssstt! If you want to give me a challenge phffttt put me back on Morrowindl.' The eyes blinked, luminous. 'On second thought, don't. I like it here, in your world.'

Wren hugged Faun into her body as the Tree Squeak tried to squirm away. 'I'm glad you're here,' she told Stresa. 'I worry about you sometimes.'

'Worry about me. Phaagg! Whatever for? After Morrowindl, nothing much frightens me. This is a good world you live in, Wren of the Elves.'

'But not so good where we're going. Do you know?'

'Hssstt. I heard. More of the dark things, the same as Morrowindl's. But how bad are these, Elf girl? Are they things like the rrowwwll Wisteron?'

The Splinterscat's nose was damp and glistening in the starlight. 'No,' she answered. 'Not yet, at least. These are men, but many more than we are and determined to destroy us.'

Stresa thought about it for a moment. 'Still, better than the monsters.'

'Yes, better.' She breathed the hot night air in a sigh. 'But some of these men make monsters, too.'

'So nothing changes, does it?' The Splinterscat ruffled its quills and rose. 'I'll be close to you hsttt but you won't see me. If you need me though, phhfftt I'll be there.'

'You could stay,' she suggested.

Stresa spit. 'I'm happier in the forest. Safer, too. Rowwlll. You'd be safer as well, but you won't go. I'll have to be your eyes. Hssstt! What I see, you'll know about first.' The tongue licked out. 'Watch yourself, Wren Elessedil. Don't forget the lessons of Morrowindl.'

She nodded. 'I won't.'

Stresa turned and started away. 'Send the Squeak ssttt if you need me,' he whispered back, and then was gone.

She stared after him into the darkness for a time, Faun

217

cradled in her arms, small and warm. Finally she lay back again, smiled, and closed her eyes. She felt better for knowing that the Splinterscat was there for her.

In seconds she was asleep once more. She did not wake again until morning.

17

At daybreak, the vanguard of the Elven army prepared to set out again. Wren summoned Tib Arne and advised him that she was sending him back to the free-born to make certain that they knew he had found them and to urge them to come as quickly as possible. She assured him that it was important that he go or she would have honored his request to stay. She told him he was welcome to return when the message was delivered. Tib pouted a bit and expressed his disappointment, but in the end he agreed that she was right and promised to do his best to hurry the free-born to their aid. Desidio gave him a pair of Elven Hunters to act as escorts and protectors – despite his repeated protests that he needed no one – and the trio set out through the valley to the Streleheim Plains. Gloon did not make an appearance, and Wren was just as glad.

It took the Elves the better part of two days to close the gap between themselves and the Federation. They traveled swiftly and steadily, using the open grasslands to speed their passage, relying on the Wing Riders and the cavalry scouts to keep from being discovered. The Wing Riders brought back regular reports of the Southland army's progress, which had slowed. One day had been used in crossing the Mermidon and a second in repairs to equipment caused by water damage. The Federation had not traveled far beyond the north bank of the

Mermidon when, by midafternoon of the second day, the Elves found themselves within striking distance.

The Wing Riders brought word of the contact, two of them, speeding out of the sun where it hung against the sky in a blazing white heat. The Elves were spread out along the edges of the Westland forests not far from where the Mermidon bent back upon itself coming out of the Pykon. When Wren was informed that the approaching army was no more than five miles distant and closing, she had Desidio order the Elves back into the shelter of the trees to wait for nightfall. There, in the cool of the shade, she called together the expedition's commanders.

'We have a choice to make,' she informed them.

They were five in all, Triss, Desidio, Tiger Ty, Erring Rift, and herself. Rift was a tall, stoop-shouldered Elf with a shaggy black beard and thinning hair and eyes like chips of obsidian. As the leader of the Wing Riders, his presence was essential. Tiger Ty was there as a personal courtesy and because Wren trusted his judgment. They were gathered in a loose circle under an aging shagbark hickory, nudging at nut shells and twigs with their boots as they listened to her speak.

'We've found them,' she continued, 'but that's not enough. Now we have to decide what to do about it. I think we all realize what sort of progress they are making. A massive army, but moving at a decent rate of speed – much quicker than we had anticipated. Five days, and they have already crossed the Mermidon and gotten here. Our own army is at least a week away from where we sit. The Federation is not going to wait on us. Left alone, they will reach the Rhenn in that week's time, and we will be making our first stand in the place where we had hoped to make our last.'

'The heat might slow them some on these open grasslands,' Desidio observed.

'A fire would slow them worse,' Rift suggested. He rubbed at his beard. 'Set properly, the wind would carry it right into them.'

'And right into the Westland forests as well,' Triss finished.

'Or the wind could shift it into us,' Wren shook her head. 'Too risky, except as a last resort. No, I think we have a better choice.'

'An engagement,' Desidio declared quietly. 'What you have planned for all along, my lady. What I am forbidden by order of the general to do.'

Wren smiled and faced him squarely. 'I told you there would come a time when it was necessary for you to hear me out. The time is now, Commander. I know what your orders are. I know what I promised General Oridio. I also know what I didn't promise him.'

She shifted her weight and leaned forward. 'If we sit here and do nothing, the Federation will reach the Rhenn before we do and bottle us up. Arborlon will be finished. There will be no time for anyone to come to our aid, free-born or otherwise. We need to slow this army down, to give our own time to come forward where it can be effective. Orders are orders, Commander, but in the field events dictate how closely those orders must be adhered to.'

Desidio said nothing.

'We both promised that the vanguard would not be taken into battle against the Federation army until General Oridio arrived. Very well, we'll keep that promise. But nothing binds the actions of the Home Guard, which I command, or the Wing Riders, who are free to act on their own. I think we should consider ways in which they might be used against this enemy.'

'A dozen Wing Riders and a hundred Home Guard?' Desidio raised his eyebrows questioningly.

'More than enough for what I think she's got in mind,' Tiger Ty interjected defensively. 'Let's hear her out.'

Desidio nodded. Erring Rift was rubbing his chin harder, eyes intent. Triss looked as if they were discussing the weather.

'We are too small to engage the Federation army openly,'

she said, her eyes sweeping their faces. 'But we have speed and quickness and surprise on our side, and these could be valuable weapons in a night attack designed to disrupt and confuse. Wing Riders can strike from anywhere, and the Home Guard are trained to be present without being seen. What if we were to come at them in the dark, when they do not expect it? What if we strike at them where they are vulnerable?'

Triss nodded. 'Their wagons and supplies.'

Erring Rift clapped his hands. 'Their siege machines!'

'Set fire to them,' Tiger Ty whispered eagerly. 'Burn them to the ground while they sleep!'

'More than that,' Wren interjected quickly, drawing them back to her. 'Confuse them. Frighten them. At night, they cannot see. Let's take advantage of that. Do all you've suggested, but make them think there is an entire army out there doing it. Come at them all at once from a dozen directions and be gone again before they can determine what has happened. Leave them with the impression that they are besieged on all sides. They won't proceed so quickly after that. Even after they repair the damage, they will be working harder at looking for us and that will slow them down.'

Erring Rift laughed. 'Spoken like a true Rover girl!' he exclaimed enthusiastically, then added, rather quickly, 'My lady.'

'And what is to be my part in this?' Desidio asked quietly. 'And that of the vanguard?'

Wren might have been mistaken, but she thought she caught a hint of anticipation in the other's voice, as if perhaps he was actually hoping she had something in mind. She did not wish to disappoint him.

'Supplies and siege machines will be kept to the army's rear. The Wing Riders and Home Guard will come from that direction. If you can see your way clear, Commander, a strike by your archers and cavalry along the front and flank would provide no small amount of additional confusion.'

Desidio considered. 'They may be more awake than you think. They may be better prepared.'

'Within the borders of their own protectorate? Without having seen a single Elf during the entire course of their march north?' She shook her head. 'By now, they are wondering if there is anyone at all to find.'

'There may be Shadowen,' Triss said quietly.

Wren nodded. 'But the Shadowen will be disguised as men and will not wish to reveal themselves to the army. Remember, Triss – they manipulate by staying hidden. If they show themselves, they lose their anonymity and panic their army. I don't think they will risk it. I don't think they will have time even to think about it if we catch them off guard.'

'We will only be able to do that once.'

She smiled faintly. 'So we had better make the most of it, hadn't we?' She looked at Desidio. 'Can you help us?'

He gave her a rueful look. 'What you mean is, can I go against my orders from General Oridio?' He sighed. 'They are explicit, but then there is a certain amount of independent thinking permitted a commander in the field. Besides, you are correct in your assessment of how matters stand if we do nothing.'

He looked to the others. 'You are all committed to this?' They nodded, each of them. He looked back again at Wren. 'Then I must do what I can to save you from yourselves, even if it means taking the field. The general will not approve, but he will accept the logic, I hope. He knows I have no authority over the Wing Riders or the Home Guard and certainly none over you, my lady.' He paused, then added ruefully, 'I confess I am surprised at how easily I am persuaded by you.'

'You are persuaded by reason, Commander,' she corrected. 'There is a difference.'

There was an exchange of looks. 'Is the matter settled?' Tiger Ty asked gruffly.

'Except for strategy,' Wren replied. 'I leave that to you. But understand that I will be going with you. No, Tiger Ty, no arguments. Look to Triss – he doesn't even bother trying anymore.'

The Wing Rider gave her a black look and bit back whatever objection he had been about to make.

'When do we do it, my lady?' Erring Rift asked. His black eyes sparkled.

Wren came to her feet. 'Tonight, of course. As soon as they are sleeping.' She stepped around them and began walking away. 'I'm going to wash up and have something to eat. Let me know when your plan is in place.'

She smiled in satisfaction at the silence that followed after her and did not look back.

The day closed with the western horizon colored red and purple and the clouds forming and reforming in a slowly changing panorama. The heat lingered on as the sun disappeared and the colors faded, a fetid dampness in the windless air that caused clothes to stick and skin to itch. The Elves ate early and tried to sleep, but even in the shade of the forests there was little comfort to be found. As midnight approached, Desidio's Elven Hunters were awakened, told to dress and arm, and taken from the trees onto the grasslands, slipping silently toward the rise north that overlooked the sleeping Federation army.

Wren went with them, anxious for a look at ground level before she took to the air with the Wing Riders. She went out with a detachment of Home Guard, Desidio and Triss leading, all of them dressed for concealment in green and brown forest colors with high boots, belts, and gloves for protection against brush and scrub. She was wearing a backpack to carry Faun (who would not be left behind) and had strung a leather pouch about her neck to keep the Elfstones close. A brace of long knives were strapped about her waist and a dagger was in one boot. Armed for anything, she thought. They rode a short distance onto the plains, then dismounted and made their way on foot to where the forward lines of Elven Hunters crouched in the dark.

Alone with Triss and Desidio, she crept forward to where she could look down on the Federation encampment.

Their army was enormous. Even though she had seen it from the air with Tiger Ty, she was not prepared for how huge it looked now. It sprawled in a maze of hundreds of cooking fires for as far as the eye could see, a wash of light that crowded out the stars with its brilliance. Talk and laughter drifted off the plains as clear as if the voices came from only yards away. Outlined against the sky by the firelight were the huge siege machines, great skeletal bulks of wooden bones and iron joints, rising up like misshapen giants. Wagons huddled in clusters, piled with stores and weapons, and the smell of oil and pitch drifted on the wind. Even though it was by now after midnight, there were many who still did not sleep, wandering from fire to fire, spurred by the clink of glasses and tin cups, drawn by calls and shouts and the promise of drink and companionship.

Wren glanced at Triss. The Federation was at ease with itself, satisfied that its size and strength would ward it from any danger. She mouthed the word 'guards' questioningly. Triss shrugged, pointed left and then right, picking out the sentries that the Federation commanders had placed. They were few and widely scattered. She had been right in her assessment; the Southlanders were not expecting trouble.

They slipped back down the rise until they were out of view of the camp, then rose and retraced their steps through the lines of bowmen and cavalry. When they were safely away, she drew Triss and Desidio close.

'Get as close as you can, Commander,' she whispered to the latter. 'Wait for the Wing Riders to strike at them from the rear. Look for the fires, then attack. Archers followed by cavalry, as we planned, then quickly away. Take no chances. Don't let them see any more of you than necessary. We want them to use their imaginations as to how many of us there are.'

Desidio nodded. He knew his job better than she, but she was the queen and he was not about to tell her so. She smiled faintly, took his hand in her own to express her confidence, then turned with Triss and crept away. Their escort was waiting, and they remounted and rode back into the forests.

The Wing Riders and the main body of the Home Guard were waiting in a clearing. A dozen baskets had been woven from branches and tied together with leather cords, each large enough to hold a dozen men. The Elven Hunters climbed aboard, armed with longbows and short swords, dark and silent forms in the night. Each basket would be carried by a Roc onto the plains behind the Federation army. Wren hurried to Tiger Ty, who was already seated atop Spirit, and pulled herself up behind him. Securing the straps that would hold her in place. Triss climbed into the basket set in front. Erring Rift gave a low whistle, and one by one the Rocs rose skyward, claws fastened to straps that held the baskets at four corners, lifting them gently, carefully away from the earth, carrying them up through the trees and into the darkened skies.

Wind rushed in cool waves across Wren Elessedil's face as Spirit cleared the trees and swept east toward the plains. The fires of the Federation army became visible almost immediately, and their sweep seemed even larger from here. Erring Rift took the lead aboard his Roc Grayl, turning the formation south along the line of the forests and as far away from the light as he could manage. They flew silently down the tree line, watching the fires widen and then shrink again as they passed beyond their glow and back into the darkness. When they were far enough down, Rift led them back again toward the light, swinging wide onto the plains so that they would come up from the center rear.

Wren clung to Tiger Ty with one hand to steady herself and to maintain contact. The Wing Rider was solid and steady in his seat, hunched over as he flew, face turned away. Neither of them spoke.

When they were as close as they could safely manage without being seen, the Rocs settled earthward. The baskets were lowered, and the straps released. The Home Guard scattered from the carriers and disappeared into the night. The Rocs rose again, Wren still riding behind Tiger Ty, and swept wide in an arc that carried them out and away. A few minutes for Triss to dispose of the sentries, and then it would be time.

The Rocs swung back again, leveled out, and headed directly into the Federation camp, picking up speed as they went. This was the most dangerous part – so dangerous that Tiger Ty was forbidden to do more than to carry the Queen of the Elves as an observer. Whatever else might happen, she was to come away safe. They sped toward the Federation encampment, flattening out some fifty feet above the ground as they passed over the first of the fires.

Then down they went, dark arrows out of the night, all but Spirit. Eleven strong, the Rocs hurtled into the Federation camp, streaking toward the watch fires. At the last instant they were spotted, and howls of surprise rose from the men below. The warnings came too late. Wings extended, the Rocs skimmed the watch fires, choosing those that were close to dying, and snatched up bunches of the burning embers with their hardened claws. Why bring fire for the burning when there was fire already at hand? Erring Rift had argued. Away flew the Rocs, wheeling right and left toward the siege machines. The Federation soldiers were turning out of their blankets and bedding in swarms, trying to decipher from the jumble of words being shouted at them by those already awake what was happening. By now the Rocs had reached the siege machines and supply wagons. Burning brands tumbled from their claws onto the dry, seasoned wood. The wind fanned the embers in falling, and the wood burst instantly into flames. Some of the brands were dropped onto dusty canvas tarpaulins, some onto the shingle-roofed cabins atop the giant scaling towers, some into the vats of pitch that served to coat the missiles of the catapults.

Fire roared into the air from a dozen quarters, licking hungrily. Shouts turned to screams of fury and cries for water, but the flames were everywhere at once. The Rocs swept down on those who tried to smother the flames early, driving them away.

Then the Home Guard attacked from out of the night, longbows sending a hail of arrows into the milling Federation soldiers, dropping them as they struggled for their weapons, killing them before they knew what was happening. Swordsmen appeared, materializing all along the encampment's edges, cutting loose war horses and pack animals and driving them into the night, spilling sacks of grain and overturning water casks, and shredding whoever stood in their way.

The Federation army was in total disarray. Men charged about wildly, striking out at anyone or anything they encountered, frequently themselves. Officers tried to restore order, but no one was certain who was who, and the effort was swept away in the tide of confusion.

Now Desidio's Elven Hunters struck from the front, bowmen first, raining arrows into the camp, one volley after another. Then the cavalry swept out of the night with a terrifying howl. From high overhead Wren watched the Elven horses cut a swath through the front ranks of the Federation, charging deep into the camp and then out again, scattering watch fires and men, sending soldiers and retainers fleeing into the darkness.

But the Federation army was huge, and the attacks barely scratched its edges. Already ranks of men had formed at its center, where calm still prevailed, and were beginning a slow, steady march outward toward the source of the trouble. Hundreds of foot soldiers armed with shields and short swords trooped through the melee, shoving aside or trampling their own men, seeking out the intruders. In moments they were at the camp's perimeter, the light of burning wagons and siege machines reflecting off their armored bodies like blood.

Wren searched the darkness to discover what had become of her Elves. The Rocs were already winging south again, and Tiger Ty had turned Spirit to follow. She scanned the camp over her shoulder as they sped away into the dark, and there was no sign of Desidio's Hunters or the Home Guard. The Federation soldiers were advancing from out of the firelight, searching in vain for an enemy that had already vanished. Behind, the entire siege and pack train was in flames, pyramids of fire that burned hundreds of feet into the night sky and gave off a heat so intense that Wren could feel it even from where she flew. The stench of ash and smoke was thick in her nostrils, and the cries of the injured filled her ears. Men lay everywhere, bloodied and still.

We have our victory, she thought, but felt the intensity of her initial satisfaction diminish.

Away they flew, Spirit trailing the others momentarily before catching up. Spread out, they descended to where the makeshift baskets waited, found the Home Guard already in place, snatched up the retaining straps, lifted the baskets into the air, and sped away west toward the forests. It was all accomplished in a few moments, and then they were passing over the trees, far from the madness of the Federation camp, back into the shelter from which they had come.

When they set down again within the forest, Wren summoned her commanders to discover the extent of their own losses. The Rocs had passed through the strike unscathed. All of the Home Guard were safely returned save one. Only three of the Elven Hunters had been lost, cavalry pulled from their horses. There were a number of injuries, but only one was serious. The attack had been a complete success.

Wren thanked Triss, Desidio, and Erring Rift, and ordered the vanguard to pack up. They would slip north now before the Federation could begin to search for them, choosing a new spot within the Westland forests to hide. Come morning, they would scout the damage to the enemy and decide what to do next. Tonight had been a good beginning, but the end was still far from sight.

Quickly the Elves prepared to move out. Whispers of satisfaction and handclasps passed from man to man as they

worked. The Elves had fought their first battle in their home-
land in more than a hundred years and won. Morrowindl's
long night was finally behind them, and some small part of the
rage and frustration that they had lived with all their lives had
been released. For many, there was a renewed sense of being
set free.

Wren Elessedil understood. As Queen of the Elves that
night in more than name, as her grandmother's hope of what
she could be and Garth's promise of what she would be,
something in her had been set free as well. She could feel
the way the Elves looked at her. She could sense their respect.
She belonged to them now. She was one of them.

Within an hour, all was ready. In stealth and silence, the
Elves of Morrowindl's past melted away into the night.

18

After an hour's steady march, the Elves spent the remainder of that· night in a forest just north of the Pykon that was backed up against the larger mass of Drey Wood and faced south toward the plains on which the Federation camp was settled. All night they could see the fires from the burning siege machines and supply wagons lighting the horizon in a bright glow, and in the still of their forest concealment they could hear faint shouts and cries.

They slept fitfully and rose again at dawn to wash, eat, and be dispatched to their duties. Desidio sent riders north to Arborlon with news of the attack and Wren's personal request to Barsimmon Oridio that the balance of the army proceed south as soon as possible. Cavalry patrols were dispatched in all directions with orders to make certain that no other Southland force was in the field besides the one they knew about. Special attention was to be given to the garrisons within the cities of Callahorn. Wing Riders flew south to assess the extent of the damage inflicted in last night's strike, with a particular eye toward determining how soon the column would be able to move again. The day was clouded and gray, and the Rocs would fly unseen against the dark backdrop of the Westland mountains and forest. The remainder of the Elves, after seeing to the care and feeding of their animals and the cleaning and

231

repair of their battle gear, were sent back to sleep until mid-day.

Wren spent the morning with her commanders – Desidio, Triss, and Erring Rift. Tiger Ty had flown south, determined that any assessment made of the condition of the Federation army should be subject to his personal verification. Wren was both tired and excited, flushed with energy and taut with fatigue, and she knew that she needed a few hours' sleep herself before she would be clear-headed again. Nevertheless, she wanted her commanders – and especially Desidio, now that she had won him over – to start considering what their small force should do next. To a great extent, that depended on what the Federation did. Still, there were only so many possibilities, and Wren wanted to steer the thinking regarding those possibilities in the right direction. With luck the South-landers would be unable to start moving again for several days, and that would give the main body of the Elven army time to reach the Rhenn. But if they did begin to move, it would be up to Wren and the vanguard to find a way to slow them once more. Under no circumstances did she intend that they should do nothing. Standing fast was out of the question. They had won an important victory over their larger foe with last night's strike, and she did not intend to lose the advantage that victory had established. The Federation would be looking over its collective shoulder now; she wanted to keep it looking for as long as possible. It was important that her commanders think the same way she did.

She was satisfied she had accomplished this when they were done conferring, and she went off to sleep. She slept until it was nearing midday and woke to find Tiger Ty and the Wing Rider patrol returned. The news they carried was good. The Federation army was making no attempt to advance. All of its siege equipment and most of its supplies had been reduced to ashes. The camp was sitting exactly where they had left it last night, and all of the army's efforts seemed to be directed toward caring for the injured, burying the dead, and culling through what remained of their stores. Scouts were patrolling the perimeter and foraging parties were canvassing the countryside, but the main body of the army was still picking itself up off the ground.

Still, Tiger Ty wasn't satisfied.

'It's one thing to find them regrouping today,' he declared to Wren, out of hearing of the others. 'You expect them to sit tight after an attack like that one. They suffered real damage, and they need to lick their wounds a bit. But don't be fooled. They'll be doing what we're doing – thinking about how to react to this. If they're still sitting there tomorrow, it'll be time for a closer look. Because they'll be up to something by then. You can depend on it.'

Wren nodded, then led him off to join Triss for lunch. Triss, apprised of Tiger Ty's thinking, agreed. This was a seasoned army they faced, and its commanders would work hard at finding a way to take back the momentary advantage the Elves had won.

They had just finished eating when an Elven patrol rode in with a battered and disheveled Tib Arne in tow. The patrol had been scouting the low end of the Streleheim toward Callahorn when they had come across the boy wandering the plains in search of the Elves. Finding him alone and injured, they had picked him up and brought him directly here.

Tib was cut and bruised about the face, and covered from head to foot with dirt and dust. He was very distressed and could barely speak at first. Wren brought him over to sit, and cleaned off his face with a damp cloth. Triss and Tiger Ty stood close to listen to what he had to say.

'Tell me what happened,' she urged him after she had calmed him down sufficiently to speak.

'I am sorry, my queen,' he apologized, shamefaced now at his loss of control. 'I have been out there for a day and a night with nothing to eat or drink and I haven't had any sleep.'

'What happened to you?' she repeated.

'We were attacked, myself and the men you sent with me, not far from the Dragon's Teeth. It was night when they came, more than a dozen of them. We were camped, and they charged out at us. The men you sent, they fought as hard as they could. But they were killed. I would have been killed as well, but for Gloon. He came to my aid, striking at my attackers, and I ran away into the dark. I could hear Gloon's shriek, the shouts of the men fighting him, and then nothing. I hid in the darkness all night, then started back to find you. I was afraid to go on without Gloon, afraid that there were other patrols searching for me.'

'The shrike is dead?' Tiger Ty asked abruptly.

Tib dissolved into tears. 'I think so. I didn't see him again. I whistled for him when it was light, but he didn't come.' He looked at Wren, stricken. 'I'm sorry I failed you, my lady. I don't know how they found us so easily. It was as if they knew!'

'Never mind, Tib,' she comforted him, placing her hand on his shoulder. 'You did your best. I'm sorry about Gloon.'

'I know,' he murmured, composing himself once more.

'You'll stay here with us now,' she told him. 'We'll find another way to get word to the free-born, or if not, we'll just wait for them to find us.'

She ordered food and drink for the boy, wrapped him in a woolen blanket, then pulled Tiger Ty and Triss aside. They stood beneath a towering oak with acorn shells carpeting the forest floor and clouds screening away the skies overhead and leaving the light faint and gray.

'What do you think?' she asked them.

Triss shook his head. 'Those were experienced men that went with the boy. They shouldn't have been caught unprepared. I think they were either very unlucky or the boy is right and someone was waiting for them.'

'I'll tell you what I think,' Tiger Ty said. 'I think it's pretty hard to kill a war shrike even when you can see it, let alone when you can't.'

She looked at him. 'What does that mean?'

His frown deepened. 'It means that there's something about all this that bothers me. Don't you think this boy is an odd choice for the job of carrying word to us about the free-born?'

She stared at him wordlessly for a moment, considering. 'He's young, yes. But he would be less likely to be noticed because of it. And he seems confident enough about himself.' She paused. 'You don't trust him, Tiger Ty?'

'I'm not saying that.' The other's brows knitted fiercely. 'I just think we ought to be careful.'

She nodded, knowing better than to dismiss Tiger Ty's suspicion out of hand. 'Triss?'

The Captain of the Home Guard was tugging at the bindings on his broken arm. The sling had come off yesterday before the attack, and all that remained was a pair of narrow splints laced about his forearm.

He did not glance up as he tightened a loosening knot. 'I think Tiger Ty is right. It doesn't hurt to be careful.'

She folded her arms. 'All right. Assign someone to keep an eye on him.' She turned to Tiger Ty. 'I have something important I want you to do. I want you to pick up where Tib left off. Take Spirit and fly east. See if you can find the free-born and lead them here, just in case they're having trouble reaching us. It may take you several days, and you'll have to track them without much help from us. I don't have any idea where to tell you to start, but if there are five thousand of them they shouldn't be hard to find.'

Tiger Ty frowned anew. 'I don't like leaving you. Send someone else.'

She shook her head. 'No, it has to be you. I can trust you to make certain the search is successful. Don't worry about me. Triss and the Home Guard will keep me safe. I'll be fine.'

The gnarled Wing Rider shook his head. 'I don't like it, but I'll go if you tell me to.'

On the chance that he might encounter Par or Coll Ohmsford or Walker Boh or even Morgan Leah in his travels, she gave him a brief description of each and a means by which he could be certain who they were. When she had finished, she gave him her hand and wished him well.

'Be careful, Wren of the Elves,' he cautioned gruffly, keeping her hand firmly tucked in his own for a moment. 'The dangers of this world are not so different from Morrowindl's.'

She smiled, nodded, and he was gone. She watched him gather a pack of stores and blankets together, strap them atop Spirit, board, and wing off into the gray. She stared skyward for a long time after he was lost from sight. The clouds were turning darker. It would be raining by nightfall.

We'll need better shelter, she thought. We'll need to move.

'Call Desidio over,' she ordered Triss.

A heavy enough rain would mire the whole of the grasslands on which the Federation camped. It was too much to hope for, but she couldn't help herself.

Just give us a week, she begged, eyes fixed on the roiling gray. Just a week.

The first drop of rain splashed on her face.

The elven vanguard assembled, packed up, and moved back into the heavy trees within Drey Wood, there to wait for the storm to pass. It began to rain more heavily as the day edged toward nightfall, and by dusk it was pouring. The Wing Riders had tethered their Rocs apart from the horses, and the men had stretched canvas sheets between trees to keep themselves and their stores dry. The patrols had come in, returned from everywhere but Arborlon, with word that nothing was approaching from any direction and there was no sign of any other Federation force.

They ate a hot meal, the smoke concealed by the downpour, and retired to sleep. Wren was preoccupied with dozens of possibilities of what might happen next and thought she would be awake for hours, but she fell asleep almost instantly, her last conscious thought of Triss and the two Home Guard who stood watch close by.

It was still raining when she awoke, as steady as before. The skies were clouded, and the earth was sodden and turning to mud. It rained all that day and into the next. Scouts went forth to check on the Federation army's progress and returned to advise that there was none. As Wren had hoped, the grasslands were soggy and treacherous, and the Southland army had pulled up its collective collar and was waiting out the storm. She remembered Tiger Ty's admonition not to be fooled into thinking that the Federation was doing nothing simply because it was not moving, but the weather was so bad that the Wing Riders did not wish to fly and there was little to discover while they were grounded.

Word arrived from Arborlon that the main body of the Elven army was still several days from being ready to begin its march south. Wren ground her teeth in frustration. The weather wasn't helping the Elves either.

She spent some of her time with Tib, curious to know more about him, wondering if there was any basis for Tiger Ty's suspicions. Tib was open and cheerful, except when Gloon was mentioned. Encouraged by her attention, he was eager to talk about himself. He told her he had grown up in Varfleet, subsequently lost his parents to the Federation prisons, had been recruited by the free-born to help in the Resistance, and had lived with the outlaws ever since. He carried messages mostly, able to pass almost anywhere because he looked as if he wasn't a danger to anyone. He laughed about that, and made Wren laugh, too. He said he had traveled north once or twice to the outlaw strongholds in the Dragon's Teeth, but hadn't gone there to live because he was too valuable in the cities. He spoke glowingly of the free-born cause and of the need to free the Borderlands from Federation rule. He did not speak of the Shadowen or indicate that he knew anything about them. She listened carefully to everything he said and heard nothing that suggested Tib was anything other than what he claimed.

She asked Triss to speak with the boy as well so that he might decide. Triss did, and his opinion was the same as her own. Tib Arne seemed to be who and what he claimed. Wren was persuaded. After that, she let the matter drop.

The rain ended on the third day, disappearing at midmorning as clouds dispersed and skies cleared into bright sunlight. Water dripped off leaves and puddled in hollows, and the air turned steamy and damp. Desidio sent riders back to the plains, and Erring Rift dispatched a pair of Wing Riders south. The Elves moved out of the deep forest to the edge of the grasslands and settled down to wait.

The scouts and the Wing Riders returned at midday with varying reports. The Elven Hunters had found nothing, but the Wing Riders reported that the Federation camp was being struck, and the army was preparing to move. As it was already midday, it was uncertain as to what this meant since the army could not hope to progress more than a few miles before dusk. Wren listened to all the reports, had them repeated a second time, thought the matter through, then summoned Erring Rift.

'I want to go up for a look,' she advised him. 'Can you choose someone to take me?'

The black-bearded Rift laughed. 'And have to face Tiger Ty if something goes wrong? Not a chance! I'll take you myself, my queen. That way if anything bad happens at least I won't be around to answer for it!'

She told Triss what she was about, declined his offer to accompany her, and moved to where Rift was strapping himself onto Grayl. Tib caught up with her, wide-eyed and anxious, and asked if he might go as well. She laughed and told him no, but spurred by his mix of eagerness and disappointment promised that he might go another time.

Minutes later she was winging her way southward atop

238

Grayl, peering down at the damp canopy of the forests below and the windswept carpet of the grasslands east. Mist rose off the land in steamy waves, and the air shimmered like bright cloth. Grayl sped quickly down the forest line past the Pykon until they were within sight of the Federation army. Rift guided the Roc close against the backdrop of trees and mountains, keeping between the Southlanders and the glare of the midafternoon sun.

Wren peered down at the sprawling camp. The report had been right. The army was mobilizing, packing up goods, forming up columns of men, and preparing to move out. Some soldiers were already under way, the lead-most divisions, and they were heading north. Whatever else the Elf attack might have done, it had not discouraged the army's original purpose. The march to Arborlon was under way once more.

Grayl swept past, and as Rift was about to swing the giant Roc back again, Wren caught his arm and gestured for them to continue on. She was not sure what she was looking for, only that she wanted to be certain she wasn't missing anything. Were there riders coming up from the Southland cities, reports being exchanged, reinforcements being sent? Tiger Ty's warning whispered in her ear.

They flew on, following the muddy ribbon of the Mermidon where it flowed south out of the Pykon along the plains before turning east above the Shroudslip toward Kern. The grasslands stretched away south and east, empty and green and sweltering in the summer heat. The wind blew across her face, whipping at her eyes until they teared. Erring Rift hunched forward, hands resting on Grayl's neck, as steady as stone, guiding by touch.

Ahead, the Mermidon swung sharply east, narrowed, and then widened again as it disappeared into the grasslands. The river was sluggish and swollen by the rains, clogged with debris from the mountains and woodlands, churning its way steadily on through its worn channel.

On the river's far bank a glint of sunlight reflected off metal as something moved. Wren blinked, then touched Rift's shoulder. The Wing Rider nodded. He had seen it, too. He slowed Grayl's flight and guided the Roc closer to the concealment of the trees by the northern edge of the Irrybis.

Another glint of light flashed sharply, and Wren peered ahead carefully. There was something big down there. No, several somethings, she corrected. All of them moving, lumbering along like giant ants . . .

And then she got a good look at them, hunched down at the riverbank as they prepared to cross at a narrows, coming out of the Tirfing on their way north.

Creepers.

Eight of them.

She took a quick breath, seeing clearly now the armored bodies studded with spikes and cutting edges, the insect legs and mandibles, the mix of flesh and iron formed of the Shadowen magic.

She knew about Creepers.

Rift swung Grayl sharply back into the trees, away from the view of the things on the riverbank, away from the revealing sunlight. Wren glanced back over her shoulder to make certain she had not made a mistake. Creepers, come out of the Southland, sent to give aid to the Federation army that marched on Arborlon – it was the Shadowen answer to her disruption of the Federation army's march. She remembered the history Garth had taught her as a child, a history that the people of the Four Lands had whispered rather than told for more than fifty years, tales of how the Dwarves had resisted the Federation advance into the Eastland until the Creepers had been sent to destroy them.

Creepers. Sent now, it seemed, to destroy the Elves.

A pit opened in the center of her stomach, chill and dark. Erring Rift was looking at her, waiting for her to tell him what to do. She pointed back the way they had come. Rift nodded and urged Grayl ahead. Wren stole a final look back and watched the Creepers disappear into the heat.

Gone for the moment, she thought darkly.

But what would the Elves do when they reappeared?

19

Walker Boh blinked. It was a crystalline clear day, the
kind of day in which the sunlight is so bright and the
colors so brilliant that it almost hurts the eyes to
look. The skies were empty of clouds from horizon to horizon,
a deep blue void that stretched away forever. Out of that void
and those skies blazed the sun at midday, a white-hot glare that
could only be seen by squinting and quickly looking away
again. It flooded down upon the Four Lands, bringing out the
colors of late summer with startling clarity, even the dull
browns of dried grasses and dusty earth, but especially the
greens of the forests and grasslands, the blues of the rivers and
lakes, and the iron grays and burnt coppers of the mountains
and flats. The sun's heat rose in waves in those quarters where
winds did not cool, but even there everything seemed etched
and defined with a craftsman's precision, and there was the
sense that even a sharp cry might shatter it all.

It was a day for living, where all the promises ever made
might find fulfillment and all the hopes and dreams conceived
might come to pass. It was a day for thinking about life, and
thoughts of death seemed oddly out of place.

Walker's smile was faint and bitter. He wished he could find
a way to make such thoughts disappear.

He stood alone outside Paranor's walls, just at their northwest corner beneath a configuration in the parapets that jutted

out to form a shallow overhang, staring out across the sweep of the land. He had been there since sunrise, having slipped out through the north gates while the Four Horsemen were gathered at the west sounding their daily challenge. Almost six hours had passed, and the Shadowen hadn't discovered him. He was cloaked once again in a spell of invisibility. The spell had worked before, he had argued to Cogline while laying out his plan. No reason it shouldn't work again.

So far, it had.

Sunlight washed the walls of the Dragon's Teeth, chasing even the most persistent of shadows, stripping clean the flat, barren surface of the rocks. He could see north above the tree-line to the empty stretches of the Streleheim. He could see east to the Jannisson and south to the Kennon. Streams and ponds were a glimmering of blue through the trees that circled the Keep, and songbirds flew in brilliant bursts of color that surprised and delighted.

Walker Boh breathed deeply the midday air. Anything was possible on a day like this one. Anything.

He was dressed in loose-fitting gray robes cinched about his waist, the hood pulled down so that his black hair hung loose to his shoulders. He was bearded, but trimmed and combed. Nothing of this was visible, of course. To anyone passing, and particularly to the Shadowen, he was just another part of the wall. Rest and nourishment had restored his strength. The wounds he had suffered three days earlier were mostly healed, if not forgotten. He did not give thought to what had befallen him then except in passing. He was focused on what was to happen now, this day, this hour.

It was the tenth day of the Shadowen siege. It was the day he meant for that siege to end.

He glanced back over his shoulder along the castle wall as another of the Four Horsemen circled into view. It was Famine, edging around the turn that would take it along the north wall, skeletal frame hunched over its serpent mount, looking neither left nor right as it proceeded, lost in its own peculiar form of madness. Gray as ashes and ephemeral as smoke, it slouched along the pathway. It passed within several feet of Walker Boh and did not look up.

Today, the newest of the Druids thought to himself.

He looked out again across the valley, thinking of other times and places, of the history that had preceded him, of all the Druids who had come to Paranor and made it their home. Once there had been hundreds, but they had all died save one when the Warlock Lord had trapped them there a thousand years ago. Bremen alone had survived to carry on, a solitary bearer of hope for the Races and wielder of the Druid magic. Then Bremen had passed away, and Allanon had come. Now Allanon was gone, and there was only Walker Boh.

The empty sleeve of his missing arm was drawn back and pinned against his body. He reached across to test the fitting, to touch experimentally his shoulder and the scarred flesh that ended only inches below. He could barely remember any more what it had been like to have two arms. It seemed odd to him that it should be so difficult. But much had happened to him in the weeks since his encounter with the Asphinx, and it might be argued that he could not be expected to remember anything of his old life, so completely had he changed. Even the anger and mistrust he had felt for the Druids had dissipated, useless now to one who had become their successor. The Druids he had despised belonged to the past. Gone, too, was the fury he had borne for the Grimpond, relegated to that same past. The Grimpond had tried its best to destroy him and failed. It would not have another chance. The Grimpond was a shadow in a shadowland. It could never come out, and Walker would never go back to see it. The past had carried away Pe Ell and the Stone King as well. Walker had found the strength to survive all of the enemies that had been set against him, and now they were memories that barely mattered in the scheme of his life's present demands.

Walker breathed the air, closed his eyes, and drifted away into a place deep inside him. War was passing now, all sharp edges and spikes, glinting armored plates and black breathing holes. Walker ignored the Shadowen. Settling into the silence and the calm that lay within, he played out once more what was to happen. Step by step, he went over the plan he had formed while he lay healing, taking himself through the events he would precipitate and the consequences he would control. There would be nothing left to chance this time. There would be no testing, no halfway measures, no quarter given. He would succeed, or he would . . .

He almost smiled.

Or he would not.

He opened his eyes and glanced skyward. The midday was past now, edging on toward afternoon. But the light was not yet at its brightest and the heat not yet at its greatest, and so he would wait a little longer still. Light and heat would serve him better than it would the Shadowen, and that was why he was out there at midday. Before, he had thought to slip away in darkness. But darkness was the ally of the Horsemen, for they were creatures born of it and took their strength therefrom. Walker, with his Druid magic, would find his strength in brightness.

It was to be a testing of strengths, after all, that would determine who lived and died this day.

Strengths of all kinds.

He remembered his last conversation with Cogline. It was nearing dawn and he was preparing to go out. There was movement on the steps leading down through the gate towers to the entry court where he was positioned, and Cogline appeared. His stick-thin body slipped from the stairwall shadows in a soft flutter of robes and labored breathing. The seamed, whiskered face glanced at Walker briefly from beneath the edges of his frayed cowl, then looked away again. He approached and stopped, turning toward the door that led out.

'Are you ready?' he asked.

Walker nodded. They had discussed it all – or as much of it

as Walker was willing to discuss. There was nothing more to say.

The old man's hands rested on the stone bulwarks that shielded and supported the iron-bound entry, so thin that they seemed almost transparent. 'Let me come with you,' he said quietly.

Walker shook his head. 'We have discussed this already.'

'Change your mind, Walker. Let me come. You will have need of me.'

He sounded so sure, Walker recalled thinking. 'No. You and Rumor will wait here. Stay by the door – let me back in if this fails.'

Cogline's jaw tightened. 'If this fails, you won't need me to let you back in.'

True, Walker thought. But that didn't change things. He wasn't going to let the old man and the moor cat go out there with him. He wasn't going to be responsible for their lives as well. It would be enough that he would have to worry about keeping himself whole.

'You think I can't look after myself,' the old man said, as if reading his thoughts. 'You forget I took care of myself for years before you came along – before there were any Druids. I took care of you as well, once.'

Walker nodded. 'I know that.'

The old man fidgeted. 'Could be I was meant to take care of you again, you know. Could be you'll have need of me out there.' He turned his face within the cowl to look at Walker. 'I'm an old man, Walker. I've lived a long time – lived a full life. It doesn't matter so much what happens to me anymore.'

'It matters to me.'

'It shouldn't. It shouldn't matter a whit.' Cogline was emphatic. 'Why should it matter? Since when did you like me all that much anyway? I was the one who dragged you into this business. I was the one who persuaded you to visit the Hadeshorn, then to read the Druid History. Have you forgotten?'

246

Walker shook his head. 'No, I haven't forgotten any of it. But it was me who made the choices that mattered – not you. We've talked all this out, too. You were as much a pawn of the Druids as I was. Everything was decided three hundred years ago when Allanon bestowed the blood trust on Brin Ohmsford. You are not to blame for any of it.'

Cogline's eyes turned filmy and distant. 'I am to blame for everything that has happened in my life and yours as well, Walker Boh. I chose early on to take up the Druid way and chose after to discard it. I chose the old sciences to learn, to recover in small part. I made myself a creature of both worlds, Druid and Man, taking what I needed, keeping what I coveted, stealing from both. I am the link between the past and the present, the new and the old, and Allanon was able to use me as such. How much of what I am has made your own transformation possible, Walker? How far would you have gone without me there to prod you on? Do you think for a moment that I wasn't aware of that? Or that Allanon was blind to it? No, I cannot be absolved from my blame. You cannot absolve me by taking it upon yourself.'

Walker remembered the vehemency in the other's voice, the hard edge it had revealed, the insistence it had conveyed. 'Then I shall not attempt to absolve you, old man,' he replied. 'But neither shall I absolve myself. You did not make the choices for me; nor did you hinder me in making them. Yes, there were compelling reasons to choose as I did, but those reasons were not suggested by you before I had considered them myself. Besides, I could claim as you do, if I wished. Without me, what part would you have had in all of this? Would you have been more than a messenger to Par and Wren if you had not been tied to me as well? I don't think that you can say so.'

The old man's face was lowered into shadow by then, seeing the other's inflexibility, hearing his resolve.

'You will help me best by waiting here,' Walker finished, reaching out to touch the other's arm. 'Always before, you

247

have understood the importance of knowing when to act and when not to. Do so again for me now.'

It had ended there, Cogline standing with him until the sound of the Shadowen challenge had reverberated through Paranor's stone walls and Walker had gone out into the gloomy dawn to meet it.

Strengths of all kinds, he repeated as he stood now in the lee of the castle wall and listened to the approach of the next of the circling Shadowen. He would need especially a resolve of the sort that Cogline possessed – a fierce determination not to give in to the hardest and most certain of life's dictates – if he was to survive this day. Famine, Pestilence, War, and Death – the Four Horsemen of the Apocalypse, come to claim his soul. But on this day he was Fate, and Fate would determine the destiny of all.

He looked up as Pestilence appeared, then straightened perceptibly. It was time.

Walker Boh waited in the shadow of the wall, an invisible presence, while the Horseman approached. It came disinterestedly, lethargically, borne on its serpent mount, a swarm of buzzing, plague-ridden insects gathered in the shape of a man. Pestilence lacked features and therefore expression, and Walker could not tell what it was seeing or thinking. It passed without slowing, serpent claws scraping roughly on the path. Walker fell into step behind it. The spell of invisibility kept him from being seen, and the sound of the serpent's own passage kept him from being heard. Walker had considered using the spell of invisibility to slip clear of the Shadowen entirely. But they had been quick enough to find him when he had tried to escape through Paranor's underground tunnels, even though he had been as silent as thought, and he believed that they could sense him when he was far enough from the Keep, from his sanctuary and the source of his Druid power. Even invisibility might not protect him then. Better, he had decided, to use his advantage where it could be relied upon and put an end to the Horsemen once and for all.

In the wake of Pestilence he circled the castle walls, the silence of midday broken only by the scrabble of serpent claws and the buzzing of caged insects. They moved out of the cooler north wall and down along the west, passing the gates at which each morning the Horsemen gathered to issue challenge to him. He had chosen the north wall in which to hide, aware that he would be out there for hours in the heat, hoping that the castle's lee shadows might give him some protection. But the south wall was where he would fight these Shadowen – south, where the sunlight was strongest. Already it was brightening ahead as they passed from the last shade offered by the castle ramparts and edged out into the light.

They rounded the corner of the south wall, a towering, flat expanse of burning stone that faced out across a broad sweep of forestland towards the densely clustered peaks of the Dragon's Teeth. A worn, dusty stretch of bluff offered what passageway there was below the wall, barren save for a smattering of scrub and a few stunted trees that fell away in a steep slide toward the cooler woodlands. The heat rose in a swelter that threatened to suck the air from Walker's lungs, but he held himself steady against the burning rush, trailing Pestilence at the same distance, catching sight momentarily of Famine far ahead disappearing into the shadows formed by the parapet arch beneath the eastern fasthold.

The seconds slipped away. Walker could feel the tension build inside. Be patient, he reminded himself. Wait until it is time.

Within, his magic began to come together.

When Pestilence was midway between the near watchtower and the south gates, Walker Boh struck. Still concealed within the spell of invisibility, he unleashed a thunderbolt at Pestilence that sent both rider and mount tumbling to the earth. The Horseman tried to rise, and Walker struck again, the magic a cool heat lancing from his hands, slamming the Shadowen backward in shock. Already Walker could hear the sound of the others coming, a shriek in his mind. Already he could feel their anger.

Famine appeared first, wheeling through the arch of the fasthold that had momentarily swallowed it, closer to the struggle than the others. Skeletal frame hunched low, bony hands stretched forth, the Horseman charged ahead. But there was a cloud of dust and smoke in its way, stirred by Walker in anticipation of its coming, and it could not see clearly what was happening. When it broke through the screen, it found itself right on top of its prey. Walker Boh was struggling with Pestilence, grappling with the Shadowen, trying to wrest it from atop its writhing serpent, fighting to keep either from rising.

Famine swept past, finger bones raking Walker across the face.

Missing him completely.

Catching Pestilence instead. And being caught by the other in turn.

Both of the Horsemen screamed as the magic of each attacked the other. Pestilence fell back, weakened by hunger and want. Famine lurched away, sickened and retching.

Fire exploded out of the stone walls between them, dealing Famine a ferocious blow that sent the Shadowen reeling.

Now War appeared, come around the west end of the wall, the huge mace raised overhead as the Horseman thundered to the fray. Its serpent breathed flames, and there was a glimmer of fire in the eye slits beneath the armor. It saw Walker Boh clearly, saw the Druid grappling with Famine, and it attacked at once. It might have heard Famine scream in warning, but if it did it failed to heed. It brought the mace down with a crunching blow, intending to finish Walker Boh with a single pass. But Walker had disappeared, and the blow struck Famine instead, hammering right through the Shadowen and deep into his serpent. Famine wailed in anguish and collapsed in a pile of bones. Serpent and rider lay unmoving in the dust.

War wheeled back, and suddenly there were plague flies all over it, stinging and biting past weapons and armor. War shrieked, but the strike was quick and certain. Pestilence had seen Walker Boh dodge the blow that had felled Famine, seen him launch himself onto War and begin to strangle the Shadowen. Pestilence, dazed and battered, had reacted out of instinct, sending fever and sickness in a swift counterattack. But somehow things had gone awry; it was not Walker Boh who was struck, but the Horseman War.

Flattened against the castle wall, Walker withdrew the image of himself into a cloud of dust behind the thrashing War and sent a bolt of fire into Pestilence that threw the Shadowen from his mount completely. The entire stretch of bluff was a haze of dust and heat thrown up by the twisting, snarling serpents and their maddened riders. The images were an old trick, one that a young Jair Ohmsford had perfected three centuries ago in his battle with the Mord Wraiths. Walker had remembered and used the trick to good purpose this day, sending the Shadowen wheeling this way and that, overlaying an image of himself on first one and then another, all the while keeping his back firmly planted against the castle wall.

Mirrors and light, but it was proving to be enough.

Stricken with a dozen killing fevers, War wheeled its serpent about. Walker Boh had appeared again, straddling the fallen Pestilence, trying to smother the Shadowen. War charged, half-blinded and crazed, a great battle-axe drawn. It was on the Druid in seconds, and the axe swept down, cutting him apart.

Except that he wasn't there again, and the blade sliced through Pestilence and his serpent instead.

From his place against the castle wall, Walker sent fire hammering into War. The Shadowen went down, separated from his mount. When the mount tried to rise, Walker burned it to ash.

The mounts, he had discovered, did not share their riders'

resiliency. And the Four Horsemen, while able to recover from his magic, were not immune to their own. He had not missed the way they had attacked him each time out – one at a time, one after the other, never all at once. A sustained rush would have finished him, and there had been none. The Four Horsemen were deadly not only to their enemies, but to one another. Flawed imitations of the legends, their magics were anathema. He had counted on that. He had depended on it like he had depended on the midday light and heat weakening these things born of darkness. He had been right.

There was a desperate thrashing from where War lay writhing within its armor, fighting the sickness that raged through it. Famine and Pestilence were unmoving heaps. Their serpents lay still beside them, greenish ichor seeping from their bodies into the ground. The hazy air was clearing, dust and grit settling to the earth. Patches of sky and mountain and forest were coming back into view.

Walker stepped away from the wall. One left. Where was –

The weighted black cord whistled out of the haze with a hawk's shriek, slamming into Walker and whipping about him as he sagged from the blow. Tangled, he dropped to his knees, then fell onto his back. Instantly Death appeared, riding out of the sunlight's glare, the great scythe lifted. Walker gulped air into his stinging lungs. How could it have found him? How could it have seen where he was? The Horseman was bearing down on him, its serpent's claws scrabbling viciously on the rocky earth. Walker lunged back to his knees, fighting to get free. It must have come up more cautiously than the others. It must have seen him burn War's serpent, traced the fire to its source, and guessed where he was hiding.

Walker dropped the spell of invisibility, useless to him now that he had been discovered, and summoned the Druid fire in a blinding whirlwind that cut Death's cord to ribbons. Just as the Horseman reached him, Walker struggled to his feet, threw up a protective shield, and deflected the scythe as it swept down. Even so, the force of the blow knocked him sprawling. He lurched to his feet again as the Shadowen wheeled back. Walker braced. There was no one left to fight this battle for him; he had taken the image trick as far as it would go. This time he must stand alone.

He summoned the fire again. Death against Fate.

Walker crouched.

The Horseman swept past a second time, and Walker sent the fire burning into it. Death reeled away, the scythe's blade deflected just enough that it missed. But the air turned chilly at its passing, and Walker felt a wave of nausea rush through him.

Back around swung the Shadowen, and Walker counterattacked at once, the Druid fire lancing from his extended hand. Up came the scythe, catching the fire and shattering it. Death urged the serpent forward, sending it at Walker once more. Again and again Walker struck out, but the fire would not penetrate the Horseman's defenses. Death was almost on top of him now, the serpent hissing balefully through the dust and heat, the scythe glinting. Walker realized suddenly that Death had changed the form of its attack and meant simply to ride him down. Instantly he shifted the focus of the Druid fire, striking the serpent's legs, cutting them out from underneath, striking next the writhing body until everything was a mass of smoking flesh.

The serpent shuddered, twisted aside, lost its balance, and went tumbling forward. Walker threw himself out of the way as the monstrous beast slid past, engulfed in flames, screaming in fury. The tail thrashed wildly, catching Walker across the chest and slamming him down against the earth. Dust rose in clouds to mingle with the smoke from the serpent's charred body, and everything disappeared in a blinding haze.

Battered and bloodied, his robes torn, Walker forced himself to his feet. To one side the serpent lay dying, its breathing an uneven rasp in the sudden silence. Walker peered about, searching the haze.

Then Death appeared behind him, scythe swinging wickedly for his head. Walker threw up the Druid fire and blocked the strike, then straightened to meet Death's rush. His good hand locked on the handle of the scythe, and his body pressed up against Death's. Paralyzing cold surged through him. The Shadowen's cowled head lowered as they lurched back and forth across the bluff, the strange red eyes fixing him, drawing him slowly in. Walker turned his face aside quickly and sent the Druid fire spinning out from his hand and down the scythe's haft. Death jerked back, cowl lifting to the light, empty within save for the crimson eyes. One hand left the scythe and struck out at Walker, knocking him backward. Walker shrank from the blow, feeling the cold spread through him anew. His magic was failing him. Again Death struck out, a vicious blow to his throat. Walker released his hold on the scythe and fell away.

Death strode forward purposefully, a terrible blackness against the haze. Walker rolled to his knees, pain washing through him as he clutched at his chest, fighting for breath.

The blade of the scythe rose and fell.

Then suddenly Cogline was between them, come out of nowhere, a scarecrow figure, worn robes flapping and wispy hair flying. He caught the handle of the scythe and turned the blow aside, sending the blade slicing deep into the earth beside Walker. Walker twisted away and tried to regain his feet, yelling at the old man. But Cogline had thrown himself on the Shadowen and forced him further back. Death had one hand on Cogline's throat and the other on the handle of the blade, lifting it to strike. The old man was determined, fighting with every ounce of strength he possessed, but the Shadowen was too much. Slowly Cogline was forced back, the hand on his throat bending him away, the other hand shifting to get a better grip on the scythe. *Get away!* Walker pleaded in a silent mouthing, unable to speak the words. *Cogline, get away!*

Walker staggered to his feet, fighting through his exhaustion and pain, reaching down inside for the last of his strength.

Cogline's stick-thin frame was bending like deadwood in a high wind, crumpling beneath the Shadowen onslaught. Then suddenly he cried out, his hand snatched a handful of the black powder he carried from his robe, and he threw it at the Horseman with a curse.

At the same instant, the scythe swept down.

The powder exploded through Death in a flash of fire and sound, catching Cogline as well, sending both flying. Walker flinched away from the blast and the sudden glare and the glimpse of tattered bodies. Then he was stumbling forward, summoning the magic as he went, building the Druid fire in his fist. He saw Death rise from the dust, black-cloaked form singed and smoking, bits of flame spurting from the ends of its sleeve. The scythe lay shattered on the ground beside it, and its red eyes flared as it reached for what remained.

Walker sent the fire lancing into the Shadowen, down through the faceless hood, down into what lived inside. Death lurched back, stricken. Walker kept coming, the fire hammering with relentless purpose, burning and burning more. Death reeled away, trying to flee. But there was no escape. Walker caught up to it, jammed his fist into the twisting cowl, and sent everything he had left down inside.

Death shuddered once and exploded in flames.

Walker fell back, yanking his arm clear and twisting away from the light and the heat. His allies, light and heat, he thought dazedly – what he knew the Shadowen could not survive. He looked back once. Death burned in tatters on the dusty ground, lifeless and still.

Walker Boh went back then to where Cogline lay sprawled on the earth in a crumpled heap. Gently he turned the old man over, kneeling to straighten out his arms and legs and to place the blackened, singed head in his lap. Cogline's hair and beard were mostly burned away. There was blood leaking from his mouth and nostrils. He had been too close to the fire to escape what it would do.

Walker felt a tightening in his chest. The old man had

known that, of course. He had known it and used the powder anyway.

Cogline's eyes opened, startlingly white against the blackened skin. 'Walker?' he breathed.

Walker nodded. 'I'm here. It's over, old man. They are finished – all of them.'

A rattle of breath ended in a gasping for air. 'I knew you would need me.'

'You were right. I did.'

'No.' Cogline's hand reached up and gripped his arm possessively. 'I *knew*, Walker.' He coughed up blood, and his voice strengthened. 'I was told. By Allanon. At the Hadeshorn, when he warned me that my time was gone, that my life was ending. Remember, Walker? I told you only part of what I learned that day. The part about the Druid Histories. There was more that I kept secret from you. You would have need of me, I was told. I would be given a little time, here, in Paranor, to be with you. I would stay alive long enough to be of use once more.'

He coughed, doubling over with pain. 'Do you understand?'

Walker nodded. He recalled how distant and withdrawn the old man had seemed within the Druid's Keep. Something had changed, he had thought, but consumed by his struggle to escape the Shadowen he had not taken time to discover what. Now it was clear. Cogline had known his life was almost over. Allanon had given him a reprieve from death, but not a pass. The magic of the Druid Histories had saved him at Hearthstone so that he could die at Paranor. It was a trade the old man had been willing to make.

Walker glanced down at the ruined body. Where the scythe had cut through him, there was frost woven in silver streaks through the fabric of his robes.

'You should have told me,' he insisted quietly. There were tears in his eyes. He did not know when they had come. Some part of him remembered being able to cry once, a long time ago. He did not understand why he was able to do so now, but did not think after this that he would ever do so again.

256

Cogline shook his head, a slow and painful movement. 'No. A Druid doesn't tell what he doesn't have to.' He coughed again. 'You know that.'

Walker Boh couldn't speak. He simply stared down at the old man.

Cogline blinked. 'You told me that I always knew when to act and when not to.' He smiled. 'You were right.'

He swallowed once more. Then his eyes fixed and he quit breathing. Walker kept staring down at him, kneeling in the dust and heat, listening to the silence as it stretched away unbroken, thinking in bitter consolation that Allanon had used the old man for the last time.

He closed Cogline's sightless eyes.

It remained to be seen if the Druid had used him well.

20

Walker Boh buried Cogline in the woods below Paranor, laying him to rest in a glade cooled by a stream that meandered through a series of shallow rapids, a glade sheltered by oaks and hickories whose leafy branches dappled a carpet of wildflowers and green grasses with shadowy patterns that would shift and change each day with the sun's passage west. It was a setting that reminded Walker of the hidden glens at Hearthstone where they had both loved to walk. He chose a place near the center of the glade where the spires of Paranor could be clearly seen. Cogline, who to the end had thought of himself as a Druid gone astray, had come home for good.

When he was finished with the old man, Walker stayed in the clearing. He was battered and worn, but the wounds that were deepest were those he couldn't see, and it gave him a measure of comfort to stand amid the ancient trees and breathe the forest air. Birds sang, a wind rustled the leaves and grasses, the stream rippled, and the sounds were soothing and peaceful. He didn't want to go back into Paranor just yet. He didn't want to go up past the blackened, charred remains of the Four Horsemen and their serpent mounts. What he wanted was to wipe away everything that had happened in his life like chalk from a board and start over. There was a bitterness within him that he could not resolve, which gnawed and scratched at him with the persistence of a hungry animal and refused to be chased. The bitterness had many sources – he did not care to list them. Mostly, of course, he was bitter with himself. He was always bitter with himself these days, it seemed, a stranger come out of nowhere, a man whose identity he barely recognized, an all-too-willing pawn for the wants and needs of old men a thousand years gone.

He sat in the glade by the stream, staring back across the clearing and the patch of fresh-turned earth where Cogline lay, and forced himself to remember the old man. His bitterness needed a balm; perhaps memories of the old man would provide it. He took a moment to splash handfuls of the stream's cold water on his face, cleansing it of the dirt and ash and blood, then positioned himself in a patch of sun and let his thoughts drift.

Walker remembered Cogline as a teacher mostly, as the man who had come to him when his life had been jumbled and confused, when he had abandoned the Races to live in isolation at Hearthstone where he would not be stared at and whispered about, where he would not be known as the Dark Uncle. The magic had been a mystery to Walker then, the legacy of the wishsong come down through the years from Brin Ohmsford in a tangle of threads he could not unravel. Cogline had shown him ways in which he could control the magic so that he no longer would feel helpless before it. Cogline had taught him how to focus his life so that he was master of the white heat that roiled within. He removed the fear and the confusion, and he gave back to Walker a sense of purpose and self-respect.

The old man had been his friend. He had cared about him, had looked after him in ways that on reflection Walker knew were the ways that a father looked after a son. He had instructed and guided and been present when he was needed. Even when Walker was grown, and there was that distance between them that comes when fathers and sons must regard themselves as equals without ever quite believing it, Cogline stayed close in whatever ways Walker would allow. They had fought and argued, mistrusted and accused, and challenged each other to do what was right and not what was easy. But they had never given up on or forsaken each other; they had never despaired of their friendship. It helped Walker now to know that was so.

Sometimes it was easy to forget that the old man had lived other lives before this one, some of which Walker still barely knew about. Cogline had been young once. What had that been like? The old man had never said. He had studied with the Druids – with Allanon, with Bremen, with those who had gone before, perhaps, though he had never really said. How old was Cogline? How long had he been alive? Walker realized suddenly that he didn't know. Cogline had been an old man when Kimber Boh was a child and Brin Ohmsford came into Darklin Reach in search of the Ildatch. That was three hundred years ago. Walker knew about Cogline then; the old man had talked about that period of time, about the child he had raised, about the madness he had feigned and then embraced, about how he had led Brin and her companions to the Maelmord to put an end to the Mord Wraiths. Walker had heard those stories; yet it was such a small piece of the old man's life to know – one day of a year's time. What of all the rest? What parts of his life had Cogline failed to reveal – what parts that were now lost forever?

Walker shook his head and stared out across the trees at Paranor. Parts that the old man had not minded losing, he decided. Walker could not begrudge that Cogline had chosen to keep them secret. It was that way with everyone's life. All people kept parts of who and what they were and how they had lived to themselves, things that belonged only to them, things that no one else was meant to share. At death, those things were dark holes in the memories of those who lived on, but that was the way it must be.

He pictured the old man's whiskered face. He listened for the sound of his voice in the silence. Cogline had lived a long time. He had lived any number of lives. He had lived longer than he should have, spared at Hearthstone to come into Paranor and see it brought back again, and he had died in the way he chose, giving up his own life so that Walker could keep his. It would be wrong for Walker to regret that gift, because in regretting it he was necessarily diminishing its worth. Cogline had lived to see him transformed into the Druid the old man had never become. He had lived to see him through growing up to the dreams of Allanon and the fulfillment of Brin Ohmsford's trust. Whether it was for good or bad, Walker had gotten safely through because of Cogline.

He felt some of the bitterness beginning to fade. The bitterness was wrong. Regrets were wrong. They were chains that bound you tight and dragged you down. Nothing good could come of them. What was needed was balance and perspective if the future was to have meaning. Walker could remember – and should. But memories were for shaping what would come, for taking the possibilities that lay ahead and turning them to the uses for which they were intended. He thought again of the Druids and their machinations, of the ways they had shaped the history of the Races. He had despised their efforts. Now he was one of them. Cogline had lived and died so that he could be so. The chance was his to do better what he had been so quick to criticize in those who had gone before. He must make the most of that chance. Cogline would expect him to do so.

The sun was slipping beneath the canopy of the forest west when he rose and stood a final time before the ground in which the old man lay. He was better reconciled to what had happened than before, more at peace with the hard fact of it. Cogline was gone. Walker remained. He would take strength and courage and resolve from the old man's example. He would carry his memory in his heart.

With the light turning crimson and gold and purple in the haze of summer heat, he made his way back through the darkening forests to Paranor.

*   *   *

261

That night he dreamed of Allanon.

It was the first time he had done so since Hearthstone. His sleep was deep and sound, and the dream did not wake him though he thought afterward it might have come close once or twice. He was exhausted from his struggle, and he had eaten little. He had bathed, changed, then drank a cup of ale as he sat within the study that Cogline had favored. Rumor lay curled up at his feet, the luminous eyes glancing toward him now and then as if to ask what had become of the old man. When he had grown so tired he could barely hold himself upright, he had gone to his sleeping chamber, crawled beneath the blankets, and let himself drift away.

The dream seemed to come instantly. It was night, and he walked alone upon the shiny black rock that littered the floor of the Valley of Shale. The sky was clear and filled with stars. A full moon shone white as fresh linen against the jagged ridge of the Dragon's Teeth. The air smelled clean and new as it had of old, and a wind brushed his face with a cooling touch. Walker was dressed in black, robe and cowl, belt and boots, a Druid passing in the wake of Druids gone before. He did not question who he was, come out of the darkness of the Black Elfstone, come through the fire of the transformation in the well of the Keep, come back into the world of men. He was master of Paranor and servant to the Races. It was a strange, exhilarating feeling. The feeling seemed to belong.

Languid moments slipped past in the dream and then he neared the Hadeshorn, its waters black and still in the night. Like glass the lake shone in the moonlight, smooth and polished, reflecting the sky and the stars. The stone crunched beneath his feet as he walked, but beyond that single sound there was only silence. It was as if he were alone in the world, the last man to walk it, keeper of a solitary vigil over the emptiness that remained.

He reached the Hadeshorn and stopped, standing perfectly still at its edge. The wind died as he did so, and the silence pressed in about him. He reached up and pulled back the hood of his cloak; he did not know why. Head bared, he waited.

The wait lasted only a moment. Almost instantly the Hadeshorn began to churn, its waters boiling as if heated in a kettle. Then they began to swirl, a slow and steady clockwise sweep that extended from shoreline to shoreline. Walker recognized what was happening. He had seen it happen before. The Hadeshorn hissed, and spray lifted in geysers that towered above the surface and fell away in a tumble of diamonds. Wailing began, the sound of voices trapped in a faraway place, begging for release. The valley shuddered as if recognizing the cries, as if cringing away from them. Walker Boh held his ground.

Then Allanon appeared, rising out of the black waters to a chorus of cries, a cloaked and hooded gray ghost come out of the netherworld to speak with the man who had been chosen as his successor. He shimmered as he rose, translucent in the moonlight, the flesh and bone of his mortal body faded into dust long ago, a pale image of who he had been. He ascended from the depths until he stood upon the surface of the waters, there to settle into stillness facing out at Walker Boh.

'Allanon,' the Dark Uncle greeted in a voice he did not recognize as his own.

– You have done well, Walker Boh –

The voice was deep and sonorous, welling up from far inside some cavernous space within the shade.

Walker Boh shook his head. 'Not so well. Only adequately. I have done what I must. I have given up who I was for who you would have me be. I was angry at first that it should be so, but I have put that anger behind me.'

The waters of the Hadeshorn roiled and hissed anew as the shade came forward, gliding on the surface without seeming to move. It stopped when it was within ten feet of Walker.

– Life is a time for making choices, Walker Boh. Death is a time for remembering how we chose. Sometimes the memories are not always pleasant –

263

Walker nodded. 'I know that it must be so.'

– Are you sad for Cogline –

Walker nodded again. 'But that, too, is behind me. The choices he made were good ones. Even this last.'

The shade's arm lifted, trailing a glitter of spray that fell away like silver dust.

– I could not save him. Even Druids do not have the power to stay death. I was told by Bremen when my time was near. Cogline was told by me. I gave him what help I could – a chance to come back into the Four Lands with Paranor restored – a chance to help you one last time in your battle with the Shadowen. It was all I could do –

Walker did not speak, staring at the apparition, staring right through him, looking far away at events come and gone, at Cogline's final stand. Death had claimed the old man, but it had claimed him on his terms.

– If I could, I would give you back all those you have lost, Walker Boh. But I cannot. I can give you nothing of what is gone and nothing of what will yet be lost. A Druid's life sees many passings –

In his dream the valley was darkened by a wash of mistiness that swept like rain through a forest or clouds across the sun. It was a slow, soft passage, and it carried with it a sense that lives had come into being and run their course, all in a matter of seconds. There were faces, all unknown; there were voices that called out in laughter and pain. Time stretched away, hours to days, days to years, and Walker was there, unchanged, through it all, constantly left behind, eternally alone.

– It will be like that for you. Remember –

But Walker did not need to remember. He had Allanon's memories for that. The transformation had given them to him. He had the memories of all the Druids who had gone before. He knew what his life would be like. He understood what he was facing.

– Remember –

The shade's whisper brought time to a halt again, the Valley of Shale back into focus, and the flow of Walker's thoughts to bear on the dream's intent once more.

'Why am I here, Allanon?' he asked.

– You are complete now, Walker Boh. You have become what you were intended to be, and there is nothing more that remains to be done. You bear the Druid mantle; you will wear it in my stead. Carry it now from Paranor into the Four Lands. You are needed there –

'I know.'

Spray hissed and sang. Allanon's hooded face lowered.

– You do not know. You are transformed, Walker Boh, but that is only the beginning. You have become a Druid, yes – but becoming is not being. Yours is the responsibility of the Races, of their well-being, Dark Uncle. Those from whom you once sought to isolate yourself must now be your charge. They wait –

'To be free of the Shadowen.'

– For you to show them *how* to be free. For you to set them on the path. For you to guide them from the darkness –

Walker Boh shook his head, confused. 'But I don't know the way any better than they do.'

The surface of the Hadeshorn steamed, and the air was filled with mist. The dampness settled on Walker's face like the chill of an early winter's morning. It was death to touch the waters of the Hadeshorn, but not for him. For the Druids had discovered secrets long ago that enabled them to transcend death.

Allanon's voice was dark and certain.

– You will find the way. You have the strength and the wisdom of all those who have gone before. You have the magic of the ages. Take yourself out from Paranor and find the other children of Shannara. Each of you was sent to fulfill a charge. Each of you has done so. You are bearers of talismans, Walker Boh. Those talismans shall sustain you –

Walker shook his head in confusion. 'What talisman do I bear?'

The shade of Allanon shimmered momentarily in a wailing of cries that rose out of the lake, threatening to disappear.

– The most powerful talisman of all: the Druid mantle which you have assumed. It can never be seen, but it is always there and it is yours alone. Its power increases as you wield it; it strengthens with each use. Think, Walker Boh. Before you fought and destroyed the Horsemen, you were less than what you are now. So shall it be with each challenge you face and overcome. You are in your infancy, and you are just beginning to discover what it is to be a Druid. With time, you will grow –

'But for now . . . ?'

– The charges are enough. The charges yield talismans, and the talismans yield magic. Magic combined with knowledge shall see the end of the Shadowen. It was thus when I first spoke to you. It is thus now. If I could, I would give you more, Walker Boh. But I have given you all I can, all that I know. Remember, Dark Uncle. I am gone from your world and placed within another. I am without substance. I am now of other things. I see imperfectly from where I stand. I see only shadows of what would be and must rely on those. Yours is the vision that can be relied upon. Go, Walker. Find the scions of Shannara and discover what they have done. In their stories and in your own you will find what you need. You must believe –

Walker said nothing then, thinking for a moment that he was being asked once again to proceed on faith alone. But, of course, that was what he had been doing ever since the dreams had first appeared to him and he had been persuaded to travel to the Hadeshorn and Allanon. Was it really so difficult to accept that faith must guide him anew?

He looked at the pale figure before him, all lines about transparency, all memories of life gone before. 'I believe,' he said to Allanon's shade, and meant it.

– Walker Boh –

The shade's voice was soft and filled with regrets that words could not speak.

– Find the children of Shannara. You have the Druid sight. You have the wisdom they need. Do not fail them –

'No,' Walker said hoarsely. 'I will not.'

– Put an end to the Shadowen before they destroy the Four Lands completely. I feel their sickness spreading even here. They steal the earth's life. Stop them, Walker Boh –

'Yes, Allanon, I will.'

– Bend to me then, Dark Uncle. Bend to me one final time before you go. Sleep carries us towards daybreak, and we must travel different paths. Hear the last of what I would tell you, and let your wisdom and your reason divine what remains concealed from us both. Bend to me, Walker Boh, and listen –

The shade approached, steam upon the waters of the Hadeshorn in human shape, a cloaking of mist and gray light, a wraith formed of sounds come out of terrifying darkness.

Tense and uncertain, Walker Boh waited, eyes lowered to the boiling waters, to the reflection of stars and sky, until both disappeared in the blackness of shadow.

Then he felt the other's touch against his skin, and he shuddered uncontrollably.

He came awake at sunrise, the light a faint creeping from the hallway beyond his darkened room. He lay without moving for a time, thinking of the dream and what it had shown him. Allanon had sent the dream so that he would have a place to begin his new life. The dream had reinforced his intention to seek out Par and Wren, but it had also given him reason to believe in himself. He could accept who and what he had become if there was at least a chance that he could bring the ravaged lands and their people safely out of the Shadowen thrall.

Find the children of Shannara. Do not fail them.

He rose then from his bed, washed, dressed, and ate breakfast on the castle battlements looking out over the land in the light of the new day. He thought again of Cogline, of all that the old man had taught him. He recited to himself the litany of rules and understandings that his transformation from mortal man to Druid had given him, the whole of the history of the Druids come and gone. He worked his way carefully through the teachings of his magic's use – some already put to the test, some that remained untried.

Last of all, he recounted the events of the dream and the secrets it had shown him. And there had been secrets – a few, important ones, there at the last, when Allanon had touched him. What he had learned was already beginning to suggest answers to his heretofore-unanswered questions. The whole of the history of the Four Lands since the time of the First Council at Paranor formed a pattern for what was happening now. The events of weeks past gave color and shape to that pattern. But it was the dream and the insights with which it provided him that thrust that pattern into the light where it could be clearly seen.

What was missing still was the reason that Wren had been charged with bringing back the Elves.

What was missing was the reason Par had been sent to find the Sword of Shannara.

Most of all what was missing was the truth behind the secret of the Shadowen power.

He rose finally and went down into the depths of the castle, Rumor trailing silently, a shadow at his back. He would take the moor cat with him, he decided. Cogline had given him the cat, after all; it was his responsibility to see that it was looked after. It could not be left locked up within the Keep, and the closeness they shared might prove useful. He smiled as he examined his thinking. The truth was that Rumor would provide a little of the companionship he would miss without Cogline.

Down into the well of the Keep he descended, there to place his hands on the walls of stone, reaching inward to the life that rested there. The magic came to him, obedient to his summons, and he set in place a bar to any but himself so that none could enter until he returned.

Then he closed Paranor's gates and went out into the world again. He went down from the bluff and into the forests where the heat was screened away and it was shady and cool. Rumor went with him, grateful to be free again of the confining walls, slipping into the shadows to forage and track, returning now and again to Walker's side to be certain he was still there. They traveled north of the place where Cogline lay, and Walker did not turn aside. He had said goodbye already to the old man; it was best to leave it at that.

The day eased away toward nightfall, the sun's fiery glare slipping west toward the Dragon's Teeth, the heat dissipating slowly into the cool of the evening shadows. Walker and the moor cat traveled steadily on. Ahead, the watch fires of the Federation soldiers camped within the Kennon Pass were lit, meals were consumed, and guards sent to their posts.

By midnight Walker and the cat had slipped by them unseen and were on their way south.

21

The rains that had inundated the Westland Elves and the pursuing Federation army were still thunderheads on the western horizon the morning the two ragged scrapwomen led their elderly blind father through the gates of Tyrsis with the other tradesmen, merchants, drummers, peddlers, and itinerant hucksters who had come in from the outlying communities to barter their wares. As with most of the others that sought entry, they had spent the night camped before the gates, anxious to enter early so as to secure the best stalls in the open market where the trading and bartering took place. They shuffled along as quickly as they could manage, the women slowed by the old man as he groped his way uncertainly, supported on either side, his feet directed carefully along the dusty way.

Federation guards lined the entries through the outer and inner walls, checking everyone who passed, pulling aside those who seemed suspicious. It was unusual for them to worry about who was entering the city, for the emphasis in the past had been directed toward worrying about who might leave. But Padishar Creel, the leader of the free-born, was to be executed at noon of the following day, and the Federation was concerned that an attempt would be made to rescue him. It was believed that such a rescue would fail, no matter how well conceived, because the city garrison was at full strength, some five thousand men strong, and security measures were extraordinary. Still, nothing was to be left to chance, so the guards at the gates had been given explicit instructions to make certain of everyone.

They chose to pull aside the scrapwomen and the old man. It was a random selection, an approach the guard commander had settled on early, a compromise between stopping everyone, which would take forever, and no one, which would seem a dereliction of his duty. The three were ordered to stand apart from the throng, to occupy a space in the center of the court between the city's walls, there to wait for questioning. Scattered glances from the crowd were directed their way, furtive and suspicious. Better you than me, they seemed to say. Dust rose with the crowd's passing, and even now, before the heat of the day had settled in, the air had a hot, sticky feel to it.

'Names,' the duty officer said to the scrapwomen and the old man.

'Asra, Wintath, and our father, Criape,' the one with the ragged, tangled reddish hair said. Sores dappled the skin of her face, and she smelled like old rubbish.

The officer glanced at the other woman, who promptly opened her mouth to reveal blackened teeth and a raw, red throat in which the tongue was missing. The officer swallowed.

'She can't speak,' the first said, grinning.

'What's your village?'

'Spekese Run,' said the woman. 'Know of it?'

The officer shook his head. He studied the piles of rags they carried strapped to their backs. Worthless stuff. He glanced at the old man, whose head was lowered into his cowl. Couldn't see much of his face. The officer stepped forward and pushed back the cowl. The old man's head jerked up and his blackened lids snapped back to reveal a thick, milky fluid where his eyes should have been. The officer gagged.

'On with you.' He beckoned, moving quickly away to question the next unfortunate.

271

The women and the old man shuffled off obediently, slipping back into the crowd, passing through the cordon of guards that lined the gates of the inner wall, moving on from there into the city. They were well off the Tyrsian Way and into the side streets where there were no Federation guards before Matty Roh spit out the dyed fruit skin pasted to the inside of her mouth and said, 'I told you this was too risky!'

'We got through, didn't we?' Morgan snapped irritably. 'Stop complaining and get me where I can wash this stuff out of my eyes!'

'Be silent, the both of you!' Damson Rhee ordered, and hurried them on.

Tempers were short by now. They had fought bitterly about who was to come into the city, a fight precipitated by the news of Padishar Creel's impending execution. A day and a half was not nearly enough time to effect a rescue, but it was all they had to work with and Morgan had decided that his original plan needed changing. Instead of Matty and Damson going into the city and finding the Mole on their own, he would enter as well. At best they had today and tonight to track down the Mole, bring Chandos and the others of the free-born in through the underground tunnels, devise a rescue plan for Padishar, and set it in motion. Morgan insisted that he needed to get inside the city immediately in order to determine what must be done. He could not afford to wait for nightfall and the Mole to get a look at things. Damson and Matty were equally insistent that any attempt to sneak him past the guards would jeopardize them all. It would be hard enough for just the two of them, but doubly dangerous if they were forced to take him in as well. Why couldn't he do his thinking where he was? Hadn't he spent enough time in the city by now to know where everything was?

So it had gone, but in the end Morgan won the argument by pointing out that he couldn't do any thinking at all until he knew where Padishar was being kept, and he couldn't know that unless he went into the city. The price for his victory was an implacable demand by both women that he leave his Sword behind. A disguise would possibly work, but not if he carried that weapon. Chances of discovery were simply too great. Despite his protests, neither woman would budge. The Sword of Leah had stayed behind with Chandos.

Damson took them down an alleyway to a side door in an abandoned building, pushed open the door, and guided them inside. The interior was close and airless, and dust hung in the air in visible layers. She closed the door behind them. They moved across the room to a second door and from there into another room, equally stifling. A tiny courtyard opened beyond, and they crossed through the early morning shadows and the faint scent of wildflowers inexplicably growing in one sundrenched corner of the otherwise withered yard to an openfronted shed filled with old tools and workbenches. Damson left her companions there and went off with a tin bowl. When she returned, the bowl was filled with water, and the three sat down to wash themselves off.

When they were scrubbed clean again, they dug through the bundles of rags and pulled out their good clothes. Stripping off the old, they redressed and sat down on a pair of the workbenches to discuss what would happen next.

'I'll go out first to try to make contact with the Mole,' Damson said, still combing out the knots from her tangled red hair. Carefully she tied it all back and tucked it into a scarf. 'There are signs I can leave that he will understand. When that's done, I'll come back and we'll see what we can discover about Padishar. Then I'll have to put you somewhere while I go wait for the Mole. He might not come if he sees all of us – he doesn't know either of you and he will be very careful after what's happened. If he comes, he and I will go after Chandos and the rest, and we will meet up with you again by dawn. If he doesn't come – '

'Don't say it,' Morgan cut her short. 'Just do the best you can.'

Damson looked at Matty. 'How well do you know the city?'

'Well enough to stay out of trouble.'

Damson nodded. 'If anything happens to me, you will have to get Morgan out of here.'

'Wait a minute!' Morgan exclaimed. 'I'm not going to – '

'You are going to do what you are told. Your plans count for nothing if I fail. If the Federation has the Mole or if they capture me, there isn't anything more to be done.'

Morgan stared at her, silenced by the anger and determination he found in her green eyes.

Matty took his arm and moved him back a step. 'I'll look after him,' she promised.

Damson nodded, and her face softened a shade. She rose, wrapped her cloak about, gave them a short nod, and disappeared back the way she had come. Morgan stared after her, feeling helpless. She was right. There was nothing he could do if she failed. The success of any plan he devised depended on the girl and the Mole bringing Chandos and the free-born into the city. Without the free-born or the magic of his Sword, he would not be able to help Padishar. Such a slender thread for events to hang upon, he thought grimly.

'Care for something to eat?' Matty Roh asked cheerfully, her dark eyes questioning, and offered him an apple.

They waited within the shade of the storage shed, secluded and alone in the little, closed-about courtyard until almost mid-day. The air grew steamy and thick with heat, and the sun burned a slow trail across the stones and withered grass, climbing the north wall east to west like the spread of spilled paint. Morgan dozed for a time, weary from the long march in and the uncertain night sleeping before the gates in his uncomfortable disguise. He found himself thinking of Par and Coll and the days before the Shadowen and Allanon, of the times they had spent hunting and fishing in the Highlands, of his own boyhood, of the long slow days when life had seemed an exciting game. He thought of Steff and Granny Elise and Auntie Jilt. He thought of Quickening. They were memories of a past that lost a little of its color with the passing of every day. They all seemed to have disappeared from his life a very long time ago.

The sun was directly overhead when Damson Rhee finally returned. She was flushed with the heat and covered with dust, but there was excitement in her eyes.

'They have Padishar within the same watchtower where they held me,' she announced, dropping down on one of the benches and peeling off her cloak. She took a long drink from the cup of water Matty Roh offered her. 'It seems to be common knowledge. They plan to take him to the main gates at noon tomorrow and hang him in view of the city.'

'How is he?' Morgan asked quickly. 'Did anyone say?'

She shook her head, swallowing. 'No one has seen him. But talk among the soldiers is that he'll walk to his end.'

She glanced at Matty Roh. The other woman frowned. 'Common knowledge, is it?' She gave Damson a thoughtful look. 'I don't much trust common knowledge. Common knowledge often ends up meaning 'false rumor' in my experience.'

Damson hesitated. 'Everyone seemed so sure.' She cut herself short. 'But I guess we have to make certain, don't we?'

Matty Roh leaned forward, elbows on knees, chin in hands, her boyish face intense. 'You've told me how they used you to trap Padishar.' Morgan stared. This was the first he'd heard of that. How much more had Damson told her that he didn't know? 'It worked once, so chances are pretty good they'll try it again. But they'll change the rules. They'll make sure no one gets away this time. Instead of using live bait, maybe they'll use . . . common knowledge.'

Morgan nodded. He should have thought of that. 'A decoy. They expect a rescue attempt, so they misdirect it. They keep Padishar somewhere else.'

Matty nodded solemnly. 'I would guess.'

Damson came back to her feet. 'I've left signs for the Mole that he can't miss. If he's coming, he'll come tonight. I've got until then to go back out and try to find where Padishar really is.'

275

'I'm coming as well.' Morgan rose and reached for his cloak.

'No.' Matty Roh's voice was sudden and firm. She stood up and came between them. 'Neither of you is going.' She reached for her cloak. 'I am.' She looked at Morgan. 'You might be recognized, now that you've shed your disguise, and you can't go where you might learn anything in any case. You are better off staying here.' She turned to Damson. 'And you can't afford to risk yourself further. After all, they know who you are, too. It was chancy enough going out this morning. Whatever happens, you have to stay safe until you can meet the Mole and bring the others in. You can't do that if you're discovered and find yourself in Padishar Creel's company. Besides, I'm better at this sort of thing than you are. I know how to listen, how to find things out. Discovering secrets is what I do.'

They stared at her without speaking for a moment. When Morgan started to object, Damson silenced him with a look. 'She's right. Padishar would agree.'

Again Morgan tried to speak, but Damson overrode him, saying, 'We'll wait here for you, Matty. Be careful.'

Matty nodded and slung her cloak over her shoulder. Her slim face was tight and smooth across the set of her jaw. 'Don't wait if I'm not back by dark.' She gave Morgan a quick, ironic smile. 'Keep me safe in your thoughts, Highlander.'

Then she was across the courtyard and through the door of the room beyond and gone.

They waited for Matty Roh all day, hunched down in the shelter of the shed, trying to take what small comfort they could from the shade it provided. The sun passed slowly west, the heat building in its wake, the air still and dusty within the airless court.

To help pass the time, Morgan began telling Damson how Padishar and he had fought together against the Federation at the Jut. But talking of it did not ease his boredom as he had hoped. Instead it brought back a memory he had hoped forgotten – not of Steff or Teel or the Creeper or even his shattering battle within the catacombs, but of the terrible, frightening sense of incompleteness he had felt when deprived of the magic of the Sword of Leah. Discovering its magic again after years of dormancy through generations of his family had opened doors that he could not help but feel had been better left closed. The magic had saddled him with such dependency, an elixir of power that was stronger than reason or self-denial, that was insidious in its intent to dominate, that was absolute in its need to command. He remembered how that power had bound him, how he had suffered its loss afterward, how it had stripped him of his courage and resolve when he had needed both – until now, in possession of that power once more, he was terrified of what its renewed use would cost him. It made him think again of Par, cursed, not blessed, with the magic of the wishsong, a magic potentially ten times stronger than that of the Sword of Leah, a magic with which he had been forced to contend since his birth, and which now had evolved in some frightening way so that it threatened to consume him completely. Morgan thought he had been lucky in a way the Valeman had not. There had been many to give aid to the Highlander – Steff, Padishar, Walker, Quickening, Horner Dees, and now Damson and Matty Roh. Each had brought a measure of reason and balance to his life, keeping him from losing himself in the despair that might otherwise have claimed him. Some had been taken from him forever, and some were distanced by events. But they had been there when he had needed them. Whom had Par been able to rely upon? Coll, stripped away by Shadowen trickery? Padishar, gone as well? Walker or Wren or any of the others who had started out on this endless journey? Cogline? Himself? Certainly not himself. No, there had been only Damson and the Mole – and mostly only Damson. Now she was gone, too, and Par was alone again.

One thought led to another, and although he had started

talking of Padishar and the Jut, he found himself turned about in the end, speaking once more of what haunted him most, of Par, his friend, whom he had failed, he felt, over and over again. He had promised Par he would stay with him, he had sworn to come north as his protector. He had failed to keep that promise, and he found himself wishing that he might have another chance, just one, to make up for what he had given away.

Damson spoke of the Valeman as well, and the timbre of her voice betrayed her feelings more surely than any words, a whisper of her own sense of loss, of her own perceived failing. She had chosen Padishar Creel over Par, and while the choice could be justified, there was no comfort for her in the knowledge.

'I am tired of making choices, Morgan Leah,' she whispered to him at one point. They had not spoken for a time, lying back within their shelter, sipping at warm water to keep their bodies from dehydrating. Her hand gestured futilely. 'I am tired of being forced to choose, or constantly having to make decisions I do not want to make, because whatever I decide, I know I am going to hurt someone.' She shook her head, lines of pain etched across her brow. 'I am just plain tired, Morgan, and I don't know if I can go on anymore.'

There were tears in her eyes, generated by thoughts and feelings hidden from him. He shook his head. 'You will go on because you must, Damson. People depend on you to do so. You know that. Padishar now. Par later.' He straightened. 'Don't worry, we'll find him, you and I. We won't stop until we do. We can't be tired before then, can we?'

He sounded condescending to himself and didn't like it. But she nodded in response and brushed away the tears, and they went back to waiting for Matty Roh.

Nightfall came, and she still hadn't returned. Shadows blotted away the light, and the sky was darkening quickly and filling with stars. West, beyond where they could see, the storm front continued to approach, and within the walls of the city the air began to cool with its coming.

Damson rose. 'I can't wait any longer, Highlander. I have to go now if I am to find the Mole and still have time to bring the free-born into the city.' She pulled on her cloak and tied it about her. 'Wait here for Matty. When she comes, find out what you can that will help us.'

'When she comes,' Morgan repeated. 'Assuming she does.'

She reached down to touch him lightly on the shoulder. 'Whatever happens, I will come back for you as quickly as I can.'

He nodded. 'Good luck, Damson. Be careful.'

She smiled and disappeared across the darkening courtyard into the shadows. The sound of her footsteps echoed on the stone and faded away into silence.

Morgan sat alone in the gloom and listened to the sounds of the city slowly quiet and die. Overhead, clouds moved across the stars and began to screen them away. The night darkened, and a strange hush settled over the bluff. Padishar, he thought, hang on, we're coming. Somehow, we're coming.

He tried sleeping and could not. He tried thinking of something he could do, but everything involved going out from his hiding place, and if he did that he might not get back again. He would have to wait. Rescue plans crowded his mind, but they were as ephemeral as smoke, based on speculation, not on fact, and useless. He wished he had brought the Sword of Leah so that he would not feel so defenseless. He wished he had made better choices in his efforts to aid his friends. He wished himself into a dark corner and was forced to stop wishing for fear that he would find himself paralyzed by regrets.

It was nearing midnight when he heard the scrape of boots on the stone of the courtyard and looked up from his light doze to see Matty Roh materialize in the fading starlight. He jerked upright, and she hushed him to silence. She crossed to where he waited and sat next to him, breathing heavily.

'I ran the last mile,' she said. 'I was afraid you would be gone.'

'No.' He waited. 'Are you all right?'

She looked at him, and her eyes were haunted.

'Damson?'

'Gone in search of the Mole, then off to bring Chandos and the rest through the tunnels. She'll meet us back here by dawn.'

The smile she gave was anxious and searching. 'I'm glad you're here.'

He smiled back, but the smile seemed wrong, and he let it drop. 'What happened, Matty?'

'I found him.'

Morgan took a deep breath. 'Tell me,' he urged softly, sensing she should not be rushed. There was a sheen of sweat on her skin, and that strange look in her eyes.

She bent so that their shoulders touched. Her boyish, delicate features were taut, and there was an urgency that radiated as surely as light. 'I began at the ale houses, looking and listening. I made some easy friends, soldiers, a junior officer. I got what I could from them and kept moving. Padishar's name was mentioned, but just in passing, in connection with the execution. Night came, and I still hadn't learned where they were keeping him.'

She swallowed, reached for the water tin, scooped out a cup, and drank deeply. He could feel the strength in her slim body as it moved against his own.

She turned back. 'I was certain they were keeping him somewhere people would avoid. The watchtower was a ruse, so where else would he be? There are prisons, but word would leak from there. It had to be someplace else, a place no one would want to go.'

Morgan paled. 'The Pit.'

She nodded. 'Yes.' She kept her eyes fixed on him. 'I went into the People's Park and found the Gatehouse heavily guarded. Why would that be? I wondered. I waited until an officer emerged, one highly placed, one who shares. I followed him, then sat with him to drink. I let him persuade me to go with him to a private place. When I had him alone, I put a knife to his throat and asked him questions. He was evasive, but I was able to persuade him to admit what I already knew – that Padishar was being held in his cells.'

'But he is alive?'

'Alive so that he can be executed publicly. They don't want rumors floating about afterwards that he might have escaped. They want everyone to see him die.'

They stared at each other in the dark. The Pit, Morgan was thinking, a sinking feeling in his stomach. He had hoped never to go back there again, never even to come close. He thought of the things that lived there, the Shadowen misfits, the monsters trapped by the barrier of magic that had shattered the Sword of Leah . . .

He brushed the thought aside. The Pit. At least he knew what he was up against. He could devise a plan with that.

'Did you learn anything else?' he asked quietly.

She shook her head. He could see the pulse beat at her throat, the black helmet of her hair a frame about her delicate face.

'And the officer?'

There was a long silence as she looked into his eyes, seeing something beyond and far away. Then she gave him an empty smile.

'When I was finished with him, I cut his throat.'

22

They sat without speaking after that, side by side on the workbench, still touching, looking out at the darkness. Several times Morgan thought to rise and move away, but he was afraid that she would mistake the reason for it and so stayed where he was. The sound of laughter penetrated the silence of the open court from somewhere without, harsh and unwelcome, and it seemed to rub raw even further nerves that were already frayed. Morgan did not know how much time passed. He should say something, he knew. He should confront the dark image of her words. But he did not know how to do so.

A dog barked in the distance, a long staccato peal that died away with jarring sharpness.

'You don't like it that I killed him,' she said finally. It was not a question; it was a statement of fact.

'No, I don't.'

'You think I should have done something else?'

'Yes.' He didn't like making the admission. He didn't like the way he sounded. But he couldn't help himself.

'What would you have done?'

'I don't know.'

She put her hands on his shoulders and turned him until they were facing. Her eyes were pinpricks of blue light. 'Look at me.' He did. 'You would have done the same thing.'

He nodded, but was not convinced.

'You would have, because if you stop to think about it, there wasn't any other choice. This man knew who I was. He knew what I was up to. He couldn't have mistaken that. If I had let him live, even if I had tied him up and hidden him away somewhere, he might have escaped. Or been found. Or anything. If that had happened, we would have been finished. Your plans, whatever they might be, wouldn't stand a chance. And I have to return to Varfleet. If he ever saw me there, he would know. Do you see?'

He nodded again. 'Yes.'

'But you still don't like it.' Her rough, low voice was a whisper. She shook her head, her black hair shimmering. There was an unmistakable sadness in her voice. 'I don't either, Morgan Leah. But I learned a long time ago that there are a lot of things I have to do to survive that I don't like. And I can't help that. It has been a long time since I have had a home or a family or a country or anything or anyone but myself to rely on.'

He stopped her, suddenly ashamed. 'I know.'

She shook her head. 'No, you don't.'

'I do. What you did was necessary, and I shouldn't find fault. What bothers me is the idea of it, I suppose. I think of you in another way, a different way.'

She smiled sadly. 'That is only because you really don't know me, Morgan. You see me one way, for a short time, and that is how I am for you. But I am a good many more things than what you have seen. I've killed men before. I've killed them face to face and out of hiding. I've done it to stay alive.' There were tears in her eyes. 'If you can't understand that . . .'

She stopped, bit down on her lip, rose abruptly, and moved away. He did not try to stop her. He watched her walk to the far side of the courtyard and seat herself on the stones with her back against the wall in the deep shadows. She stayed there, motionless in the dark. Time slipped away, and Morgan's eyes grew heavy. He had not slept since the previous night and then poorly. Dawn would be there before he knew it, and he would be exhausted. He had not yet devised a plan for rescuing Padishar Creel – had not even considered the matter. He felt bereft of ideas and hope.

Finally he spread his cloak on the floor of the shed, made a pillow with the rags that the three of them had carried in, and lay down. He tried to think about Padishar, but he was asleep almost at once.

Sometime during the night he was awakened by a stirring next to him. He felt Matty Roh curl up against him, her body pressing close against his own. One slender arm reached around him, and her hand found his.

They lay together like that for the remainder of the night.

It was nearing dawn when Damson's touch on his shoulder brought him awake. There was a lightening in the spaces between the shadows that told of day's coming, faint and silvery lines against the building walls surrounding where he lay. He blinked the sleep from his eyes and recognized who it was crouching next to him. He was still tangled with Matty, and he nudged her gently awake. Together they rose stiffly, awkwardly, to their feet.

'They're here,' Damson said simply. Her eyes revealed nothing of what she thought, finding them together. She gestured over her shoulder. 'The Mole has them hidden in a cellar not far away. he found me last night shortly after I left you, took me through the tunnels, and together we brought Chandos and the others in. We're ready. Did you find Padishar?'

Morgan nodded, fully awake now. 'Matty found him.' He looked back at the elfin face. 'I wouldn't have been able to, I don't think.'

Damson smiled gratefully at the tall girl and clasped her

slender hands in her own. 'Thank you, Matty. I was afraid this was all going to be for nothing.'

Matty's cobalt eyes glinted like stone. 'Don't thank me yet. We still have to get him out. He's being held in the Gatehouse cells at the Pit.'

Damson's jaw tightened. 'Of course. They would take him there, wouldn't they?' She wheeled back. 'Morgan, how are we going to — '

'We'd better hurry,' he said, cutting her short. 'I'll tell you when we reach the others.'

If I can think of something by then, he added silently. But the beginnings of an idea were forming in the back of his mind, a plan that had come to him all at once upon waking. He threw on his cloak, and together the three of them abandoned the tiny court, went back through the rooms that led in, and stepped out into the street.

It was silent and empty there, the street a black corridor that sliced through building walls until it disappeared into a tangle of crossroads and alleyways. They moved quickly ahead, skimming along the stone in tandem with their shadows, pressing through the blackness of the dying night. Morgan's mind was working now, turning over possibilities, examining ways, considering alternatives. They would execute Padishar at midday. He would be hanged at the city gates. To do that, they would have to transport him from the Gatehouse at the Pit to the outer wall. How would they do that? They would take him down the Tyrsian Way, which was broad and easily watched. Would he walk? No, too slow. On horseback or in a wagon? Yes, standing in a wagon so that he could be seen by everyone . . .

They turned into a passage that ran back between two buildings to a dead end. There was a door halfway down, and they entered. Inside, it was black, but they groped their way to a door on the far wall that opened to a flicker of lamplight. Chandos stood in the door, sword in hand, black beard bristling. He looked ferocious in the shadows, all bulk and iron. But his smile was quick and welcoming, and he guided them down the steps into the cellar below where the others waited.

There were greetings and handshakes, a sense of anticipation, of readiness. It had taken the little band of twenty-four almost the entire night to come into Tyrsis through the tunnels, but they seemed fresh and eager, and there was determination in their eyes. Chandos handed Morgan the Sword of Leah, and the Highlander strapped it across his back. He was as anxious as they.

He looked for the Mole and could not find him. When asked about him, Damson said he was keeping watch.

'I'll need him to show me where the tunnels run beneath the streets,' he announced. 'And I'll need you to draw a map of the city so that he can do that.'

'Have you a plan, Highlander?' Chandos asked, pressing close.

Good question, Morgan thought. 'I do,' he replied, hoping he was right.

Then he drew them close and told them what it was.

The dawn was gray and oppressive, the thunderheads moved close to the edge of Callahorn, roiling black clouds that cast their dark shadow east to the Runne. It was hot and windless in the city of Tyrsis as its citizens woke to begin their day's work, the air thick with the taste of sweat and dust and old smells. Men and women glanced skyward, anxious for the impending rain to begin so that it might give them some small measure of relief.

As morning slid toward midday, excitement over the impending execution of the outlaw Padishar Creel began to build. Crowds gathered at the city gates in anticipation, irritable and weary from the heat, anxious for any distraction. Shops closed, vendors cleaned out their stalls, and work was set aside in what soon became a carnival atmosphere.

There were clowns and tricksters, sellers of drink and sweets, hucksters and mimes, and cordons of Federation soldiers everywhere, dressed in their black and scarlet uniforms as they lined the Tyrsian Way from inner to outer wall. It grew darker with midday's approach as the thunderheads crowded the skies from horizon to horizon and rain began to fall in a thin haze.

At the center of the city, the People's Park sat silent and deserted. Wind from the approaching storm rustled the leaves of the trees and stirred the banners at the Gatehouse entrance. A wagon had arrived, drawn by a team of horses and surrounded by Federation guards. Canvas stretched over metal hoops covered its wooden bed, and iron bound its wheels and sides. The horses stamped and grew lathered in their traces, and the heat brought a sheen of sweat to the faces of the uniformed men. Eyes searched the trees and pathways of the Park, the walls that ringed the Pit, and the shadows that gathered in clumps all about. The iron heads of pikes and axes glinted dully. Voices were kept low and furtive, as if someone might hear.

Then the Gatehouse doors swung open, and a team of soldiers emerged with Padishar Creel in tow. The leader of the free-born had his arms bound tightly behind him and his mouth securely gagged. He walked unsteadily, his gait halting and painful. There was blood on his face and bruises and cuts everywhere. He lifted his head despite his obvious pain, and his eyes were hard and fierce as he surveyed his captors. Few met that gaze, keeping their attention trained elsewhere, waiting until he was past to sneak a furtive glance. The outlaw was taken to the back of the wagon and pushed inside. Canvas flaps were drawn in place, the wagon was turned about, and the soldiers began to assemble in lines on either side. When all was in readiness, the procession began to move slowly ahead.

It took a long time to complete the journey out of the park, the horses held carefully in check, the lines of soldiers surrounding the wagon in a solid wall. There were more than fifty of them, armed and hard-faced, spearing a path through the trees and out onto the Tyrsian Way. The few people they encountered were moved quickly back, and the wagon lurched slowly into the city. Buildings rose to either side, and heads leaned out of windows. The soldiers deployed teams moving ahead to search doorways and alcoves, to check cross streets and alleys, to move aside any obstruction they found. Rain was falling steadily now, spattering on the stones of the roadway, staining them dark and beginning to puddle. Thunder boomed from somewhere distant, a long steady peal that echoed through the city walls. The rain fell harder, and it grew increasingly difficult to see.

The wagon had reached a commons where a series of cross streets intersected when the woman appeared. She was crying hysterically, calling out to the soldiers to stop. Her clothes were in disarray and there were tears on her face. They had the outlaw leader with them, didn't they? They were taking him to be hanged, weren't they? Good, she cried out vehemently, for he was responsible for the deaths of her husband and son, good men who had fought in the Federation cause. She wanted to see him hang. She wanted to make certain she was there when it happened.

The procession lurched to an uncertain stop as others appeared to take up the cry, stirred by the woman's fiery speech. Hang the outlaw leader, they cried out angrily. They pressed forward, a ragged bunch, throwing up their hands and gesturing wildly. The soldiers held them away with pikes and spears, and the unit's commanding officer ordered them to move back.

No one noticed the sewer grate slide away from its seating under where the wagon was stopped or saw the shadowy forms that slid out of the darkness one by one to crouch beneath.

Hang him here and now! the crowd was crying, continuing to press up against the soldiers massed before it. The Federation officer had drawn his sword and was shouting angrily for his men to clear the way.

Then abruptly the forms beneath the wagon sprang up on all sides, some onto the driver's seat, some into the bed. The drivers and the officer were thrown to the street, clutching their throats. More soldiers were thrown, out the back to land in crumpled heaps, bloodied and still. The soldiers surrounding the wagon turned instinctively to see what was happening, and in an instant's time half fell dying as the free-born, who at that point made up the bulk of the crowd, killed them with the daggers they had kept hidden. Screams and shouts rose up, and the soldiers surged back and forth wildly, trying to bring their weapons to bear.

Morgan Leah appeared on the driver's seat of the wagon, snatched up the reins, and shouted at the horses. The wagon lurched forward, the horses wild-eyed. Soldiers flung themselves at the Highlander, trying to claw their way up to stop him, but Matty Roh was there instantly, her blade swift and deadly as it cut them down. The wagon broke through the leading edge of the column, the team trampling some men beneath its hoofs, the wagon wheels crushing more. Morgan sawed on the reins and turned the team onto a side street. Behind, the fighting continued, men grappling with one another and striking out with their weapons. The Federation column was decimated. No more than a handful still stood, and those few had backed themselves against a building wall and were battering at the doors.

Damson Rhee raced up, finished now with her deception as the grieving widow. She reached for the seat rail and pulled herself aboard as the wagon rolled past. The free-born were charging after them as well, swiftly closing the gap between themselves and the wagon. For a second it seemed that Morgan's plan was going to work. Then something moved in the shadows to one side, and Morgan, distracted momentarily, turned to look. As he did, the wagon struck a water-filled hole, an axle broke, a wheel flew off, and the traces snapped. The wagon lurched wildly to one side, and a split second later it upended, sending everyone sprawling into the street.

Morgan lay in a tangle with Damson and Matty Roh. Slowly they picked themselves up, muddied and bruised. The wagon was ruined, the canvas shredded and the wooden box splintered and cracked. In the distance, the terrified team disappeared into the gloom. Chandos crawled from beneath the wreckage with his burly arms wrapped about Padishar. The outlaw leader had freed his hands and removed the gag. There was fire in his eyes as he tried to stand on his own.

'Don't stop!' he rasped. 'Keep moving!'

The others of the free-born reached them, their clothing bloodstained and torn. There were fewer than before, and some were wounded. Shouts and cries trailed after them, and a fresh body of soldiers surged into the square.

'Hurry! This way!' Damson called urgently, and began to run.

They slogged after her down the muddied street through a maze of rain-soaked buildings. Mist rose off the damp, heated stone as the air cooled and everything father than twenty feet away disappeared in a haze. More Federation soldiers appeared, surging out of side streets with their weapons drawn. The free-born met them head-on and thrust them back, struggling to get clear. Matty Roh battled at the forefront of the charge, cat-quick and deadly as she opened a path for the rest. Chandos and Morgan fought on either side of Padishar, who, though game enough to try, lacked sufficient strength to protect himself. He fell continually, and finally Chandos was forced to pick him up and carry him.

They reached a bridge that spanned a dry riverbed and stumbled across wearily. Without the wagon to carry them, they were tiring quickly. Almost half of those who had come into the city to rescue Padishar were dead. Several of those who remained were wounded so badly they could no longer

fight. Federation soldiers were coming at them from everywhere, summoned from the gates where news of the escape
had carried. The little party fought valiantly to go on, but
time was running out. Soon there would be too many soldiers
to avoid. Even the mist and the rain would not hide them
then.

A body of horsemen charged out of the mist, appearing so
swiftly that there was no chance to get clear. Morgan saw
Matty fling herself aside and tried to do the same. Bodies
went flying as the free-born were overrun. The horses
stumbled and went down in the melee and their riders went
flying as well. Screams and shouts rose from the struggling
mass. Chandos was gone, buried in a pile of bodies. Padishar
lurched to one side and fell to his knees. Morgan rose and
stood centermost on the bridge, virtually alone, and swung
the Sword of Leah at everything that came within reach. He
gave his family's battle cry, 'Leah, Leah,' seeking strength in
the sound of it, and fought to rally those who were left to
stand with him.

For a second he thought they were lost.

Then Chandos surged back into view, bloodied and terrible,
thrusting Federation soldiers aside like deadwood as he
stumbled to where Padishar leaned against the bridge wall
and pulled the leader of the free-born back to his feet. Damson
was calling out from somewhere ahead, urging them on. Matty
Roh reappeared, darted at the last Federation soldier standing,
killed him with a single pass, and sped on. Morgan and the
free-born followed, skidding in the mix of rain and blood that
coated the bridge surface.

On the low end of the causeway they found Damson waiting
in the open doors of a large warehouse, gesturing for them to
hurry. They struggled to reach her, hearing the sounds of
pursuit – booted feet pounding through the mud, weapons
clanging against armor, curses and shouts of rage. They
entered the gloom-filled building in a rush, and Damson
slammed and barred the doors behind them. The Mole poked

his head out of a trapdoor that was all but lost in the shadows at the building's rear and disappeared again.

'Down into the tunnels!' Damson ordered, pointing after the Mole. 'Quick!'

The free-born hastened to comply, those who were able giving what support they could to the injured. Chandos went first, half dragging, half carrying Padishar Creel, and disappeared from sight. The shouts of their pursuers reached the doors of the warehouse, and a violent pounding began. Pikes and spears slammed into the barrier, splitting the wood. Morgan paused, halfway to the tunnel. Matty Roh stood alone before the impending rush, sword held ready.

'Matty!' he called out.

The last of the free-born dropped through the trapdoor. Battle-axes split the crossbar that braced the warehouse entrance, and the heavy doors sagged. Matty Roh backed away slowly, reluctant even now to give ground. She seemed small and vulnerable before the crush that surely faced her, but held herself as if made of iron.

'Matty!' Morgan shouted again, then raced back for her. Seizing her arm, he dragged her toward the tunnel entry just as the warehouse doors gave way, and Federation soldiers poured into the room. Foremost were Seekers, hooded and cloaked, the wolf's-head insignia gleaming on their uniforms. Their cries at seeing him were hisses of delight.

Morgan turned to face them, standing before the tunnel entrance. It was too late to flee. If he tried, they would cut him down from behind and then catch the others as well. If he stayed, he could slow the rush and the others would gain a few precious moments. Matty Roh crouched at his elbow. He thought momentarily to tell her to run, but a furtive glance at her face told him he would be wasting his time.

The rush came from three sides, but Morgan and the girl fought with a ferocity born of desperation and threw it back. The Sword of Leah turned to blue fire as it met the Seeker strike, hammering past the Shadowen defense and turning the

292

black things to ash. Some of the Federation soldiers saw what was happening and fell back with whispered cries and oaths. Matty Roh attacked at the first indication of a weakening in the ranks, her slender sword snaking out so quickly that it could barely be seen, her movements fluid and efficient as she followed her weapon into the crush. Morgan went with her, fighting to cover her back, impelled by the sudden rush of magic that surged from the Leah talisman into his limbs. He howled out his battle cry anew, 'Leah, Leah,' and threw himself at the men before him. The Seekers died immediately, and the soldiers who had followed them in tripped and fell over one another in their haste to get away. Matty Roh was crying out as well, a shriek that pierced the cacophony of screams rising from the dead and wounded. Morgan felt light-headed, empty of thought, of needs and wants, of everything but the magic's fire.

Then suddenly the Federation attack gave way completely, and the last of those who still lived fled back through the warehouse doors into the streets of Tyrsis. Morgan whirled in fury, driven by the magic, and the Sword of Leah radiating fire. Swinging the talisman like a scythe, he cut into the upright beams that braced the ceiling supports, cut so deep that he severed them, and the entire building began to collapse.

'Enough!' Matty screamed, catching hold of his arm and pulling him away.

He fought her for an instant, then realized what he was doing and gave in. They rushed for the trapdoor and scrambled to safety just as the ceiling gave way and buried everything in a thunderous crash.

Below, they ran through the blackness of the tunnels, charging ahead recklessly, heedless of where they were going. Light glimmered in the distance, faint and beckoning, and they raced wildly to reach it. The strange wholeness that Morgan felt when using the Sword's magic began to dissipate, opening a pit within that widened into a hunger, into a familiar sense of loss, into the beginnings of a desperate need. He fought against it, warning himself that he must not let the magic rule him as it had before, calling up images of Par and Walker and finally Quickening to strengthen his resolve. He reached out for Matty and caught hold of her hand. Her grip tightened on his own, as if she sensed his fear, and she held him fast.

Don't let me go, he prayed silently. Don't let me fall.

Dust and dampness filled his lungs, and he coughed against the air's thickness, fighting to catch his breath. His weariness weighed him down, chains on his limbs and body. They ran on, the light stronger now, closer. Matty's ragged breathing matched the pounding of their boots on the stone. The blood pulsed in his ears.

Then they were within the light, a shaft of brightness from a drainage-grate opening in the street above. Rain cascaded down through the gaps and formed a silver curtain, and thunder rolled across the skies. Matty collapsed against one wall, pulling him down with her. They sat with their backs against the cool stone, gasping.

She turned to him, and her cobalt eyes were wild and fierce and her waiflike features were shining. She looked as if she wanted to howl with glee. She looked as if she had discovered something that she had believed forever lost.

'That was wonderful!' she breathed, and laughed like a child.

When she saw the astonishment mirrored on his face, she leaned over quickly and kissed him hard on the mouth. She held the kiss for a long time, her arms wrapping about him and holding him fast.

Then she released him, laughed again, and pulled him to his feet. 'Come on, we have to catch the others! Come on, Morgan Leah! Run!'

They continued down the tunnel, the sounds of the storm trailing after them into the black. They did not run far, slowing quickly to a walk as their wind gave out. Their eyesight adjusted to the gloom, and they could pick out the movement of rats. Rainwater sloshed down the grates in an increasingly heavy flow, and soon they were ankle-deep. From light shaft to light shaft they made their way, listening for the sounds of those who might be following as well as for those they sought. They heard shouts and cries from the streets, the gallop of horses, the rumble of wagons, and the thudding of booted feet. The city was swarming with soldiers hunting for them, but for now the sounds were all above ground.

Still there was no sign of Damson and the free-born.

Finally they reached a divergence in the passageway that forced them to choose. Morgan did the best he could, but there was nothing to help him decide. If the rainwater hadn't flooded the sewer floor, there might have been tracks. They pressed on, side by side, Matty Roh holding onto him as if frightened she might lose him to the dark. The distance between the grates began to widen until the tunnel was so black they could barely see.

'I think we missed a turn,' Morgan said softly, angrily.

They backtracked and tried again. The new passage angled sharply one way and then another, and again the distance between grates widened and the light began to fail. They found a blackened torch wedged in the rock wall and managed to light it using a strip of cloth and Matty's fire-making stones. It took a long time to get a flame in the dampness, and by the time they had the torch burning, they could hear movement in the watery corridors behind them.

'They've dug through – or found another way,' the girl whispered, and gave him a secretive smile. 'But they won't catch us – or if they do, they'll wish they hadn't. Come on!'

They pushed ahead into tunnels that grew increasingly narrow. The grates finally disappeared entirely and the torch became their only light. The hours wore on, and it became obvious that they were hopelessly lost. Neither said so, but both knew. Somehow they had chosen the wrong direction. It was still possible that they would find their way clear, but Morgan didn't care for the odds. Even Damson, who lived in the city and came down into the tunnels often, did not feel she could navigate the maze of corridors without the Mole. He wondered what had become of her and the others of the freeborn. He wondered if they thought Matty and he were dead.

They found another torch, this one in better condition, and took it with them as a spare. When the pitch-coated length of the first was burned away, Morgan used the stub to light the spare and they continued on. They were angling deeper into the bluff and could no longer see or hear the rain. Sounds grew muffled and then disappeared; there was only their breathing and their footsteps. Morgan tried to set a direct course, but the tunnels intersected and cut back so often that he gave it up. Time ticked away, but there was no way to be certain how much of it had passed. They grew hungry and thirsty, but there was nothing to eat or drink.

Finally Morgan stopped and turned to Matty. 'We're not getting anywhere. We have to try something else. Let's find our way back up to the first level. Maybe we can slip out into the city tonight and sneak through the gates tomorrow.'

It was a faint hope at best – the Federation would be looking for them everywhere – but anything was better than wandering around hopelessly in the dark. Night would be coming soon, and Morgan kept thinking about the Shadowen that Damson had told him prowled the tunnels closest to the Pit. Suppose they stumbled into one of those. It was too dangerous for them to remain down here any longer.

They worked their way back toward the bluff face, choosing tunnels that angled upward, winding about with their torch slowly burning away. They knew they were running out of time; if they did not regain the streets of the city soon, their light would be used up and they would be stuck there in the dark. But now they were hearing continual sounds in the distance, the movement of men through water and damp, the whisper of voices. Their hunters were out in force, and they were no closer than before to finding a way past them.

It was a long time before they reached the sewers again and caught a glimpse of daylight through a street grating. The light was thin and fading now, the day easing quickly toward dark. The rain had turned to a slow drizzle, and the city was silent and empty feeling. They walked until they found a ladder leading up, and Morgan took a deep breath and climbed. When he peered out from between the bars he saw Federation soldiers stationed across from him, grim and silent in the gloom. He climbed back down noiselessly, and they continued on.

Their torch burned out, the daylight turned to dark – the skies so clouded that almost no light showed down into the tunnels, and the sound of their hunters faded away and was replaced by the scurrying of rats and the drip of runoff. All of the grate openings they checked were under watch. They kept moving because there was nothing else for them to do, afraid that if they stopped they might not be able to start again.

Morgan was beginning to despair when the eyes appeared in front of him. Cat's eyes, they gleamed in the darkness and then disappeared.

Morgan came to an immediate stop. 'Did you see that?' he whispered to Matty Roh.

He felt, rather than saw, her nod. They stood frozen for a long time, not wanting to move until they knew what was out there. Those eyes had not belonged to any rat.

Then there was a whisper of water disturbed and a scrape of boots.

'Morgan?' someone called softly. 'Is that you?'

It was Damson. Morgan answered, and an instant later she was hugging him, then Matty, telling them she had been looking for them for hours, searching the tunnels from end to end, trying to find their trail.

'Alone?' Morgan asked incredulously. He was so relieved to see her he was almost giddy. 'Do you have any food or water?'

She gave them both an aleskin and bread and cheese from her pack. 'I had the Mole to help me,' she said, keeping her voice at a whisper. 'When you collapsed the ceiling to the warehouse, a part of the tunnel went with it. Maybe you didn't even notice. At any rate, we were cut off from you, and you ended up going the wrong way.' She shook back her fiery hair and sighed. 'We had to get Padishar and the others out first. There was no time to look for you then. When they were safe, the Mole and I came back for you.'

In the darkness to one side, the Mole's bright eyes blinked and gleamed. Morgan was dumbfounded. 'But how did you find us? We were completely lost, Damson. How could you . . . ?'

'You left a trail,' she said, clutching at his arm to slow his argument.

'A trail? But the rainwater washed everything away!'

She smiled, although she was clearly trying not to. 'Not in the earth, Morgan – in the air.' He shook his head in confusion. 'Mole?' she called. 'Tell him.'

The Mole's furry face eased into the light. He blinked almost sleepily, and his nose twitched as he sniffed at the Highlander. 'Your smell is very strong,' he said. 'All through the tunnels. Lovely Damson is right. You were easy to track.'

Morgan stared. He could hear Matty Roh's smothered laughter, and he turned bright red.

They rested only long enough to eat, then set out again, this time with the Mole as their guide. There were no encounters with either Federation soldiers or Shadowen wraiths and their passage was smooth and easy. As he walked, Morgan's thoughts wandered into the past and out again, a slow, deliberate journey of self-evaluation. He looked at himself and the ways he had changed. When he was done, he found he was not displeased. The lessons he had learned were important ones, and he was better for having traveled the road that had brought him north from Leah.

When they emerged from the side of the mountain north, the skies were clear once more and filled with light from the moon and stars. The air was rain-washed and smelled of the forest, and the breeze that blew out of the west was cool and soft as down. They stood together in grasses still damp with the storm, looking out across the plains and hills to the Dragon's Teeth and the horizon beyond.

Morgan glanced at Matty Roh and found her studying him, smiling slightly, her thoughts private and secretive and strangely compelling. She was plain and pretty, reticent and forward, and a dozen other contradictions, a paradox of moods and behavior he did not understand but wanted to. He saw her in fragments of memory – as the boy he had believed her to be at the Whistledown, as the girl with the ruined feet and shattered past at Firerim Reach, as the deadly quick swordswoman standing against the Federation and the Shadowen at Tyrsis, and as the quixotic waif who could be either demon or sprite at a moment's passing.

He could not help himself. He smiled back at her, trying to share a secret that only she knew.

Damson was kneeling before the Mole. 'Won't you come with us this time?' she was asking him. The Mole was shaking his head. 'It grows more dangerous for you every time you go back.'

The Mole considered. 'I am not afraid for myself, lovely Damson. I am afraid only for you.'

'The monsters, the Shadowen, are in the city,' she reminded him gently.

He gave her a small shrug and a serious look. 'The monsters are everywhere.'

Damson sighed, nodded, reached out carefully, put her arms around the little fellow, and hugged him. 'Goodbye, Mole. Thank you for everything. Thank you for Padishar. I owe you so much.'

The Mole blinked. His bright eyes glistened.

She released him and rose. 'I will come back for you when I can,' she said. 'I promise.'

'When you find the Valeman?' The Mole suddenly looked embarrassed.

'Yes, when I find Par Ohmsford. We will both come back.'

The Mole brushed at his face. 'I will wait for you, lovely Damson. I will always wait for you.'

Then he turned and disappeared back into the rocks, melting away like one of night's shadows. Morgan stood with Matty Roh and stared after him, not quite believing he was really gone. The night was still and cool, empty of sound and filled with memories that jumbled together like words spoken too fast, and it seemed as if everything was a dream that could end in the blink of a waking eye.

Damson turned to look at him. 'I'm going after Par,' she announced quietly. 'Chandos has taken Padishar and the others back to Firerim Reach where they will rest a day or two before making their journey north to meet with the Trolls. I have done what I can for him, Morgan. He doesn't need me for anything more. But Par Ohmsford does, and I intend to keep my promise to him.'

Morgan nodded. 'I understand. I'm going with you.'

Matty Roh looked inexplicably defiant. 'Well, I'm going, too,' she declared. She searched first one face and then the other for an objection, found none, and then asked in a more reasonable tone, 'Who is Par Ohmsford?'

Morgan almost laughed. He had forgotten that Matty knew only a little of what was going on. There was no reason, he guessed, that she shouldn't know it all. She had earned the right by coming with them into Tyrsis after Padishar Creel.

'Tell her on the way,' Damson interjected suddenly, and gave an uneasy glance over her shoulder. 'We're too exposed, standing about out here. Don't forget they're still hunting for us.'

Within moments they were moving east away from the bluff

and toward the Mermidon. An hour's walk would bring them to the shelter of the forests and a few hours' sleep. It was the best that they could hope for this night.

As they traveled, Morgan told again the story of Par Ohmsford and the dreams of Allanon. The three figures receded slowly into the distance, midnight came and went, and the new day began.

23

23

They spent what remained of the night in an arbor of white oaks bordering the Mermidon a few miles below the Kennon Pass. It was cool and shady where they slept, protected from the late summer heat that gathered early on the open grasslands, and they did not wake until well after sunrise. They washed and ate from the supplies that Damson carried, listening to the steady flow of the river and an effervescent birdsong. Morgan rubbed sleep from his eyes and tried to remember everything that had happened the previous day, but it was already growing vague in his mind, a memory that seemed to have been stored away a long time ago. That Padishar Creel was safe again, however distant the event, was all that mattered, he told himself wearily, and he let the matter slide into the distance of yesterday.

He pulled on his boots as he munched on bread and cheese and considered what lay ahead. Today was a hot, sultry expectation that shimmered through the dappled shadows of the leaves and branches, and it might take him anywhere. The past was a reminder of the vicissitudes of life, chance playing off opportunity and giving back what she would. The hardships and losses that Morgan had experienced had tempered him like iron run through the fire, and a vacuum had formed around him that he did not think anything would ever get past again, a dead place where hurt and disappointment and fear could not survive, a shield that let him keep everything away so that he might go on when sometimes he did not think he could. The problem, of course, was that it kept other things away as well – hope and caring and love among them. He could admit them when he chose, but there was always the danger that the other feelings would come in as well. When you let in one, you always risked letting in the others. It was his legacy from Steff and Quickening, from the Jut and Eldwist, from Druid wraiths and Shadowen. It was a truth that haunted him.

He brushed aside the musings and speculation, finished off his meal, and stood and stretched.

'Ready?' Damson Rhee asked. She was flushed from cold water splashed on her skin, and her fiery hair was brushed out so that it shone. She was pretty and vital and filled with a determination that radiated like heat from a flame. Morgan looked at her and thought again how lucky Par was to have someone like that in love with him.

Matty Roh finished washing off her plate and handed it over to Damson to pack. 'Where do we go from here?' she asked in her customarily blunt fashion. 'How do we go about finding Par Ohmsford?'

Damson shoved the plate in with the others. 'We track him.' She tightened the stays on the pack and stood up. 'With this.'

She reached down inside her tunic front and pulled out what looked to be half of a medallion threaded on a leather thong. Morgan and Matty bent close. The medallion – a metal disk, actually – had no markings or insignia, and the jagged sharpness of the straight edge indicated that it had been broken recently.

'It is called a Skree,' Damson explained, holding it up to the light where it gleamed a copper gold. 'I gave the other half to Par when we separated. The disk was fashioned out of one metal, one forging, and can only be used once. The halves draw the holders to each other. They give off light when they are brought close.'

Matty Roh looked skeptical. 'How close do you have to be?' Her black hair was short and straight about her elfin face, and her eyes were deep and searching. She looked fresh-scrubbed and new – younger than she was, Morgan thought, and nothing of who she could be.

Damson smiled. 'The Skree is a street magic. I have seen it work; I know what it can do.' The smile tightened. 'Shall we try it out?'

She held it outstretched in her palm and faced west, north, and then east. The Skree did nothing. Damson glanced at them quickly. 'He was traveling south,' she explained. 'I saved that for last.'

She pointed her hand south. The coppery face of the Skree might have pulsed faintly, but Morgan really wasn't sure. Damson, however, nodded in satisfaction.

'He's a long way away, it seems.' Her smile was hesitant as she let her eyes meet theirs. 'You have to know how to read it.' She stuffed the disk back inside her tunic. 'We had better start walking.'

She reached down for her pack and swung it over her shoulders. Matty Roh gave Morgan a sideways glance and a shake of her head that said, *Did you see something I missed?* Morgan shrugged. He wasn't sure.

They set out into the heat, following the Mermidon on its winding path east toward Varfleet, keeping as much as they could to the shade of the trees. A breeze blew off the water and helped cool them, but the surrounding countryside was empty and still. The peaks of the Dragon's Teeth north were barren and gray with the summer's swelter, and the mix of hills and low mountains south were burned out and dry. The sun lifted in the cloudless sky, and the heat beat down in waves. Dead animals lay scattered on the open plains, their twisted bodies rotting. Vast stretches of Callahorn's woods had been sickened and the earth beneath left bare. Pools of stagnant, dull-green water stood listless and stinking. Trees were ravaged and withered like the carcasses of creatures hung out to dry. Often

304

the stretches of ruined earth lasted for miles. Morgan could smell the decay in the air. This was more than the summer heat and dryness; this was the Shadowen poisoning that he had witnessed time and again since coming north, a devastation of the land that the dark things were somehow causing. And it was growing worse.

Midday faded into afternoon, and they skirted Varfleet to the north, still following the Mermidon as it began to bend south. They encountered a handful of peddlers and other tradesmen on their way, but the heat kept most would-be travelers out of the sun, so they had the river road pretty much to themselves. They spotted their first Federation patrol as they neared Varfleet and stepped back into the trees to let it pass.

Damson used the Skree again while they waited, and the result was the same. The disk glowed faintly when pointed south – or it might have been nothing more than a glimmer of sunlight. Again Morgan and Matty Roh exchanged a surreptitious look. It was hot, and they were tired. They were wondering if this was leading somewhere or if Damson was just being hopeful. There were other ways to track Par if the disk wasn't working, but neither of them was ready to challenge Damson on the matter just yet.

They needed a boat to travel down the Mermidon to the Rainbow Lake, she advised, tucking the Skree away once more. It would be quicker by three times than trying to make the journey afoot. Matty shrugged and said she would go into the city, since it was less dangerous for her to do so than for them, and she would meet them here again as soon as she had found what they needed. She put down the bedroll she had been carrying and disappeared into the swelter.

Morgan sat with Damson in the shade of an ancient willow close by the riverbank where they could see anyone approaching from either direction. The river was muddy and clogged with debris in the wake of last night's storm, and they watched it flow past in sluggish, deliberate fashion, a bearer of discards and old news. Morgan's eyes were heavy with lack of sleep, and he closed them against the light.

'You're still not certain of me, are you?' he heard Damson ask after a time.

He looked over at her. 'What do you mean?'

'I saw the look you exchanged with Matty when I used the Skree.'

He sighed. 'That doesn't mean I'm not certain of you, Damson. It means I didn't see anything and that worries me.'

'You have to know how to use it.'

'So you said. But what if you're wrong? You can't blame me for being skeptical.'

She smiled ironically. 'Yes, I can. Somewhere along the way we have to start trusting each other, all three of us. If we don't, we're going to get into a lot of trouble. You think about it, Morgan.'

He did and was still thinking on it when dusk settled over the borderlands and Matty trudged back out of the haze with a tired look on her face.

'We have a boat,' she announced, dropping wearily into the shadow of the willow and reaching for the water cup Damson offered. She splashed water on her dust-streaked face and let it run off. 'A boat, supplies, and weapons, all tucked away at the waterfront. We can pick them up after dark when we won't be seen.'

'Any problems?' Morgan asked.

She gave him a hard look. 'I didn't have to kill anyone, if that's what you mean.' She glowered at him, then settled back and wouldn't say another word.

Now they were both mad at him, he thought, and decided he didn't care.

When night came, they followed the riverbank down into the city until they reached the docks north where Matty had secured the boat. It was an older craft, a flat-bottomed skiff with poles, oars, a mast, and a canvas sail, and was supplied with food and weapons as Matty had promised. They climbed

306

aboard without saying anything and shoved off, rode the skiff down-river to the first unoccupied cove, then beached their craft and went immediately to sleep. At sunrise they were up again and off. They rode the Mermidon south toward the Runne until sunset and made camp in a wedge of rocks that opened onto a narrow sand bar fronting a grove of ash. They ate dinner cold, rolled into their blankets, and slept once more. Two days had passed without anyone saying much of anything. Tempers were frayed, and uncertainty over the direction they were taking had shut down any real effort at communication. There had been a bonding in Tyrsis that was lacking here – perhaps because of the doubts they were feeling about one another, perhaps because of their uneasiness over what might be waiting for them. In Tyrsis there had been a plan – or at least the rudiments of one. Here there was only a vague determination to keep hunting for Par Ohmsford until he was found. They had known where Padishar was, and there had been a sense of having some control over reaching him. But Par could be anywhere, and there was nothing to suggest that they were not already too late to do him any good.

It was with immense relief, then, that when Damson brought out the Skree the following morning and pointed her hand south, the copper metal gleamed bright even in the shadow of the rocks that hemmed them about. There was a moment's hesitation, and then they smiled like old friends rediscovering one another and pushed off into the channel with fresh determination.

The tension eased after that and the sense of companionship they had shared in rescuing Padishar returned once more. The skiff eased its way down the channel, borne steadily south on waters that had turned calm and smooth once more. The day was hot and windless, and the journey was slow, but the free-born women and the Highlander passed the time exchanging thoughts and dreams, working their way past the barriers they had allowed to form between them, conversing until they were comfortable with one another once more.

Nightfall found them deep within the Runne, the mountains a shadowy wall in the growing dark that blocked the starlight and left them with only a narrow corridor of sky overhead. They camped on an island that was mostly sandy beach and bleached driftwood encircling a stand of scrub pine. The air stayed sultry and was thick with pungent river smells – dead fish, mud flats, and rushes. Morgan fished, and they ate what he caught over a small fire, drank a little of the ale Damson carried, and watched the river flow past like a silver ribbon. Damson used the Skree, and it glowed bright copper when pointed south. So far, so good. They were less than a day's journey from where the Mermidon emptied into the Rainbow Lake. Perhaps there they would learn something of the whereabouts of Par.

After a time Damson and Matty stretched out on their blankets to sleep while Morgan ambled down to the water's edge and sat thinking of other times and places. He wanted to pull together the threads of all that had happened in an effort to make some sense out of what was to come. He was tired of running from an enemy he still knew almost nothing about, and in typical fashion believed that if he considered the matter hard enough he was bound to learn something. But the threads trailed away from him as if blown in a wind, and he could not seem to gather them up. They drifted and strayed, and the questions that had plagued him for weeks remained unanswered.

He was digging in the sand with a stick when Matty appeared and sat down next to him.

'I couldn't sleep,' she offered. Her face was pale and cool-looking in the starlight, and her eyes were depthless. 'What are you doing?'

He shook his head. 'Thinking.'

'What about?'

'Everything and nothing.' He gave her a quick smile. 'I can't seem to settle on much. I thought I might try to reason out a few things, but my mind just keeps wandering.'

She didn't say anything for a moment, her eyes turning away to look out over the river. 'You try too hard,' she said finally.

He looked at her.

'You work at everything like it was the last chance you were ever going to get. You're like a little boy with a chore his mother has given him to do. It means so much to you that you can't afford to make even the smallest mistake.'

He shrugged. 'Well, that's not how I am. Maybe that's how I seem at the moment, but that isn't really me. Besides, now who's judging who?'

She met his gaze squarely. 'I'm not judging you; I'm giving you my impression. That's different from what you were doing. You were judging me.'

'Oh.' He didn't believe it for a moment. His face said so, and he didn't bother to hide it. 'Anyway, trying hard isn't a bad thing.'

'Do you remember when I told you that I had killed a lot of men?' He nodded. 'That was a lie. Or at least an exaggeration. I just said that because you made me mad.' She looked away again, thoughtful. 'There's a lot you don't understand about me. I don't think I can explain it all to you.'

He stared at her hard, but she refused to look at him. 'Well, I didn't ask you to explain,' he replied defensively.

She ignored him. 'You're very good with that sword. Almost as good as I am. I could teach you to be better if you'd let me. I could teach you a lot. Remember what happened to you at the Whistledown when you grabbed me. I could teach you to do that, too.'

He flushed. 'That wouldn't have happened if . . .'

'. . . you had been ready.' She smiled. 'I know, you said so before. But the point is, you weren't ready – and look what happened. Besides, being ready is what counts. Padishar taught me that. Being ready is certainly more important than trying hard.'

His jaw tightened. 'Are you about finished detailing what's wrong with me? Or is there something else you'd like to add?'

The smile disappeared from her face. She did not look at him, keeping her eyes on the river. He started to say something more, then thought better of it. She seemed strangely vulnerable all of a sudden. He watched her draw up her knees, clasp her arms about them, and lower her head into the darkened space between. He could hear the sound of her breathing, slow and even.

'I like you a lot,' she said finally. She kept her face hidden. 'I don't want anything to happen to you.'

He didn't know what to say. He just stared at her.

'That's why I'm here,' she said. 'That's why I came.' she lifted her head to look at him. 'What do you think about that?'

He shook his head. 'I don't know what I think.'

She took a deep breath. 'Damson told me about Quickening.'

She said it as if the words might catch fire in her mouth. Her eyes searched his, and he saw that she was frightened of what he might be thinking but determined that she would finish anyway. 'Damson said you were in love with Quickening, that losing her was the worst thing that had ever happened to you. She told me about it because I asked her. I wanted to know something about you that you wouldn't tell me yourself. Then I wanted to talk to you about it, but I didn't know how. I'm very good at listening, but not so good at asking.'

Morgan blinked. He saw Quickening in his mind, a flawless, silver-haired vision as ephemeral as smoke. The pain he felt in remembering was palpable. He tried to shut it away, but it was pointless. He did not want to remember, but the memory was always there, just at the edges of his thinking.

Matty Roh put her hand over his, impulsive, hesitant. 'I could listen now, if you would let me,' she said. 'I would like it if I could.'

He thought, No, I don't want to talk about it, I don't even want to think about it, not with you, not with anybody! But then he saw her again in his mind bathing her ruined feet in the stream and telling him how she had come to be disfigured, how

310

the poisoning of the land had changed her life forever. Was the pain of her memories any less than his own? He thought, too, of Quickening as she lay dying, healing the shattered Sword of Leah, giving him a part of herself to take with him, something that would transcend her death. What she had left behind was not meant to be kept secret or hidden. It was meant to be shared.

And memories, he knew, were not glass treasures to be kept locked within a box. They were bright ribbons to be hung in the wind.

He turned his hand over and clasped hers. Then he leaned close so that he could see her face clearly and began to speak. He talked for a long time, finding it hard at first and then easier, working his way through the maze of emotions that rose within him, searching for the words that sometimes would not come, forcing himself to go on even when he thought that maybe he could not.

When he was done, she held him close and some of the pain slipped away.

They set out again at dawn, the daylight gray and misty with a promise of rain. Clouds rolled out of the west, a heavy, dark avalanche that sealed away everything in its path. It was hot and still on the river, and the slap of the water against the canyon walls echoed sharply as they wound their way down-river. Morgan put up the mast and sail, but there was little wind to help, and after a while he took it down again and let the current carry them. It was nearing midday when they passed beneath Southwatch, the black obelisk towering over them, vast and silent and impenetrable, its shadow cast like a For-bidding across the Mermidon. They stared at it with loathing as they passed, imagining the dark things that waited within, uneasy with the possibility that they might be watched. But no one appeared, and they sailed by unchallenged. Southwatch receded into the distance, melted into the haze, and was gone.

They reached the mouth of the river shortly after, the waters widening and stretching away to become the Rainbow Lake, smoothing into a glassy surface and brightening into a richer blue. The rainbow from which the lake took its name was in pale evidence, shimmering in the heat and mist, suspended above the water like a weathered, faded banner whose stays had come loose so that it floated free. They guided the skiff to the west bank, beached it, and walked out onto a barren flat that dropped away east and south into the water and spread northwest across a plain empty of everything but scrub grass and stunted, leafless ironwood to where a line of hills shadowed the horizon. They breathed the air and looked about, finding no sign of anything for as far as they could see.

Damson brushed back her fiery hair, tied it in place with a bandanna across her forehead, and drew out the Skree. Holding it forth in her open palm, she faced south. Morgan watched as the half disk glimmered bright copper.

She began to put it away, apparently had second thoughts, and tested each of the other compass points. When she faced north, the direction from which they had come, the Skree glimmered a second time, a small, weak pulsing. Damson stared at it in disbelief, closed her hand over it, turned away and then back once more, and reopened her hand. Again the Skree glimmered fitfully.

'Why is it doing that?' Matty asked immediately.

Damson shook her head. 'I don't know. I've never heard of it behaving like this.'

She faced south again and carefully let her palm travel the horizon from east to west and back again. Then she did the same thing facing north, reading the Skree's hammered surface as she turned. There was no mistake in what they were seeing. The Skree brightened both ways.

'Could it have been broken again and the pieces carried in two directions?' Morgan asked.

'No. It can only be divided once. Another breaking would render it useless. That hasn't happened.' Damson looked worried. 'But something has. The reading south points towards the Silver River country west of Culhaven above the

Battle-mound. It is the stronger of the two.' She looked over her shoulder. 'The reading north is centered on Southwatch.'

There was a long silence as they considered what that meant. A heron cried out from over the lake, swept out of the haze in a flash of silver brightness, and disappeared again.

'Two readings,' Morgan said, and put his hands on his hips and shook his head. 'And one of them is a fake.'

'So which one do we believe?' Matty asked. She started away a few steps as if she had something in mind, then turned abruptly and came back again. 'Which is the real one?'

Again Damson shook her head. 'I don't know.'

Matty's cobalt eyes glanced toward the horizon where the clouds were building. 'Then we will have to check them both.'

Damson nodded. 'I think so. I don't know any other way.'

Morgan exhaled in frustration. 'All right. We'll go south first. That reading is the stronger of the two.'

'And abandon Southwatch?' Matty shook her head. 'We can't do that. Someone has to stay here in case Par Ohmsford is inside. Think about it, Highlander. What if he's in there and they try to move him? What if a chance to rescue him comes along and no one is here to do anything about it? We might lose him and have to start all over again. I don't think we can take that chance.'

'She's right,' Damson agreed.

'Fine, you stay, Damson and I will go south,' Morgan declared, irritated that he hadn't thought of it first.

But Matty shook her head again. 'You have to be the one who stays. Your sword is the only effective weapon we have against the Shadowen. If a rescue is needed, if any sort of confrontation comes about, your Sword is a talisman against their magic. My skills are good, Morgan Leah, but I also know when I'm overmatched. I don't like this any better than you do, but it can't be helped. Damson and I will go south.'

There was a long silence as they faced each other, Morgan fighting to control an almost irresistible urge to reject flatly what he perceived to be the madness of her suggestion, Matty

313

with her cobalt eyes steady and determined, the weight of her arguments mirrored in their blue light.

Finally Morgan looked away, reason winning out over passion, a reluctant submission to necessity and hope. 'All right,' he said softly. The words were bitter and harsh sounding. 'All right. I don't like it, but all right.' He looked back again. 'But if you find Par and there's to be a fight, you come back for me.'

Matty nodded. 'If we can.'

Morgan winced at the qualification, shook his head angrily, and glanced at Damson in challenge. But Damson simply nodded in agreement. Morgan exhaled slowly. 'If you can,' he repeated dully.

They conferred a moment more, agreeing on what they would do if time and circumstance allowed. Morgan scanned the countryside and then pointed west to where a bluff fronting the lake looked out across the surrounding land. From there he would be able to see anything coming to or going from Southwatch. If nothing happened in the time between, that was where they would find him when they returned.

He walked back with them to the skiff and retrieved supplies sufficient to last him a week. Then he embraced them hesitantly, Damson first, then Matty. The tall girl held him tightly against her, almost as if to persuade him of her reluctance to leave. She did not speak, but her hands pressed into his back, and her lips brushed his cheek. She looked hard at him as she broke away, and he had the feeling that she was leaving something of herself behind with him in that look. He started to give her a reassuring smile in reply, but she had already turned away.

When they were gone, faded into the mist that had settled over the river, he turned west toward his selected watch post and trudged into the growing dark. The clouds blanketed the skies from horizon to horizon, and the air had begun to cool. A wind had sprung up, gusting across the flats, sending dust and silt swirling into his eyes. Far west, the rain was a dark curtain moving toward him. He pulled up the hood of his forest cloak and lowered his eyes to the ground.

He had just reached his destination when the rain arrived, a downpour that swept across the plains in a rush and covered everything in an instant's time. Morgan burrowed deep within the shelter of a broad-limbed fir and settled down against the base of the trunk. It was dry and protected there, and the storm rolled past leaving him untouched. The rain continued for several hours, then turned to drizzle, and finally stopped. The thunderheads passed east, the skies cleared, and the sunset was a red and purple blaze in the fading light.

Morgan left the shelter of the fir and found a stand of broadleaf maple that allowed him to remain hidden while at the same time giving him a clear view of Southwatch and the Mermidon east, a large stretch of the Rainbow Lake south, and a cut through the hills below the Runne that funneled any land traffic that might approach the Shadowen keep from the north and west. It was an ideal position to observe everything for nearly a dozen miles. Good enough, he decided, and settled in to await the night.

He ate a little of the food he had brought and drank some water. He wondered if Damson and Matty had attempted a crossing of the Rainbow Lake before the storm had struck or if they had decided to wait. He wondered if they were camped somewhere along the river looking back across at him.

The light faded to gray, and the stars began to appear. Morgan stared down at Southwatch and wished he could see inside. He tried not to think too closely about what might be happening there. Too much imagination could be a dangerous thing. He studied the plains east, barren and stripped of life, a wasteland of brown earth and gray deadwood that radiated out from the tower of the Shadowen like a stain. The fringes, he noted, were already darkening as well, infected by the poison as it spread. Trees rotted and grasses withered. The bluff on which he sat was an island already at risk.

315

He unstrapped the Sword of Leah from his back and cradled it in his arms. A talisman against the Shadowen, Matty Roh had called it. But it was power, too, that stole your soul, and there was little that could be done to protect against it. Each time he used the magic, a test of wills resumed, his own and the Sword's, both fighting for supremacy, struggling for control. Three hundred years ago Allanon had answered Rone Leah's desperate, angry plea by bestowing a tiny part of the Druid magic on the ancient weapon, and the legacy of that gift or curse – take your choice – was a bittersweet taste that once experienced cried out for more.

As did the wishsong for Par. As did all the magic that ever was or had ever been – siren songs of power that transcended everything in their compelling, inexorable need to be sung.

He smiled darkly. Be careful what you wish for. Wasn't that the old admonition to those who begged for what they did not have?

The smile faded. Maybe he would find out when it came time to summon the Sword's magic again – as summon it he surely must, sooner or later. Maybe Quickening's healing touch, the magic that had restored his talisman, would prove in the end to be as killing as that of the Shadowen.

The thought left him feeling cold and empty and impossibly alone. He sat motionless in the shadows, staring out across the countryside, waiting for the darkness to claim it.

24

Three days earlier another storm had passed, one markedly more violent, a torrential downpour riddled by explosions of thunder and flashes of lightning and driven by a rough-faced howling wind, the sort of deluge that came and went regularly in the Borderlands with the buildup of late summer pressure and heat. It swept into Callahorn at dusk, inundated the land through the night, and disappeared south with the coming of dawn.

In the wake of its passing a solitary figure rose from the sodden earth at the edge of the Rainbow Lake, muddied beyond recognition and stooped as if weighed down with chains.

Dark eyes blinked and tried to focus. The day was late in waking, worried perhaps that the storm might return, dark-edged clouds lingering fitfully in the leaden skies, sunrise iron-gray and cautious as it eased back the night's stubborn shadows. The figure stared out at the flat expanse of the lake, at the light east, at the skies, at a world that was clearly unfamiliar. One hand held a sword that glimmered faintly where the grass and mire caked on it were scraped down to the metal. The figure hesitated uncertainly, then stumbled to the edge of the lake and submerged hands and face and finally body as well, washing and rinsing down to a tangle of rags and bare skin.

Mud and debris swirled away in the dark waters, and Coll Ohmsford rose to look about.

At first he could not remember anything beyond who he was – though he was quite determined of that, as if perhaps his identity had been in doubt once. He recognized the Rainbow Lake, the ground upon which he stood, and the country that surrounded him. He was standing on the lake's southern shore west of Culhaven and north of the Battlemound. But he did not know how he had gotten there.

He looked down at the blade in his hand (Had he managed to wash himself without releasing it?) and realized that he was holding the Sword of Shannara.

And then the memories came back in a rush that caused him to gasp and double over as if a blow had been delivered to his stomach. The images hammered at him. He had been captured by the Shadowen and imprisoned at Southwatch. He had managed an escape, but in truth Rimmer Dall had managed it for him. He had been tricked into believing that the Mirrorshroud would conceal him when in truth it had subverted him in ways he did not care to recall, turning him into one of them, making him over in their image. He had lost control of himself, becoming something very close to animal, scouring the countryside in search of his brother, Par, seeking him without clear reason or purpose beyond a vague intention to cause him harm. Cloaked in the Mirrorshroud's dark folds, he had tracked, found, and attacked his brother . . .

He was breathing rapidly through his mouth. His chest tightened and his stomach churned.

His brother.

. . . and tried to kill him – and would have, if something hadn't stopped him, hadn't driven him away.

He shook his head, fighting through the maze of memories. He had fled from Par confused and maddened, torn between who he had been and what he had become. He had drawn Par after, barely aware of what he was doing, fleeing by day, seeking by night, hunting always, lost somewhere deep within

318

himself. Hatred and fear drove him, but their source was never clear. He could feel the Mirrorshroud's hold on him beginning to loosen, yet was undecided whether or not that was good. He was changing back again, but could not come the whole distance, still bound by the Shadowen magic, still held within its thrall. In darkness he would return to find his brother, thinking to kill him, thinking at the same time to find salvation, the thoughts twisting about each other like snakes. *Follow me!* he had prayed to Par – then sought to run so fast and so far that his brother couldn't.

He hugged himself against the chills that swept through him, looking out across the hazy expanse of the lake, remembering. How many days had he run? How much time had been lost?

Follow me!

He had stolen the metal disk then, the one that Par wore hung about his neck – had stolen it without knowing why, but only from seeing him hold and caress it in the twilight shadows and sensing its importance, thinking to hurt Par by taking it, but thinking, too, that stealing the disk would make his brother follow after him.

As it had.

To the ruined land below Southwatch.

Why had he run there? The reason eluded him, an evasive whisper in his subconscious. His brow furrowed deeply as he struggled to understand. He had been driven by the Mirrorshroud's magic, compelled to return . . .

His eyes widened. To bring Par, because . . .

And Par had caught up with him there beneath that ancient, blasted oak, found him exhausted and beaten and ruined. They had fought one final time, grappling for the Sword of Shannara, trying to break through the barriers that separated them, each in his own way – Par struggling to summon the Sword's magic so that Coll could be free, Coll battling in turn to . . . to . . .

What?

319

To tell Par. To tell him.

'Par,' he whispered in horror, and his memory of what the Sword's truth had revealed to him burned through him like white fire. He looked down at the mud-streaked blade, at the carving beneath his fingers – the hand that held aloft a burning torch. He stared at it in recognition and wonder, and his fingers moved along the emblem as if finding secrets still.

All those months spent searching for the Sword of Shannara, he thought, and they had never realized. So much effort expended to recover it, a struggle marked by desperate battles and lost lives, and they had never once suspected. Allanon's charge had swept them on, heedless. It had driven Par, and Coll had been swift to follow. Find the Sword of Shannara, the Druid shade had instructed. Only then can the Four Lands be made whole. Find the Sword, he had whispered in the whirl-wind of cries that echoed from the Hadeshorn.

And Par Ohmsford had done so – without once suspecting that it was never to be his to use.

Coll Ohmsford's heart was racing, and he took slow, deep breaths to steady himself against the pounding of his blood. He experienced an almost overpowering urge to despair be-cause of what the deception might have cost them, but he would not let himself be drawn to that precipice. With both hands wrapped about the talisman, he moved back from the Rainbow Lake to where a stand of maple trees spread dappled shadows across a grassy knoll. Dazed and weakened, he sat where the sun's light could find him through the branches and tried to sort through the images he had unlocked from his memory.

Par had tracked him to that plain west of Southwatch and they had done battle a final time, brother against brother. Par had come for him because the Mirrorshroud was a Shadowen magic from which Coll could not free himself. Par had sought to use the Sword of Shannara to give Coll what he needed to break his shackles – recognition of who and what he had become, understanding of how he had been subverted. Truth, the special province of the Sword, would help him to escape. Par had been certain that it really was the Sword of Shannara he possessed because the magic had revealed itself when Coll had come at him above Tyrsis. Triggered in the heat of their struggle, it had spiraled down through them both, letting Par know that Coll was alive and giving Coll a terrifying glimpse of what he had become. Let the magic of the Sword come into his brother, Par had believed, and Coll would be set free.

There were tears in his eyes as he remembered the intensity in Par's face as they stood locked in battle in the fury of that storm. Again he saw his brother's lips move, whispering to him. *Coll. Listen to me, Coll. Listen to the truth.*

And the truth had come, blazing out of the Sword of Shannara in a cleansing, white heat, winding down into Coll and shattering the Shadowen magic so that he could tear off the Mirrorshroud and cast it away forever. The truth had come, and Coll had indeed been set free.

But the truth had never been Par's truth – and never Par's to give. It had been Coll's – and his alone to take.

East, the sun was breaking through the diminishing storm clouds, the grayness of dawn giving way to golden daylight. Coll stared at it and felt as if all the sadness he had ever known had been compressed into this single moment in time.

Par hadn't summoned the magic of the Sword of Shannara. Coll had. Not once, but both times, and each time without realizing what he was doing or that it was his to command. Coll, not Par, was the Ohmsford for whom the Sword was meant. But the truth here, as in so many things, was as elusive as smoke and took time to understand. Allanon had given Coll no charge when they had gathered at the Hadeshorn – yet the power to summon the Sword of Shannara's magic was his. It was reasonable that it should be, when you thought about it. He was Par's brother, and like Par an heir to the Elven magic. They shared the same Elven blood and birthright. But it was to Par that the charge had been given, and it was on Par that everything had subsequently focused. Par had been sent to recover the Sword, armored in his own magic and in his unyielding resolve, certain of his purpose even when the others in the little company had doubted. Par had been sent, and Allanon must have known he would not fail. But why had they not been told that the Sword was meant for Coll? Why had nothing been asked of him?

His hands clasped and knotted before him. He remembered how it had felt when he had brought the Sword's magic to life, an inexplicably cool white fire. Even trapped as he was in the thrall of the Mirrorshroud he had felt it come, a flood washing through him, sweeping everything before it. Truths broke down the barriers of the Shadowen magic, small ones first, remembrances of childhood and youth, then larger ones, harsher and more insistent, blows that stiffened his resolve, that toughened him little by little against what was to follow. The truths were painful, but they were healing as well, and when the last of them was brought before him – the truth of who and what he had become – he was able to accept it and to put an end to the charade being played on him.

He had told the story of the Sword of Shannara a thousand times – how the talisman had come to life in the hands of Shea Ohmsford five hundred years earlier, how it had revealed the Valeman to himself and then unmasked the Warlock Lord. He had told the story so often that he could recite it in his sleep.

But even that had not prepared him for what he felt now in the aftermath of the magic's use. Exposure to the truth had drained him of illusions and conceits that had sheltered him for his entire life. He had been stripped of the protective barriers he had erected for himself against the harshest of his mistakes and failings. He had been left naked and exposed. He had been left feeling foolish and ashamed.

And terrified for Par.

For the Sword of Shannara in freeing him had revealed truths about Par as well. One of them was that Par could not use the Sword. Another was that he did not realize this. A third was that the wishsong was the cause of his brother's problems.

Secrets revealed – he had seen them all. But Par had not. For reasons still unknown, the wishsong would not let Par summon the Sword's magic, would not let him bring the magic into himself, and would not let him see any truths about himself. The wishsong was a wall that kept the Sword's magic out, hiding what it would reveal, keeping his brother a prisoner. Coll didn't know why that was – only that it was so. The wishsong was doing something to Par, and Coll was not certain what it was. He had felt its resistance to the power of the Sword when he had struggled with his brother for possession of the blade. He had felt it force the magic away, keeping it inside Coll, making certain that the truths revealed were his and not his brother's.

Why? he wondered. Why would that be? Why hadn't Allanon told them anything about this, or about who could use the Sword, or about what the Sword was needed to do? What *was* the Sword's purpose? They had been sent to retrieve it and had done so. Now what were they supposed to do with it?

What was *he* supposed to do with it?

Sunlight brushed his face, and he closed his eyes and leaned into it. The warmth was soothing, and he let it envelop him like a blanket. He was tired and confused, but he was safe as well and that was more than could be said for Par.

He backed out of the light and opened his eyes anew. The King of the Silver River had tried to take them both, but the effort had failed. Par had panicked and used the wishsong, and his magic had counteracted that of their rescuer. Coll had been carried up into the light and safely away, but Par had fallen back into the darkness and the waiting hands of the Shadowen.

Rimmer Dall had him now.

Coll's mouth tightened. He had screamed after Par as he had watched him fall, then felt himself wrapped about and soothed by the light that bore him away. The King of the Silver River had spoken to him, words of reassurance and comfort, words of promise. The old man's voice had been soft in his ear. He would be safe, it whispered. He would sleep and momentarily forget, but when he woke he would remember again. He would keep as his own the Sword of Shannara, for it was his to wield. He would carry it in search of his brother, and he would use it to save him.

Coll nodded at the memory. Use it to save him. Do for Par what Par had done for him. Seek Par out and by invoking the magic of the Sword of Shannara force him to confront the truths that the wishsong was hiding and set him free.

But free from what?

A dark uneasiness stirred inside him as he remembered Par's fears about the way the wishsong's magic was evolving. Rimmer Dall had warned both Ohmsfords that Par was a Shadowen, that the wishsong made him so, and that he was in danger of being consumed by the magic because he did not understand how to control it. He had warned that only he could keep the Valeman from being destroyed. There was no reason to believe anything the First Seeker said, of course. But what if he was even a little bit right? That would surely be reason enough for the wishsong to block the Sword's truth from Par. Because if Par really was a Shadowen . . .

Coll exhaled sharply, furiously. He would not let himself finish the thought, could not accept its possibility. How could Par be a Shadowen? How could he be one of those monsters? There was some other reason for what was happening. There had to be.

Stop debating the matter! You know what you have to do! You have to find Par!

He rose to his feet and stood staring out at the misted lake, battered and worn from his struggle to stay alive and from the revelations of the Sword. He thought of the years he had spent looking after his brother while they were growing up – Par so volatile and contentious, fighting to understand and control the magic that lived within him, and Coll the peacemaker, using his size and calming disposition to keep things from getting out of hand. How many times had he stood up for Par, shielded him from punishments and retributions, and kept him safe from harm? How often had he compromised his own misgivings so that he could stand with his brother and protect him? He couldn't begin to count them. He didn't want to. It was simply something he'd had to do. It was something he would do again now. Par and he were brothers, and brothers stood up for one another when it was needed. The choice had been made a long time ago.

Find Par and set him free.

Before it is too late.

He looked down at the Sword of Shannara and fingered its pommel experimentally, remembering the feel of the magic coursing through him. His magic. The magic he had thought he would never have. It was an odd sensation, knowing that its power was his. He remembered how much he had wanted it once, wanted it not so much for what it could do but because he had believed it would bring him closer to Par. He remembered how alone he had felt after the meeting with Allanon – the only member of the Ohmsford family to whom no charge had been given. He remembered thinking that he might just as well not have been there. The memory burned even now.

So what would he make of the chance that had been given him?

He looked at himself, ragged and battered, without food or water, without weapons (save for the Sword), without coins or possessions to trade. He looked back across the lake again, at the mist beginning to burn off as the sunlight strengthened.

Find Par.

His brother would be at Southwatch. But would he be his brother still? Coll believed he could reach Par, that he could find a way to overcome any obstacles set against him, but what would have happened to his brother in the meantime? Would the Sword of Shannara help against what the Shadowen might have done to Par? Would the magic be of any use if Par had become one of them?

The questions were troubling. If he considered them further, he might change his mind about going.

But was it any different when Par came in search of me?
Did he ask if I was still his brother?

He brushed the questions aside, took a firm grip on the Sword of Shannara, and started walking.

He traveled east, following the shoreline toward the mouth of the Silver River. Going west was out of the question, because it meant navigating the Mist Marsh and he knew better than to try that. The clouds disappeared, the sun came out, and the land turned molten. Steamy dampness rose in waves from the sodden earth, and the puddles and streams created by the storm dried back into the dust. Herons and cranes flew over the lake in long swooping glides, and the waters turned silver-tipped in the wake of their passing.

A stranger still to his new life, he thought long and hard about everything that had happened, trying to piece together the parts of the puzzle that still didn't fit. Chief among those was Rimmer Dall's obsession with Par. That the First Seeker had such an obsession was now beyond dispute. Too much time and effort had been expended to think otherwise. First there had been his elaborate hoax to make Par think Coll was dead. Then Coll had been allowed to come back to life, subverted by the Mirrorshroud, and sent to find Par. And there was the whole business of giving the Sword of Shannara to Par when Par couldn't use it. What was it all about? Why was his brother so important to Rimmer Dall? If he had been an obstacle in the First Seeker's path, he would have been killed long ago. Instead Dall seemed content with elaborate gamesplaying – with the search for the Sword of Shannara, with orchestrating Coll's death and subversion, and with suggesting repeatedly the possibility that Par was the very thing he sought to destroy. What was Rimmer Dall trying to do?

Somehow, Coll knew, it was tied to the charge that Allanon had given his brother to bring back the Sword of Shannara. Perhaps the Sword was meant to reveal the truth behind all the deceptions. Perhaps it was meant for something else. Whatever the case, there were schemes and maneuverings at work here that neither he nor Par yet understood, and somehow they must unravel them.

He rested at midday, drinking water from a stream and wishing he had something to eat. He was nearing the Silver River and would soon turn north toward the Rabb. He had grown strong at Southwatch training with Ulfkingroh, but his subversion by the Mirrorshroud had weakened him considerably. His hunger worked through him, and he finally gave in to it. Using the Sword, he fashioned a spear from a willow stick and went fishing. Walking through the shallows of the lake to a quiet cove, he stood knee-deep in the clear waters until a fish passed and stabbed at it. It took him a dozen tries, but finally he had his catch. He carried it ashore, then remembered he had no way to cook it. He could not eat it raw – not after his days in the thrall of the Mirrorshroud. He searched his clothing for fire-making materials, but found only the strange disk he had stolen from Par stuffed down into one pocket. Angry and frustrated, he threw the fish back into the lake and began walking once more.

The afternoon dragged by. Coll rested more frequently now, light-headed in the swelter, his concentration wavering. Sleep would help, but he had determined to go on until nightfall. He saw Par appear now and again in the shimmer of heat that rose off the saw grass, heard him speaking and saw him move. Memories came and went, mixing with the images and evaporating when he tried to venture too close. He needed a better plan, he told himself. It was not enough simply to return to Southwatch. He would never be able to rescue Par on his own. He needed help. What, he wondered, had happened to Morgan Leah and the others? What had become of Walker Boh and Wren? Where was Damson? Was she searching for Par, too? Padishar Creel would help if Coll could find him. But Padishar could be anywhere.

He walked into the early twilight and saw the Silver River appear ahead, a bright thread weaving inland. He skirted a mire formed by the poisoning of a shallow inlet, tepid waters green and murky, vegetation gray with sickness, the stench of its dying heavy on the air. Breathing through his mouth, he forced his way past, anxious to get on.

As he came out from a stand of pine he saw a wagon and stopped.

Five men seated about a cooking fire looked up. Hard-faced and rough, they stared at him without moving. There was meat cooking on a spit and broth in a pot. The smells reached out to Coll enticingly. A team of mules unhitched from the wagon grazed on a tether. Bedrolls lay scattered on the ground in preparation for sleep. The men were in the process of passing an aleskin back and forth.

One of them motioned for Coll to join them. Coll hesitated. The others waved him over, telling him to come on in, to have something to eat and drink, and what in the name of everything sane had happened to him?

Coll went, aware of how strange he must look, but desperate for food. He was seated among them, given a plate and bowl and a cup of the ale. He had barely taken his first bite when the first blow struck him behind the ear and they were all over him. He fought to rise, to free himself and flee, but there were too many hands holding him back. He was pummeled and kicked nearly unconscious. The Sword of Shannara was stripped from him. Chains were locked about his wrists and ankles, and he was thrown into the back of the wagon. He pleaded with them not to do this. He begged them to set him free, telling them that he was searching for his brother, that he had to find him, that they had to let him go. They laughed at him, scorned him, and told him to keep quiet or he would be gagged. He was propped upright and given a cup of broth and a blanket.

His weapon, he was told, would fetch a good price. But he would fetch an even better one when they sold him to the Federation to work in the slave mines at Dechtera.

25

Par Ohmsford dreamed. He ran through a forest black
with shadows and empty of life. It was night, the sky
through the leafy canopy of boughs a deep blue bereft of
stars and moon. Par could see clearly as he ran, but he could
not determine the source of his vision's light. The trunks of
the trees shifted before him, waving like stalks of grass in a
wind, forcing him to dodge and weave to avoid them. Branches
reached down and brushed against his face and arms, trying to
hold him back. Voices whispered, calling out to him over and
over again.

Shadowen. Shadowen.

He was terrified.

The clothes he wore were damp with his sweat, and he could
feel the chafing of his boots against his ankles. Now and again
there would be streams and ponds, and he was forced to leap
them or turn aside because he knew instinctively that they
were quagmires that if stepped in would pull him down. He
listened as he ran for the sounds of other living things. He kept
thinking that he could not be this alone, that a forest must have
other creatures living within it. He kept thinking, too, that the
forest must eventually end, that it could not go on indefinitely.
But the farther he ran, the deeper grew the silence and the
darker the trees. No sound broke the stillness. No light
penetrated the woods.

After a time he became aware of something following him, a nameless black thing that ran as swiftly as he, following as surely as his shadow. He sought to outdistance it by running faster and could not. He sought to lose it by turning aside, first this way and then that, and the thing turned with him. He sought to flatten himself against a monstrous old trunk of indistinguishable origin, and the thing stopped with him and waited.

It was the thing that whispered to him.

Shadowen. Shadowen.

He ran on, not knowing what to do, panic rushing through him, despair washing away hope. He was trapped by the trees and the darkness and could not escape, and he knew that sooner or later the thing would have him. He could feel the blood pounding in his ears and hear the ragged tremor of his breathing. His chest heaved and his legs ached, and he did not think he could go on but knew he could not stop. He reached down for his weapons and found he carried none. He tried to bring someone to help him by sheer force of will, but the names and faces of those he would call upon would not come.

Then he was at the bank of a river, black and swift in the night, racing with the force of floodwaters down a broad, straight channel. He knew it was not really a river, that it was something else, but he did not know what. He saw a bridge spanning it and raced to cross. Behind, he could hear the thing following. He leaped onto the bridge, a wide arching span built of timbers and iron nails. His boots made no sound as he ran. His footfalls were silent. The bridge had seemed an avenue of escape when he had started across it, but now he found he could not see the far shore. He looked back, and the forest had disappeared as well. The sky had lowered and the water had risen, and suddenly he was in a box that was closing tightly about.

The thing that followed him hissed. It was gaining quickly, and it was growing as the box shrank.

Par turned then, knowing he would not escape, that he had

been led into a trap, that whatever he had hoped to gain by running had been lost. He turned, and as he did so he remembered that he was not defenseless after all, that he possessed the power of the wishsong, and that the Elven magic could protect him against anything. A surge of hope flooded through him, and he summoned the magic to his defense. It exploded through him in a wild, euphoric rush, a white light that turned his blood to fire and his body to ice. He felt it fill him, felt it sheathe him in the armor of its power and turn him indestructible.

He waited for the thing that followed with anticipation.

It crept out of the night like a cat, a creature without form or substance. He could feel it long before he saw it. He could sense it watching, then breathing, then drawing itself up. It was first to one side and then to the other and finally all about. But he knew somehow that he was not in danger until he could see its face. It twisted and swirled about him, staying carefully out of reach, and he waited for it to tire.

Then it began to materialize, and it was not strange or misshapen or even so large. Its body was the size and shape of his own, and it stood just before him, fully revealed save for its face. He brought the wishsong's magic to his fingertips and held it there like an arrow drawn back in a bowstring, taut, straining for release, razor-sharp. The thing before him watched. Its head was turned toward him now, but its face was clouded and dim. Its voice whispered again.

Shadowen. Shadowen.

Then its face came together and Par was looking at himself.

Shadowen. Shadowen.

Par shuddered and sent the magic of the wishsong flying into the thing. The thing caught it, and it was gone. Par sent the magic a second time, a hammer-blow of power that would smash the creature back into smoke. The thing swallowed it as if it were air. His face smiled back at him, hollow-looking and ragged about the edges, a mirage threatening to disappear back into the heat.

332

Don't you know?

Don't you see?

The voice whispered, sly, condescending, and hateful, and he attacked again, over and over, the magic flying out of him. But something strange was happening. The more he called upon the magic, the more pleased the thing seemed. He could feel its satisfaction as if it were palpable. He could sense its pleasure. The thing was changing, growing more substantial rather than less, feeding on the magic, drawing it in.

Don't you understand?

Par gasped and stepped back, aware now that he was changing as well, losing shape and definition, disintegrating like burned wood turned to ash. He groped at himself in despair and saw his hands pass through his body. The thing came closer, reaching out. He saw himself reflected in its eyes.

Shadowen. Shadowen.

He saw himself, and he realized that there was no longer any difference between them. He had become the thing.

He screamed as it took him in its arms and slowly drew him in.

The dream ended, and Par awoke with a lurch. He was dizzy, and his breathing was ragged and harsh in the silence. Just a dream, he thought. He put his face in his hands and waited for the spinning to stop. A nightmare, but so very real! He swallowed against his lingering fear.

He opened his eyes again and looked about. He was in a room that was as black as the forest through which he had fled. The room smelled of must and disuse. Windows on a far wall opened onto night skies that were clouded and moonless. The air felt hot and sticky, and there was no wind. He was sitting on a bed that was little more than a wooden frame and pallet, and his clothes were damp and stiff with dried mud.

He remembered then.

The plains, the storm, the battle with Coll, the triggering of the magic of the Sword of Shannara, the coming of the Shadowen, the appearance of the King of the Silver River, the light and then the dark – the images sped past him in an instant's time.

Where was he?

A light flared suddenly from across the room, a brilliant firefly that rested at the fingertips of an arm gloved to the elbow. The light settled on a lamp, and the lamp brightened, casting its glow across the shadows.

'Now that you're awake, perhaps we can talk.'

A black-cloaked form stepped into the light, tall and rangy and hooded. It moved in silence, with grace and ease. On its breast gleamed the white insignia of a wolf's head.

Rimmer Dall.

Par felt himself go cold from head to foot, and it was all he could do to keep from bolting. He looked about quickly at the stone walls, at the bars on the windows, at the iron-bound wooden door that stood closed at Rimmer Dall's back. He was at Southwatch. He looked for the Sword of Shannara. It was gone. And Coll was missing as well.

'You don't seem to have slept well.'

Rimmer Dall's whispery voice floated through the silence. He pulled back the hood and his rawboned, bearded face was caught in the light, all angles and planes, a mask devoid of expression. If he was aware of Par's distress, he did not show it. He moved to a chair and seated himself. 'Do you want something to eat?'

Par shook his head, not yet trusting himself to speak. His throat felt dry and tight, and his muscles were in knots. Don't panic, he told himself. Stay calm. He forced himself to breathe, slow and deep and regular. He brought his legs around on the bed and put his feet on the floor, but did not try to rise. Rimmer Dall watched him out of depthless eyes, his mouth a narrow, tight line, his body motionless. Like a cat waiting, Par thought.

'Where is Coll?' he asked, and his voice was steady.

'The King of the Silver River took him.' The whispery voice was smooth and oddly comforting. 'He took the Sword of Shannara as well.'

'But you managed to keep him from taking me.'

The First Seeker laughed softly. 'You did that yourself. I didn't have anything to do with it. You used the wishsong, and the magic worked against you. It forced the King of the Silver River away from you.' He paused. 'The magic grows more unpredictable, doesn't it? Remember how I warned you?'

Par nodded. 'I do. I remember everything. But what I remember doesn't matter, because I wouldn't believe you if you told me the sun came up in the east. You've lied to me from the beginning. I don't know why, but you have. And I'm through listening, so you might as well do whatever you have in mind and be done with it.'

Rimmer Dall studied him silently. Then he said, 'Tell me what I've lied to you about.'

Par was furious. He started to speak, but then stopped, suddenly aware that he couldn't remember any specific lies the big man had told. The lies were there, as clear as the wolf's head that glimmered on the black robes, but he couldn't seem to focus on them.

'I told you when we met that I was a Shadowen. I gave you the Sword of Shannara and let you test it against me to find out if I was lying. I warned you that your magic was a danger to you, that it was changing you, and that you might not be able to control it without help. Where was the lie in any of this?'

'You took my brother prisoner after making me think I had killed him!' Par howled, on his feet now in spite of his resolve, threatening. 'You let me think he was dead! Then you let him escape with the Mirrorshroud so that he would become a Shadowen and I might kill him again! You set us against each other!'

'Did I?' Rimmer Dall shook his head. 'Why would I do that? What would doing that gain me? Tell me what purpose any of that would serve.' He stayed seated and calm in the face of

Par's wrath, waiting. Par stood there glaring, but did not answer. 'No? Then listen to me. I didn't make you think you killed Coll – you did that on your own. Your magic did that, twisting you about, changing what you saw. Remember, Par? Remember the way you thought you had lost control?'

Par caught his breath. Yes, it had been exactly like that, a sense of flying out of himself, of being shifted away.

The big man nodded. 'My Seekers found your brother after you had fled and brought him to me. Yes, they were rough with him, but they did not know who he was, only that he was where he shouldn't be. I held him at Southwatch, yes – trying to persuade him to help me find you. I believed him my last chance. When he escaped, he took the Mirrorshroud with him – but I didn't help him steal it. He took it on his own. Yes, it subverted him; the magic is too strong for a normal man. You, Par, could have worn it without being affected. And I didn't set you against each other – you did that yourselves. Each time I came to you I tried to help, and each time you ran from me. It is time the running stopped.'

'I'm sure you would like that!' Par snapped furiously. 'It would make things so much easier!'

'Think what you are saying, Par. It lacks reason.'

Par clenched his teeth. 'Lacks reason? Everywhere I go there are Shadowen waiting, trying to kill me and my friends. What of Damson Rhee and Padishar Creel at Tyrsis? I suppose that was all a mistake?'

'A mistake, but not mine,' Rimmer Dall answered calmly. 'The Federation pursued you there, took the girl and then subsequently the free-born leader. The Seekers you destroyed in the watchtower when you freed the girl were there on Federation orders. They did not know who you were, only that you were an intruder. They paid for it with their lives. You must answer for the fairness of that.'

Par shook his head. 'I don't believe you. I don't believe anything you say.'

Rimmer Dall shifted slightly in the chair, a ripple of black.

'So you have said each time we have talked. But you seem to lack any concrete reason for your stance. When have I done anything to threaten you? When have I done anything but be forthright? I told you the history of the Shadowen. I told you that the magic is our birthright, a gift that can help, that can save. I told you that the Federation is the enemy, that it has hunted us and destroyed us at every turn because it fears and hates what it cannot or will not understand. Enemies, Par? Not you and I. We are kindred. We are the same.'

Par saw the dream suddenly, and its memory sparked something dark and inexorable inside. Running from himself, from the magic, from his birthright, from his destiny — it was possible, wasn't it?

'If we are kindred, if you are not the enemy, then you will let me go,' he insisted.

'Oh, no, not this time.' The big man shook his head and his smile was a twitch at the corners of his mouth. 'I did so before, and you almost destroyed yourself. I won't be so foolish again. This time we will try my way. We will talk, visit, explore, discover, and hopefully learn. After that, you can go.'

Par shook his head angrily. 'I don't want to talk or visit or any of the rest. There's nothing to talk about.' He glared. 'If you try to hold me, I will use the wishsong.'

Rimmer Dall nodded. 'Go ahead, use it.' He paused. 'But remember what the magic is doing to you.'

Changing me, Par thought in recognition of the warning's import. Each time I use it, it changes me further. Each time, I lose a little more control. I try not to let that happen, but I can't seem to prevent it. And I don't know what the consequences will be, but they do not feel as if they will be pleasant.

'I am not a Shadowen,' he said dully.

Rimmer Dall's gaze was flat and steady. 'It is only a word.'

'I don't care. I am not.'

The First Seeker rose and walked over to the window. He stared out at the night, distracted and distant. 'I used to be

337

bothered by who I was and what I was called,' he said. 'I considered myself a freak, a dangerous aberration. But I learned that was wrong. It was not what other people thought of me that mattered; it was what I thought of myself. If I allowed myself to be shaped by other people's opinions, I would become what they wished me to become.'

He turned back to Par. 'The Shadowen are being destroyed without reason. We are being blamed without cause. We have magic that can help in many ways, and we are not being allowed to use it. Ask yourself, Par – how is it any different for you?'

Par was suddenly exhausted, weighed down by the impact of what had happened to him and his confusion over what it might mean. Rimmer Dall was calm and smooth and unshakable. His arguments were persuasive. Par could not think how the First Seeker had lied. He could not focus on when he had tried to cause harm. It had always seemed that he was the enemy – and Allanon and Cogline had said so – but where was the proof of it? Where, for that matter, were the Druid and the old man? Where was anyone who could help him?

His memory of the dream haunted him. How much truth had the dream told?

He turned back to the bed from which he had risen and sat down again. It seemed as if nothing had gone right for him from the moment he had accepted Allanon's charge to recover the Sword of Shannara. Not even the Sword itself had proved to be of any use. He was alone and abandoned and helpless. He did not know what to do.

'Why not sleep a bit more,' Rimmer Dall suggested quietly. He was already moving for the door. 'I'll have food and drink sent up to you in a little while, and we can talk again later.'

He was through the door and gone almost before Par thought to look up. The Valeman rose quickly to stop him, then sat down again. The spinning sensation had returned. His body felt weak and leaden. Perhaps he should sleep again. Perhaps he would be able to reason things through better if he did.

Shadowen. Shadowen.

Was it possible that he was?

He curled up on the pallet and drifted away.

He dreamed again, and this second dream was a variation of the first, dark and terrifying. He woke in a sweat, shaking and raw-nerved, and saw daylight brightening the skies through his windows. Food and drink were brought by a black-robed, silent Shadowen, and he thought for a moment to smash the creature with his magic and flee. But he hesitated, uncertain of the wisdom of this course of action, the moment passed, and the door closed on him once more.

He ate and drank and did not feel better. He sat in the gloom of his prison and listened to the silence. Now and again he could hear the cries of herons and cranes from somewhere without, and there was a low whistling of wind against the castle stone. He walked to the windows and peered out. He was facing east into the sun. Below, the Mermidon wound its way down out of the Runne to the Rainbow Lake, its waters swollen from the storm and clogged with debris. The windows were deep-set and did not allow for more than a glimpse of the land about, but he could smell the trees and the grasses and he could hear the river's flow.

He sat on his bed again afterward, trying to think what to do. As he did so, he became aware of a thrumming sound from deep within the castle, an odd vibration that ran through the stone and the iron like thunder in a storm, low and insistent. It seemed that it ran in a steady, unbroken wave, but once in a while he thought he could feel it break and hear something different in its whine. He listened to it carefully, feeling its movement in his body, and he wondered what it was.

The day eased toward noon, and Rimmer Dall returned. So black that he seemed to absorb the light around him, he slipped through the door like a shadow and materialized in the chair once more. He asked Par how he was feeling, how he had slept, whether the food and drink had been sufficient. He was pleasant and calm and anxious to converse, yet distant, too, as if fearing that any attempt to get close would exacerbate wounds already opened. He talked again of the Shadowen and the Federation, of the mistake that Par was making in confusing the two, of the danger in believing that both were enemies. He spoke again of his mistrust of the Druids, of the ways they manipulated and deceived, of their obsession with power and its uses. He reminded Par of the history of his family – how the Druids had used the Ohmsfords to achieve ends they believed necessary and in the process changed forever the lives of those so employed.

'You would not be suffering the vicissitudes of the wish-song's magic if not for what was done to Wil Ohmsford years ago,' he declared, his voice, as always, low and compelling. 'You can reason it through as well as I, Par. All that you have endured these past few weeks was brought about by the Druids and their magic. Where does the blame for that lie?'

He talked then of the sickening of the Four Lands and the steps that needed to be taken to hasten a recovery. It was not the Shadowen who caused the sickness. It was the neglect of the Races, of those who had once been so careful to protect and preserve. Where were the Elves when they were needed? Gone, because the Federation had driven them away, frightened of their heritage of magic. Where were the Dwarves, always the best of tenders? In slavery, subdued by the Federation so that they could pose no threat to the Southland government.

He spoke for some time, and then suddenly he was gone again, faded back into the stone and silence of the castle. Par sat where he had been left and did not move, hearing the First Seeker's whisper in his mind – the cadence of his voice, the sound of his words, and the litany of his arguments as they began and ended and began again. The afternoon passed away, and the sun faded west. Twilight fell, and dinner arrived. He accepted what he was offered by the silent bearer and this time did not think of trying to escape. He ate and drank without paying attention, staring at the walls of his room, thinking.

Nightfall came, and with it came Rimmer Dall once more. Par was looking for him this time, expecting him, anticipating him as he would thunder in a rainstorm. He heard the door latch give, saw it open, and watched the First Seeker come through. The black-cloaked figure moved to his chair without speaking and sat. They stared at each other in the silence, measuring.

'What have I not told you that I should?' Rimmer Dall asked finally, motionless in the growing shadows. 'What answers can I give?'

Par shook his head. The First Seeker had given him too many answers and too much to consider, and it tumbled about in his mind like colored glass in a kaleidoscope. A part of him continued to resist everything he heard, stubborn and intractable. It would not let him believe; it would not even let him consider. He wished that it would. His sleep was filled with nightmares, and his waking was crowded with a senseless warring of possibilities. He wanted it all to end.

He did not say this to Rimmer Dall. He asked instead about the sounds from within the castle, the thrumming through the walls, the pitch and whine, the sense of something stirring. The First Seeker smiled. The explanation was simple. What Par was hearing was the Mermidon passing through an underground channel that ran beneath the keep, its waters crashing against the walls of ancient caves below. At times you could feel the vibrations for miles about. At times you could feel them in your bones.

'Does it disturb your sleep?' the big man asked.

Par shook his head. The nightmares disturbed his sleep. 'If I were to decide to believe you,' he said, letting the words slip free before his stubborn side could think better of it, 'what would you do to help me control the magic of the wishsong?'

Rimmer Dall sat perfectly still. 'I would teach you to

manage it. I would teach you to be comfortable with it. You could learn how to use it safely again.'

Par stared straight ahead without seeing. He wanted to believe. 'You think you could do that?'

'I have had years to learn how. I was forced to do so with my own magic, and the lessons have not been lost on me. The magic is a powerful weapon, Par, and it can turn against you. You need discipline and understanding to rule it properly. I can give you that.'

Par's mind felt leaden and his eyes drooped. His weariness was a dark cloud that would not let him think. 'We could talk about it, I guess,' he said.

'Talk, yes. But experiment, too.' Rimmer Dall was leaning forward, intense. 'Control of the magic comes from practice; it is an acquired skill. The magic is a birthright, but it needs training.'

'Training?'

'I could show you. I could let you see inside my mind, let you see how the magic functions within me. I could give you access to the ways in which I block it and channel it. Then you could do the same for me.'

Par looked up. 'How?'

'You could let me see inside your mind. You could let me explore and help set in place the protections you need. We could work together.'

He went on, explaining carefully, persuasively, but Par had ceased to hear, locked on something vaguely alarming, something that lacked an identity, but was there nevertheless. The stubborn part that refused to believe anything the First Seeker said had risen up with a gasp and closed down his mind like a trapdoor. He pretended to listen, heard bits and pieces of what the other was saying, and gave responses that committed nothing.

What was it? What was the matter?

After a time, Rimmer Dall left him alone. 'Think about what I have told you,' he urged. 'Consider what might be done.' The night settled in, and the darkness of Par's chamber was complete. He lay down to sleep, exhausted without reason, then fought against the urge to close his eyes because he did not want the nightmares to come again. He stared at the ceiling and then out the windows at a sky that was clear and filled with stars. He thought of his brother and the Sword of Shannara, and he wondered what the King of the Silver River had done with them. He thought of Damson and Padishar, Walker and Wren, and all the others who had been involved in his struggle. He wondered vaguely what the struggle had been for.

He slept finally, drifting off before he knew what was happening, sinking into a soothing blackness. But the nightmare surfaced instantly, and he experienced for the third time a confrontation with himself as a Shadowen wraith. He thrashed and twisted and fought to come awake, and afterward lay sweating and gasping in the dark.

He realized then, with chilling certainty, that something was dreadfully wrong.

Look at what was happening to him. He could not sleep without dreaming, and the dream was always the same. He ate, but he lost strength. He spent his time in his room doing nothing, yet he was always tired. He could not think straight. He could not concentrate. His energy was being sapped away.

This wasn't happening by chance, he admonished himself. Something was causing it.

He sat upright on the bed, swung his legs to the floor, and stared into the room's shadows. *Think!* He fought back against his exhaustion, against the chains of his lethargy and disorientation. Recognition came, a slow untangling of threads that had knotted. There were two possibilities. The first was that the magic of the wishsong was infecting him in some new way, and he needed to do what Rimmer Dall was urging. The second was that the magic infecting him was Shadowen, that Rimmer Dall was working to break down his defenses, and that all his talk about helping him was some sort of trick.

But a trick to do what?

Par took a deep, steadying breath. He wanted to crawl back beneath the covers but would not let himself. He felt an urge to scream and choked it down. Was Rimmer Dall lying or telling the truth? What were his real intentions in all this? Par clasped his hands together to keep them from shaking. He was falling apart. He could feel himself unraveling, and he did not know how to stop it. If Rimmer Dall was telling the truth about the wishsong, then he needed his help. If he was lying, it was a deception so intricate and so vast that it dwarfed anything the Valeman could imagine, because it had to have been at work from the moment the First Seeker had come looking for him weeks ago at the Blue Whisker Ale House.

Shades! I need to know!

Par rose, walked to the windows, and stood looking out at the night, breathing the cool air. He was paralyzed with indecision. How was he going to learn the truth? Was there some way to see past his own uncertainty, to recognize if there was a deception being played? The Sword of Shannara had showed him nothing, he reminded himself. Nothing! What else was there to try?

He watched shadows thrown by the night clouds shift like animals through the trees across the river. He would have to stall, he told himself. He could listen and talk, but he could not allow anything to happen. He would have to find a way to dispel his confusion so that he could recognize what was truth and what a lie, and at the same time he would have to find a way to keep himself from disintegrating completely.

He closed his eyes, put his face in his hands, and wondered how he was going to do that.

26

Heat rose off the grasslands east of Drey Wood in sweltering waves, the midday sun a fiery ball in the cloudless sky, the air thick with the smell and taste of sweat and dust. Wren Elessedil lay flat against the crest of a rise and watched the Federation army toil its way across the plains like a slow-moving, many-legged insect.

Mindless and persistent, she thought bleakly.

She did not bother glancing over at the others – Triss, Erring Rift, and Desidio. She already knew what she would see in their faces. She already knew what they were thinking.

They had been watching the Federation's progress for more than an hour – not with any expectation that they would learn anything, but out of a need to do something besides sit around and wait for the inevitable. The Elves were in trouble. The Federation march north to the Rhenn had resumed two days ago, and time was running out. Barsimmon Oridio had finally completed the mobilization and provisioning of the main body of the Elven army and was headed east to the pass, a forced march that would bring the Elves into the Rhenn at least three days ahead of the enemy. But the Elves were still outnumbered ten to one, and any kind of direct engagement would result in their annihilation. Worse, the Creepers continued their approach, closer now than before, catching up quickly to the slower Southlanders. In four, maybe five days, the Creepers would overtake them and become their vanguard, the advance for a search-and-destroy action. When that happened, it would be the end of the Elves.

Wren felt a vague hopelessness nudging at her, and she angrily thrust it away.

What can I do to save my people?

She focused again on the crawling army and tried to think. Another midnight raid was out of the question. The Federation was alerted to them now and would not be caught napping twice. Cavalry patrols rode day and night all around the main body of the army, scouring the countryside for any sign of the Elves. Once or twice riders more bold than smart had even ventured into the forests. Wren had let them pass, the Elves melting back into the trees, invisible in the shadows. She did not want the Federation to know where they were. She did not want to give them anything she didn't have to. Not that it mattered. The patrols kept them at bay, and sentry lines were extended a quarter-mile out from the camp once darkness fell. The Wing Riders could come in from overhead, but she did not care to risk her most valuable weapon when she could bring no strength to bear in its support.

Besides, it made little difference what she did about the Federation army if she did not first find a way to stop the Creepers. Though still distant, the Creepers were the most dangerous and immediate threat. If they were allowed to reach the Rhenn, or even the Westland forests immediately south, there would be nothing to stop them from carving a path straight through to Arborlon. The Creepers wouldn't worry about finding a roadway leading in. They wouldn't concern themselves with ambushes and traps. They didn't need scouts or patrols to search out the enemy. The Creepers would find the Elves wherever they tried to hide and destroy them in the same manner they had destroyed the Dwarves fifty years earlier. Wren knew the stories. She knew what kind of enemy they were up against.

The sweat lay against her face like a damp mask. She exhaled slowly, beckoned to the others, and began backing off the rise. When they were safely within the shelter of the trees once more, they rose and walked to where their horses were held by the Elven Hunters who had come with them. No one spoke. No one had anything to say. Wren led the way, trying to look as if she had something in mind even though she didn't, worried that she was beginning to lose the confidence she had won in leading the attack three nights earlier, confidence that she needed if she was to control events once Barsimmon Oridio arrived. She was Queen of the Elves, she told herself. But even a queen could fail.

They mounted and rode back to the Elven camp. Wren thought back over all that had happened since the coming of Cogline, wondering what had become of the old man – what, for that matter, had become of the others he had gathered at the Hadeshorn to speak with the shade of Allanon. She experienced a vague sense of regret that she knew so little of their fates. She should be searching for them, seeking them out and telling them the truth about the Shadowen origins. It was important that they know, she sensed. Something about who and what the Shadowen were would lead to their destruction. Allanon had known as much, she believed. But if he had known, why hadn't he simply told them? She shook her head. It was more complex than that; it had to be. But wasn't everything in this struggle?

They reached the vanguard camp, settled several miles north, dismounted, and handed over their horses. Wren strode away from the others, still without speaking, took food from a table not because she was hungry but because she knew she must eat, and sat alone at one end of a bench and stared off into the trees. The answers were out there somewhere, she told herself. She kept thinking that they were tied to the past, that history repeats, that you learn from what has gone before. Morrowind's lessons paraded themselves before her eyes in

347

the form of dead faces and brief images of unending sacrifice. So much had been given up to get the Elves safely away from that deathtrap; it could not have been simply for this. It had to have been for something more than dying here instead of there.

She wished suddenly for Garth. She missed his steadying presence, the way he could take any problem and make it seem solvable. No matter how dark things had gotten, Garth had always gone on, taking her with him when she was little, letting her lead when she was grown. She missed him so. Tears came to her eyes, and she brushed them away self-consciously. She would not cry for him again. She had promised she would not.

She rose and carried her plate back to the table, looking about for Erring Rift. She would fly south again, she decided, for another look at the Creepers. There had to be a way to stop or at least slow them. Maybe something would suggest itself. It was a faint hope, but it was all she had. She wished Tiger Ty was there; he provided some of the same steadiness that she had gotten from Garth. But the gnarled Wing Rider had not returned from his search for the free-born, and bringing the free-born to the aid of the Elves was more important than providing solace for her.

She caught sight of Rift and whistled him over.

'We're going up for another look at the Creepers,' she announced, keeping her gaze steady as she faced him. His bearded face clouded. 'I need to do this. Don't argue with me.'

Rift shook his head. 'I wouldn't dream of it,' he muttered. 'My lady.'

She took his arm and walked him through the camp. 'We won't stay out long. Let's just see where they are, all right?'

Obsidian eyes glanced over and away again. 'They're too confounded close, is where they are. We both know that already.' He rubbed at his beard. 'There's no mystery to this. We have to stop them. You don't happen to have a plan for doing that, do you?'

She gave him a faint smile. 'You'll be the first to know.'

They were moving toward the clearing where the Rocs were settled when Tib Arne came running up, breathless and flushed.

'My lady! My lady! Are you flying one of the great birds? Take me with you this time, please? You said you would, my lady. The next time you went out, you said you would. Please? I'm tried of sitting about doing nothing.'

She turned to face him. 'Tib,' she began.

'Please?' he begged, coming to a ragged stop in front of her. He brushed back his shock of blond hair. His blue eyes sparkled with anticipation. 'I won't be any trouble.'

She glanced at Rift, who gave her a black look of warning. But she was feeling at loose ends with herself, strangely disconnected from everything, and she needed to regain her perspective. Why not? She thought. Perhaps having Tib along would help. Perhaps it would suggest something.

She nodded. 'All right. You can come.'

Tib's smile spread from ear to ear. It just about matched Erring Rift's scowl.

They flew south against the backdrop of the mountains, the Elf Queen, the leader of the Wing Riders, and the boy, staying low and tight against the land. They passed the laboring Federation army, strung out across the empty plains in a massive cloud of dust, and continued on past the bleak expanse of the Matted Brakes toward the blue ribbon of the Mermidon. The wind blew at them in soothing, cooling waves, and the land spread away in a patchwork of earth colors dotted with bright flashes of sunlight reflecting off ponds and streams. Wren sat behind Erring Rift, and Tib Arne sat behind her. She could feel the tension in the boy as he strained to look down past Grayl's wings, taking in the land below, seeking first to one side and then to the other, small exclamations of excitement escaping his lips. She smiled, and lost herself in memories.

Only once did her thoughts stray back to the present. For the second time in a row, she had not brought Faun with her on a flight with Erring Rift. Faun had begged to go, and she had refused. Maybe she was afraid for the Tree Squeak, frightened that it would fall from the Roc's back. Maybe it was something more. She really wasn't sure.

The hours slipped away. They reached the Pykon, picked up the winding channel of the Mermidon, and sped south. Still no sign of the Creepers. Wren scanned the countryside, afraid that the monsters had slipped into the trees where they could no longer be followed. But seconds later a glint of metal flashed out of the distance, and Erring Rift swung Grayl into a sweeping loop that carried them away from the Mermidon and closer to the mountains west. They hugged the rocks as they came up on the Creepers, who were bunched east of the river, lurching after the Federation army. Wren watched the insect things move tirelessly through the heat and dust, monsters that served inhuman masters and insupportable needs. She thought of the things she had left behind on Morrowindl and realized that she had not really left them behind after all. The dark creatures that the Elven magic had created there had simply been recreated here in another form. History repeating again, she thought. So what were the lessons she needed to learn?

They flew past twice, and then Wren had Erring Rift land them on a bluff amid a series of forested foothills backed up against the Rock Spur. From there they could watch the progress of the Creepers as they labored on across the grasslands, disjointed legs rising and falling in steady cadence.

Wren seated herself without comment. Tib Arne sat next to her, knees drawn up, arms wrapped about his legs, face intense as he stared out at the Creepers. *Creepers.* She mouthed the word without saying it. How could they be stopped? She dug at the ground with the heels of her boots, thinking. Behind her, Erring Rift was checking the harness straps on Grayl. Wind blew gently through the trees, soothing and cool on her skin. She thought of the Wisteron, a distant cousin to the Creepers, sunk finally into the mire close to where it had made its lair.

Rift touched her shoulder, handing down a waterskin. She took it, drank, and offered it to Tib, who declined. She rose and walked with Rift to the edge of the rise, staring out again at the Creepers. What was out there that could hurt these things? did they eat and sleep like other creatures? Did they need water? Did they breathe air?

She brushed at the sweat on her face.

'We should start back,' Rift said quietly.

She nodded and didn't move. Below, the Creepers lumbered on, sunlight glinting off their armor, dust rising from their heavy tread.

The Wisteron, she was thinking. *Sunk into the earth.*

She blinked. There was something there for her, she realized. Something useful . . .

Then she heard a familiar, low whistle, and started to turn. Tib Arne appeared next to her, blond-haired and blue-eyed, smiling and excited. He came up with a laugh and pointed out toward the plains. 'Look.'

She stared out into the swelter, seeing nothing.

Beside her, Erring Rift grunted sharply and lurched forward. Behind, there was a heavy clump, as if a tree had fallen, and a shriek that froze her blood.

She turned, something slammed against her head, and everything went black.

Far to the east, the Dragon's Teeth had begun already to cast their shadows with the failing of the late afternoon light. Tiger Ty rode Spirit on a slow, steady wind that bore them north across the tallest of the peaks toward the parched and scorching plains. The Wing Rider's day had been fruitless – the same as every day since he had set out in search of the free-born. From dawn to dusk he scoured the land for an indication of the promised army and found nothing. There were Federation patrols everywhere, some of considerable size, like the one blocking the pass at the south end of the mountains. He had left Spirit long enough to visit with people on the road, asking for news, learning of a prison break in a city called Tyrsis, where the leader of the free-born, Padishar Creel, had been held for execution until his followers managed to free him. It was quite an accomplishment, and everyone was talking about it. But no one seemed to know where he was now or where any of the free-born were, for that matter.

Or at least they weren't saying.

The fact that Tiger Ty was an Elf and knew almost nothing of the Four Lands didn't help matters. Constricted by his ignorance, he was reduced to searching blindly. He had managed to discover that the outlaws had probably gone to ground in the mountains he now sailed across, but the peaks were vast and filled with places to hide, and he might spend fifty years looking and never find anyone.

In point of fact, he was beginning to think that it was hopeless. But he had given his promise to Wren that he would find the free-born, and he was no less determined than she had been when she had flown to Morrowindl in search of the Elves.

He stared down at the empty, blasted rock, his leathery face furrowed and dark. It all looked the same; there was nothing to see. As the mountains spread farther north, he banked Spirit left, tracking their line yet again. He had made this same sweep twice now, taking a slightly different tack each time so as to cover a fresh stretch of the vast range, knowing even as he did that there were still hundreds of places he was missing.

His body knotted with frustration and weariness. If there was a free-born army out there, why was it so confounded hard to find?

He thought momentarily of Wren and the Land Elves, and he wondered if the Federation army had recovered sufficiently to continue its pursuit. He smiled, remembering the night attack. The girl was something, all right. She was all grit and hard edges. Barely grown, and already a leader. The Land Elves, he thought, would go exactly as far as they would allow her to take them. If they didn't listen to her, they were foolish beyond –

A flash of light from the rocks below disrupted his train of thought. He stared downward intently. The flash came again, quick and certain. A signal, sure enough. But from who? Tiger Ty nudged Spirit, spiraling outward so that he could study better what they were flying toward. The flash came a third and fourth time, and then stopped, as if whoever had given it was satisfied that it had been seen. The source of the signal was a bluff high in the north central peaks, and as he approached he could see a knot of four men standing at the bluff's center, waiting. They were out in the open and not trying to hide, and it did not appear that there were any others about or any places that they might be hiding. A good sign, the Wing Rider thought. But he would be careful anyway.

He settled Spirit onto the bluff, alert for any deception. The giant Roc came to rest at the edge, well away from the four. Tiger Ty sat where he was for a moment, studying the terrain. The men across from him waited patiently. Tiger Ty satisfied himself, loosened the retaining straps, and climbed down. He spoke a word of caution to Spirit, then ambled forward across a stretch of dried saw grass and broken rock. Two of the four came to meet him, one tall and lean and chiseled like stone, the other black-bearded and ferocious. The tall one limped.

When they were less than six paces from each other, Tiger Ty stopped. The two men did the same.

'That was your signal?' Tiger Ty asked.

The tall one nodded. 'You've been flying past for two days

353

now, searching for something. We decided it was time to find out what. Legend has it that only Wing Riders fly the giant Rocs. Is that so? Have you come from the Elves?'

Tiger Ty folded his arms. 'Depends on who's asking. There's a lot of people not to be trusted these days. Are you one of them?'

The black-bearded man flushed and started forward a step, but a glance from the other stopped him in his tracks. 'No,' he answered, lifting an eyebrow quizzically. 'Are you?'

Tiger Ty smiled. 'Guess this game could go on awhile, couldn't it? Are you free-born?'

'Now and forever,' said the tall man.

'Then you're who I'm looking for. I'm called Tiger Ty. I've been sent by Wren Elessedil, Queen of the Land Elves.'

'Then the Elves are truly back?'

Tiger Ty nodded.

The tall man smiled in satisfaction. 'I'm Padishar Creel, leader of the free-born. My friend is called Chandos. Welcome back to the Four Lands, Tiger Ty. We need you.'

Tiger Ty grunted. 'We need you worse. Where's your army?'

Padishar Creel looked confused. 'My army?'

'The one that's supposed to be marching to our rescue! We're under attack by a Federation force ten times our size – cavalry, foot soldiers, archers, siege equipment – well, not so much of that anymore, but enough armor and weapons to roll us up like ants under a broom. The boy said you were on your way to help us with five thousand men. Not enough by half, but any help would be welcome.'

Chandos frowned darkly, rubbing at his beard. 'Just a minute. What boy are you talking about?'

Tiger Ty stared. 'The one with the war shrike.' A sudden uneasiness gripped the Wing Rider. 'Tib Arne.' He looked from one face to the other. 'Blue eyes, towheaded, kind of small. You did send him, didn't you?'

The men across from him exchanged a hurried glance. 'We

354

sent a man who was forty if he was a day. His name was Sennepon Kipp,' Chandos said carefully. 'I should know. I made the choice myself.'

Tiger Ty went cold all the way through. 'But the boy? You don't know the boy at all?'

Padishar Creel's hard eyes fixed him. 'Not before this. Tiger Ty. But I'd be willing to bet we know him now.'

Bright light seared the slits of Wren's eyes as she regained consciousness, and she turned her head away, blinking. A fist knotted in her hair and jerked her upright, and the voice that whispered in her ear was filled with hatred and disdain.

'Awake, awake, Queen of the Elves.'

The hand released, letting her slump forward on her knees, her head aching from the blow that had felled her. A gag filled her mouth, secured so tightly that she could only breathe through her nose. Her hands were tied behind her back, her wrists lashed with cord that cut the flesh. Dust and the smell of her own sweat and fear filled her nostrils.

'Ah, lady, my lady, the fairest of the fair, ruler of the Westland Elves – you are such a fool!' The voice became a hiss. 'Sit up and look at me!'

She was struck a blow to the side of the head that spilled her back to the ground, and again the fist closed on her hair and yanked her upright. 'Look at me!'

She lifted her head and stared into Tib Arne's blue eyes. There was no laughter in them now, nothing of the boy that he had seemed. They were hard and cold and filled with menace.

'Cat got your tongue?' he sneered, and gave her a mirthless smile. There was blood on his hands. 'Cat got your tongue, and I've got the rest. But what to do with you? What duty shall I render to the Queen of the Elves?'

He wheeled away, laughing softly, shaking his head, hugging himself with glee. Wren looked around in dismal recognition. Erring Rift lay dead on the ground next to her, the killing blade still jammed to the hilt in his back. Grayl lay a little further off, lifeless as well, most of his head missing. Towering over him was Gloon, grown somehow as large as the Roc, feathers bristling from his sinewy body like quills. Talons and beak already red with blood ripped at the dead Roc, tearing out new chunks of flesh. In the midst of eating, Gloon paused and stared directly at her, crested brows furrowing, and what she saw in the war shrike's eyes was an undisguised hunger.

Her breath caught in her throat, and she could not look away.

'Larger than you remember him, isn't he?' Tib Arne said, suddenly very close again, his shadow enveloping her as he bent down. His boyish voice was all wrong for the hardened face. 'That was your first mistake – thinking that we were what we seemed. You were very stupid.'

He seized her neck and twisted her to face him. 'It was easy, really. I could have come into the camp at any time, could have told you I was anyone. But I waited, patient and smart. I saw the free-born messenger, and I intercepted him. He told me everything before he died. Then I took his place. All I needed to do was to get you alone for a few moments, you see. That was all.'

His eyes danced. Suddenly he began hitting her with his free hand, holding her upright as he did so that she would not fall. 'But you wouldn't give me that!' He stopped hitting her, jerking her bloodied face about so that she could see him again. His blond hair was awry and his blue eyes sparkled, but the winning boy could not conceal the monster that seethed just beneath the surface of the skin, tensed to break forth. 'You tried to send me away, and while I was gone you led that night attack on the Federation army! Stupid, stupid girl! They're nothing! All you did was slow things up a bit, force us to bring the Creepers just that much sooner, require us to work just that much harder!'

He dropped to his knees in front of her, hand still clenched about her neck in a grip of iron. A single word repeated itself over and over in her pain-fogged mind. *Shadowen*.

'But I killed those men – or rather Gloon did for me. Tore them to shreds, and I listened to them scream and did nothing to quicken their death. But it was your fault they died, not mine. I sent Gloon to hide and came back – too late to stop your foolish night raid, but soon enough to make certain it would not happen again. And then I waited, knowing a chance would come to get you alone, knowing it must!'

He gave her his little-boy look of pleading, and his voice grew mocking. 'Oh, Lady, please, please take me with you? You promised you would? Please? I won't be any trouble?'

She breathed sharply through her nose, fighting to clear the blood and dust, struggling to stay conscious.

'Oh, I'm sorry. Are you uncomfortable?' He slapped her lightly on one cheek and then the other. 'There! Is that better?' He laughed. 'Where was I? Oh, yes – waiting. And today marks the end of that, doesn't it? You turned your back, I whistled in Gloon to finish the Roc, kept your attention fixed on the Creepers while I stabbed the Wing Rider, then knocked you out. So quick, so easy. Over and done with in seconds.'

He released her and stood up. Wren slumped but refused to fall, to give him the satisfaction. Her own rage was building, fighting through the weariness and pain, giving her strength enough to focus on the boy.

The Shadowen.

Tib Arne snickered. 'No hope for you now, is there, Queen of the Elves? Not the least. They'll hunt for you, but they won't find you. Not you, not the Wing Rider, not the Roc. You will all simply disappear.' He smiled. 'Want to know where? Of course you do. Doesn't matter with the other two, but you . . .'

He put his hands on his hips and cocked his head, his casual stance betrayed by the hardness in his eyes and the malice in

357

his voice. 'You will go to Southwatch and Rimmer Dall – with these!'

He reached into his pocket and pulled out the leather pouch that held the Elfstones. Her heart lurched. The Elfstones, her only weapon against the Shadowen.

'We've known about them since you killed our brother at the Wing Hove. Such power – but it is no longer yours. It belongs to the First Seeker now. And so will you, my lady. Until he's done with you, and then I'll ask that you be given back to me!'

He shoved the pouch back into his pocket. 'You should have let things be, Elf Queen. It would have been better for you if you had. You should have remembered that we are all of a common origin – Elves, come out of the old world where we were kings. You should have asked to be one of us. Your magic would have let you. Shadowen are what Elves were destined to become. Some of us knew. Some of us listened to the earth's whisper!'

What is he talking about? she wondered. But her thinking was muddled and dull.

He turned away, watched Gloon eat for a time, then whistled the war shrike over. Gloon came reluctantly, pieces of Grayl still clutched in his hooked beak. Tib Arne patted and soothed the giant bird, talking quietly with it, laughing and joking. Gloon listened intently, eyes fixed on the boy, head dipped obediently. Wren stayed where she was, trying to think what she might do to help herself.

Then Tib came for her, picked her up easily, slung her over Gloon's slate-gray back like a sack of grain, and strapped her in place. The boy went back for Erring Rift, and threw the Wing Rider's body from the bluff into the dense thickets below. On command, Gloon buried his blood-streaked yellow beak in Grayl, dragged the unfortunate Roc to the edge, and dropped him after. Wren closed her eyes against what she was feeling. Tib Arne was right; she had been stupid beyond reason.

The boy came back to her then and pulled himself aboard Gloon.

'You see, the magic allows us anything, Elf Queen,' he snapped over his shoulder as he settled himself in place. 'Gloon can make himself large or small as he chooses, cloaked in the shrike's feathers, come out of the Shadowen form he took when he embraced the magic. And I can be the son you'll never have. Have I been a good son, mother? Have I?' He laughed. 'You never suspected, did you? Rimmer Dall said you wouldn't. He said you'd want to like and trust me, that you needed someone after losing your big friend on Morrowindl.'

Wren felt bitterness rise within to mix with humiliation and despair. Tib Arne watched her for a moment and laughed.

Then Gloon spread his wings and they were flying east across the plains, speeding away from the Westland forests, the Creepers, the Federation army, and the Elves. She watched everything disappear gradually into the sunset and then into shadows, night descending in a hazy, gray light. They flew into darkness, following lowing the line of the Mermidon into Callahorn, past Kern and Tyrsis, down through the grasslands south.

Midnight came, and they descended to a darkened flat on which a wagon and horsemen waited. How they had come to be there, Wren didn't know. The men were black-cloaked and bore the wolf's-head insignia of Seekers. There were eight, all dark and voiceless within their garb, wraiths in the silence of the night. They looked as if they had been expecting Tib Arne and Gloon. Tib gave the pouch with the Elfstones to one, and two others lifted her from Gloon and placed her inside the wagon. No words were spoken. Wren twisted about in an effort to see, but the canvas flaps had already been drawn and secured.

Lying in blackness and silence, she heard the sound of Gloon's wings as he rose back into the air. Then the wagon gave a lurch and started forward. Wheels creaked, traces jangled, and horses' hooves clumped in steady rhythm through the night.

She was on her way to Southwatch and Rimmer Dall, she knew, and felt as if a great hole had opened in the earth to swallow her.

27

It was nearing dawn when Morgan Leah saw the wagon and riders come out of the grasslands west, slowing to begin the climb into the hills that led to Southwatch. He stood on the bluff south, his watch post for three days past now, staring out across the awakening land. Stars and moon were fading in a cloudless night sky, but the hills were thick with patches of mist that clung to the hollows and draws. The earth was a repository for predawn shadows melting into the gray of the disappearing night, still and lifeless husks that would be swallowed whole when morning arrived.

Except, of course, for the wagon and the horsemen, shadows of substance whose movements stood out against the frozen dark. Morgan watched them silently, motionlessly, as if any sound or movement on his part might cause them to vanish in the haze. They were still a fair distance away, nearly lost in the gloom, shimmering like dark ghosts against the night.

They were the first sign of life he had seen since he had begun his vigil. They were, he knew instantly, what he had been waiting for.

Three days gone, and no one had gone into or come out of Southwatch. No one had even gone near. The land might have been devoid of life but for a handful of birds that sped in and out of view with single-minded concentration. There had been skiffs upon the Mermidon and the Rainbow Lake, but all had passed south, well clear of the Shadowen citadel, well away from any contact. Morgan had watched long and carefully for signs of life within the obelisk, but there had been none. He had slept in snatches, staying awake a portion of the day and night both so that he could minimize the chance that something might get by him. He had watched and waited, and nothing had appeared.

But now there was a wagon and horsemen, and he was certain already that they were bound for Southwatch.

He studied them further and knew as well that they were Seekers. He could tell from the black cloaks and hoods, from the way they held themselves, and from the dark secrecy of their approach. They came in stealth and under cover of night, and whatever they were about they did not want it known. There were six riders, four in front and two behind, and there were at least two drivers. In the odd hush of night's leaving, they were a whisper across the empty land, creeping in and out of the haze and shadows, inching toward the coming light.

He took a deep breath. They were, he repeated, what he had been waiting for. He did not know why. He did not understand their purpose or fathom their intent. They might be carrying Par Ohmsford within the wagon. They might not. It didn't matter. Something inside him whispered that he must not let them pass. It spoke in a voice so clear and certain that he could not ignore it.

This is what you have been waiting for. Do something.

It had been five days since Damson Rhee and Matty Roh had departed in search of Par, following the brightening Skree in hopes that it would lead them to the Valeman. The storm had swept away all trace of what had gone before, so the Skree was all they had to help them track. Morgan had remained at Southwatch to wait for their return. But they were not yet back, and there was no indication that they would be coming anytime soon. It had been left to Morgan to determine if Par was a prisoner of the Shadowen, a task that seemed virtually impossible in the absence of an opportunity to enter and have a look around.

But now . . .

He took a deep breath. Now, it might be different.

But he would have to decide quickly what he was going to do. He would have to act at once.

He was already tracing the wagon's route as it wound ahead through the misted hills. He could intercept it if he chose. He could reach it before it arrived at Southwatch, cut across its path while it was still several miles away. With his eyes he followed the rutted track it must stay on to reach the citadel, a path that other wagons had worn before. He was close enough, he decided. He could stop it.

If he chose.

One man against eight – and those eight Seekers, and probably Shadowen as well. His jaw tightened, and he smiled sardonically. He had better be sure.

East, the first faint tinges of silvery light began to peek out from behind the forested horizon, sending gleaming spiderwebs across the flat, dark surface of the Rainbow Lake. The silence deepened, a hush of expectation, waiting, waiting.

Standing motionless on the bluff, staring out across the hills at the wagon and the horsemen, Morgan found himself looking beyond the here and now into the past, seeing himself again in Leah, in the Highlands in which his family had lived for centuries, picturing what his life had been like such a short time ago. He remembered how he had described it to Matty – standing in place. He had spent his time nipping at the heels of the Federation officials quartered in what had once been his family home, content with creating annoying distractions, satisfied with causing mischief and discontent. He had come a long way from that, gone north to the Hadeshorn and the shade of Allanon, gone beyond to Tyrsis and the Pit, to the Dragon's Teeth and the Jut, to Padishar Creel and the freeborn, gone farther still to Eldwist and the Stone King, to the Black Elfstone and the Maw Grint. He had fought the Sha-

363

dowen and their minions and survived what no one should have. He had taken himself out of one life and emerged changed forever in another. He would never be the same again – but then he would never want to be. A lifetime had passed since his departure from the Highlands, and his experiences had strengthened him in ways that once he could only have imagined.

His vision cleared, the past fading back into memory, the present a steady and certain conviction of what was needed. He stared out at the wagon and the horsemen and listened to the whisper in his mind. He knew what he must do.

He moved quickly then, the decision made. He left everything behind but the Sword of Leah. Stripped of his pack and great cloak, the Sword strapped securely across his back, he slipped down through the trees on the bluff's north slope, keeping his goal in sight as he went. He reached the hills below and raced through them, pointing north to the narrows through which the wagon and horsemen must pass to reach Southwatch, thinking to himself that he could still change his mind once he got there if it seemed wrong then, thinking as well that he needed a plan if he was to have any chance of surviving a fight against so many. The ground was hard and hollow feeling beneath his feet, but the grasses were damp with morning dew and made a wet, slapping sound as he passed through them. He smelled the earth and the trees in the windless air, their scents thick and pungent. The haze deepened as he wound ahead, reaching out to enfold him one moment, slipping free again the next. He would have to be quick, he thought to himself – as swift as thought and as certain as fate. He would have to kill most of them before they knew he was there. He would have to be darker than they were. He would have to be more deadly.

He came out of a hollow into a stand of black walnut shot through with cherry, bent heavy with dewy leaves, and he stared out across the hills, listening. He could hear the wagon, its creak and groan soft in the mist. He was well ahead of it, close to where he would make his intercept, and the night's gloom lingered on against the coming dawn. He glanced east and found the sun still down within the trees, its light no more than a faint brightening against the sky. Time enough remained for him to act before the sunrise revealed him. He would have his chance.

He started out again, keeping to cover where he could, staying silent in his passage. He had hunted the Highlands for years before coming north, rising before dawn to set out with his ash bow, alone in a world in which he was an intruder, learning to make himself one with the animals he hunted. Sometimes he shot them for food; more often, he simply stalked them, not needing to kill them to teach himself their ways, to discover their secrets. He became good at it; he was good now. But the Shadowen were hunters, too. They could sense what was out there better than he. He would have to remember that. He would have to be careful.

Because if they found him first . . .

He breathed deeply through his mouth, steadying the pounding of his heart as he moved ahead. What was his plan? What was it that he intended to do? Stop them, kill them, have a look at what was in the wagon? What if nothing was in the wagon? Did it matter? How much would he give away if this was all for nothing?

But it wasn't for nothing. He knew it wasn't. The wagon wasn't empty. There was no reason for Seekers to escort an empty wagon to Southwatch. The wagon would carry something. The voice inside, the voice that urged him on, promised him so.

This is what you have been waiting for.

For an instant it occurred to him that it might be Quickening's voice he heard, that spoke to him from out of some netherworld or perhaps out of the earth into which she had returned, guiding him, shepherding him, leading him on to what she alone could see. But the idea seemed wishful and somehow dangerous, and he discarded it immediately. The voice was his own and no one else's, he told himself. The decision and its consequences must be his.

He reached the draw through which the horsemen and their wagon would pass, the place where he would stop them, and he drew up sharply in the stillness to listen. Distantly, from somewhere back in the haze, came the sounds of their approach. He stood in the center of the draw and tried to judge the time that remained to him. Then he walked its length, staying in the shadows to one side so that his damp footprints would not be visible against the light, breathing the hazy coolness to clear his head. Plans came and went in a flurry, sorted out and cast aside as quickly as dreams upon waking. None suited him; none seemed right. He reached the end of the draw and started back, then stopped.

He stood at the entrance to the narrowest part of the draw.

Here, he told himself. This is where it would begin, after the wagon was within the draw, after the lead horsemen were trapped in front and could not get back to help those behind. That would give him precious moments to dispatch at least two riders and perhaps those who drove the wagon as well, reaching whoever or whatever lay within. If he found nothing, he could be gone again swiftly . . .

Yet he knew even as he thought it that he could not, for the others would track him. No, he would have to stand and fight, whatever he found within the wagon. He would have to kill them or be killed. There would be no running, no escape.

He felt as if the pounding in his chest would explode his heart within him, and there was a hollow place in his stomach that lurched and heaved. He was dizzy with the thought of what he was planning, terrified and excited both at once, unable to contain any of the dozen emotions that ripped through him.

But still the voice whispered. *This is what you have been waiting for. This.*

The sound of the Shadowen approach grew louder. East, the light remained faint and distant. Here, the haze hung thick and unmoving in the draw. He would have cover enough, he decided. He moved back into the trees, unsheathed the Sword of Leah, and crouched down.

Please, be right. Please, don't be wrong. Let it be Par in that wagon. Let this be for something good.

The words repeated themselves, a litany in his mind, mixing with the whisper that held him bound to his course of action, to the certainty that it was right. He could not explain the feeling, could not justify it beyond the belief that sometimes you did not question, you simply accepted. He was torn by the truth he sensed in its and the possibility of its fraud. Reason advised caution, but passion insisted on blind commitment. The feelings warred within him as he waited, pulling and twisting into knots.

Abruptly he sprang up again and sped back through the trees and up the hill behind, keeping to the deepest shadows as he went, breathing through his mouth to take in quick gulps of air. At the summit he crept to where he could see west, his body heated and tensed. The riders and their wagon appeared out of a curtain of white frost, slow and steady in their coming, strung out along the divide. They showed no hesitation or concern; they did not glance about or ride alert. Too close to home to worry, Morgan thought. He wished he could tell what was in the wagon. He peered down at it as if by doing so he might penetrate the canvas that wrapped its bed, but nothing revealed itself. He felt a fire burn inside, the struggle between doubt and certainty continuing.

He slid back into the shadows and hunched down there, sweating. What was he to do? It was his last chance to change his mind, to reconsider the wisdom of his decision. How true was the voice that whispered to him? What were the chances that it deceived?

Then he was up and moving, slipping down again through the shadows to the narrows, all his thinking behind him, his course of action fixed. *Do something. Do something.* The whisper became a shout. He embraced it, wrapping it about him like armor.

He reached his concealment and dropped to his knees. Both hands gripped the pommel of his Sword, the talisman he had forsworn so often and must now rely upon once again. How quickly and easily he had come back to it, he thought in wonder. Sweat ran down his brow, tickling him, and he wiped it away. The cool dawn air did not seem to soothe his body's heat, and he gulped air in deep breaths to slow his heart. He felt as if he were coming apart at the seams. What would the sword's magic do – save him or consume him? Which, this time?

The sound of the wagon's approach was quite clear now, wheels bumping and thudding over the uneven trail, horses huffing in the silence. He froze in the shadows of his hiding place, eyes fixed on the curtain of mist. One hand trailed down the obsidian surface of the Sword of Leah, and he remembered how the Sword's magic had come about, how his ancestor Rone Leah had asked Allanon for magic to protect Brin Ohmsford, how the Druid had granted his wish by dipping the Sword's blade in the waters of the Hadeshorn. So much had come to pass in the wake of that single act. So many lives had been changed.

He brought both hands to the carved handle and tightened his grip until his knuckles were white.

The mist broke apart before him, and the black-cloaked riders appeared, hooded and faceless and somehow much larger than he had expected. The horses' breath clouded the air, and steam rose off their heated flanks. Down into the draw they came, four leading, followed by the creaking, swaying wagon and its drivers, and two trailing. Morgan Leah was calm now, the anticipation behind him, the event at hand. The wraiths hunched down atop their mounts and atop the wagon seat, silent and motionless, showing nothing of their faces, nothing of their thoughts. On each breast, the wolf's-head insignia gleamed like white metal. Morgan counted them again, eight in all. But there might be more inside the canvas tent of the wagon, the flaps to which remained drawn and tied. The wagon might be filled with them.

He took a deep breath and let it out slowly. Could he do this? His jaw tightened. He had fought Federation Seekers and Shadowen from one end of Callahorn to the other and survived. He was no callow, inexperienced youth. He would do what he must.

The horsemen passed and the wagon thudded by, entering the narrows of the draw. Morgan rose, silent and fluid, and brought up the Sword of Leah. *Be swift. Be sure. Don't hesitate.*

He left his cover and moved in behind the trailing riders. The leaders and the wagon had entered the narrows. He caught the trailing riders at its mouth, brought his blade around in an arc, the whole of his strength behind it, and cut them apart at the waist. They toppled from their horses like logs falling, soundless after a single surprised grunt, dead instantly. Their blood was greenish and thick on their robes as they tumbled down, and some of it smeared on Morgan's hands. The horses shied, pulling to either side as the Highlander surged past, springing for the wagon. Ahead, the draw was shadowed and thick with brush and trees, and the procession did not slow. Morgan reached the wagon, leaped for the canvas flaps, and pulled himself aboard. He sliced through the ties and jumped inside. The faint dawn light revealed a single figure lying motionless in the bed, hands and feet bound. He went past without slowing, seeing the dark figures seated ahead beginning to turn. His momentum carried him to the wagon front in a rush, his body twisting as he brought back his Sword. Somebody spoke, a cry of warning, and then he was ripping through the canvas with a fury, shredding it as if it weren't there, slashing the Seekers as they tried to free their weapons. They screamed and toppled from view, and in Morgan's hands the Sword of Leah began to glow like fire.

He pushed past the shredded flaps onto the wagon seat, kicking off what remained of one Seeker. He snatched up the reins, howled in fury, and whipped at the team. The horses screamed and bolted ahead, charging into the lead riders, who were in the process of turning about to see what was happening. The wagon bore down on them, still within the narrows, and there was no place for them to go. They tried to turn back again, tried to spring out of the way, lunged and twisted in the narrowing gap like contortionists, black robes flying. But the wagon hammered into them, taking two down instantly, crushing one Seeker beneath the wheels, slamming the other back into the trees. The wagon lurched and bucked, and the horses shied at the contact. Morgan rose in the seat as he swept past the two riders who remained, the Sword of Leah lifting to block the blows directed at him.

Thundering out of the draw and onto the flats beyond, he yanked on the reins and brought the team about, nearly overturning the wagon in the effort. The wheels skidded on the damp grass, and Morgan dropped his Sword into the boot to free both hands to control the team. Behind, the remaining two riders came at him, dark shapes materializing out of the mist. One of the two riders who had fallen appeared as well, now afoot. Morgan whipped the team toward them, building speed. Sweat ran down his face, and his vision blurred. He reached back into the boot for the Sword of Leah and brought it up, the magic racing down its length like fire. The mounted Seekers reached him first, splitting to either side, blades drawn. He pushed himself as far to the right as he could, concentrating on the horseman closest, hammering past the other's defenses and crushing his skull. He felt a red-hot searing in his shoulder as the other Seeker leaped from his horse onto the wagon seat and struck him a slashing, off-balance blow. He reeled away, nearly falling off, kicking out with his boot to knock the other back. The wagon swung wide and this time did not correct. It snapped loose from its traces and tongue and went over, throwing the combatants to the earth.

Morgan landed hard, a red mist sweeping across his vision, pain lancing through his body, but came back to his feet instantly.

The Seeker who had wounded him was waiting, and the one afoot was coming up fast. Both were reverting to Shadowen, lifting from their black-robed bodies in a mist of darkness, eyes red and chilling. They had seen the fire race the length of his sword and knew Morgan possessed the magic. Shedding their Seeker disguise, they were calling up magic of their own. Crimson fire launched from their weapons at Morgan, but he blocked it, rushing them with single-minded determination, no longer thinking, acting now out of need. He slammed into the first and bowled him over. The Sword of Leah swept down, shattering the other's weapon, and the fire burned from throat to stomach, through one side and out the other. The Shadowen screamed, shuddered, and went still.

Morgan went after the other without slowing, consumed by the magic's elixir, driven by forces he no longer controlled. The Shadowen hesitated, seeing his face, realizing belatedly that he was overmatched. He threw up the fire, and it splintered apart on Morgan's blade. Then Morgan was on top of him, striking once, twice, three times, the magic racing up and down the talisman, a sudden white heat. The Shadowen shrieked, tearing to get free, and then the fire exploded through him in a brilliant flash of light, and he was gone.

Morgan whirled about, searching the gloom – left, right, behind, in front again. The land was still and empty. East, the sun crested the horizon in a burst of silver gold, light streaming through the trees to penetrate the shadows and mist. The draw was a dark tunnel in which nothing moved. The Shadowen lay lifeless about him. A single horse remained, a dark blur some fifty feet off, reins trailing as it shook its head and stamped the earth, uncertain of what to do. Morgan looked at it, steadied his sweating hands, and slowly straightened. The magic of the Sword faded, and the blade turned depthless black again.

Close at hand, a thrush called once. Morgan Leah listened without moving, and his breath whistled harshly in his ears.

371

The Shadowen at Southwatch will have heard. They will come for you. Move!

He sheathed the Sword of Leah and hurried over to the collapsed wagon, remembering Par, anxious to discover if the Valeman was all right. It was Par in there, he insisted to himself. It had to be. He was dazed and bleeding, his clothing torn and soiled, his skin coated in dust and sweat. He felt light-headed and dangerously invincible.

Of course it was Par!

He climbed into the upended wagon and moved to the bound figure, who was slumped against one splintered side, looking up at him. Shadows hid the other's face, and he bent close, blinked, and stared.

It wasn't Par he had rescued.

It was Wren.

28

Wren was as surprised to see Morgan Leah as he was to see her. Tall and lean and quick-eyed, he was exactly as she remembered him – and at the same time he was different. He seemed older somehow, more worn. And there was something in the look he gave her. She blinked up at him. What was he doing here? She tried to straighten up, but her strength failed her and she would have fallen back again if the Highlander hadn't reached down to catch her. He knelt at her side, withdrew a hunting knife from his belt, and severed her bonds and gag.

'Morgan,' she breathed, relieved beyond measure, and reached up to embrace him. 'I'm sure glad to see you.'

He managed a quick, tight smile, and a bit of the mischievousness returned to his haggard face. 'You look a wreck, Wren. What happened?'

She smiled back wearily, aware of how she must appear, her face all bruised and swollen. 'I made a serious error in judgment, I'm afraid. Don't worry, I'm all right now.'

He picked her up anyway and carried her from the ruins of the wagon into the dawn light, setting her gingerly back on her feet. She rubbed her wrists and ankles to restore the circulation, then knelt to wet her hands with dew from the still-damp grasses and dabbed tentatively at her injured face.

She looked up at him. 'I thought there was no hope for me at all. How did you find me?'

He shook his head. 'Blind luck. I wasn't even looking for you. I was looking for Par. I thought the Shadowen were transporting him in the wagon. I had no idea at all it was you.'

There had been disappointment in his eyes when he had recognized her. She understood now why. He had been certain it was Par he had rescued.

'I'm sorry I'm not Par,' she told him. 'But thanks anyway.'

He shrugged, and grimaced with the movement, and she saw the mix of red and green blood on his clothing. 'What are you doing here, Wren?'

She rose to face him. 'It's a long story. How much time do we have?'

He glanced over his shoulder. 'Not much. Southwatch is only a few miles away. The Shadowen will have heard the fighting. We have to get away as soon as we can.'

'Then I'll keep it short.' She felt stronger now, flushed with urgency and renewed determination. She was free again, and she intended to make the most of it. 'The Elves have returned to the Four Lands, Morgan. I found them on an island in the Blue Divide where they've been living for almost a hundred years, and I brought them back. It was Allanon's charge to me, and I finally accepted it. Their queen, Ellenroh Elessedil was my grandmother. She died on the way, and now I am queen.' She saw the astonishment in his eyes and gripped his arm to silence him. 'Just listen. The Elves are besieged by a Federation army ten times their size. They fight a delaying action just south of the Valley of Rhenn. I have to get back to them at once. Do you want to come with me?'

The Highlander stared. 'Wren Elessedil,' he said softly, trying the name out. Then he shook his head, and his voice tightened. 'No, I can't, Wren. I have to find Par. He may be a prisoner of the Shadowen at Southwatch. There are others out looking for him as well. I promised to wait for them.'

His voice had an edge to it that did not allow for argument, but he added reluctantly, 'But if you really need me . . .'

She stopped him with a squeeze of her hand. 'I can make it back on my own. But there is something I have to tell you first, and you have to promise me that you will tell the others when you see them again.' Her grip tightened. 'Where are they, anyway? What's become of them? What's happened with Allanon's charges? Did the others fulfill them as well?' She was speaking too rapidly, and she forced herself to slow down, to stay calm, not to look off to the east and the brightening sky. 'Here, sit down. Let me have a look at your wound.'

She took his arm and led him to a moss-covered log where she seated him, stripped off his shirt, tore it in strips, and cleaned and bound the sword slash as best she could.

'Par and Coll found the Sword of Shannara, but then they disappeared,' he told her as she worked. 'It's too long a story for now. I've been tracking Par; he may be tracking Coll. I don't know who has the Sword. As for Walker, I was with him when he went north to recover a magic that would restore Paranor and the Druids. He was successful, and we came back together, but I haven't seen him since.' He shook his head. 'Paranor's back. The Sword's found. The charges are all fulfilled, but I don't know what difference it makes.'

She finished tying up his wound and moved back around in front of him. 'Neither do I. But in some way it does. We just have to find out how.' She swallowed against the dryness in her throat, and her hazel eyes fixed him. 'Now, listen. This is what you are to tell the others.' She took a deep breath. 'The Shadowen are Elves. They are Elves who rediscovered the old magic and thought to use it recklessly. They stayed behind when the rest of the Elven nation fled the Four Lands and the Federation. The magic subverted them as it does everything; it made them into the Shadowen. They are another form of the Skull Bearers of old, dark wraiths for which the magic is a craving they cannot resist. I don't know how they can be destroyed, but it must be done. Allanon was right – they are an evil that threatens us all. The answers we need lie in the purpose of fulfilling the charges that we were given. One of us will discover the truth. We must. Tell them what I've told to you, Morgan. Promise me.'

Morgan rose. 'I'll tell them.'

A heron's cry pierced the morning stillness, and Wren jerked about. 'Wait here,' she said.

She hobbled over to the fallen Shadowen and began rifling through their clothing. One of them, she knew, had the Elfstones, stolen from her by Tib Arne. Her anger at him burned anew. She searched the closest two and found nothing. She stirred the ashes of the one Morgan had burned through and found nothing there either. Then she went back to the driver and his companion, to their severed bodies, and ignoring what had been done to them, she worked her way carefully through their robes.

In the cloak pocket of one she found the pouch and the Stones. Exhaling sharply, she stuffed the pouch into her tunic and limped back toward Morgan.

Halfway there, she saw the Shadowen horse that hadn't run grazing at the edge of the trees. She stopped, considered momentarily, then put her fingers to her mouth and gave a strange, low-pitched whistle. The horse looked up, ears pricking toward the sound. She whistled again, varying the pitch slightly. The horse stared at her, then pawed the earth. She walked over to the animal slowly, talking softly and holding out her hand. The horse sniffed at her, and she reached out to stroke his neck and flank. For a few moments they tested each other, and then suddenly she was on his back, still talking soothingly, the reins in her hands.

The horse whinnied and pranced at her touch. She guided him back to where Morgan waited and climbed down.

'I'll need him if I expect to make any time,' she said, one hand still firmly gripping the reins. 'What we find belongs to us, the Rovers used to say. Guess I haven't forgotten everything they taught me.' She smiled and reached out to touch his arm. 'I don't know when we'll meet up again, Morgan.'

He nodded. 'You better get going.'

'I owe you, Highlander. I won't forget.' She vaulted back into the saddle. 'We've come a long way from the Hadeshorn, haven't we?'

'From the Hadeshorn, from everything. Farther than I would have dreamed. Watch out for yourself, Wren.'

'And you. Good luck to us both.'

She met his eyes a moment longer, drawing on the strength she found there, taking heart in the fact that she was not as alone as she had believed, that help sometimes came from unexpected sources.

Then she dug her boots into the horse's flanks and galloped away.

She rode west after the retreating night until daylight overtook her, then stopped to rest the horse and let him drink from a pool of water. She rubbed at her wrists and ankles some more, washing clean the deep cuts and dark bruises, and swore to herself that when she caught up with Tib Arne she would make him pay dearly. She had not eaten or drunk in almost twelve hours, but there was no time to search for food or drinking water now. Once the Shadowen discovered she had escaped, they would be after her. They would be after Morgan Leah as well, she thought, and hoped he knew a good hiding place.

She remounted and rode on, following the grasslands out of the hill country to the plains below Tyrsis that led into the Tirfing. The day was turning hot and humid, the sky a cloudless blue and the sun a white-fire furnace. The trees thinned into scattered groves and then into stands of two and three and finally disappeared altogether. Midday arrived, and she crossed the Mermidon at a narrows, the river's waters low and sluggish here, dwindling away into the flats. Her body and face ached from the beating and the trussing, but she ignored her discomfort, thinking instead of the havoc that her disappearance must have caused. By now they would be searching for her everywhere. Perhaps they had found Erring Rift and Grayl and thought her dead as well. Perhaps they had given up on her, choosing to concentrate on the Federation army and the Creepers. Some would surely recommend that she be forgotten. Some would find her disappearance a blessing . . .

She brushed the prospect aside. She had nothing to prove to anyone. The fact remained that she needed to get back. Barsimmon Oridio would be nearing the Rhenn with the main body of the Elven army. With luck, Tiger Ty would be returning with the Federation. If she could reach them before any fighting began . . .

She stopped herself.

What?

What would she do?

She blocked the question away. It didn't matter what she did. It would be enough that she was there, that the Elves knew they had their queen back, that the Federation must deal with her anew.

She turned north to follow the Mermidon and found water for the horse on the plains, but none for herself. The sun beat down overhead, and the air sucked the moisture from her body. She was tired, and the horse was tiring as well. She could not keep on much longer. She would have to stop and wait out the heat. The thought made her grind her teeth. She didn't have time for that! She didn't have time for anything but going on!

She rested finally, knowing she must, finding a grove of ash close to the riverbank where it was cool enough to escape the worst of the heat. She found some berries that were more bitter than sweet and a gum root that gave her something to chew on. She stripped the horse of his saddle and tethered him. Resting back within the trees, she watched the river flow past, and though she did not mean to do so she fell asleep.

It was late in the afternoon when she woke again, startled out of a restless doze by the soft whicker of her horse. She came to her feet instantly, seeing its shaggy head pointed south, and she looked off across the plains and river to find horsemen coming toward her from several miles off – black-cloaked, hooded horsemen, whose identity was no secret.

She saddled her mount and was off. She rode several miles along the riverbank at a quick trot, glancing back to see if her pursuers were following. They were, of course, and she had the feeling that more might be waiting ahead at Tyrsis. The light faded west, turning silver, then rose, then gray, and when the haze of early twilight set in, she turned away from the river and headed west onto the plains. She would have a better chance of losing her pursuit there, she reasoned. She was a Rover, after all. Once it was dark, no one would be able to track her. All she needed was a little time and luck.

She found neither. Shortly after, her horse began to falter. She urged him on with whispered promises and encouraging pats about the neck and ears, but he was played out. Behind, her pursuers had fanned out across the horizon, distant still, but coming on. The haze was deepening, but the moon and first stars were out, and there would be light enough for a hunter to see by. She stiffened her resolve and rode on.

When her horse stumbled and went down, she rolled free, rose, went back to him, got him to his feet again, unstrapped his saddle and bridle, and set him free. She began walking, limping because her injuries were still painful and inhibiting, angry and tired and determined not to be taken again. She walked without looking back for a long time, until the night had settled in completely, and the whole of the plains were bathed in white light. The plains were silent and empty, and she knew her pursuers were not close enough yet to worry about or she would have heard them, and so she concentrated on putting one foot in front of the other and simply going on.

When she finally did look back, no one was there.

She stared in disbelief. There wasn't one rider, not a single horse, no one afoot, nothing. She took a deep breath to calm herself and looked again – not just east, but all about this time, thinking in sudden fear that she had been flanked. But there was no one out there. She was alone.

She smiled in bewilderment.

And then she saw the dark shadow high overhead winging its way toward her, slow and lazy and as inevitable as winter cold. Her heart lurched in dismay as she watched it take shape. Not for a second did she think it was one of the Wing Riders come in search of her. Not for an instant did she mistake it for a friend. It was Gloon she was seeing. She knew him instantly. She recognized the blocky muscled body, the jut of the war shrike's fierce crested head, the sharp hook of the broad wings. She swallowed against her fear. No wonder the Seekers had fallen back. There was no need to hurry with Gloon to hunt her down.

Tib Arne would be riding him, of course. In her mind she saw the boy's chameleon face, first friend, then foe; human, then Shadowen. She could hear his grating laughter, feel the heat of his breath on her face as he struck her, taste the blood in her mouth from the blows . . .

She looked about for a place to hide and quickly discarded the idea. She was already seen, and wherever she hid she would be found. She could either run or fight – and she was tired of running.

She reached down into her tunic and took out the Elfstones. She balanced them in her hand, as if the weight of their magic could be determined and so the outcome of her battle decided early. She glanced west to the horizon, but there was nothing to see, the forests still lost below the horizon. No one would be searching for her anyway – not this far out and not at night. She gritted her teeth, thinking of Garth again, wondering what he would do. She watched Gloon wing his way closer, taking his time, riding the wind currents smoothly, easily, confident in his power and skill, in what he could do. The war shrike would try to take her on his first pass, she thought – quick and decisive before she could bring the magic of the Elfstones to bear. And it would not be easy using the Elfstones against a moving target.

She edged across the plains to put a small rise at her back. Better than nothing, she told herself, keeping her eyes on Gloon. She thought of what the war shrike had done to Grayl. She felt small and cold and vulnerable, alone in the vastness of the grasslands, nothing for as far as she could see, no one to help her. No Morgan Leah this time. No reprieve from an unexpected source. She would fight on her own, and how well she fought – and how lucky she was – would determine whether she lived or died.

Her hand tightened on the Elfstones. *Come see me, Gloon. Come see what I have for you.* The war shrike soared and dipped, sweeping out and back again, rising and falling in careless disregard, a dark motion against the sky's blue velvet. Wren waited impatiently. *Come on! Come on!*

Then abruptly Gloon dropped like a stone and was gone.

Wren jerked forward, startled. The night spread away before her, vast and dark and empty. What had happened? She felt sweat run down her back. Where had the shrike gone? Not into the earth, it wouldn't have driven itself into the earth, that didn't make any sense . . .

And then she realized what was happening. Gloon was attacking. He had dropped level with the ground so that his shadow could no longer be seen, and he was coming at her. How fast? How soon? She panicked, staggering backward in fear. She couldn't see him! She tried to pick out the shrike against the dark horizon, but could see nothing. She tried to hear him, but there was only silence.

Where is it? Where . . . ?

Instinct alone saved her. She threw herself aside on impulse and felt the massive weight of the shrike rip past her, talons tearing at the air inches away. She struck and rolled wildly, tasting dust and blood in her mouth, feeling the pain of her injured body rush through her anew.

She came back to her feet instantly, whirled in the direction she thought the shrike had gone, summoned the magic of the Elfstones, and sent it careening out into the night in a fan of blue fire. But the fire blazed into the void and struck nothing. Wren dropped into a crouch, desperately scanning the moonlit blackness. It would be coming back – but she couldn't see it! She had lost it! Below the horizon it was invisible. Despair raced through her. *Which way was it coming? Which way?*

She struck out blindly, right and then left, and threw herself down, rolling, coming up and striking out again. She heard the magic collide with something. There was a shriek, followed by Gloon's heavy passage as the shrike winged off to her left, hissing like steam. She peered after the sound, wiping at the dust in her eyes. Nothing.

She got up and ran. Forcing down all thoughts of pain, she sprinted across the empty grasslands to a wash that lay some hundred feet away. She reached it and dove into it on a dead run. There was the now-familiar rush of wind and the passing of something dark overhead. Gloon had just missed her again. She flattened herself in the wash and peered skyward. The moon was there, and the stars, and nothing else. *Shades!* She came to her knees. The wash offered her some protection, but not nearly enough. And the night was no friend, for the war shrike's eye-sight was ten times better than her own. It could see her clearly in the wash, and she could see nothing of it.

She rose and sent the Elven magic stabbing out, hoping to get lucky. The fire raced away, working across the flats, and she felt the power rush through her. She howled in exhilaration, unable to help herself, saw the war shrike coming just an instant before it reached her, swung the magic about furiously – too late – and threw herself down once more. But her quickness saved her, the blue fire of the Elfstones forcing the shrike to change direction at the last minute, causing it to miss her once again.

She saw Tib Arne this time, just a glimpse as he streaked past, blond hair flying. She heard his cry of rage and frustration, and she shrieked out after him, furious, taunting.

The skies went still, the land silent. She huddled in the wash, shaking and sweating, the Elfstones clenched in her hand. She was going to lose this fight if she didn't do something to change the odds. Sooner or later, Gloon was going to get through.

Then she heard a new cry, this one far off to the west, a wild shriek that pierced the suffocating silence. She turned toward it, recognizing it yet unable to place it. A bird, a Roc. It came again, quick and challenging.

Spirit! It was Spirit!

She watched his dark shadow race out of the night, coming down from high up, as swift as thought. Spirit, she thought – and that meant Tiger Ty! Hope surged through her. She started to rise, to cry out in response, then flattened herself again quickly. Gloon was still out there, looking for an opportunity to finish her off. Her eyes swept the darkness, searching in vain. Where was the shrike?

Then Gloon rose out of the dark to meet this new challenger, thick black body gathering speed. Wren scrambled to her feet, shouting in warning. Spirit came on, then at the last possible moment veered aside so that the war shrike swept past harmlessly and wheeled about to give chase. The giant birds circled each other cautiously, feinting and dodging, working for an advantage. Wren gritted her teeth, earthbound and helpless. Gloon was bigger than Spirit and trained to kill. Gloon was a Shadowen, and had the magic to sustain him. Spirit was brave and quick, but what chance did he stand?

There was a flurry of movement as the birds came at each other, locked momentarily in a shriek of rage, and then broke apart again. Once more they began to circle, each trying to get above the other. Wren came out of the wash and back onto the flat of the plain. She moved after them as they edged away, following because she did not want to lose contact, still determined to help. She could not leave this battle to Tiger Ty and the Roc. This was not their fight. It was hers.

Again the birds dove at each other and locked, talons and beaks tearing and ripping. Black shadows against the moonlit sky, they twisted and turned, their wings flailing madly as they spiraled down. Wren raced after them, Elfstones in hand. *Just let me get close enough!* was all she could think.

At what seemed the last possible second the birds broke apart, staggering rather than flying away from each other, feathers and gristle and blood falling away from their tattered bodies. Wren gritted her teeth in rage. Gloon shook himself and rose, flattening out in a long slow spiral. Spirit arced upward and fell back, wobbly and unsure. He tried to right himself, shuddered once, dropped earthward, and vanished. Wren gasped in dismay – then caught her breath in wonder as Spirit suddenly reappeared, steady once more, miraculously recovered. A feint! Directly under Gloon now, he rose from the ground like a missile, hurtling through the night to slam into the war shrike. It sounded like rocks crunching, a sharp grating. Both birds cried out and then broke apart, talons raking the air.

Then one of the riders fell, dislodged by the impact. Arms and legs flailing the air, shrieking in horror, he plummeted earthward. He fell like a stone, unable to help himself, and struck with an audible thud. Overhead, the struggle continued, the Roc and war shrike battling on across the skies as if the loss of a rider made no difference. Wren could not tell who had fallen. She ran across the flats, her heart pumping wildly, her throat closing in fear. She ran for a long time without seeing anything. Then all at once there was a crumpled heap in front of her, a bloodied, ragged form trying to rise off the ground, somehow still alive.

She slowed her rush, and a shattered, broken visage turned toward her. She shuddered as the eyes met her own. It was Tib Arne. He tried to speak, a thick gurgle that would not let the words form, and she could hear his hatred of her in the sound. He was a boy still beneath the leaking wounds, but it was the Shadowen that broke free finally, rising like black smoke to come at her. She brought up the Elfstones instantly, and the blue fire tore through the dark thing and consumed it.

When she looked again, Tib Arne's blue eyes were staring up at her sightlessly.

She heard a shriek from overhead then, either war shrike or Roc, and looked up just in time to see Gloon descending with Spirit in pursuit. The shrike had abandoned his sky battle and was coming for her. She crouched beneath its shadow, no place to hide now, the wash too far away to reach. She brought up the Elfstones, but her movements were leaden, and she knew she didn't have enough time to save herself.

And then Spirit gave a final surge and caught Gloon from behind, hammering into the war shrike, knocking it off balance and away. Gloon whipped about, tearing at the Roc, and in that instant Wren unleashed the magic of the Elfstones a final time. It caught Gloon full on, enfolded the shrike, and began to burn it apart, eating at it even as it tried to escape. Gloon shrieked in rage, twisted wildly, and tried to fly. But the Elven magic had set the bird afire, and the flames were everywhere. It rolled and straightened, wings beating. Wren struck it again, the blue fire turning white hot. Down went the war shrike, flames trailing from its body. It struck the earth, shuddered, and went still.

In seconds, the fire had turned it to ash.

In the hush that followed, Spirit made a silent descent to the grasslands. Tiger Ty climbed down and came over to Wren, walking in that shuffling, bowlegged gait, leathery face streaked with sweat. She reached out her hands to clasp his.

'Are you all right, girl?' he asked quietly, and she could see the deep concern in his sharp eyes.

She smiled. 'Thanks to you. That's twice in one day I've been saved by friends I'd thought I'd lost.' And she told him of Morgan Leah and the Shadowen at Southwatch.

'I found the free-born in the Dragon's Teeth yesterday morning.' The gnarled hands would not release her, holding on as if afraid she might fade away. 'Their leader told me he didn't send the boy, that he'd sent someone else. I knew what had happened. I left them to follow when they could and came back for you. Too late, I thought. You were already missing. We searched for you all day. Found Rift and Grayl, but there was no sign of you. I knew the boy had taken you. But I knew as well that if there was a way, you'd escape. I took Spirit out alone after the others gave it up for the night and kept looking.' He gave her a hard look. 'Good thing I did.'

'Good thing,' she agreed.

'Confound it, what did I tell you about going up with anybody but me?'

She leaned close, and for a moment the emotions were so strong she couldn't speak. 'Don't make me say it,' she whispered.

Perhaps he saw the pain in her eyes. Perhaps he heard it in her voice. He held her gaze a moment longer, then released her hands and stepped back. 'Just so you don't ever do it again. I've got a lot of time and effort invested in you.' He cleared his throat. 'Let me see to Spirit, make sure there's no real damage.'

He spent a few minutes checking the big Roc, hands moving carefully over the dark feathered body. Spirit watched him with a fierce eye. When the Wing Rider spoke to him, the Roc dipped his beak, spread his great wings, and shook himself.

Satisfied, Tiger Ty beckoned her over. He gave the bird a proud glare. 'He would have won, you know,' he said gruffly.

Wren didn't say anything for a moment. Then she smiled. 'I thought he did.'

Tiger Ty helped her aboard and strapped her in. He stroked Spirit appreciatively, nodded to himself, and joined her. Wren glanced out across the night-frozen landscape, empty and still save where Gloon's remains smoldered and steamed. She felt light-headed and worn, but she felt alive, too. The effects of the Elven magic lingered, racing through her like sparks of fire.

She had survived again, she thought, and wondered how long she could keep doing it.

'They're not going to win,' she said suddenly. 'I won't let them.'

He did not ask her what she meant. He did not speak at all. He just looked at her and nodded once. Then he whistled Spirit into the air, and the great bird rose and flew swiftly away into the dark.

29

Morgan Leah watched wren disappear into night's retreating darkness, his disappointment at not finding Par tempered by the satisfaction he felt in knowing that his efforts hadn't been wasted. Imagine – finding Wren, of all people! It made him think that the world was a smaller place than it seemed, and that because it was, perhaps the children of Shannara and their allies had a chance against the Shadowen after all.

He turned back east then, looking off to the brightening skyline, to the silver-gray light spilling down through the treetops and mountain slopes in slowly widening pools. Daybreak was upon him. The cover of night that had protected him was already gone, and he was at risk beyond what he had planned.

He glanced briefly at the shell of the toppled wagon and the black tangle of the fallen Shadowen and could not help thinking, I did it. I stood up against them all.

But where was he to go now? The Shadowen at Southwatch would be coming. They would have no trouble finding his tracks, and they would hunt him down and repay him for what he had done. He took a deep breath and looked about some more, as if in looking he might find the escape he needed. He could not go back to the bluff; that would be the first place they would look. They would find his trail and retrace his steps, hoping he was stupid enough to return to wherever he had been hiding.

He smiled faintly. He wasn't that stupid, of course, but it wasn't a bad idea to make them think he was.

He recrossed the narrows to where he had first come in and retraced his steps back through the trees and hills, not bothering to hide his tracks but messing them up as best he could to disguise how many of him there were, then turned and came back again, more cautious now because the Shadowen might have arrived in his absence. They had not, however; the narrows and the flats beyond remained empty save for the dead. He moved back up the trail that had brought the wagon in, using the ruts to hide his bootprints, following the wheel marks for several miles through the hills before turning abruptly north into high grass where he edged carefully away into the rocks of a ridgeline. If he was lucky, they would not find where he had broken off and would be forced to scour the countryside blindly. That might give him the extra time he needed to get to where he had decided to go.

Of course, none of this meant anything if the Shadowen could track by smell. If they could hunt like animals, then he was in trouble whatever he did short of rolling in mud and applying stinkweed, and he was not prepared for that. What could these quasi-Elves do? He wished he knew more about them, wished he had taken time to ask Wren, but there was no help for it now. He would have to take his chances. He breathed in the morning air and thought how lucky he was to have the Sword of Leah's magic to protect him, then realized that he had been given an answer to his question of whether the power would save or consume him. Of course, it didn't mean that he was safe with it, that he could relax in its use, that he could even be assured things would turn out the same way next time. It only meant he had survived for now, but it was becoming increasingly clear that survival on any terms was the most he could hope for – that any of them could hope for – in their battle against the Shadowen.

One day it will be different, he told himself – but wondered if it was so.

The country before him tightened into a mass of hills, ridges, scrub-choked hollows, and dense forests backed up against the Runne. He was moving over rock, taking his time, working at stepping lightly where scuffed stones and bent twigs might give him away. He had reasoned it through like this. South lay the bluff where he had kept watch, and the Shadowen, if hunting him, would start there. West was the direction in which Wren had ridden, and they would surely hunt him there as well. North lay the cities of Callahorn – Tyrsis, Kern, and Varfleet – and that would be the next logical choice. The last place they would look was east in the country surrounding Southwatch, their fortress citadel, because it would not seem likely to them that someone who had just destroyed one of their patrols to rescue the Queen of the Elves would head for the very same place the patrol had been going.

Queen of the Elves, he mused, interrupting his thinking. Wren Elessedil. Little Wren. He shook his head. He had barely known her when she was growing up with Par and Coll at Shady Vale. It was hard to believe who she had become.

He grimaced. That was true, of course, he thought ruefully, of all of them, and he shrugged the matter aside.

The sun was above the horizon now, night's shadows gone back into hiding, the swelter of summer's heat rising up through the grasses and trees with a thickening of fetid air and dry earth. Morgan found a stream running down out of the rocks, followed it to a rapids where the water was clean, and drank. He had neither food nor water to sustain him, and he would have to obtain both if he was to survive for very long. He thought momentarily of Damson and Matty, and he hoped they did not choose this day to return from their search south. They would expect to find him on that bluff, but would likely find the Shadowen waiting instead. Not a pleasant thought. He would have to warn them, of course – but he would have to stay alive to do so.

He left the stream and worked his way to high ground. From the shelter of a stand of pine, he looked back across the hills south, searching for signs of pursuit. He stayed there a long time, scanning the countryside. Nothing showed itself. Finally he went on, moving east now toward the mountains and the river and Southwatch. He was above the citadel, deep enough within the concealing trees to keep from being seen but close enough so as not to lose contact. He made steady progress despite his wound, the pain a dull throbbing he had relegated to the back of his mind, working his way ahead with the practice and determination of an experienced woodsman, able to sense what was happening about him, to feel a part of the land. He listened to the sounds of the birds and animals, sensing what they were about, knowing that nothing was amiss.

The day edged on toward noon, and still there was no sign of any pursuit. He began to hope that perhaps he had avoided it completely. He found fruit and wild greens to chew on and more drinking water, and when he reached the wall of the Runne, he turned south again. He shifted the Sword of Leah to take the strain off his wound and thought on its history. So many years of dormancy, a relic of another time, its magic forgotten until his encounter with the Shadowen during the journey to Culhaven. Happenstance, and nothing more. Strange how things worked out. He pondered the effect that the Sword had had upon his life, of the ways it had worked both for and against him, and of the legacy of hope and despair it had bequeathed. He thought that it no longer mattered whether he approved of it or not, whether he believed his link with the magic was a good or bad thing, because in the final analysis it didn't matter – the magic simply was. Quickening, he thought, had recognized the inevitability of it better than he, and she had given back the Sword whole because she knew that if the magic was to be his, it should be his complete and not diminished or failed. Quickening had understood how the game was played; her legacy to him had been to teach him the rules.

He stopped to rest when the heat of the day was at its peak, a scathing, burning glare that rose off the parched earth in a white-hot shimmer. He sat in the shade of an aging maple, broadleaved boughs canopied above him like a tent, squirrels and birds moving through the sheltering branches in apparent disregard of his presence, bound up in their own pursuits. He stared out through the trees to the hills and grasslands south and east, the Sword of Leah propped blade down between his legs, his arms folded across its hilt and grips. He wondered if Wren was safe. He wondered where everybody was, all those who had started out with him on this adventure and been lost somewhere along the way. Some, of course, were dead. But what of the others? He scuffed at the earth with his boot heel and wished he could see things that were hidden from him, then thought that maybe it was better that he couldn't.

Late afternoon brought the temperature back down to bearable, and he resumed walking. Shadows were lengthening again, easing away from the trees and rocks and gullies and ridges behind which they had been hiding. Southwatch came into view, its dark obelisk rising up out of the poisoned flats that bridged the mouth of the Mermidon with the Rainbow Lake. The lake itself was flat and silvery, a mirror of the sky and the land, and the colors of its bow were pale and washed out in the fading light. Cranes and herons swooped and glided above its surface, vague flashes of white against the gray haze of an approaching dusk.

He stopped to watch, and it probably saved his life.

The birds went suddenly still, and there was movement ahead in the trees, barely perceptible, but there nevertheless, distant and indistinct in the failing light. Morgan eased back into the brush, as silent as shadows falling, and froze. After a moment, Shadowen appeared, one, two, then four more, a patrol working its way soundlessly through the trees. They did not seem to be tracking, merely searching, and the idea that they might be using their sense of smell to hunt turned Morgan cold. They were several hundred yards away still and moving along the slope. Their path would take them below where he hid – but across the trail he had left. He wanted to run, to fly out of there as swiftly as the wind, but he knew he could not, and forced himself to wait. The hunters were black-robed and hooded and did not wear the emblem of Seekers. There was no pretense here, and that meant they either did not feel threatened or did not care. Neither prospect was reassuring.

Morgan watched them ease through the trees like bits of coming night and disappear from view.

Instantly he was moving again, gliding forward quickly, anxious to put as much distance as possible between himself and the black-garbed hunters. Were they searching for him or for someone else – for anyone, perhaps, after what had been done to their patrol, worried that there were others in hiding? It didn't matter, he decided quickly. It was enough that they were out there and that sooner or later they were likely to find him.

He revised his previous plan, thinking on his feet, not slowing for an instant. He would not stay on this side of the Mermidon. He would cross the river and wait on the far bank where he could watch the shoreline and the lake for Damson and Matty to return. It was unfortunate that he could not position himself to keep an eye on Southwatch as well, but it was too dangerous to stick around. Best to wait for Damson to report what the Skree had shown on her journey south. Let her try its magic out again if necessary then. That would have to do.

He was very close to Southwatch now and saw that he could not reach the Mermidon to try a crossing without coming down out of the concealment of the trees. That meant he must wait for darkness, and darkness was still several hours away. Too long to stay in one place, he knew. He crouched in the shadows and studied the land below, looking for a reason to reconsider his assessment. The trees thinned as they broke from the Runne, melting away south so that there was no cover

393

on the plains that stretched east to the river. He ground his teeth in frustration. It was too risky to try. He would have to backtrack into the mountains and try to find a pass leading east or circle all the way back the way he had come. The latter was impossible, the former chancy.

But as he pondered the alternatives, he caught sight of new movement in the trees ahead. Again he froze, searching the shadows. He might have been mistaken, he told himself. There seemed to be nothing there.

Then the black-cloaked figure eased into the light momentarily before fading away again.

Shadowen.

He scooted back into the deep cover, his mind made up for him. He began to double back, working his way higher into the rocks. He would look for a pass through the Runne and take his chances with the river. If he failed to find a way through, he would retrace his steps under cover of darkness. He did not like the thought of being out there at night with the Shadowen still searching for him, but his choices were being stripped from him with alarming rapidity. He forced himself to breathe deeply and slowly as he slipped back through the trees, trying to stay calm. There were too many Shadowen hunting about for it to be anything but a deliberate search. Somehow they had found out where he was and were closing in. He felt his throat tighten. He had survived one battle this day, but he did not feel comfortable with the prospect of having to survive another.

Sunset was approaching, and the mountain forest was cloaked in a windless hush. He kept his movements methodical and noiseless, knowing that any small sound could give him away. He felt the weight of the Sword of Leah pressing into his back, and resisted the temptation to reach back for it. It was there if he needed it, he told himself – and he'd better hope the need didn't arise.

He was crossing a ridgeline when he saw the shadow shift in the trees far ahead across a scrub-choked ravine. The shadow was there and gone again in an instant's time, and he had the impression that he had sensed it more than seen it. But there was no mistaking what it was, and he went into a low crouch and wormed his way into the deep brush to his right, angling higher into the rocks. One of them, he concluded – only one. A solitary hunter. The sweat on his face and neck left his skin warm and sticky, and the muscles of his back were knotted so tight they hurt. He felt his wound throb with fresh pain and wished he had a drink of ale to soothe his parched throat. He found the way up blocked by a cliff wall, and he turned back reluctantly. He had the sense of being herded, and he was beginning to think that eventually he would find walls everywhere he looked.

He paused at the edge of a low precipice and looked back into the velvet-cloaked trees. Nothing moved, but something was there anyway, coming on with steady deliberation. Morgan considered lying in wait for it. But any sort of struggle would bring every Shadowen in the forest down on him. Better to go on; he could always fight later.

The trees ahead were thinning as the rocks broke through in ragged clusters and the slopes steepened into cliffs. He was as high as he could go without leaving the cover of the trees and still there was no pass to take him through the mountains. He thought he could hear the sound of the river churning along its banks somewhere beyond the wall of rock, but it might have been his imagination. He found a stand of heavy spruce and took cover, listening to the forest about him. There was movement ahead and below now as well. The Shadowen were all about him. They must have found his trail. It was still light enough to track, and they were coming for him. They might not catch up to him before it grew too dark to follow his footprints, but he did not think it would matter if they were this close. They were more at home in the dark than he, and it would just be a matter of time before they snared him.

For the first time he let himself consider the possibility that he was not going to escape.

He reached back and drew out his Sword. The obsidian blade gleamed faintly in the dusky twilight and felt comfortable in his hand. He imagined he could feel its magic responding to him with whispered assurances that it would be there when he called for it. His talisman against the dark. He lowered his head and closed his eyes. All come to this? Another fight in an endless series of fights to stay alive? He was growing tired of it all. He couldn't help thinking it. He was tired, and he was sick at heart.

Let it go!

He opened his eyes, rose, and glided ahead through the trees, south again toward the plains that led down to Southwatch, changing his mind about staying hidden. He felt better moving, as if movement was more natural, more protective in some way. He slipped down through the forest, picking his way cautiously, listening for those who sought to trap him. Shadows shifted about him, small changes in the light, little movements that kept his heart pumping. Somewhere in the distance an owl hooted softly. The forest was a night river in slow, constant flux that shimmered and spun.

He glanced back repeatedly searching for the solitary hunter behind him and saw nothing. The Shadowen ahead were equally invisible, but he thought they might not know his whereabouts quite so surely as the other. He hoped they could not communicate by thought, but he would not have be against it. There seemed to be few limitations to the magic they wielded. Ah, but that was wrongheaded thinking, he chided. There were always limitations. The trick was in finding out what they were.

He reached a clump of cedar backed up against a cliff and turned into it, dropping again into a crouch to listen. He remained as still as the stone behind him for long minutes and heard nothing. But the Shadowen were still out there, he knew. They were still searching, still scouring . . .

And then he saw them, two close at hand, easing through the trees less than a hundred yards below, black-cloaked shadows, advancing on his concealment. He felt his heart drop. If he moved now, they would see him. If he stayed where he was, they would find him. A great set of choices, he thought bitterly. He still held the Sword of Leah, and his hands tightened on the grip. He would have to stand and fight. He would have to, and he knew how it was likely to end.

He thought back to the Jut, Tyrsis, Eldwist, Culhaven, and all the other places he'd been trapped and brought to bay when trying to escape, and he thought in despair and anger, You would think that just once . . .

And then the hand closed over his mouth like an iron clamp, and he was yanked backward into the trees.

30

Dusk came to the country south of the Rainbow Lake in a purple and silver haze that crept like a cat out of the Anar to chase a fiery sunset west into the Black Oaks and the lands beyond. Twilight was smooth and silky as it eased the day's swelter with a breeze out of the deep forest, soothing and cool. Farms dotting the lands above the Battlemound were bathed in a mixture of shadows and light and assumed the look of paintings. Animals stood with their faces pointed into the breeze, motionless against the darkening green pastures. Tenders and hands came in from their work, and there was the sound of water splashing in basins and the smell of food cooking on stoves. There was a serenity in the lengthening shadows and a relief in the cooling of the air. There was a hush that gathered and comforted and promised rest for those who had completed another day.

In a stand of hardwood on a low rise close against the fringe of the Anar just north of the Battlemound, smoke rose from the crumbling chimney of an old hunter's cabin. The cabin consisted of four timbered walls splintered and aged by weather and time, a shingled roof patched and worn, a covered porch that sagged at one end, and a stone well set back into the deepest shadows in the trees behind. A wagon was pulled up close to one side of the cabin, and the team of mules that pulled it was staked out on a picket line at the edge of the trees. The men who owned both were clustered inside, seated on benches at a table with their dinner, all save one who kept watch from the stone porch steps, looking off into the valley south and east.

They were five in number, counting the one outside, and they were shabby and dirty and hard-eyed men. They wore swords and knives and bore the scars of many battles. When they spoke, their voices were coarse and loud; and when they laughed, there was no mirth.

They did not look to Damson Rhee and Matty Roh like anyone who could be reasoned with.

The women crouched in a wash west where a covering of brush screened their movements, and stared at each other.

'Are you sure?' the taller, leaner woman asked softly.

Damson nodded. 'He's there, inside.'

They went silent, as if both lacked words to carry the conversation further. They had been tracking the wagon all day, ever since they had come upon its wheel marks while following the Skree south from the Rainbow Lake. They had crossed the lake three days earlier, sailing out of the mouth of the Mermidon just ahead of the approaching storm after leaving Morgan Leah. The winds fronting the storm had pushed them swiftly across the lake, and the storm itself had not caught them until they were almost to the far shore. Then they had been swept away, buffeted so badly they had capsized east of the Mist Marsh and been forced to swim to shore. They had escaped with the better part of their supplies in tow, waterlogged and weary, and had slept the night in a grove of ash that offered little shelter from the damp. They had walked from there south, drawn on by the Skree's light, searching for some sign of Par Ohmsford. There had been none until the wagon tracks, and now the men who had made them.

'I don't like it,' Matty Roh said softly.

Damson Rhee took out the broken half of the Skree, cupped it in her hand, and held it out toward the cabin. It burned like copper fire, bright and steady. She looked at Matty. 'He's there.'

The other nodded. Her clothing was rumpled from wear and weather and torn by brambles and rocks, and washing it had cleaned it but not improved its appearance. Her boyish face was sun-browned and sweat-streaked, and her brow furrowed as she considered the glowing half moon of metal.

'We'll need a closer look,' she said. 'After it gets dark.'

Damson nodded. Her red hair was braided and tied back with a band about her forehead, and her clothing was a mirror of Matty's. She was tired and hungry for a hot meal and in need of a bath, but she knew she would have to do without all of them for now.

They eased back along the wash to where they had left their gear and settled down to eat some fruit and cheese and drink some water. Neither spoke as the meal was consumed and the shadows lengthened. Darkness closed about, the moon and stars came out, and the air cooled so that it was almost pleasant. They were very unlike each other, these two. Damson was fiery and outgoing and certain of what she was about; Matty was cool and aloof and believed nothing should be taken for granted. What bound them beyond their common enterprise was an iron determination forged out of years of working to stay alive in the service of the free-born. Three days alone together searching for Par Ohmsford had fostered a mutual respect. They had known little of each other when they had started out and in truth knew little still. But what they did know was enough to convince each that she could depend on the other when it counted.

'Damson.' Matty Roh spoke her name suddenly. The silence had deepened, and she whispered. 'Do you know how you sometimes find yourself in the middle of something and wonder how it happened?' She seemed almost embarrassed. 'That's how I feel right now. I'm here, but I'm not sure why.'

Damson eased close. 'Do you wish you were somewhere else?'

'I don't know. No, I suppose not.' Her lips pursed. 'But I'm confused about what I'm doing here. I know why I came, but I don't understand what made me decide to do it.'

'Maybe the reason isn't important. Maybe being here is all that counts.'

Matty shook her head. 'I don't think so.'

'Maybe it's not all that difficult to figure out. I'm here because of Par. Because I promised him I would come.'

'Because you're in love with him.'

'Yes.'

'I don't even know him.'

'But you know Morgan.'

Matty sighed. 'I know him better than he knows himself. But I'm not in love with him.' She paused. 'I don't think.' She looked away, distressed by the admission. 'I came because I was bored with standing around. That was what I told the Highlander. It was true. But I came for something more. I just don't know what it is.'

'I think it might be Morgan Leah.'

'It isn't.'

'I think you need him.'

'I need him?' Matty was incredulous. 'It's the other way around, don't you think? He needs me!'

'That, too. You need each other. I've watched you, Matty – you and Morgan. I've seen the way you look at him when he doesn't see. I've seen how he looks at you. There is more between you than you realize.'

The tall girl shook her head. 'No.'

'You care about him, don't you?'

'That's not the same. That's different.'

Damson watched her for a moment without saying anything. Matty's gaze was fixed on a point in space somewhere between them, the cobalt eyes depthless and still. She was seeing something no one else could see.

When she looked up again, her eyes were empty and sad. 'He's still in love with Quickening.'

Damson nodded slowly. 'I suppose he is.'

'He will always be in love with her.'

'Maybe so, Matty. But Quickening is dead.'

'It doesn't matter. Have you heard how he speaks of her? She was beautiful and magic, and she was in love with him, too.' The blue eyes blinked. 'It's too hard to try to compete with that.'

'You don't have to. It's not necessary.'

'It is.'

'He will forget her in time. He won't be able to help it.'

'No, he won't. Not ever. He won't let himself.'

Damson sighed and looked away. The night was deep and still about them, hushed with expectation. 'He needs you,' she whispered finally, not knowing what else to say. She looked back again. 'Quickening is gone, Matty, and Morgan Leah needs you.'

They stared at each other in the darkness, measuring the truth of the words, weighing their strength. Neither spoke. Then Matty rose and looked back across the grassland toward the cabin. 'We have to go down for a look.'

'I'll go.' Damson rose with her. 'You wait here.'

Matty took her arm. 'Why not me?'

'Because I know what Par looks like and you don't.'

'Then both of us should go.'

'And put both at risk?' Damson held the other girl's eyes. 'You know better.'

Matty stared at her defensively for a moment, then released her arm. 'You're right. I'll wait here. But be careful.'

Damson smiled, turned, and slipped away into the dark. She moved easily down the wash until she was north of the cabin. Lamplight burned from within, a yellowish wash through the shutterless side windows and open front door. She paused, thinking. The sound of the men's voices came from within, but the red glow of a pipe bowl and the smell of tobacco warned that the sentry still occupied the porch steps. She watched the dark shapes of the mules shifting on the line next

402

to the cabin wall, then heard the sound of breaking glass and swearing inside. The men were drinking and arguing.

She moved on down the wash to the forest and came around behind the cabin, intent on approaching from the south wall, afraid the animals might give her away if she went in from the north. Clouds glided like phantoms overhead, changing the intensity of the light as they passed across moon and stars. Damson edged along the fringe of the trees, lost in shadow, placing her feet carefully even though the voices and laughter likely would drown out other sounds. When she was behind the cabin, she left the trees and came swiftly to the rear wall, then inched along the back and started forward toward the south window. She could hear the voices plainly now, could sense their anger and menace. Hard men, these, and no mistake about it.

She moved to the window in a crouch, rose up carefully, and looked inside.

Coll Ohmsford lay at the back of the musty, weathered cabin and listened to the men arguing as they rolled dice for coins. He was wrapped in a blanket and had turned himself toward the wall. His hands and feet were chained together and to a ring they had hammered into the boards. They had given him food and water and then forgotten about him. Which was just as well, he thought wearily, given their present unpleasant state of mind. Drinking and gambling had turned them meaner than usual, and he had no desire to discover what the result might be if they remembered he was there. He had been beaten twice already since he had been captured – once for trying to escape and once because one of them got mad about something and decided to take it out on him. He was bruised and cut and sore all over, and after being bounced about all day in the back of the wagon he just wanted to be left alone to sleep.

The problem, of course, was that there was no sleep to be had under these conditions. His fatigue and pain were not enough to overcome the noise. He lay listening and wondering what he could do to help himself. He thought again about escape. They were traveling slowly with the wagon and mules, but they were only three or four days out of Dechtera and once there he was finished. He had heard of the slave mines, worked principally by Dwarves. Morgan had described the mines after learning of them from Steff. They were used as a dumping ground for Dwarves who antagonized the Federation occupiers and most particularly for those captured in the Resistance. The Dwarves sent to the mines never returned. No one ever returned. Morgan had heard rumors of Southlanders being sent to work the mines, but until now Coll had never believed it could be so.

He stared at the cracked and splintered wallboards. It seemed he was destined to learn a lot of truths the hard way.

He took a deep breath, held it, and exhaled slowly, wearily. Time was running out and luck had long since disappeared. He was in better shape than he had a right to be, his training at Southwatch with Ulfkingroh having seen him through the worst. But that was of little consolation now, trussed up the way he was. He saw no hope of gaining release from his chains without a key. He had tried to pick the locks, but they were heavy and strong. He had tried to persuade his captors to take them off so he could walk around, but they had just laughed. His plan to rescue Par from Rimmer Dall and the Shadowen was a dim memory. He was as far from that as he was from his home in Shady Vale, and he was so far from there that he sensed he was almost beyond the point of return.

One of the men kicked over a chair, stood up, and walked from the room. Coll risked a quick look out from his coverings. The Sword of Shannara lay on the table. They were gambling for it, or for one another's shares in it. The three still at the table snarled something ugly after the one leaving but did not look away from each other.

Coll turned back to the wall again and closed his eyes. It didn't help that these men had no idea of the Sword's real value. It didn't help that only he could use the magic and that so much might depend on his doing so. At this point, he thought in despair, nothing short of a miracle would help.

He knotted his hands together beneath the blanket and descended into a black place.

What am I going to do?

'Is it him?'

Moonlight reflected off Matty Roh's smooth face, giving it a ghostly look beneath the short-cropped black hair. Damson drank from the water skin she offered and glanced back the way she had come, half thinking she might have been followed. But the night was still and the land empty and frozen beneath the stars.

'Is it?' Matty repeated, anxious, persistent.

Damson nodded. 'It has to be. He was huddled in the back of the room under a blanket and I couldn't see his face, but it doesn't matter. The Sword of Shannara was lying on the table, and there's no mistaking it. It's him, all right. They've got him chained up. They're slavers, Matty. I looked in the wagon on my way back and it was full of shackles and chains.' She paused, uneasiness darting across her face. 'I don't know how he stumbled onto them or how he let them capture him, but it shouldn't have happened. The magic of the wishsong should have been more than a match for men like these. I don't understand it. Something's wrong.'

Matty said nothing, waiting.

Damson handed back the water skin and sighed. 'I wish I could have seen his face. He looked up once, just for a moment, but it was too dark to see clearly.' She shook her head. 'Slavers – there won't be any reasoning with them.'

Matty shifted her feet. 'Reasoning isn't something men like this understand. We're women. If given half a chance, they'd seize us, use us for their own pleasure, and then cut our throats. Or if we were really unlucky, they'd sell us along with the Valeman.' She looked out at the night. 'How many did you count?'

'Five. Four inside, one standing watch. They're drinking and throwing dice and fighting among themselves.' She paused hopefully. 'When they sleep, we might be able to slip past them and free Par.'

Matty gave her a steady look. 'That would be chancy in the dark. We wouldn't be able to tell them from us if it came to a fight. And if the Valeman is chained to the wall, it would take too much time and make too much noise to try to free him. Besides, they might be up all night the way things are going. There isn't any way to know.'

'We could wait a bit. A day or two if we must. There will be a chance sooner or later.'

Matty shook her head. 'We don't have the time. We don't know how long it will be until they get to where they're going. There may be more of them ahead. No. We have to do it now. Tonight.'

Now it was Damson's turn to stare. 'Tonight,' she repeated. 'How?'

'How do you think? If they've found a way to capture the Valeman in spite of his magic, they're too dangerous to fool around with.' Matty Roh seemed to be measuring her. 'If we're quick, they'll be dead before they know what happened. Can you do it?'

Damson took a deep breath. 'Can you?'

'Just follow me in and stay behind me. Watch my back. Remember how many there are. Don't lose count. If I go down, get out of there.' She straightened. 'Are you ready?'

'Now?'

'The quicker we start, the quicker we finish.'

Damson nodded without speaking, feeling distanced from what was happening, as if she were watching it from some other vantage point. 'I only have a hunting knife.'

'Use whatever you have. Just remember what I said.'

The tall girl dropped her cloak and reached down into her

gear for the slender fighting sword and strapped it over her back, wearing it the same way Morgan Leah wore his. She fastened a brace of throwing knives to her waist and slipped a broad-bladed hunting knife down into her boot. Damson watched and did not speak. Two against five, she was thinking. But the odds were greater than that. These men were seasoned fighters, cutthroats who would kill them without a second thought. What are we to them? she wondered, and decided it was a stupid question.

They moved off into the night, slipping across the grasslands like ghosts, Damson leading Matty back the same way she had gone earlier, watching the light from the oil lamps hung within the cabin grow brighter as they neared. The voices of the men reached out to greet them, coarse and raucous. Damson could no longer see the glow of the pipe on the porch steps, but that didn't mean the sentry wasn't still there. They moved north of the cabin into the trees and came up from behind, flattening themselves against the rough board wall. Inside, the sounds of gambling and drinking continued.

They peered around the south side of the cabin toward the front. There was no sign of the sentry. With Matty leading now, her sword drawn and held before her, they eased up to the window and took a quick look inside. The scene was unchanged. The prisoner was still wrapped in his blanket and lying on the floor at the rear of the cabin. Four of the men still sat at the table. Damson and Matty exchanged a quick glance, then started toward the front. They reached the corner and looked onto the sagging porch.

The sentry was gone.

Matty's face clouded, but she edged into the light anyway, sword held ready, and moved for the open door. Damson followed, glancing left and right, thinking, Where is he? They were almost to the door when the sentry reappeared out of the dark, come from checking the animals perhaps, looking off that way and muttering to himself. He didn't see the women until he stepped onto the porch, then grunted in surprise and reached for his weapons. Matty was quicker. She shifted the sword to her left hand, reached down with her right, brought out one of the throwing knives, and flung it at the man. The blade caught him in the chest and he went back off the porch with a hiss of pain.

Then they were through the door and inside the cabin, Matty leading, Damson at her back. The room was small and smoky and cramped, and it seemed as if they were right on top of the slavers. Damson could see their faces clearly, the sweat on their skin, the anger and surprise in their eyes. The men leaped up from the table, weapons wrenched free of belts and sheaths. Shouts and oaths rose up, glasses and tin cups tipped away, and ale spilled onto the floor. Matty killed the nearest man and went for the next. The table flipped over, scattering debris everywhere. One of the men turned toward the captive, but Matty was too close to be ignored, and he twisted back to meet her rush. A second man went down, blood pouring from his throat, clawing at the air and then tumbling away. The two who remained rushed Matty Roh with swords and knives glinting wickedly in the lamplight and forced her back toward the wall. Damson stepped away, looking for an opening. Someone grabbed her from behind, and the fifth man, blood leaking from his chest wound, lurched through the doorway, clutching at her with his fingers. She twisted away, slippery with his blood, then shoved him back out the door and down the steps. Outside, the mules brayed and kicked at the cabin wall in terror.

Matty darted and cut at the men before her, fighting to keep from being cornered, yelling for Damson. A lamp shattered, spilling oil everywhere, and flames spread across the cabin floor. Damson threw herself onto the back of the man nearest, tearing at his eyes. He howled in pain, dropped his weapons, and fought with his bare hands to fling her away. She let go, throwing herself clear, reaching for her knife. The man went for her in a frenzy, heedless of everything else, tripped, and went down in the fire. It caught on his clothing and began to burn, and he ran screaming out the door and into the night.

The last man held his ground a moment longer, then bolted for the door as well. Flames were racing up the walls now, streaking across the rafters, eating hungrily at the dry wood. Damson and Matty raced for the back of the cabin where the captive had risen to his knees and was tearing at the ring that chained him to the wall. Matty shoved him down wordlessly, brought the big hunting knife out from her boot, and hacked and cut and pried at the wall until the ring broke loose. Then in a knot they rushed for the cabin door, the flames all about them, the heat singeing their hair and flesh. They were almost clear when the captive twisted free and turned back, charging into the smoke and fire with the chains trailing behind him, searching the debris on the floor until he came up with the Sword of Shannara.

It wasn't until they were all outside, gasping for air and coughing up smoke and dust as the cabin burned behind them, that Damson realized it was not Par Ohmsford they had rescued after all, but his brother, Coll.

They took just long enough to break loose the shackles from Coll's wrists and ankles, casting anxious glances over their shoulders into the night as they did so, then slipped quickly away, leaving behind the smoking ruins of the cabin, the empty wagon, and the bodies of the dead. The mules had long since run off, the remaining slavers had vanished with them, and the land was empty of life. The Valeman and the women smelled of fire and ashes, their eyes watered from the smoke, and they were smeared with the blood of the men they had killed. Matty had received several minor cuts, and Damson was scratched about the face, but both had escaped serious injury. Coll Ohmsford walked like a man whose legs had been broken.

In the shelter of the trees where they had left their gear, they cleaned themselves up as best they could, ate some food and drank some water, and tried to figure out what had happened. They discovered quickly enough that Coll carried the other half of the Skree, the half he had stolen from Par while under the influence of the Mirrorshroud, and that explained why Damson and Matty had thought they were tracking Par. It did not explain why the Skree had brightened in two directions when Damson had used it at Southwatch, although after hearing Coll's story of what had befallen the brothers earlier it could be assumed that Par's magic had affected the disk in some way. Par's magic seemed to affect almost everything with which it came in contact, Coll noted. Something was happening to the Valeman, and if they didn't get to him soon and piece together what it was that was tearing at him, they were going to lose him for good. Coll couldn't tell Damson and Matty why that was so, but he was convinced of it. His triggering of the magic of the Sword of Shannara had revealed a good many truths previously hidden from him, and this was one.

There was no debate about what they would do next. They were of a common purpose, even Matty Roh. They packed up what gear they had and set out across the grasslands north again, heading for the Rainbow Lake and the country beyond, pointing themselves toward a confrontation with the Shadowen and Rimmer Dall. Morgan Leah would be there waiting for them, and together they would attempt another rescue. Four of them, when it came time to stand against their enemies, sustained by their talismans and their small magics, by their courage and determination, and by little else. What they were doing was more than a little mad, but they had left reason behind a long time ago. They accepted it as they did the approach of the new day east, its first faint glimmerings painting the darkened horizon with golden streaks. They accepted it as they did the way in which the disparate directions of their lives had brought them to a crossroads in which they would share a common destiny. There were inevitabilities to life that could not be altered, they knew, and this was surely among them.

They hoped, each in the silence of their unshared thoughts, that this particular inevitability would result in something good.

Morgan Leah barely had time to gasp.

The attack was so swift and unexpected that he was on the ground before he could even think to act, the hand still clamped tightly to his mouth, a dark-cloaked form swinging about to pin him flat. He had lost his Sword, the one thing that might have helped him, and he was so astonished to have been caught off guard that even though his mind screamed at him to move he froze in the manner of a small animal trapped in a snare. His throat constricted, and he stopped breathing. He knew he was dead.

A huge whiskered face pushed close to his own, as if curious to discover what manner of creature he might be, and the luminous yellow eyes of a moor cat blinked down at him.

'Easy, Highlander,' a familiar voice whispered in his ear, soft and reassuring. 'You're safe. It's only me.'

The hand eased away, and Morgan began breathing again, quick and uneven. He felt the knots in his body loosen and the chill in his stomach fade. 'Quiet, now,' the voice whispered. 'They're still close.'

Then the cat face eased away, and he was looking at Walker Boh.

31

S tresa did not come to Wren Elessedil until it was almost
dawn. Stars still lingered in the velvet black skies, and
the forest was thick with shadows. Only a faint brightening east through the trees revealed the approach of the new
day. She rose when he appeared, anxious and relieved. She
had been waiting for him all night, even though it could easily
have taken him another day to reach her. Her Elven hearing
picked up his movements before he emerged from the dark,
and she called out to him.

'Stresa,' she whispered. 'Over here.'

He trundled forward obediently, spikes laid back against his
muscular body, snout lifted to test the air, eyes glittering like
candles.

'I can see you well enough, Elf Queen,' the Splinterscat
muttered as he came up to her. 'And hear you well enough, too.'

Wren smiled at the sound of the familiar voice. It had not
been three days ago that she thought she would never hear it
again. Her ordeal with Tib Arne and Gloon had given her a
new appreciation for the things she had once been too quick to
take for granted. It was strange how death's whisper suddenly
made you hear better. She wondered how many times she
would need to listen to it before she remembered its lesson.

'What did you find?' she asked him, dropping into a crouch
so that she could better see his face.

Stresa sniffed. 'A way in for them and one out for us. Phfffft. It can be done.' He glanced around. 'Where's the sstttpp Squeak?'

She gestured. 'Watching east, where the others wait. I didn't want anyone to hear what we said. Funny how much better she and I have become at communicating.'

The Splinterscat's spines rose and fell back again. 'That is hardly an accomplishment. Squeaks haven't much to say. Hsssttt. Keep your conversation brief, Elf Queen.'

Wren refrained from smiling. No point in encouraging him. 'So we can do this, you and I?'

'This isn't Morrowindl, and the Brakes aren't the In Ju. Of course we can do it. Sppptt!' He spit. 'Should have thought of the idea myself.'

Barely three days gone since her escape from the Shadowen, and Wren was about to challenge them again. She had flown into camp with Tiger Ty and been greeted with elation and astonishment by the Elves of the advance guard, who had given her up for lost. They were settled still within the fringes of Drey Wood, watching the continuing advance of the Federation army, shadowing the Southlanders from cover while they awaited Barsimmon Oridio and the balance of the Elven army. Desidio was effusive in his welcome, telling her straight out that the Elves needed her leadership and he was hers to command, saying more in that single moment than he had said the entire time they had been gone from Arborlon. Triss was furious with her, pointing out that her impulsiveness had caused her abduction, warning her that she was not to go off without the Home Guard ever, that in fact she was not to go off without him personally. She greeted them both with a handclasp and assurances that she would not take such a risk again – already knowing that she intended to do so.

In her absence, the advance guard had been busy. Desidio and Triss had put aside any differences on strategy to continue what she had begun so successfully, sending a second raiding party at the Federation the very night after she was taken, setting fire to supplies and wagons, driving off stock, harassing sleeping troops, doing everything they could think of to cause their enemies discomfort and confusion and to keep them from advancing. With the death of Erring Rift, command of the Wing Riders had passed to Tiger Ty, the most experienced among them and a leader with whom they felt comfortable. Tiger Ty, gruff and abrasive, but up to the challenge, had sent the Wing Riders in support of the Land Elves. The Federation army had been better prepared than before, but still not well enough to prevent considerable damage to supplies and stock. The Elves had lost more than a dozen men this time, but the Federation juggernaut had been brought to a halt once more, forced to stay their march long enough to allow recovery of horses, foraging for food and water, and treatment of their wounded.

Barsimmon Oridio had reached the Valley of Rhenn and was starting down to meet them. Messengers had arrived from the old general to announce that help was on the way. Desidio and Triss had dispatched the messengers back again with the queen's greetings – unwilling to reveal just yet that the queen herself was missing. Neither had been prepared to concede that she was gone for good, despite what had happened to Erring Rift and Grayl. Wren was pleased to discover that they had kept her disappearance quiet.

But she had already decided that the advance guard must do more than just wait for Bar and the rest of the army to reach them. She had thought it through on the flight in from the grasslands, her body weary from the battle with Tib Arne and Gloon, but her mind strangely sharp and clear. She knew what had to be done, and it had to be done regardless of anything else that happened. The Creepers had to be stopped. They would be gaining rapidly on the Federation army now, come out of the Tirfing and across the Mermidon and into the grasslands east of the Pykon. They would catch up in another few days and join with their allies in the hunt for the Elves. When that happened, it was all over. The Elves had no defense against the Creepers, not in numbers, skills, or strength, and the Shadowen machines would track them through the Westland forests to Arborlon and put a quick end to them.

She was not going to let that happen, she had promised, and she had thought back to Morrowindl and the things that had hunted her there and then back to the things that had hunted Ohmsfords down through the years in their service to the Druids, until surprisingly, unexpectedly, she had found the answer she needed.

But once again it would put her at risk, and once again it would require use of the Elfstones.

She had told Tiger Ty, Triss, and Desidio of her plan that very night, and all three were aghast. They had pleaded with her to give it up, to think of something else, to try a different tactic. They had beseeched her to consider what it would mean to the Elves if she was lost again – this time for good. But she had held them off with reason and hard fact, with strength of will and argument, and in the end they had been forced to accept her decision, however reluctantly. They had managed to wring one concession – Tiger Ty and Triss would go with her for however long it was possible.

That had been two days ago. She had come south that same day with Triss, Tiger Ty, fifty Home Guard, and half-a-dozen Wing Riders. The Rocs had carried the Home Guard in the giant baskets, keeping well back within the shelter of the trees and mountains where they could not be seen from the plains, and Wren had ridden with Tiger Ty. She had held everyone in place just long enough to dispatch Faun into Drey Wood to locate and bring back Stresa. She had told the Splinterscat what she intended, and because so much depended on him she had waited for his assurance that her plan could work. When he had agreed that it might, she had scooped him up, strapped him in place on Spirit's back, tucked Faun into her pack, and off they had gone.

Desidio and the rest of the advance force had been sent north to meet with Barsimmon Oridio to await her return.

415

Two days ago. They had traveled all night to get here and spent the first of those two days without sleep. They had all gone exploring instead.

She shook her head, looking off into the darkened trees, smelling moss and bark mold and wildflowers and wondering that so much could happen in such a little time. She heard Stresa shift in the darkness before her, restless, and she looked back again.

'Did you find the Thing?' she asked him, not knowing what else to call it.

'Hssstt.' Stresa was laughing. 'Not *Thing*, Wren Elessedil. *Things!* There have been some changes in three hundred years, it seems. There are more than the one now.'

And perhaps always were, and only one was ever seen, she thought suddenly. She rose, contemplating the advent of the new day. Before her, east, waited the Wing Riders and the Home Guard, and beyond them, somewhere on the grasslands, the Creepers. Behind her, west, lay the Matted Brakes.

More than one. Well, now.

'Wait for me, Stresa,' she ordered, rising again, anxious now to begin. 'The valley opens into a draw that will bring them right through here. It shouldn't be long.'

Stresa turned and moved back into the shadows. 'I'll take a nap. I'm tired from all this rooting about. It stinks in the Brakes, you know. Pfffttt. Watch yourself until you get back here, Queen of the Elves.'

She let him go without comment, then turned into the trees east and made her way back toward the dawn's brightening light. The forest was thin here, the draw she had described a broad wash down out of the higher ground where runoff and wind had swept away most of the cover. She found Faun almost immediately, the little creature leaping onto her shoulder and riding there as she slipped ahead through the trees. The plan would work, she told herself, and to make certain, she went over it again in her mind. The mechanics were simple enough. It was the execution that would make the difference. And the execution was almost entirely in her hands.

She moved down into the valley, following the north slope where the shadows were deepest in the growing light, peering out onto the plains beyond where a faint haze concealed what lay there. They had scouted everything thoroughly the day before in preparation. The Home Guard knew the terrain well enough to take advantage of it, and the Wing Riders had found hiding places within the trees close by the Brakes. Games within games, she thought. Wheels within wheels. She thought back to Morrowindl, where she had learned to play cat and mouse with the Shadowen creatures, to put into practice all that Rover knowledge Garth had imparted to her. She thought how farsighted her mother and father had been to give her into Garth's keeping, knowing how life must one day be for her. It was strange even now to think how much had been given up for her, but it was no longer so difficult to accept. Life delegated responsibility as need required and never in equal shares. The trick was in not being afraid when you learned that this was so.

Faun chittered softly in her ear, and she reached up to stroke the warm, fuzzy face. We must look after each other, she thought to herself. We must nurture and love, if life is to have any real meaning. But first, unfortunately, we must find a way to survive against the things that would prevent us from doing so.

She found Triss and the Home Guard hidden at the mouth of the valley within a cluster of pine and heavy brush. It was still and hazy on the plains beyond, the coming light diffuse within the ground mist, giving it the look of snow. There was a dampness in the air, and it had a pungent, coppery taste.

'They are no more than a mile below where we wait,' Triss advised quietly, calm and steady-eyed as he faced her. The way Garth had once been. 'Scouts screen their coming so that we will not be surprised. Are you ready, my lady?'

She nodded, and tucked Faun down into the backpack she

had brought for her to ride in. Faun would not leave her either. 'Send someone to Tiger Ty and let's be off.'

A messenger was dispatched, and the remainder of the Home Guard, armed with longbows and quivers of arrows, slipped out of their concealment and onto the plains, working their way through the heavy grasses and scrub. The plains were wet with dew, but the ground beneath as hard as stone. They moved slowly, cautiously, dropping into a crouch when the lead men signaled to do so, watchful for the monsters that approached.

As it was, they heard them before they saw them, the heavy armored bodies shaking the ground, more quiet nevertheless in their movement than Wren would have thought. The forward scouts dropped back to report that the Creepers were ahead and to the east, not more than five hundred yards away, eight strong, marching two abreast. There were Seekers with them, black-robed and bearing the wolf's-head marking so that there could be no mistake. Wren was surprised. She had seen no Seekers before. But their presence changed nothing, and so she gave Triss the order to deploy. Silently, the Home Guard slipped away into the haze, fanning out like ghosts.

Then they could only wait. The second slipped by, agonizingly slow. They listened to the sounds of the Creepers and to the sudden silence of the land about that marked their coming. Triss muttered something about the mist. He glanced at her, and she smiled. Triss looked away. Even now, after all they had been through together, he kept his distance. She was queen, after all. She must always stand apart.

The sky continued to brighten and the mist to dissipate.

The first pair of Creepers appeared, materializing like spectral apparitions, huge and monstrous, dwarfing the black-cloaked figures that marched beside them. Twenty or so of the latter, Wren counted rapidly.

She reached down into her tunic and took out the Elfstones. The Stones lay comfortably within her palm and glittered like bits of blue fire. Mine alone to use, she thought. She closed her fingers over them and waited.

When the second pair of Creepers was directly abreast, she rose, held out the Elfstones, summoned the power within, and sent the blue fire streaking out. It lanced through the half light and mist and hammered into the closest of the Shadowen monsters. The Creepers jerked in shock, and one went down, smoking and burning. The others wheeled toward her, and instantly the Home Guard attacked. A rain of arrows showered down on the Creepers and the Shadowen, and shouts rose up from the Elves. There were a few moments of confusion while the Creepers and their tenders milled about uncertainly, and then they counterattacked in a lumbering rush, pounding across the grasslands in search of their assailants.

But the Home Guard were already falling back toward the treeline, firing arrows, screaming oaths, and running for their lives. The Creepers were huge, but very quick, and they began to close the gap. Wren slowed them with a rush of blue fire from the Stones, retreating as she did. Triss at her side. The Creeper who had gone down was back up again, and all eight were coming on. It was what she had hoped for, what she had expected, but now that it was happening it was terrifying. As they lurched through the mist she saw again the Wisteron on Morrowindl, replicated eight times over, and she had to fight down the fear that the memory engendered. She could hear the scrape of claws and the click of mandibles and pincers. She saw the trees west come into view, pocketed the Elfstones, and made a dash for them.

They entered the valley ahead of the Creepers, not bothering to slow yet to see if they were being followed because the sounds of pursuit were unmistakable. Midway through the valley, Wren turned, brought out the Elfstones once more, and sent a wall of blue flame back across the entrance. She could hear the Creepers scream in fury, the sound like the scrape of rusting metal, shrill and inhuman. The Creepers came through the wall with flesh smoking and armor steaming.

She sent another strike into them, rising up on her toes with the force of it, so buoyed by the magic that she thought she could float on air. Filled with its power, she began screaming in challenge.

'Enough!' Triss cried, yanking her back. 'Run, now!'

Anger flared in her eyes at the intrusion. She closed her fingers over the Elfstones and jerked around with a gasp, tearing free. But she did as he urged, running with him into the draw beyond, into the trees and cool shadows. She breathed as if she could never again get enough air into her lungs, feeling the magic race through her body, anxious and demanding, asking to be freed, begging to be used. *So much power!* She clenched her hands into fists and ran on.

They raced up through the draw and into the trees beyond, the Elven Hunters leading the way for Wren and Triss and a handful of rear guard. The Creepers came on, tearing apart everything in their path from brush to full-grown trees, the sounds of the destruction frightening. It was working, Wren thought. It was going as planned. But the Creepers were too quick by half!

At a clearing ahead, the Wing Riders waited with their carrying baskets. The Home Guard climbed in, all but Triss, who had insisted he stay with Wren. The Rocs rose skyward and disappeared west. Wren crossed the clearing into the trees and brought out the Elfstones once again. When the Creepers appeared, shouldering their way furiously through the undergrowth, a jumble of jagged metal and spiky limbs, she sent the fire into them once more, burning everything across the clearing, obliterating all traces of the Home Guard escape while drawing the monsters on.

Then she was back within the trees, racing with Triss for the darkness that lay ahead. Stresa appeared suddenly, cutting across their path, taking the lead. He said nothing, did not even look back at them, his blocky form moving far more swiftly than seemed possible as he took them directly toward the gloom that marked the eastern edge of the swamp they called the Matted Brakes.

Wren glanced back once to make certain that the Creepers were still following, and then ran on. In moments, they were within the Brakes. *Come after me, come after me,* she repeated over and over in her mind, willing that it should be so. The plan she had devised to destroy the Creepers was simple. Attack them on the plains with enough men that they would think it was the vanguard of the Elven army or a significant part thereof, draw them into the trees and the Matted Brakes beyond, take them down a trail that Stresa had chosen and knew and they did not, lead them into a trap they could not escape – a trap where their strength and cunning would prove useless.

Like so many things, the answers to the present lay rooted in the past, and in this case in the songs of Par Ohmsford and the legends of their Shannara ancestors.

With Stresa leading and Triss keeping pace, she drew the Shadowen things deeper into the swamp, never letting them know that they no longer chased an army but only a girl, a man, and a creature from another world. She sent the fire of the Elfstones lancing into them, the earth over which they lumbered, the trees thick with vines and moss, and the fetid, green waters surrounding. She used it to confuse and anger them, to keep them off balance and intent on their chase. Once, she had been afraid to use the Elven magic. But that seemed a long time ago, as distant as the life she had known before her journey to Morrowindl and the discovery of her heritage. She had been freed of her fears when she had accepted her birthright as Queen of the Elves and brought her people out of Morrowindl. The magic now was an extension of herself, a part of the trust bequeathed to her by her grandmother, the fire come from the blood of her ancestors to shield her against whatever threatened. If she was strong, she believed, she could not be harmed.

The day brightened and eased toward noon. They ate and drank when they could, mostly when they paused in their flight, brief stops to listen and make certain of their pursuit.

The Brakes thickened in a morass of tangled roots, trees whose branches hung down like corpses, still, depthless waters, and quicksand that would swallow you in an instant. Stresa chose their path carefully, finding the solid ground, moving steadily ahead. Twice the Creepers caught up with them unexpectedly, once on a flanking maneuver that almost trapped them, the second time in a rush that brought the iron-clad horrors barreling through the trees so quickly that they barely escaped being trampled. The swamp seemed to offer no deterrent; the Creepers crossed it as if it were all solid ground. Wren could not tell if any had been lost or had turned back. She hoped not. She hoped she had them all with her still, hunting. They were formed for that purpose and no other, and she prayed that their instinct for it would lead them on when more reasonable, less powerful creatures would turn back.

It was just after midday when they reached the lake.

They slowed as they came up to it, changing their movements so that they approached with as little noise as possible. Behind, the sounds of pursuit echoed through the cavernous trees, rough and heedless, closing rapidly. The lake was huge and stagnant green and as silent as a tomb. It stretched away into a cloud of mist that hung across it like a shroud. The near shoreline faded to either side into the mist. The far shoreline was hidden entirely. Vines and moss hung from the surrounding trees in curtains of lacy green, and roots tangled and twisted down into the waters like feeding snakes. Everywhere there was silence; no birds, no insects, no fish, not even the whisper of a breeze to disturb the hush. There was the sense of time having come to a standstill here, of life having frozen in place, of everything waiting expectantly.

Here, Wren thought, catching her breath involuntarily. Here is where it will end.

But there was no time to contemplate further. The Creepers were coming, rolling on through the swamp, slashing and hacking and crushing what would not give way. Stresa was already moving right, down the shoreline to a narrow strip of land formed of earth and roots that angled its way out into the center of the vast lake. Wren and Triss hurried after. They turned onto the bridge and began moving toward the wall of mist. Wren glanced skyward once, allowing herself to do so for the first time since they had begun running. But the sky was empty. Too soon yet. They hurried on, stepping lightly, silently, listening to the sound of the Creepers. She looked out across the lake, looking for the Things, but there was nothing to be seen but the flat, opaque surface of the frozen waters.

They were almost into the mist when the Creepers appeared from out of the trees, lurching to a stop, their iron-plated bodies trailing vines and branches and steaming with the heat. They flattened everything close to them as they pushed together at the lake's edge. The Seekers were with them. Catching sight of Wren, they moved swiftly to follow after her.

'There,' Stresa hissed suddenly, head swinging left.

She looked and saw the ridge that lay within the waters – what appeared to be crusted rock grown thick with moss and lichen until you saw the twin jets of steam that rose from one end and realized you were looking at breathing holes. There were two of them, and beyond, almost lost in the haze, another. Still here, just as they had been in the time of Wil Ohmsford, monsters from the deep waters of the Matted Brakes, the Things.

Stresa was moving again, and she hurried after, trying to keep from rushing, trying to keep her passage as silent as that of a cloud across the sky. Do nothing to disturb them, she told herself. Let them sleep a little while more. The haze billowed about, but it was not thick enough to hide them from the creatures following. The Creepers were on the bridge as well, she saw, glancing hurriedly back.

But only two of them!

She stopped abruptly, hissing Stresa and Triss to a stop with her. Two were not enough! She needed them all! She wheeled back, brought out the Elfstones, and held them forth.

'*No!*' she heard Stresa cry out harshly, hissing the word. But she sent the fire forth anyway, flying over the still swamp waters, lancing into the Creepers that hunched down upon the shores, scattering flames into them like arrows, burning and singeing. The Creepers reared back, tearing at the earth. She felt something in the lake stir. Not yet! The Creepers on the shore milled about, their black-cloaked tenders trying to calm them. One of the Seekers disappeared under a flurry of iron claws, screaming.

Ripples spread slowly across the mirrored green waters. Wren took a deep breath. Steady, steady.

Then she struck again, the Elven fire exploding into the Creepers, and this time they all came for her, thundering onto the bridge in a furious rush.

There was movement everywhere in the lake now, a slow shifting of the ridges, a gathering of dark shapes. She saw it out of the corner of her eye as she raced on behind Triss and Stresa – saw it on either side and then ahead and behind, too, and she realized the danger she was in. If the Things attacked now, none of them would escape. Monsters of the swamp, older than the Shadowen spawn and as implacable as time, these were what she had brought the Creepers to face. They had been there when Wil Ohmsford and Amberle Elessedil had passed through the Brakes more than three hundred years earlier in search of the Bloodfire. They had devoured two of the Elven Hunters sent to keep the Valeman and the Chosen safe. She hoped now they would devour the Creepers as well.

Ahead, there was an island, little more than a flat stretch of rock-encrusted earth dotted with scrub and a small stand of cypress. The bridge ran to it and then wound away again beyond. It stood alone in the haze, empty of life.

'*Hurry!*' she heard Stresa hiss.

She looked back again and saw the Creepers, all eight of them, clawing their way across the root-entangled strip of land that stretched away behind her. The Seekers ran after, some crying out, most struggling to keep from being crushed. The

Creepers were out of control, seeing their prey so close at hand, sensing that they would have them in moments. They were closing quickly, heedless of the dangers about, confident of their strength and armor. The Elven magic might burn, but it could not destroy. Hunters, they thought only to hunt, never to hide, never to turn back. One slipped and fell, floundering momentarily in the stagnant lake waters before struggling back out again.

Come after me, she hissed soundlessly at them. *Come see what I have planned for you.*

Then she was on the island and turning back once more, the fire from the Elfstones already building in her hand. She went cold as she realized that she might have waited too long, that the closest of the Creepers was less than fifty yards away. She willed forth the magic quickly, and sent the fire not into the Creepers but into the lake about them, into the ridges with their breathing holes, into the Things.

The lake exploded in geysers that shot hundreds of feet into the air as dark shapes lifted skyward like whales breaching. On the bridge, the Creepers slowed, confused by what was happening, iron jaws clicking, claws scraping. The lake boiled and churned about them, and then the Things attacked. They swept out of the stagnant green, out of the depthless shadowed dark, and tore the Creepers from the bridge. The Creepers thrashed and flailed but could find no purchase in the waters and were dragged from sight. The Seekers went with them, screaming. It happened so fast that it was over almost before it had begun. It took only seconds, a vast roiling of the lake, a rising up of darkness, a thrashing of iron and flesh, and the Creepers were gone.

Save one – the one that had been closest to the island. That one came on, thundering across what remained of the narrow bridge, shaking the earth with the fury of its attack. Wren shifted the fire to meet it, but it came through the flames as if they were nothing more than gold and scarlet leaves. It was on the island an instant later, so huge that it blocked away the

425

whole of the swamp behind where the last ripples were dying back into stillness across the empty surface. Triss cried out and leaped to Wren's defense, sword drawn. Stresa was shouting wildly, and even Faun had appeared, working free of the backpack, screaming in fear.

Then a dark shape flashed down out of the haze, swifter than thought, and Spirit's claws tore at the Creeper's head and back and knocked the beast aside. The Creeper lurched to its feet and twisted away in rage. Spirit swept past, banked, swung around, and struck the Creeper a second time, knocking it farther back. Triss caught Wren about the waist, flung her over his shoulder and raced across the island and back onto the bridge. *No!* she wanted to warn him. *The Things are still out there!* But the breath had been knocked from her lungs, and she could only claw futilely at him. Faun skittered ahead with Stresa, the bunch of them strung out like mice on a rope.

In the lake's deep shadows, there was new movement.

But Tiger Ty had not forgotten the task Wren had assigned him, and Spirit swept back a third time, ignoring the Creeper and coming for the bridge. Tracking them ever since they had come into the Brakes, Spirit was ready now to fly them to safety. Claws reached down to secure a grip on the causeway, and the great Roc clung there long enough for Triss to toss Wren like a sack of feathers to Tiger Ty and follow her up, for Faun to scurry after, and even for Stresa to be hauled aboard. Then Spirit rose again, just avoiding the monstrous jaws that rose from the swamp to sweep across the bridge in their wake, snapping at the empty air.

They ascended slowly, and Wren righted herself, secured her safety straps, and looked down. The last of the Creepers crouched upon the island, trapped on all sides by the horrors in the lake. Shadows dappled it like a sickness. It could not escape. It would die there in the swamp like the others. Wren stared fixedly at it and felt nothing.

Spirit broke clear of the mist and into the sunlight above, causing Wren to blink from the sudden brightness. The

Matted Brakes and what lay hidden within the mist and gloom receded below.

Like Morrowindl, relegated to the past . . .

Wren turned her face to the sun and did not look back.

32

32

wilight shadows lengthened into night, and the sky over
Southwatch grew thick with clouds that screened away
the stars and moon and promised showers before dawn.
The day's heat cooled, the dust and grime settling back to
earth in motes that danced like fairies as the air lost some of its
thickness. Improbably, the barest trace of a breeze wafted
down out of the Runne. Silence fell across the land, as smooth
as satin and as fragile as glass. Mist clung to the earth in long
tendrils that snaked through gullies and across ridges and
turned the poisoned grasslands surrounding the Shadowen
keep into a vast white sea.

Foaming and swirling, the sea began to roil.

It was a time for phantoms, for ghosts that sailed on the
wind like ships at sea, for things that could walk and leave no
footprints with their passing. It was a time for the day's hopes
and expectations and fears and doubts to take shape and come
forth, searching for a voice with which to speak, seeking
redemption out of newfound belief. It was a time for reason
to give way to what imagination alone would permit. It was a
time for dreams.

Walker Boh summoned his and watched it come, swift and
certain, a hawk sweeping down, and when it reached him he
stretched to meet it, rising up out of his body as light as air,
catching hold and lifting away. Voiceless, invisible, as one with

the wraiths of the night, he went down out of the forests on the slopes of the Runne, speeding through the dark trunks and leafy boughs, through the silence and the black with the grim certainty of death's coming. He held himself as still as ice in winter, easing out onto the blasted, empty flats beyond, crossing through the brume toward the waiting black obelisk. He went in the manner of the Druids, in the way Allanon had taught him, a spirit out of flesh. His memories twisted and tugged at him, those of Allanon and those of the man he had been. He remembered both at once, and saw himself again as the outcast who would not believe, who had fought against the transition that the Druid magic had inevitably wrought. And again, too, Walker Boh saw himself as the Druid shade who had set in motion the events that would culminate in that transition by bestowing on Brin Ohmsford the blood trust that ultimately would find its purpose in him. It was strange to be more than one, and yet it was fitting, too. He had never been at peace with himself, and his dissatisfaction came in large part from feeling incomplete. Now he was fulfilled, one man made out of many, one formed of all. He was still learning to be what he had become, to be comfortable with what he was, but it began with feeling whole, and he thought he was that at least if nothing else.

The earth beneath was blackened and bare, stripped of life, burned away and scorched, empty and razed. The Shadowen had done that, but he did not understand yet the nature of their poison. Tonight, he thought, he might.

Southwatch loomed ahead, its black pinnacle towering over him, its knife-edged spire reaching for the sky. He could feel the life within it. He could feel its pulse. Southwatch was alive. There was magic in its walls, magic that had formed and now sustained and protected it. The magic was powerful, but reluctant. He could sense that. He could feel the strain of its effort to be free. Deep inside the black stone it crouched, an animal caged. Shadowen walked within and without, barely visible against the black, keeping watch. The magic fled from them.

A part of the mist, a part of the night, as silent as drifting ash, he came up to the walls. Oblivious, the Shadowen did not sense him passing close and moving on. He came to the gates of the keep and slid swiftly away. They were too well protected to venture through, even as a spirit. He waited for one of the dark things to enter through a crack in the stone skin and followed. He felt the weight of the tower close about him as he did so, a palpable thing. He hugged himself against the evil that raged through the air, a mix of terrible anger and hatred and despair. Where, he wondered in surprise, did it come from?

He hesitated in his choice of directions, and then impulsively followed the magic toward its source. *Just for a moment, just to have a look.* The magic emanated from below, from deep within the earth beneath the keep, all darkness and blind fury. He slipped along the corridors of the fortress, careful not to brush against the walls, against anything of substance, for even in his spirit form he might be sensed. The wards were powerful here, greater than had been those of Uhl Belk at Eldwist, greater even than those of the Druids in the Hall of Kings. The magic was powerful beyond belief, a great crushing force that could destroy anything.

Anything, he corrected, but the bonds that secured it and made it serve the Shadowen.

He followed a stairwell down, winding and twisting through the black, hearing for the first time the sound of something grinding and huffing, the sound of something at labor. It had the feel of a dragon chained. It had the taste and smell of sweat. It strained and lifted like a bellows at work within a forge – and yet it was nothing so simple as that. It was from here that the magic took its life, he sensed. It was from here that it was given birth.

Then he reached wards that even a spirit could not pass undetected, and he was forced to turn aside. He was close to what lay trapped within the cellars of Southwatch, close to the source of the magic, to the secret the Shadowen kept so carefully hidden. But he could go no closer, and so the secret would have to keep.

He turned back up the stairway, speeding quickly through the gloom, a brief glimmer of thought and nothing more. He passed more of the Shadowen wraiths as he went, and one or two slowed before going on, but none discovered him. He went now in search of Par, knowing the Valeman was a prisoner, anxious to discover where he was being kept and whether he was still himself. For there was reason to believe he might not be. There was reason to believe that he had been subverted and was lost.

Walker Boh's heart was as stone as he considered the possibility. The signs were there that it was happening. It had begun with the changing of Par's magic, the evolution of the wishsong into something more than what it had been when he had begun his journey to the Hadeshorn and Allanon. It had continued with the breaking down of his confidence in its use, the sense that somehow the magic was getting away from him. It would terminate here, in the Shadowen keep, if Par embraced their cause, if he accepted that he was one of them.

As he was, Walker Boh thought darkly.

And yet wasn't.

Games within games. He knew some of their rules, but not yet all.

He ascended the stairwells of the keep in steady search of the Valeman, seeking down the dark corridors and into the darker rooms, swiftly and silently. He remembered how Par had convinced him to come to the Hadeshorn to speak with the shade of Allanon. He remembered how Par had believed. *The magic is a gift. The dreams are real.* Well, yes and no. It was so. And not. Like so many things, the truth lay somewhere in between.

Old memories triggered new, and he saw himself as Allanon leading Cogline down the corridors of Paranor when the Druid's Keep was still locked in the mists between worlds, banished by the magic to the nether reaches. He felt Cogline's mix of fear and determination, and in those emotions found mirrored anew the conflict within himself. Cogline had understood that conflict. He had tried to help Walker learn to balance the weight of it. Human and Druid – the parts that formed him would struggle with each other forever, the demands and needs of each at constant war. It would never change. It was the bargain he had struck with himself when he had agreed to accept the blood trust. The last of the old Druids or the first of the new – which was he? Both, he thought. And thought, too, that maybe this was the way it had been for Allanon and Bremen and Galaphile and all the others.

He rose high within the dark tower, and suddenly there was the barest whisper of a familiar presence. It emanated from down the corridor he faced at the head of the stairwell, a gossamer thread. He went toward it, cautious because there was a second presence as well, and this one familiar, too. He smelled Rimmer Dall as he would a swamp, vast and depthless. The leader of the Shadowen filled the air with his dark magic, the scent of it a toxic perfume. Just beneath its veil and barely recognizable, Par's own magic crouched, suppressed and raging.

Walker coasted to the door behind which they faced each other, paused without where he would not be sensed, and bent to listen.

'It would help,' Rimmer Dall said softly, 'if you were not so frightened of the word.'

Shadowen.

'What you are will not be changed by what you are called. Or even by what you call yourself. It is your fear of accepting the truth about yourself that threatens you.'

Shadowen.

Par Ohmsford heard the whisper in his mind, a repetition that would not cease, that haunted him now both on waking and in sleep. And Rimmer Dall was right – he could not escape his fear of it, his growing certainty that he was the very thing he had been fighting against from the beginning, the enemy that the shade of Allanon had sent the children of Shannara to destroy.

He rose from the edge of his bed and walked to the window to stare out into the night. The sky was clouded and the land was misted and still, a ragged shadowed playground for the phantoms of his mind. He was coming apart, he knew. He could feel it happening. His thoughts were scattered and incoherent, his reasoning cluttered with roadblocks, and his concentration fragmented to the point of uselessness. Each day it grew worse, the darkness that surrounded him filling him up like a bowl that now threatened to overflow. He could not seem to escape it. His nights were haunted by dreams of confrontations with himself as a Shadowen, and his days were ragged and weary and empty of hope. He was wracked with despair. He was slipping steadily into madness.

All the while Rimmer Dall continued to come to him, to speak with him, to offer his help. He knew how bad it was, he assured the Valeman. He understood the demands of the magic. Time and again he had warned Par that he must confront who and what he was and take the steps necessary to protect himself. If he failed to do so – and failed now to do so immediately – he would be lost.

The dark-cloaked figure moved to stand beside him, and for an instant Par wanted to seek comfort within the other's shadowy strength. The urge was so strong that he had to bite his lip to keep himself from doing so.

'Listen to me, Par,' the whispery voice urged, low and persuasive. 'Those creatures within the Pit in Tyrsis were like you once. They had use of the magic – not as you do, for their magic was of a lesser sort, but like you in that it was real. They denied who and what they were. We tried to reach them – or as many of them as we could find. We urged them to accept that they were Shadowen and to embrace the help that we could offer. They refused.'

A hand settled lightly on Par's shoulder, and he flinched from it. The hand did not move. 'The Federation found them all, one by one, and took them to Tyrsis and put them into the Pit, caging them like animals. It destroyed them. Trapped in the darkness, deprived of hope and reason, they became victims quickly. The magic consumed them and made them the monsters you found. Now they live a terrible existence. We who are Shadowen can walk among them, for we can understand them. But they can never be free again, and the Federation will leave them there until they die.'

No, Par thought. No, I do not believe you. I do not.

But he wasn't sure, just as he wasn't sure about much of anything now. Too much had happened for him to be sure. He knew he was being eaten up by magic, but he did not know whose it was. He had determined that he would stall until he could find out, but he had made no progress. He was as imprisoned as the creatures in the Pit, and though Rimmer Dall had offered him help repeatedly, he could not accept that the First Seeker's help was what he needed.

Demons wheeled before his eyes, sharp-eyed monsters that teased and laughed and danced away. They followed him everywhere. They lived within him like parasites. The magic fostered them. The magic gave them life.

Down in the depths of Southwatch, the thrumming continued, steady and inexorable.

He wheeled away from the window and the big man's touch. He wanted to bury his face in his hands. He wanted to cry or scream. But he had resolved to show nothing and he was determined to keep that promise. So much had happened to him, he thought. So much that he wished had not. Some of it was beginning to fade, dim memories lost in a haze of confusion. Some of it lingered like the acrid taste of metal on his tongue. It felt as if everything inside was roiling about like windswept clouds, shaping and reshaping and never showing anything for more than an instant.

'You must allow me to help you,' Rimmer Dall whispered,

434

and there was an urgency to his voice that Par could not ignore. 'Don't let this happen, Par. Give yourself a chance. Please. You must. You have gone on as long as you can alone. The magic is too great a burden. You cannot continue to carry it by yourself.'

The big hands settled on his shoulders once more, holding him firm, filling him with strength.

And Par felt all his resolve crumble in that instant, cracking and falling away like shards of shattered glass. He was so tired. He wanted someone to help. Anyone. He could not go on. The demons whispered insidiously. Their eyes gleamed with anticipation. He brushed at them futilely, and they only laughed. He gritted his teeth at them in fury. He felt the magic build within him and with an effort he forced it back.

'Let me help you, Par,' Rimmer Dall pleaded, holding him. 'It won't take a moment for me to do so. Remember? Let me come into you just long enough to see where the magic threatens. Let me help you find the protection you need.'

Enough of Allanon. Enough of the Druids and their warnings. Enough of everything. Where are those who said they would help me now that I need them? All gone, all lost. Even Coll. I am so tired.

'If you wish,' Rimmer Dall whispered, 'you can come into me first. It is not difficult. You can lift out of yourself quite easily if you try. I can show you how, Par. Just look at me. Turn around and look at me.'

The Sword of Shannara lost. Wren and Walker and Morgan disappeared. Where is Damson? Why am I always alone?

There were tears in his eyes, blinding him.

'Look at me, Par.'

He turned slowly and started to look up.

But in that instant a shadow passed between them, swift as light, come and gone in the blink of an eye, and in its wake Par Ohmsford thrust out violently.

No!

Fire exploded between them, generated by the friction of

435

their contact, sparking and flying out into the shadows. Rimmer Dall wheeled away, the features of his rawboned face knotted in rage. His black robes billowed out and his gloved hand lifted in a blaze of red fury. Par, still unsure about what had happened, gasped and fell back, throwing up his own protection, feeling the blue fire of the wishsong's magic rise to shield him. In an instant, he was sheathed in light, and now it was Rimmer Dall's turn to draw back.

They faced each other in the gloom, the fires of their magics gathered at the tips of their fingers, eyes mirroring anger and fear.

'Stay away from me!' Par hissed.

Rimmer Dall remained unmoving before him for an instant more, huge and black and unyielding. Then he drew back his fire, lowered his gloved hand, and stalked from the room without a word.

Par Ohmsford let the fire of his magic die as well. He stood staring into the shadows that surrounded him, wondering at what he had done.

All about him, his demons danced in seeming glee.

'How long is he going to stay like that?' Matty Roh finally asked.

Morgan Leah shook his head. Walker Boh hadn't moved for more than an hour. He was in some sort of trance, a self-induced half sleep. He sat wrapped in his dark cloak, his eyes closed, his breathing slow and barely discernible. He had told them to keep watch and wait for his return. He hadn't told them where he was going. In truth, it didn't appear that he had gone anywhere, but Morgan knew better than to question the Dark Uncle.

They were gathered in a stand of spruce high within the forests bordering the cliffs of the Runne – Morgan, Matty, Damson Rhee, Coll Ohmsford, and Walker Boh. In the darkness beyond where they waited, Rumor's eyes gleamed watchfully. The night was deep and still, the sky a blanket of clouds from horizon to horizon, the air fresh with the smell of a north wind out of the trees. Five days had passed since Walker had found Morgan and saved him from the encircling Shadowen. He had tricked the dark things by cloaking one of them in Morgan's image and letting the others tear it to pieces. It had satisfied the Shadowen that the intruder they were tracking was destroyed and they had drifted back into Southwatch. Yesterday the Valeman and his rescuers had reappeared, crossing the Rainbow Lake in a small skiff. Walker and Morgan had intercepted them at the mouth of the Mermidon and brought them here.

'What do you think he is doing?' Matty persisted, her voice anxious and uneasy.

'I don't know,' Morgan confessed.

He leaned forward for a closer look but moved quickly back again when he heard Rumor growl. He looked at Matty and shrugged. The other two sat silent, faceless in the gloom. They were better rested and fed than they had been in a while, but they were all emotionally drained and physically worn from the long struggle to stay alive. What kept them going was their common determination to find Par Ohmsford and the sense they got from Walker Boh that their journey from the Hadeshorn was coming to a close.

'He's looking for Par,' Damson said suddenly, her voice a low whisper in the silence.

He was, of course. He was following the secondary trail of the Skree to Southwatch to see if the Valeman was a prisoner there. Coll had always been certain his brother was in Shadowen hands, and so were the rest of them by now. But Walker was searching for something more, Morgan sensed. He would not talk about it yet, had been careful to keep it to himself, in fact. He knew something he wasn't telling them, but then that was the way it was with the Druids, and that was what Walker was now. A Druid. Morgan breathed deeply and relaxed, staring off into the dark. How strange. Walker Boh had become the very thing he had once abhorred. Who would have believed it? Well, they had all come from different worlds than this one, he thought philosophically. They had all lived different lives.

He was staring right at Walker when the other's eyes opened, and it startled him so he jumped. The pale face lifted within the cloak's hood, ghostly white, and the lean body shivered.

'He is alive,' the Dark Uncle whispered, coming back to himself as they stared at him. 'Rimmer Dall and the Shadowen have him imprisoned.'

He rose tentatively, hugging himself as if cold. The others rose with him, exchanging uncertain glances. Rumor moved in from the dark.

'What did you see?' Coll asked anxiously. 'Did you have a vision?'

Walker Boh shook his head. He reached down absently to stroke Rumor's broad head as the cat nuzzled up against him. 'No, Coll. I used a Druid trick and went out of my body in spirit form to enter the Shadowen keep. They could not sense me so easily that way. I found Par locked within the tower. Rimmer Dall was with him. The First Seeker was trying to persuade Par to let him take control of the wishsong's magic. He says that Par is a Shadowen like himself.'

'He has told Par that before,' Damson said quietly.

'It is a lie,' Coll insisted.

But Walker Boh shook his head. 'Perhaps not. There is some truth to what he says. I can sense it in the words. But the truth is an elusive thing here. There is more of it than is being told. Par is confused and angry and frightened. He is on the verge of accepting what the First Seeker tells him. He was close to letting the other have his way.'

'No,' Damson whispered, white-faced.

Walker breathed the night air and sighed. 'No, indeed. But time is running out for Par. His strength is fading. I risked a small intrusion to disrupt the acceptance and for now it will not happen. But we have to get to him quickly. The secret to destroying the Shadowen lies with Par. It always has. Rimmer Dall ignores everything in his efforts to win Par over. He knows of my return, of Wren's return, of our escapes from other Shadowen. He knows we draw steadily closer to him. The Shadowen are threatened, but he concentrates only on Par. Par is the key. If we can free him of his fear of the wishsong, we may have all the pieces to the puzzle. Allanon sent us to find the talismans and we have done so. He sent us to bring back the Elves and Paranor and we have done that as well. We have everything we require to defeat the Shadowen; we just need to discover how to use it. The answer lies down there.'

He looked off into the valley, down through the trees to where the dark obelisk of Southwatch rose against the horizon.

'The Sword of Shannara will free Par,' Coll promised, stepping forward determinedly. 'I know it will.'

Walker didn't seem to hear him. 'There is one thing more. The Shadowen keep something locked within the cellars of the keep, something living, chained by magic and held against its will. I don't know what it is, but I sense that it is powerful and that we have to find a way to set it free if we are to win this fight. Whatever it is, the Shadowen guard it with their lives. The wards protecting it are very strong.'

He looked back at them again. 'The Shadowen are Elven-born and use Elven magic out of the time of faerie. Their strengths and weaknesses all derive from that. Par may be one of them in some sense because he is of Elven blood. I can't be sure. But I think the question of what he will become has not yet been settled.'

'He would never turn against us,' Damson whispered, and looked away.

'What do we do, Walker?' Coll asked quietly. He held the Sword of Shannara in both hands, and his blocky face was set like a piece of granite.

'We go down after him, Valeman,' the other answered. 'We go after him now, before it is too late.'

'Not all of us,' Morgan interjected hastily, and glanced at the women.

Walker looked at him. 'They are resolved to go, Highlander.'

Morgan refused to back off. He didn't want Damson and Matty going down into the Shadowen den. The men all possessed magic of one sort or another to protect themselves. The women had nothing. It seemed a mistake.

'You're not leaving me,' Damson interjected quickly, and he saw Matty nod in agreement.

'It's too dangerous,' he heard himself object. 'We can't protect you. You have to stay here.'

They glared at him, and he faced them down. For a moment no one spoke, the three of them standing toe to toe in the darkness, daring one another to say something more.

Then Walker lifted one hand and brought Damson and Matty before him and in the same motion moved Morgan and Coll back. He was taller than Morgan remembered, and broader as well, as if he had grown and put on weight. It wasn't possible, of course, but it seemed that way. It appeared as if he were more than one man. He filled the space between them, huge and forbidding, and the night about them was hushed suddenly with expectation.

'I cannot give you magic with which to fight,' he told the women softly, 'but I can give you magic with which to shield yourselves from the Shadowen attack. Stand quiet now. Don't move.'

He reached out then and swept the air about them with his hand. The air filled with a brightness that seemed to spread and fall like dust, burning and fading away as it touched them. He brought his hand up one side and down the other, glazing them with the brightness from head to foot, leaving them momentarily shimmering and then cloaked once more in blackness.

'If you are resolved to go,' he said, 'this will help keep you safe.'

He brought them all back about him, gathering them in like small children to a father's embrace. He looked suddenly tired and lost, but he looked determined as well. 'We will do what we must and what we can,' he told them. 'Everything we have fought for, every road we have traveled, every life given up along the way, has been for this. I was told so by Allanon after the return of Paranor, after my own transformation, after Cogline had given up his life for me. The end of the Shadowen or the end of us happens here. No one has to go who doesn't choose to. But everyone is needed.'

'We're going,' Damson said quickly. 'All of us.'

The others, even Morgan Leah, nodded in agreement.

'Five, then.' Walker smiled faintly. 'We go to Par first to set him free, to give him back the use of his magic. If we succeed in that, we go down into the cellars. We leave now, so that we can enter Southwatch at dawn.' He paused as if searching for something more to say. 'Look out for yourselves. Stay close to me.'

In the darkness of the grove, the five faced one another and gave voiceless acquiescence to the pact. They would try to finish what so many had begun so long ago, and while they might have wished it otherwise, they were all that were left to do so.

Silent shadows, the three men, the two women, and the moor cat slipped out from the trees and down the mountainside ahead of the coming light.

33

Two days following the destruction of the Creepers in the Matted Brakes, the Elves attacked the Federation army on the flats below the Valley of Rhenn. They struck just before dawn when the light was weak and sleep still thick in the eyes of their enemy. The skies were clouded from a rain that had fallen all through the night, the air damp-smelling and cool, the ground sodden and treacherous underfoot, the land filled with a low-lying blanket of mist that stretched away from the Westland forests toward the sunrise. The grasslands had the look of some phantasmagoric netherworld, shadows shifting within the haze, skies black and threatening and pressing down against the earth, sounds muted and indistinct and somehow given to suggest things not really there. Everything took on the look and feel of something else. The timing was perfect for the Elves.

They had not intended to attack at all. They had planned a defense that would begin at the Valley of Rhenn and give way as required back toward the home city of Arborlon. But Barsimmon Oridio had arrived the day before, linking up at last with Wren Elessedil and the advance column, bringing the Elven army up to full strength for the first time, and after Elf Queen and General huddled with Desidio, Tiger Ty, and a handful of high-ranking commanders from the main army, it was decided that there was no point in waiting on a Federation attack, that waiting only gave the Federation time to dispatch further reinforcements, and that the best defense was an unexpected offense. It was Desidio's suggestion, and Wren was surprised to hear him offer it and even more surprised to hear Bar accept. But the old general, though conservative by nature and set in his ways, was no fool. He recognized the precariousness of their situation and was sharp enough to understand what was needed to offset the Federation's superior numbers. Handled in the right manner, an attack might succeed. He organized its execution, scouted it out personally, and at dawn of the day following set it in motion.

The Federation was still waking up, having crossed the better part of the flats south to reach the head of the valley, intent on covering the last few miles after sunrise and entering the valley at noon. They could not camp safely within the Rhenn, knowing that the Elves had settled their defenses there, and they were reasonably sure that the Elves would await them there. Once again they guessed wrong. The Elves crept out of the forest west while it was still dark, setting their bowmen in triple lines along the Federation flank and backing them with a dozen ranks of foot soldiers equipped with spears and short swords. A second set of archers and foot soldiers and all of the cavalry were sent down out of the valley east to organize a second line of attack at the northeast front of the Federation camp. It was all carried out in absolute silence, the Elves employing the stealth tactics they had perfected while still on Morrowindl – everything done in small increments, the army broken down into squads and patrols that were dispatched separately and reassembled at the point of attack. The Elves had fought together for ten years against odds as great as these. They were not deterred and they were not frightened. They were fighting for their lives, but they had been doing so for a long time.

The archers on the west flank struck first, raining arrows down into the waking camp. As the Federation soldiers sprang up, snatching for armor and weapons, the call to battle ringing out, the Elven Hunters started forward, spears lowered, passing between the archers and down into the midst of the enemy. As they carved their way through the melee, the archers above the Federation army launched a second front. By now the Southlanders were convinced they were surrounded and were attempting to defend on all sides. The Elven cavalry, a relatively small body, swept down out of the haze to rake the still-disorganized Federation defense and send it reeling back. The whole of the flats where the Federation was encamped was a sea of struggling, surging bodies.

The Elves pressed the attack for as long as they were able to do so without risking entrapment, then fell back into the mist and gloom. Barsimmon Oridio commanded personally on the west flank, Desidio on the northeast. Wren Elessedil, Triss, and a body of Home Guard watched through the shifting haze from a promontory at the mouth of the valley. Faun sat on Wren's shoulder, wide-eyed and shivering. Stresa was scouting the forests west of the valley on his own. Tiger Ty was with the Wing Riders, who were being held in reserve.

The attack broke off as planned, and the Elves shifted their positions, taking advantage of the gloom and the confusion, moving swiftly to re-form. They had been settled down in the valley for almost two weeks now, and their scouts had studied the terrain thoroughly. Callahorn might belong to the Federation, but the Elves knew this particular part of it better than the soldiers of the Southland army. The west flank moved to the front and the northeast moved directly east. Then they struck again, this time bringing archers forward to point-blank range, then sending swordsmen in their wake. The Federation army was driven backward, and men began to break and run. The center held firm, but the edges were being systematically destroyed. Men lay wounded and dying everywhere, and the chain of command of the Southland juggernaut was in almost total disarray.

It might have ended then and there, the front ranks of the

Federation army falling back across the flats in confusion, but for one of those quirks of battle that seemingly always crop up to affect the outcome. Riding in the thick of the east flank's strike, Desidio had his horse shot out from under him and went down in a tangle of bodies. His arm and leg were broken, and he was pinned beneath his horse. As he watched helplessly, the foremost of the Federation defenders, encouraged by his fall, launched a counterattack. The attacked pressed back toward the injured Elven commander, and the Elves abandoned their battle plan and rushed to protect him. Freeing him from his horse, they pulled him to safety, but the whole of their front collapsed.

Hearing shouts of victory from the right, the Federation regrouped and counterattacked Barsimmon Oridio. Without a second front, the Elven commander was forced to fall back as well or risk being overwhelmed. The Federation surged toward him, disorganized still, but numbering thousands and regaining lost ground through sheer weight of numbers. When it seemed as if Bar would not reach the safety of the Rhenn without having to stand and fight again, Wren sent the Wing Riders into the fray, sweeping down out of the clouds to rake the foremost ranks of the Federation assault and stall it out long enough for the balance of Bar's forces to escape.

The attack broke off then as both armies paused to regroup. The Elves entrenched anew along the slopes and at the head of the Rhenn, there to await the Federation advance. The Federation, for its part, sent its dead and wounded to the rear, and began to reassemble the bulk of its fighting men for a massive strike. Their plan was not complicated. They intended to come right at the Elves and simply overwhelm them. There was no reason to think they could not do so.

Wren visited Desidio and found him in severe pain, his leg and arm splinted and wrapped, his face as gray as ash. He was furious at being hurt and asked to be carried back to his soldiers. She refused his request, and bolstered by orders from Barsimmon Oridio she dispatched him back to Arborlon, his involvement in the battle ended.

Bar huffed up to her and announced that a commander named Ebben Cruenal would take over Desidio's command. Wren nodded without comment. Both knew that no one would adequately replace Desidio.

The day brightened, but the clouds and the haze hung on, leaving the land in a swelter of damp and heat. Morning edged toward midday. The Elves sent scouts east and west to check for flanking maneuvers but found none. The Federation, it seemed, was confident that a direct attack would succeed.

The attack came shortly after midday, the drums booming out of the haze as the army advanced, wave upon wave of black- and-scarlet-garbed soldiers marching to the beat, spears and swords gleaming. Archers guarded the flanks, and cavalry patrolled out along the fringes to warn against surprise attacks. But the Elves did not have enough men to chance splitting their forces, and they were forced to concentrate on holding the Rhenn. The Federation marched into the valley as if oblivious to what waited, into the teeth of the Elven weaponry.

The Elves struck from all sides. Entrenched above and under cover, the archers raked the Federation ranks until the Southlanders were forced to march over the bodies of their own men. But still they came on, carving their way forward, using their own bowmen to screen their advance. Wren watched with Bar and Triss from the head of the valley, listening to the cries and screams of the fighting men and the clash of their weapons and armor. She had never experienced anything like this, and she shrank from the fury of it. Bar stood apart, observing dispassionately, issuing orders to messengers who carried them forward, and exchanging comments with members of his staff and occasionally with Triss. The Elves had seen a lot of fighting and had fought a lot of battles. This was nothing new for them. But for Wren, it was like standing at the center of a maelstrom.

As the battle wore on, she found herself thinking of the senselessness of it all. The Federation was seeking to destroy the Elves because they believed Elven magic was destroying the Four Lands. While Elven magic was indeed at fault, it had not been conjured by the Elves under attack but by renegades. Yet the Elves under attack were responsible for allowing their magic to be subverted and the Shadowen to come into being in the first place. And the Federation was responsible for perpetuating the misguided witch hunt that would place all blame with the Westland Elves. Mistakes and contradictions, misconceptions and false beliefs – they knotted together to make the madness possible. Reason had no place here, Wren thought disgustedly. But then in war, she supposed, it seldom did.

For a time the Elves held their ground and the Federation attack stalled. But gradually the pressure of so many on so few began to tell, and the Elves were driven back, first along the slopes of the valley and then on its floor. They gave ground grudgingly, but steadily. The attack was beginning to roll them up like leaves before a broom. Bar committed the last of his reserves and left to join the fight. Triss sent the bulk of the Home Guard forward to a position on the slopes several hundred yards below where he stood with Wren. The orders he gave were simple. There was to be no retreat unless he called for it. The Home Guard would stand and die where it was to protect the queen.

Overhead, the Wing Riders were using their Rocs to carry logs and boulders to drop into the center of the Federation ranks. The damage was fearful, but the enemy archers had wounded two of the giant birds, and the others were being kept at a distance. From out of the haze south marched further reinforcements for the Southland army. There were just too many, Wren thought dismally. Too many to stop.

She had agreed to remain clear of the fighting, to save the Elfstones for when they were needed most, either against the Creepers and their Shadowen masters or against anything else the dark magic might conjure up. So far nothing of that sort had joined in the Federation attack. Even the black-cloaked Seekers had not shown themselves. It appeared they felt they were not needed, that the regular army could manage well enough alone. It appeared that they were right.

The afternoon lengthened with agonizing slowness. The Federation army now held the mouth of the valley and was moving steadily toward its head. All efforts to slow the advance had failed. The Elves were giving way before it, severely out-numbered, desperately tired, fighting for the most part on heart alone. Wren watched the black and scarlet hordes inch closer, and her hand closed over the bag that contained the Elfstones and drew it forth. She had hoped not to have to use the Stones. She was not sure even now that she could. These were not Creepers she would be destroying; they were men. It seemed wrong to use the magic against humans. It seemed unconscionable. Using the Elfstones drained her of strength and will-power; she knew that much from her encounters with the Shadowen here and on Morrowindl. But using them drained her of humanity as well, threatening each time to diminish her in a way that would not let her ever be herself again. Killing of any sort did that to you, but it would be worse if she was forced to kill human beings.

Triss moved up beside her. 'Put them away, my lady,' he said quietly. 'You don't have to use them.'

It was as if he had read her mind, but that was the way it was between them; the way it had been since Morrowindl.

'I can't let the Elves lose,' she whispered.

'You can't help them win if you lose yourself either.' He put his hand over hers. 'Put them away. Dusk approaches. We may be able to hang on until then.'

He did not mention what would happen when tomorrow arrived and the Federation juggernaut came at them again, but she knew that there was no point in dwelling on it. She did as he suggested. She slipped the Elfstones away again.

Below, the fighting had intensified. In places, the Federation soliders were breaking through the Elven lines.

'I need to send Home Guard to help them,' Triss said quickly, already moving away. 'Wait here for me.' He called to the knot of Home Guard surrounding her to keep the queen safe, and moved quickly down the slope and out of view.

Wren stood staring down at the carnage. She was alone now with Faun and eight protectors. Alone on an island of calm while all about the seas raged. She hated what she was seeing. She hated that it was happening. If she survived this, she swore, she would spend what remained of her life working to revive the Elven tradition of healing, carrying the tenants of that skill back into the Four Lands to the other Races.

Faun stirred on her shoulder, nuzzling her cheek. 'There, there, little one,' she whispered soothingly. 'It's all right.'

The valley was awash with men surging back and forth along the slopes and down the draw, and the sound of the fighting had grown louder with its approach. She glanced at the sky west in search of the darkness that would bring the battle to a close, but it was still too far removed and distant to give hope. The Elves would not last until then, she thought bleakly. They would not survive.

'We've come so far to lose now,' she murmured to herself, so low that only Faun could hear. The Tree Squeak chittered softly. 'It's not fair. It's not . . .'

Then Faun shrieked in warning, and she wheeled about to find a wave of black-cloaked Seekers breaking from cover behind her, emerging from the trees where the shadows and mist cast their deepest gloom. The Seekers came swiftly, purposefully toward her, weapons glinting wickedly in the half-light, wolf's-head insignias gleaming on their breasts. The Home Guard rushed to defend her, springing to intercept the attackers. But the Seekers were quick and merciless, cutting down the Elves almost as quickly as they reached them. Cries of warning rang out, shouts for help to those below, but the sounds of battle drowned them out completely.

Wren panicked. Six of the Home Guard were down and the last two were on the verge of falling. The Seekers must have worked their way past the scouts and into the deep forest to reach her. She was surrounded on three sides and the circle was closing. Once they had her trapped, there was no question as to what would happen. They had lost her once. They would not risk it again.

She turned to run, tripped, stumbled, and fell. The Seekers had killed the last of the Home Guard and were coming for her. She was all alone now. Faun sprang clear of her shoulder, hissing. She reached into her tunic for the bag that contained the Elfstones, her fingers closing on it, dragging it free, lifting it up. Everything took so long. She tried to breathe and found her throat frozen shut. Blades lifted before her, sweeping up as the Seekers came for her. She scrambled backward through the long grass as she fought to free the Elfstones from the bag. *No! No!* She couldn't move fast enough. She was cast in molten ore and cooling to iron. She was paralyzed. Red eyes gleamed within the hoods of the attackers who were nearest. *How could they have slipped through? How could this have happened?*

Her hands tore apart the drawstrings, frantic, wild, digging, and then digging harder. The first of the Seekers reached her, and she kicked out with her boot and knocked him aside. Grasping the bag, she scrambled to her feet, weaponless as she faced the rest. She screamed in fury, giving up on the Stones, her hand closing over the leather pouch in a fist, swinging at the Seeker closest, deflecting the blade from her throat so that it sliced down the side of her arm, shredding her cloak and drawing blood. She spun and kicked, and another of her attackers flew aside. But there were too many, too many to face alone.

Then Faun was leaping into the fray, launching her tiny body at the closest attacker, spitting and tearing with her claws and teeth. The Seekers behind slowed, not certain what it was they faced, surprised by the Tree Squeak's sudden reappearance. Wren stumbled backward again and struggled to her feet. *Faun!* she tried to call out, but her throat constricted on the cry. The Seeker Faun had attacked ripped out furiously, tearing the small body away from its face and throwing it to the ground. '*No!*' Wren howled, bringing up the arm that held the Elfstones. Faun struck the rocky earth and the Seeker brought down his boot. There was the sound of breaking bones and a high-pitched shriek.

And everything shattered inside Wren Elessedil, a whirlwind of fury and anguish and despair, and from out of its core rose the magic of the Elfstones. It exploded inside her fist, disintegrating the leather pouch, ripping through the cracks of her fingers like water squeezed through sand. It caught the Seeker standing over Faun and consumed him. It raced on to the others who were trying to reach her and hammered into them. They went down as if formed of paper, as if cut and pasted together, then hung on strings in the air and left to withstand the force and violence of a windstorm. Some got past and reached her, hands groping, tearing for her. Some fastened on her and sought to bring her down. But Wren was beyond their power, beyond feeling, beyond anything but the Elven magic as it surged through her. She was given over to its need and nothing could bring her back until that need was satisfied. The magic swung back to catch those clinging to her and ripped them away, loose threads from her clothing. She turned to destroy them, and they burned like fall leaves in the magic's flames. She made no sound as she fought them, all her words forgotten, her face twisted in a death mask. The battle between the Elves and the Federation disappeared in a haze of red. She could no longer see anything beyond the ground over which she fought. Seekers came at her and died in the fiery wake of the Elfstone magic, and the smell of their ashes was all she knew.

Then suddenly she was alone again, the last of the Seekers racing for the trees, fleeing in terror, black robes shredded and smoking. She gathered up the fire and sent it racing after them and with it went the last of her strength. Her arm dropped, and the fire faded. She fell to her knees. The grass about her was charred black and stinking. There were ash piles everywhere amid the bodies of the Home Guard. She heard shouts from the slopes below, where Triss and the balance of the Home Guard had taken up their stations to face the Federation. Don't touch me, she said in response. Don't come near me. But she wasn't sure if she had spoken the words or not. The shouts grew, resounding now from all across the Valley of Rhenn. Something was happening. Something unexpected.

She dragged herself back to her feet and looked out through the fading, misty light.

Far east, beyond where the mouth of the valley opened onto the grasslands below, an army of men had appeared. They came out in a rush, brandishing their weapons and howling their battle cries. They were mostly afoot, armed with swords and bows. They did not join the Federation forces as she had first thought they might, but instead attacked the Southlanders with unmatched fury and determination, driving into them like a rock into damp earth. The cries they gave were audible even where she stood. '*Free-born! Free-born!*' They rolled across the madness like a fresh wind across a swamp. Then over the slopes of the valley where the Elves had stood and died and been driven backward came wave upon wave of massive armored bodies that seemed chiseled from stone. Rock Trolls, bearing eight-foot spears, maces, axes, and great iron-bound shields, marched in cadence out of the gloom and down into the ranks of the Federation.

Joined together as one, free-born and Rock Troll swept into the Southland army. For several minutes the Federation soldiers held their ground, still vastly outnumbering their attackers. But this fresh onslaught was too much for men who had been fighting since sunrise. The Southland soldiers fell back slowly at first, then more quickly, and finally turned and ran. The whole of the Valley of Rhenn emptied of Southland troops as the Federation attack fell apart. Elves joined in the pursuit, and the combined armies of free-born, Trolls, and Elves drove the Federation juggernaut back into the mist and gloom south, leaving in their wake fresh carnage and destruction, soaking the ground anew in blood.

Wren turned to find Faun. She heard Triss calling to her as he scrambled up the slope from behind, heard as well the sounds of the Home Guard who accompanied him. She did not respond. She jammed the Elfstones into her tunic pocket as if they were riddled with plague and left them there, her hands still tingling with the magic's fire, her mind still loud with a strange buzzing. Faun lay crumpled amidst the piles of ashes, unmoving. There was blood all over. Wren knelt beside the Tree Squeak and lifted the shattered form in her hands.

She was still cradling the tiny creature when Triss and the Home Guard finally reached her. She did not look up. In a way she could not explain, she felt as if she were cradling the whole of the Elven nation.

34

The assault on southwatch began with less than an hour remaining before dawn. The approach was uneventful. Clouds continued to blanket the sky, shutting out the light of moon and stars, wrapping the earth below in a soft, thick blanket of gloom. Beneath the clouds, mist rose off the ground into the air and clung to trees and brush and grasses like wood smoke. The night was still and deep, empty of sound and movement, and nothing stirred on the parched and barren land that surrounded the keep.

Walker Boh led the way, easing them down out of the high country and onto the flats, taking them through the mist and shadows, using his Druid magic to cloak them in silence. They passed as phantoms through the black, as invisible as thought and as smooth as flowing water. The Shadowen were not abroad this night, or at least not where the five humans and the moor cat walked, and the land belonged only to them. Walker was thinking of his plan. He was thinking that they would never have enough time to reach Par, free him of his bonds, and descend into the cellar. The Sword of Shannara would be needed to break the wishsong's strange hold on him, and the Shadowen would be all over them the moment the Sword was used. What they needed was to bring Par out of his prison and down to the cellar before using the Sword. He was thinking of a way they might do that.

Coll Ohmsford was thinking, too. He was thinking that perhaps he was wrong in his belief that the Sword of Shannara could help his brother. It might be that the truth he sought to reveal would not free Par but drive him mad. For if the truth was that Par was a Shadowen, then it was of precious little use. Perhaps Allanon had intended the Sword for another purpose, he worried – one he had not yet recognized. Perhaps Par's condition was not something that the Sword could help.

A step behind and to one side, Morgan Leah was thinking that even with all the talismans they carried and magics they wielded, their chances of succeeding in this venture were slim. The odds had been great at Tyrsis when they had gone after Padishar Creel, but they were far greater here. They would not all survive this, he was thinking. He did not like the thought, but it was inescapable, a small whisper at the back of his mind. He wondered if it was possible that after surviving so much – the Pit, the Jut, Eldwist, and all the monsters that had inhabited each – he might end up dying here. It seemed ridiculous somehow. This was the end of their quest, the conclusion of a journey that had stripped them of everything but their determination to go on. That it should end with them dying was wrong. But he knew as well that it was possible.

Damson Rhee was thinking of her father and Par and wondering if she had traded one for the other in making her decision to let Par go on alone in search of Coll when his brother had unexpectedly reappeared among the living. She wondered if the cost of her choice would be both their lives, and she decided that if her dying was the price exacted for her choice, she would pay it only after seeing the Valeman one more time.

At her side Matty Roh was wondering how strong the magic was that the Druid had given her, if it was enough to withstand the black things they would face, if it would enable her to kill them. She believed it was. She wore about her an air of invincibility. She was where she was meant to be. Her life had been leading to this time and place and a resolution of

455

many things. She looked forward to seeing what it would bring.

Ranging off in the dark, a lean black shadow padding through the damp predawn grasses, Rumor thought nothing, untroubled by human fears and rationalizations, driven by instincts and excited by the knowledge that they were at hunt.

They passed through the gloom and came in sight of the dark tower, not pausing to consider, not even to look, but pressing on quickly so that it might be reached before fears and doubts froze them out. Southwatch rose out of the mist, faint and hazy, a dark wall against the clouds, looking as if it were something born of the night and in danger of passing back into it with the coming of dawn. It loomed immutable and fixed, the blackest dream that sleep had ever conjured, a thing of such evil that even the closeness of it was enough to poison the soul. They could feel its darkness as they approached, the measure of its purpose, the extent of its power. They could feel it breathing and watching and listening. They could sense its life.

Walker took them to its walls, to where the obsidian surface rose smooth and black out of the earth, and he placed his hands against the stone. It pulsed like a living thing, warm and damp and stretching upward as if seeking release. But how could this be so? The Dark Uncle pondered the nature of the tower again, then pressed on along its walls, anxious to find a way in. He reached out tendrils of his magic to seek the tower's dark inhabitants, but they were all busy within and not aware yet of his presence. He drew back quickly, not wanting to alert them, cautious as he continued on.

They came to an entry formed by an arched niche that sheltered a broad wedge of stone that was a door. Walker studied the entry, feeling along its borders and searching its seams. It could be breached, he decided, the locks released and the portal opened. But would the breach give them away too quickly? He looked back at the others, the two women, the Highlander, the Valeman, and the moor cat. They needed to reach Par without being discovered. They needed to gain at least that much time before having to fight.

He bent close to them. 'Hold me upright. Do not let me go and do not move from this spot.'

Then he closed his eyes and went out from himself in spirit form to enter the keep.

Within the dark confines of his prison cell Par Ohmsford sat hunched over on his pallet, trying to hold himself together. He was desperate now, feeling as if another day within the tower would mark the end of him, as if another day spent wondering if the magic was changing him irreparably would unhinge him completely. He could feel the magic working through him all the time now, racing down his limbs, boiling through his blood, nipping and scratching at his skin like an itch that could never be satisfied. He hated what was happening to him. He hated who he was. He hated Rimmer Dall and the Shadowen and Southwatch and the black hole of his life to which he had been condemned. Hope no longer had meaning for him. He had lost his belief that the magic was a gift, that Allanon's shade had dispatched him into the world to serve some important purpose, that there were lines of distinction between good and evil, and that he was meant to survive what was happening to him.

He hugged his knees to his chest and cried. He was sick at heart and filled with despair. He would never be free of this place. He would never see Coll or Damson or any of the others again – if any of them were even still alive. He looked through the bars of his narrow window and thought that the world beyond might have already become the nightmare that Allanon had shown him so long ago. He thought that perhaps it had always been like that and only his misperception of things had let him believe it was anything else.

He was careful not to fall asleep. He didn't dare sleep at all anymore because he couldn't stand the dreams that sleep brought. He could feel himself beginning to accept the dreams as fact, to believe that it must be true that he was a Shadowen. His sense of things was fragmented on waking, and he could not escape the feeling that he was no longer himself. Rimmer Dall was a dark figure promising help and offering something else. Rimmer Dall was the chance he dared not take – and the chance that he eventually must.

No. No. Never.

There was a stirring in the air where the door to his cell stood closed and barred. He sensed it before he saw it, then caught a glimpse of shadows passing across the night. He blinked, thinking it another of his demons come to haunt him, another vestige of his encroaching madness. He brushed at the air before his eyes in response, as if that might clear his vision so that he could see better what he knew wasn't there. He almost laughed when he heard the voice.

Par. Listen to me.

He shook his head. Why should he?

Par Obmsford!

The voice was sharp-edged and brittle with anger. Par's head snapped up at once.

Listen to me. Listen to my voice. Who am I? Speak my name.

Par stared at the black nothingness before him, thinking that he had gone mad indeed. The voice he was listening to was Walker Boh's.

Speak my name!

'Walker,' he whispered.

The word was a spark in the blackness of his despair, and he jerked upright at its bright flare, legs dropping back down to the floor, arms falling to his sides. He stared at the gloom in disbelief, hearing the demons shriek and scatter.

Listen to me, Par. We have come for you. We have come to set you free and take you away. Coll is with me. And Morgan. And Damson Rhee.

'No.' He could not help himself. The word was spoken before he could think better of it. But it was what he believed.

458

It could not be so. He had hoped too many times. He had hoped, and hope had failed him repeatedly.

The stirring in the air moved closer, and he sensed a presence he could not see. Walker Boh. How had he reached him? How could he be here and not be visible? Was he become . . . ?

I am. I have done as I was asked, Par. I have brought back Paranor and become the first of the new Druids. I have done as Allanon asked and carried out the charge given to me.

Par came to his feet, breathing rapidly, reaching out at the nothingness.

Listen to me. You must come down to where we wait. We cannot reach you here. You must use the magic of the wishsong. Par. Use it to break through the door that imprisons you. Break through and come down to us.

Par shook his head. Use the wishsong's magic? Now, after taking such care to prevent that use? No, he couldn't. If he did, he would be lost. The magic freed would overwhelm him and make him the thing he had struggled so to prevent himself from becoming. He would rather die.

You must, Par. Use the magic.

'No.' The word was a harsh whisper in the silence.

We cannot reach you otherwise. Use the magic, Par. If you are to be free of your prison, of the one you have constructed for yourself as well as the one in which the Shadowen have placed you, you must use the magic. Do it now, Par.

But Par had decided suddenly that this was another trick, another game being played by either his or the Shadowen magic, a conjuring of voices out of memory to torment him. He could hear his demons laugh anew. Wheeling away, he clapped his hands over his ears and shook his head violently. Walker Boh wasn't there. No one was there. He was as alone now as he had been since he had been brought to the keep. It was foolish to think otherwise. This was another facet of his growing madness, a bright polished surface that mirrored what he had once dreamed might happen but now never would.

'I won't. I can't.'

He clenched his teeth as he spoke and hissed the words as if they were anathema. He swung away from the perceived source of the false hope, the voice that wasn't, moving into deeper shadow, taking himself further into the dark.

Walker Boh's voice came again, steady and persuasive.

Par. You told me once that the magic was a gift, that it had been given to you for a reason, that it was meant to be used. You told me that I should believe in the dreams we had been shown. Have you forgotten?

Par stared into the black before him, remembering. He had said those things when he had first encountered Walker at Hearthstone, all those weeks ago, when Walker had refused to come with him to the Hadeshorn. Believe, he had urged the Dark Uncle. Believe.

Use your magic, Par. Break free.

He turned, the spark visible again in the darkness of his hopelessness, of his despair. He wanted to believe again. As he had once urged his uncle to believe. Had he forgotten how? He started across the room, gaining a measure of determination as he went. He wanted to believe. Why shouldn't he? Why not try? Why not do something, anything, but give up? He saw the door coming toward him out of the gloom, rising up, the barrier he could not get past. Unless. Unless he used the magic. Why not? What was left?

Walker Boh was beside him suddenly, close enough that he could feel him even though he was not really there. Walker Boh, come out of his own despair, his own lack of belief, to accept the charges of Allanon. Yes, Paranor and the Druids were back. Yes, he had found the Sword of Shannara. And yes, Wren had found the Elves as well – must have, would have.

Use the magic, Par.

He did not hear the admonition this time. He walked through it as if it wasn't there, the only sound the rush of his breathing as he closed on the door. Inside, something gave way. I won't die here, he was thinking. I won't.

The magic flared at his fingertips then, and he sent it hurtling into the door, blowing it off its hinges as if it had been caught in a thunderous wind. The door flew all the way across the hall and shattered on the wall beyond. Instantly Par was through the opening and moving down the hall toward the stairs, hearing Walker Boh's voice again, following the directions and urgings it was giving, but feeling nothing inside but the fire of the magic as it wheeled and crashed against his bones, released anew and determined to stay that way. He didn't care. He liked having it free. He wanted it to consume him, to consume everything that came within reach. If this was the madness he had been promised, then he was anxious to embrace it.

He went down the stairs swiftly, leaving the magic's fire in his wake, fighting to control the buildup of its power within. Dark shapes darted to meet him, and he burned them to ash. Shadowen? Something else? He didn't know. The tower had come awake in the predawn dark, its inhabitants rising up in response to the magic's presence, knowing they were invaded and quick to seek out the source of the intrusion. Fire burned down at him from above and from below, but he sensed it long before it struck, and deflected it effortlessly. There was a dark core forming within him, a dangerous mix of casual disregard and pleasure born of the magic's use, and its coming seemed to generate a falling away of caring and worry and caution. He was shedding his humanity. He could do as he pleased, he sensed. The magic gave him the right.

Walker Boh was screaming at him, but he could no longer hear the words. Nor did he care to. He pressed on, moving steadily downward, destroying everything that came into his path. Nothing could challenge him now. He sent the fire of the wishsong ahead and followed gleefully after.

Walker Boh thrashed awake again, body jerking, arms yanking free. His companions stepped back from him quickly. 'He's coming!' he hissed, his eyes snapping open. 'But he's losing himself in the magic!'

They did not have to ask who he was talking about. 'What do you mean?' Coll still gripped his cloak, and he pulled Walker about violently.

Walker's eyes were as hard as stone as they met the Valeman's. 'He has used the magic, but lost control of it. He's using it on everything. Now, get back from me!'

He shrugged free and wheeled away, put his hands on the stone door, and pushed. Light flared from his palms and streaked out of his fingertips into the seams of the massive portal, racing down through the cracks. Locks snapped apart and iron bars splintered. The time for stealth and caution was past. The doors shuddered and gave way with a crunch of metal.

They were inside at once, moving into a blackness even more intense than the night, feeling cold and damp on their skin, breathing dust and staleness through their nostrils. It wasn't age and disuse they found waiting, but a terrible foulness that spoke of something trapped and dying. They choked on it, and Walker sent light scurrying to the darkened corners of the room in which they stood. It was a massive entry to a series of halls that passed beneath a catwalk high above. Beyond, through an arched opening, stood an empty courtyard.

Somewhere in the distant black, they could hear screams and smell burning and see the white flare of Par's magic.

Rumor was already moving ahead, loping down the entry and through the opening to the courtyard. Walker and the others went after him, grim-faced and voiceless. Shadows moved at the fringes of the whirl of light and sound, but nothing attacked. They crossed the courtyard in a crouch, glancing left and right guardedly. The Shadowen were there, somewhere close. They reached the far side of the yard, still following the noises and flashes within, and pushed through into a hall.

Before them, a stairway climbed into the dark tower, winding upward into a blackness now stabbed with the bright flare of magic's white fire. Par was coming down. They stood frozen as he neared, unsure what they would find, uncertain what to do. They knew they had to reach him somehow, had to bring him back to himself, but they also knew – even Matty Roh, for whom the magic was something of an enigma – that this would not be easy, that what was happening to Par Ohmsford was harsh and terrifying and formidable. They spread out on Walker's silent command. Morgan drew free the Sword of Leah and Coll the Sword of Shannara, their talismans against the dark things, and when Matty saw this she freed her slender fighting sword as well. Walker moved a step in front of them, thinking that this was his doing, that it was up to him to find a way to break through the armor that the magic of the wishsong had thrown up around Par, that it was his responsibility to help Par discover the truth about himself.

And suddenly the Valeman came into view, gliding smoothly down the stairs, a phantom ablaze with the magic's light, the power sparking at the ends of his fingers, across his face, in the depth of his eyes. He saw them and yet did not see them. He came on without slowing and without speaking. Above, there was chaos, but it had not yet begun to descend in pursuit. Par came on, still floating, still ephemeral, moving directly toward Walker and showing no signs of slowing.

'Par Ohmsford!' Walker Boh called out.

The Valeman came on.

'Par, draw back the magic!'

Par hesitated, seeing Walker for the first time or perhaps simply recognizing him, and slowed.

'Par. Close the magic away. We don't have – '

Par sent a ribbon of fire whipping at Walker that threatened to strangle him. Walker's own magic rose in defense, brushing the ribbon back, twisting it to smoke. Par stopped completely, and the two stood facing each other in the gloom.

'Par, it's me!' Coll called out from one side.

His brother turned toward him, but there was no hint of recognition in his eyes. The magic of the wishsong hissed and sang in the air about him, snapping like a cloak caught in a wind. Morgan called out as well, pleading for him to listen, but Par didn't even look at the Highlander. He was deep in the magic's thrall now, so caught up in it that nothing else mattered and even the voices of his friends were unrecognizable. He turned from one to the other as they called to him, but the sound of their voices only served to cause the magic to draw tighter.

We can't bring him back, Walker was thinking in despair. *He won't respond to any of us*. Already he could sense the pursuit beginning again, could feel the Shadowen drawing near down the connecting halls. Once Rimmer Dall reached them . . .

And then suddenly Damson Rhee was moving forward, brushing past Walker before he could think to object, mounting the stairs and closing on Par. Par saw her coming and squared himself away to face her, the magic flaring wickedly at his fingertips. Damson approached without weapons or magic to aid her, arms lowered, hands spread open, head lifted. Walker thought momentarily to rush forward and yank her back again, but it was already too late.

'Par,' she whispered as she came up to him, stopping when she was no more than a yard away. She was on a lower step and looking up, her red hair twisted back from her face, her eyes filling with tears. 'I thought I would never see you again.'

Par Ohmsford stared.

'I am frightened I will lose you again, Par. To the magic. To your fear that it will betray you as it did when you believed Coll killed. Don't leave me, Par.'

A hint of recognition showing in the maddened eyes.

'Come close to me, Par.'

'Damson?' he whispered suddenly.

'Yes,' she answered, smiling, the tears streaking her face now. 'I love you, Par Ohmsford.'

For a long moment he did not move, standing on the stairs

in the gloom as if carved from stone while the magic raced down his limbs and about his body. Then he sobbed in response, something coming awake within him that had been sleeping before, and he squeezed his eyes shut in concentration. His body shook, convulsed, and the magic flared once and died away. His eyes opened again. 'Damson,' he whispered, seeing her now, seeing them all, and swayed forward.

She caught him as he fell, and instantly Walker was there, too, and then all of them, reaching for the Valeman and bringing him down into the hall, holding him upright, searching his ravaged face.

'I can't breathe anymore,' he whispered to them. 'I can't breathe.'

Damson was holding him close, whispering back that it was all right, that he was safe now, that they would get him away. But Walker saw the truth in Par Ohmsford's eyes. He was waging a battle with the wishsong's magic that he was losing. Whatever was happening to him, he needed to confront it now, to be set free of the fears and doubts that had plagued him for weeks.

'Coll,' he said quietly as they lowered Par to his knees and let him collapse against Damson. 'Use the Sword of Shannara. Don't wait any longer. Use it.'

Coll stared back at the Dark Uncle uncertainly. 'But I'm not sure what it will do.'

Walker Boh's voice turned as hard as iron. 'Use the Sword, Coll. Use it, or we're going to lose him!'

Coll turned away quickly and knelt next to Par and Damson. He held the Sword of Shannara before him, both hands knotting, on its handle. It was his talisman to use, but the consequences of that use his to bear.

'Morgan, watch the stairs,' Walker Boh ordered. 'Matty Roh, the halls.' He moved toward Par. 'Damson, let him go.'

Damson Rhee stared upward with stricken eyes. There was unexpected warmth in Walker's gaze, a mix of reassurance and kindness. 'Let him go, Damson,' he said gently. 'Move away.'

She released Par, and the Valeman slumped forward. Coll caught him, cradled him in his arms momentarily, then took his brother's hands and placed them on the handle of the Sword beneath his own. 'Walker,' he whispered beseechingly.

'Use it!' the Dark Uncle hissed.

Morgan glanced over uneasily. 'I don't like this, Walker . . .'

But he was too late. Coll, persuaded by the strength of Walker Boh's command, had summoned forth the magic. The Sword of Shannara flared to life, and the dark well of the Shadowen keep was flooded with light.

Wrapped in a choking cloud of paralyzing indecision and devastating fear, Par Ohmsford felt the Sword's magic penetrate like fire out of darkness, burning its way down into him. The magic of the wishsong rose to meet it, to block it, a white wall of determined silence. Protective doors flew closed within, locks turned, and the shivering of his soul rocked him back on his heels. He was aware, vaguely, that Coll had summoned the Sword's magic, that the power to do so was somehow his where it had not been Par's, and there was a sense of things being turned upside down. He retreated from the magic's approach, unable to bear the truth it might bring, wanting only to hide away forever within himself.

But the magic of the Sword of Shannara came this time with the weight of his brother's voice behind it, pressing down within him. *Listen, Par. Listen. Please, listen.* The words eased their way past the wishsong's defenses and gave entry to what followed. He thought it was Coll's words alone at first that breached his defenses, that let in the white light. But then he saw it was something more. It was his own weary need to know once and for all the worst of what there was, to be free of the doubt and terror that not knowing brought. He had lived with it too long to live with it longer. His magic had shielded him from everything, but it could not do so when he no longer

466

wished it. He was backed to the wall of his sanity, and he could not back away farther.

He reached for his brother's voice with his own, anxious and compelling. *Tell me. Tell me everything.*

The wishsong spit and hissed like a cornered cat, but it was, after all, his to command still, his birthright and his heritage, and nothing it might do could withstand both reason and need. He had bent to its will when his fear and doubt had undermined him, but he had never broken completely, and now he would be free of his uncertainty forever.

Coll, he pleaded. His brother was there, steadying him. *Coll*.

Holding on to each other and to the Sword, they locked their fingers tight and slipped down into the magic's light. There Coll soothed Par, reassuring him that the magic would heal and not harm, that whatever happened, he would not abandon his brother. The last of Par's defenses gave way, the locks releasing, the doors opening, and the darkness dispelling. Shedding the last of the wishsong's trappings, he gave himself over with a sigh.

And then the truth began, a trickle of memories that grew quickly to a flood. All that was and had ever been in Par's life, the secrets he had kept hidden even from himself, the shames and embarrassments, the failures and losses he had locked away, marched forth. They came parading into the light, and while Par shrank from them at first, the pain harsh and unending, his strength grew with each remembering, and the task of accepting what they meant and how they measured him as a man became bearable.

The light shifted then, and he saw himself now, come in search of the Sword of Shannara at Allanon's urging, anxious for the charge, eager to discover the truth about himself. But how eager, in fact? For what he found was that he might be the very thing he had committed against. What he found was Rimmer Dall waiting, telling him he was not who he thought, that he was someone else entirely, one of the dark things, one of the Shadowen. Only a word, Rimmer Dall had whispered, only a name. A Shadowen, with Shadowen magic to wield, with power no different than that of the red-eyed wraiths, able to be what they were, to do as they did.

What he saw now, in the cool white light of the Sword's truth, was that it was all true.

One of them.

He was one of them.

He lurched away from the recognition, from the inescapability of what he was being shown, and he thought he might have screamed in horror but could not tell within the light. A Shadowen! He was a Shadowen! He felt Coll flinch from him. He felt his brother jerk away. But Coll did not let go. He kept holding him. *It doesn't matter what you are, you are my brother*, he heard. *No matter what. You are my brother*. It kept Par from falling off the edge of sanity into madness. It kept him grounded in the face of his own terror, of his frightening discovery of self.

And it let him see the rest of what the truth would reveal.

He saw that his Elven blood and ancestry bound him to the Shadowen, who were Elven, too. Come from the same lineage, from the same history, they were bound as people are who share a similar past. But the choice to be something different was there as well. His ancestry was Shannara as well as Shadowen, and need not be what his magic might make him. His belief that he was predestined to be one of the dark things was the lie Rimmer Dall had planted within him, there within the vault that held the Sword of Shannara, there when he had come down into the Pit for the last time with Coll and Damson. It was Rimmer Dall who had let him try the Sword, knowing it would not work because his own magic would not let it, a barrier to a truth that might prove too unpleasant to accept. It was Rimmer Dall who had suggested he was Shadowen spawn, was one of them, was a vessel for their magic, giving him the uncertainty required to prevent the warring magics of Sword and wishsong from finding a common ground and thereby beginning the long spiral of doubt that would lead to Par's final subversion when the possibility of what he might be grew so large that it became fact.

Par gasped and reared back, seeing it now, seeing it all. Believe for long enough and it will come to pass. Believe it might be so, and it will be so. That was what he had done to himself, blanketed in magic too strong for anything to break down until he was willing to allow it, locked away by his fears and uncertainties from the truth. Rimmer Dall had known. Rimmer Dall had seen that Par would wrestle alone with the possibilities the First Seeker offered. Let him think he killed his brother with his magic. Let him think he was failing because of who he might be. As long as he unwittingly used the wishsong to keep the Sword's magic at bay, what chance did he have to resolve the conflict of his identity? Par would be savior of the Druids and pawn of the Shadowen both, and the twist of the two would tear him apart.

'But I do not have to be one of them,' he heard himself say. 'I do not have to!'

He shuddered with the weight of his words. Coll's understanding smile warmed him like the sun. As it had been for his brother when the Sword's truth tore away the dark lie of the Mirrorshroud, recognition became the pathway by which Par now came back to himself. Had Allanon known it would be like this? he wondered as he began to rise out of light. Had Allanon seen that this was the need for the Sword of Shannara?

When the magic died away and his eyes opened, he was surprised to find that he was crying.

35

Shadows and mist tangled and twisted down the length of the Valley of Rhenn, a sea of movement that rolled across the bodies of the dead and beckoned in grim invitation for the living to join them. Wren Elessedil stood at the head of the valley with the leaders of the army of the Elves and their newfound allies and pondered the lure of its call. From out of the corpses still strewn below, mostly Southlanders abandoned by their fellows, arms rose, cocked in death, signposts to the netherworld. The carnage spread south onto the flats until the dark swallowed it up, and it seemed to the Queen of the Elves that it might very well stretch away forever, a glimpse of a future waiting to claim her.

She stood apart from the others – from Triss and Barsimmon Oridio, from the free-born leader Padishar Creel and his gruff friend Chandos, and from the enigmatic Troll commander Axhind. They all faced into the valley, as if each was considering the same puzzle, the mix of mist and shadows and death. No one spoke. They had been standing there since news had arrived that the Federation was on the march once more. It was not yet dawn, the light still below the crest of the horizon east, the skies thick with clouds, the world a place of blackness.

Despair ran deep in Wren. It ran to the bone and out again, and it seemed to have no end. She had thought she had cried her last when Garth had died, but the loss of Faun had brought the tears and the grief anew, and now she believed she might never be free of them again. She felt as if the skin had been stripped from her body and the blood beneath allowed to run, leaving her nerve endings exposed and raw. She felt as if the purpose of her life had evolved into a testing of her will and endurance. She was sick at heart and empty in her soul.

'She was just a Squeak,' Stresa had hissed to her unconvincingly when he had found her toward midnight. She had told him of Faun's death, but death was nothing new to Stresa. 'They grow up to die, Wren of the Elves. Don't trouble yourself about it.'

The words were not meant to hurt, but she could not help challenging them. 'You would not be so quick with your advice if I were grieving for you.'

'Phhffft. One day you will.' The Splinterscat had shrugged. 'It is the way of things. The Squeak died saving you. It was what she wanted.'

'No one wants to die.' The words were bitter and harsh. 'Not even a Tree Squeak.'

And Stresa had replied, 'It was her choice, wasn't it?'

He had gone off again, deep into the forests west to keep watch for what might come that way, to bring warning to the Elves if the need arose. They were drifting apart, she sensed. Stresa was a creature of the wild, and she was not. He would go out one day and not come back, and the last of her ties with Morrowindl would be gone. Everything would be consigned to memory then, the beginning of who she was now, the end of who she had been.

She wondered that her life could evolve so thoroughly and she feel so much the same.

Yet perhaps she lied to herself on that count, pretending she was unchanged when in fact she was and simply could not admit it. She frowned into the gloom, searching the killing ground below, and she wondered how much of herself had survived Morrowindl's horror and how much had been lost.

She wished she had someone of whom she could ask that question. But most of those she might have asked were dead, and those still living would be reticent to answer. She would have to provide her own answer to her question and hope her answer was true.

Padishar Creel's lean face glanced in her direction, searching, but she did not acknowledge him. She had not spoken with any of them since rising, not even Triss, wrapped in her solitude as if it were armor. The free-born had come finally, bringing with them Axhind and his Rock Trolls, the reinforcements she had prayed for, but she suddenly found it difficult to care. She did not want the Elves to perish, but the killing sickened her. Yesterday's battle had ended in a draw, settling nothing, and today's did not promise a new result. The Federation had stopped running and regrouped and were coming on again. They would keep coming, she thought. There were enough that they could do so. The addition of the free-born and Trolls strengthened the Elven chances of surviving, but did not give reason to hope that the Federation could be stopped. Reinforcements would be sent from the cities south and from Tyrsis. An unending stream, if necessary. The invasion would continue, the push into the Elven Westlands, and the only thing left undecided was how long the destruction would go on.

She bit back against the bitterness and the despair, angry at her self-perceived weakness. The Queen of the Elves could not afford to give up, she chided. The Queen of the Elves must always believe.

Ah, but in what was there left to believe?

That Par and Coll Ohmsford were alive and in possession of the Sword of Shannara, she answered determinedly. That Morgan Leah followed after them. That Walker Boh had brought back Paranor and the Druids. That Allanon's charges had been fulfilled, that the secret of the Shadowen was known, and that there was hope for them. She had these to believe in, and she must find her strength there.

She wondered if her uncle and her cousins and Morgan Leah still found strength in their beliefs. She wondered if they had any beliefs left. She thought of the losses she had suffered and wondered if they had suffered as much. She wondered finally if they would have given heed to the charges of Allanon had they known from the start the price that pursuing them would exact. She did not think so.

Light broke east where the sun crested the lip of the world, a faint silver glow that outlined the Dragon's Teeth and the forestland below. The light seeped down into the valley and chased the shadows from the mist, separating the two and turning the landscape stark and certain. The sound of drums and marching feet grew audible in the distance, faint still, but recognizable in its coming. Padishar Creel was arguing with Barsimmon Oridio. They did not agree on what the combined army's strategy should be when the attack commenced. They were both strong-willed men, and they mistrusted each other. Axhind listened without saying anything, impassive, expressionless. Triss had moved away. The leader of the free-born resented Bar's insistence that overall command should be his. She had separated them once already. She might have to do so again and resented it. She did not want any part of what was happening, not anymore. She stood watching and did not move as the argument grew more heated. Triss looked over, waiting for her to step in. South, the drums grew louder.

Then suddenly Stresa appeared, bursting unexpectedly from the brush, quills lifting to shake away the dust and leaves, hurrying to reach her. Wren turned, everything else forgotten. There was an urgency to the Splinterscat's coming that was unmistakable.

'Elf Queen,' he hissed, his voice ragged and dry. 'They've brought Creepers!'

She felt her heart stop and her throat constrict. 'We left them all in the swamp,' she managed.

'They've found more! Sssttt!' The wet snout lifted, the dark eyes dilated and hard. 'From Tyrsis, it seems. Phhffttt! Sol-

473

diers, too, but it is the Creepers who matter. Five at least. I came as soon as I saw them.'

She wheeled back to the others. Padishar Creel and Bar had stopped arguing. Axhind and Chandos stood shoulder to shoulder like stone figures. Triss was already next to her.

Creepers.

The light was brightening and the haze diffusing as the army of the Federation marched out of the gloom toward the Valley of Rhenn. It came with its divisions of black and scarlet spread wide across the valley mouth and up its broadening slopes, the columns of men deep and long. Cavalry rode the flanks, and there were rolling, timbered buttresses behind which their archers could hide, with slits for firing through. There were shield walls and fire catapults, and there were black-cloaked Seekers anew at every command.

But it was toward the very center of the army that all eyes turned. There were the Creepers, glinting black metal and jagged, hairy limbs, a mesh of machine and beast, lurching toward the Elves and their allies, toward the men they had been sent to destroy.

Wren Elessedil stared at them and felt nothing. Their coming marked the end of the Elves, she knew. Their coming marked the end of everything.

She reached into her tunic for the Elfstones and stepped forward to make her final stand.

'Get up, Par!'

Coll was shouting at him, pulling on his arm and dragging him to his feet. He scrambled up obediently, still in shock from what had happened to him, stunned by the revelations of the Sword. There was a whirl of movement in the stairwell as those who had come for him – Walker, Damson, Coll, Morgan, and the tall, slight, black-haired woman whose face he did not recognize – hurried to surround him. Rumor prowled the room anxiously. There was a whisper of something coming down the stairs, but the gloom hid what crept there. The doors leading from the well were all closed save one that led back across a courtyard to walls and an opening to the land beyond. That way, at least, was clear, and in the distance he could see morning's light edging above the Runne's horizon.

Walker was looking that way as well, he saw. Walker, all in black now, bearded and pale, but looking somehow stronger than he had ever looked, filled with a fire that burned just beneath the surface. Like Allanon, Par thought. As Allanon had once been. Walker stared momentarily toward the opening, undecided, the others crouching close to Par, but facing back toward the closed doors and the open stairwell, weapons held ready.

'Which way!' hissed the dark-haired girl.

Walker turned and moved swiftly to join them, decided now. 'We came for Par and to set free what they keep imprisoned in the castle depths. We're not finished.'

Damson's arms came around Par and she was holding him as if she might never let go. Par hugged her back, telling her it was all right, that he was safe now, wondering if he really was, wondering still what had happened. The magic of the wishsong was his again, but he remained uncertain even so of what it might do.

But at least I am not a Shadowen! At least I know that!

Coll was standing close to Walker. 'The door with the crossbars – over there – leads down a corridor to the cellar steps. Do we go?'

Walker nodded. 'Quickly. Stay together!'

They went across the room in a rush, and as they did so, a black shape flung itself down the stairs and onto the dark-haired girl. She sidestepped the attack, and the thing turned on her instantly, hissing and red-eyed, flinging up hands with claws of fire. But Rumor caught it before it could strike, tearing it down the middle and throwing it aside.

Walker flung open the door with the crossbars, and they surged through, leaving the stairwell and their pursuers to follow. The corridor was high and dark, and they slipped down it cautiously, eyes skittering through the shadows. Rumor was back in front, cat eyes sharper than their own, leading the way. From somewhere below came the sound of grinding, then a long sigh, a breathing out. The castle of the Shadowen shuddered in response, like the skin of something living that flinched with a skip in the beating of its heart. What was down there? Par wondered. Not the crashing of waves on the rocks as Rimmer Dall had told him – another lie. Something more. Something so important that Walker would risk everything rather than leave it. Did he know what it was? Had Allanon given him the answers they had all been searching for?

There was no time to find that out now. Shadows filled the opening behind them, and Morgan whirled back and sent the fire of the Sword of Leah surging into them. They scattered and disappeared, but were back in a moment. Coll was whispering urgently to Walker, giving him directions to the corridor leading down, but Walker seemed to know where he was going, pulling Coll after him, keeping him close. The others followed in their wake, hugging the walls. Shadows spun out of the darkness ahead, but they were merely reflections of what followed. Par clutched Damson against him and ran on.

They reached a landing that opened onto stairs winding down into the fortress depths, and now the sounds of what was kept below became clear and distinct. It was the breathing of some great animal, rising and falling, wheezing as if the air passed through a throat parched and constricted from lack of water. The grinding was the sound of movement, like the weight of stones shifting in an avalanche.

Black-cloaked forms appeared on the stairs below, and Shadowen fire burned toward them in sharp red spears. Walker threw up a shield that shattered the attack and struck back. Other shadows came out of halls intersecting the one that brought them. The Shadowen were all around, black and soundless and frenzied in their attack. Morgan turned to protect the rear while Walker led the way, the others crouching in between. They moved quickly down the steps, feeling the castle shudder as if in response to what was happening. The breathing of the thing below quickened.

Suddenly there were flames everywhere. Coll went down, struck a glancing blow, and the Sword of Shannara fell from his hand. Without thinking, Par reached down for it and snatched it up. The Sword did not burn him as it had in the Pit. Had it all been in his fear of who he might be? He stared at the Sword in wonder, then turned to help Damson, who was pulling Coll back to his feet, and shoved the blade into his brother's hands once more. Rumor had leaped down the stairs and into the closest of their attackers. His sleek coat was singed and smoking, but he ripped into the Shadowen as if the wounds meant nothing. Walker threw white Druid light from his hands in a shroud that blanketed everything, shielding them, thrusting back the Shadowen, clearing the way for their descent.

Then Par saw Rimmer Dall. The First Seeker was below them on a catwalk across a chasm that dropped away from a landing through which the stairway passed. He stood alone, his hands gripping the railing of the walk, his rawboned face a mask of rage and disbelief. The gloved hand smoldered as if in response. He looked at Par and Par at him, and something passed between them that Par might have described as an understanding, but seemed to transcend even that.

In the next instant he was gone, and Par was struggling on through the Shadowen assault. His magic had revived, and he could feel it building within him. He would use it now, he thought. He would take his chances because at least he knew that using it would not make him one of them. The Shadowen were closing from behind, and Morgan had turned back to face them, yelling at the others to go on. The dark-haired girl stood with him, pressed against his shoulder protectively, the two of them holding the stairs against the monsters that followed.

Walker reached the landing and looked over its edge. Par joined him, then jerked hurriedly away again. Something huge was down there, something that heaved and writhed and pulsed with light.

A raging black form slammed into Rumor when he passed down the stairs below the landing, and the moor cat tumbled from view. Walker and the others raced after him, Par's magic flaring to life now, burning through him as he summoned it forth with a cry. He remembered his fear of what it would do, but the fear was only a memory now, and he banished it almost as quickly as it came. Facing across to the catwalk and the Shadowen crouched there, he tried to keep their fire from reaching Damson and Coll. Coll was hurt again, but he stumbled on, still holding the Sword of Shannara before him, still keeping Damson in his shadow.

They heard Rumor shriek, that spitting, furious cry that signaled pain and fear. Then he rose before them in a leap, the black thing clinging to him. Walker spun and sent the Druid fire lancing forth, caught the black thing's midsection, and tore it from Rumor's back. The moor cat spun in midair, locked again with its attacker, and fell from view.

Smoke rose from the walls and floor where the magic burned, and the air grew thick with ash. The depths of Southwatch were as black as pitch save for the light given off by the thing below. Gloom pressed in about the humans, and the Shadowen darted in and out at them, looking for a place to attack. Damson was struck and burned and knocked aside so quickly that Par could not prevent it. She rose and fell back again. Coll reached down for her without slowing, heaved her over one shoulder, and hurried on.

Then part of the stairs gave way, and Walker Boh disappeared in a tumbling slide of dust and rock and ash. For an instant Par, Coll, and a semiconscious Damson were alone on the crumbling stairs, staring down into the void where the light pulsed, pressed back against the wall in shock. They heard Rumor snarl below, heard Walker howl in fury, and saw the flare of the Druid magic.

'What are you doing? Move!'

It was Morgan Leah screaming at them as he appeared suddenly from out of the smoke and fire above, the Sword of Leah dark and fiery in his hand. He was limping badly and his left arm was clutched to his side. The dark-haired woman was still with him, as battered as he was, blood smeared down the side of her face. They surged out of the haze and herded the others toward the slide. Par went tumbling down the broken rock into the gloom. He landed on his feet, and was set upon instantly. Black forms closed about, but the magic of the wishsong saved him. It flared like armor all about him, then exploded outward into his attackers. The black things were thrown back into the haze. Rumor surged past, striking out, a shadow appearing and fading away again. He heard the sound of the others following him down, and in seconds they were together once more.

Ahead, the light pulsed and the sound of its breathing was a terrifying groan of frustration and pain.

They went forward once more, searching the dust and ash-filled gloom for Walker and the moor cat. The Shadowen came at them repeatedly, but Morgan and Par fought them off, keeping Coll and the women between them. Damson was stirring again, but Coll continued to carry her. The other woman stumbled forward on her own, teeth gritted, fire in her eyes. They passed down a high, narrow corridor that opened overhead into the stairwell, and suddenly they were in the room with the light.

The room was cavernous and craggy, carved out of the earth's rock long ago by time and the elements, a vast chamber from which tunnels ran in all directions. At its center rested the light. The light was a bulbous, pulsing mass wrapped all about with cords of red fire. It strained and heaved against the cords, but could not break free. It seemed to be part of the cavern floor, welded to the rock and risen from its core into the gloom. It had no shape or identity, yet something in the way it moved reminded Par of an animal snared. The breathing sound came from that movement, and the whole of the chamber rising up into Southwatch seemed to be connected to it. It would shudder, and the cavern and the walls of the keep would shudder in response. It would sigh, and the cavern and the keep would sigh as well.

'What is it?' Par heard Coll whisper next to him.

Then they saw Walker Boh. He was across the cavern floor, locked in combat with Rimmer Dall, the two dark-cloaked forms straining against each other with desperate intent. Rimmer Dall's gloved hand was red with Shadowen fire, and Walker's was sheathed in Druid white. The rock beneath them steamed with heat, and the air about them pulsed. Rimmer Dall's eyes were spots of blood, and his big, rawboned face was skinned back with fury.

To one side, Rumor fought desperately to reach Walker, Shadowen closing about to finish him.

Morgan went to their aid without pausing, howling out his battle cry, bringing up the dark blade of his talisman in a trail of fire. The dark-haired woman went with him. Coll started instead toward the chained light, thinking to strike there, then was forced to turn aside to meet an attack from Shadowen launching themselves off the catwalk. He dropped Damson, and Par racing up from behind caught her up. The Shadowen closed on Coll and forced him back. The Sword of Shannara offered no threat to them, and Coll had no other magic. Par screamed at him to get out of the way, but instead Coll bulled into the cloaked melee. Par laid Damson down hurriedly and went after him. Coll stumbled and went down, rose again momentarily, and then went down for good. The Shadowen were all over him. Par howled in fury and sent the magic of the wishsong hammering into them, thrusting them aside. Fire burned back at him from above and on all sides, but from beneath his magic's armor he shrugged it away.

Coll was on his hands and knees when Par reached him,

bloodied and torn. He lifted his face so that he could see Par and then shoved the Sword of Shannara at him.

'Go on!' he said, and collapsed.

Par snatched up the Sword and started forward, the acrid smell of ash and fire thick in his nostrils. Go on and do what? He was aware of Morgan standing alone now, the dark-haired girl fallen as well. He could no longer see Walker or Rimmer Dall. He felt his strength beginning to fail, the consequence of sustained use of his magic. He would have to be quick, whatever he did. He stumbled ahead, nearing the light, wondering anew what it was and what he was supposed to do with it. Should he free it? Wasn't that what Walker had said they had come into Southwatch to do? If it was a prisoner of the Shadowen, then it should be freed. But what was it? He was not certain of anything. He was barely free himself, and his own confusion still dragged at him with chains of its own.

He looked down at the Sword of Shannara, suddenly aware that he was carrying it, that he had taken it from Coll. Why had he done that? The Sword was not meant for him. It was meant for Coll. He wasn't even able to use it.

And then suddenly Rimmer Dall was standing before him, wolf's head gleaming in the light, dark robes shredded and falling away. His hood was thrown back, and his red-bearded, craggy face was washed in blood. He blocked Par from the light, rising up before him. The gloved hand pulsed with crimson fire. When he smiled, it was a terrifying grimace.

'Come down to find what we keep hidden here?' he asked, his voice whispery and rough.

'Get out of my way,' Par ordered.

'Not anymore,' the other said, and Par suddenly realized that the gloved arm was no longer gloved at all, that the fire he was seeing was all there was of the arm, was what had laid beneath the glove all along. 'I've given you all the chances you get, boy.'

There was no pretense of friendliness or concern now. Loathing glittered in Rimmer Dall's eyes, and his body was

481

knotted with rage. 'You belong to me! You've always belonged to me! You should have given yourself to me when you had the chance! It would have been easier that way!'

Par stared openmouthed.

'You're mine!' Rimmer Dall swore in fury. 'You still don't understand, do you? You're mine, Par Ohmsford! Your magic belongs to me!'

He came forward in a lunge, and Par barely had time to cry out and throw up the wishsong's magic to slow him. And slow him was all it did. The First Seeker came through the shield as if it were paper, and his hands locked on Par's shoulders like iron clamps. Par was vaguely aware of thinking that this was what Rimmer Dall had wanted all along – the magic of the wishsong and Par's body in which to wield it. All the pretenses of wanting to help him control the magic had been a screen designed to hide his ambition to own it. Like all the Shadowen, Rimmer Dall craved the magic in others, and few had the magic of Par.

He was thrown back by the other's weight, bent down, and forced to his knees. The Sword of Shannara dropped from his nerveless fingers. He brought his hands up to fight the other off, summoning the magic to his defense, but it was as if all his strength had been leeched from him. He could barely breathe as the other's shadow enfolded him. Rimmer Dall began to come out of his body and enter Par's. The Valeman saw it happening, felt it beginning. He screamed and fought to free himself, but he was helpless.

Not this! he thought in terror. *Don't let it happen!*

He twisted and kicked and tore at the other, but Rimmer Dall's Shadowen self was pressing into him, entering through his skin. The feeling was cold and dark and filled him with self-loathing. Once, he could have prevented this, he sensed. Once, when the magic was out of control and driven by his fear and doubt, he would have been strong enough to keep the other away. Rimmer Dall had known this. The First Seeker's thoughts brushed up against his own, and he shrank from what they revealed. *Someone help me!* He caught a glimpse of movement to his left, and Morgan Leah surged forward, howling. But Rimmer Dall struck out with his gloved hand, releasing Par for the barest instant, and Morgan disappeared in a flash of red fire, tumbling away again into the dark. The hand returned, fastening on Par anew. The Valeman had retreated down inside himself where his magic was strongest, gathering it into an iron core. But Rimmer Dall closed on it relentlessly, pressing in, squeezing. Par could feel even that part of himself giving way . . .

Then abruptly the First Seeker was jerked backward, and his Shadowen self tore free of Par. Par gasped and blinked and saw Walker Boh with his good hand closed on Rimmer Dall's throat, the Druid fire racing down its length. He was singed and scraped, and his face was as white as chalk beneath the black beard and streaks of blood. But Walker Boh was a study in raw determination as he brought the force of his magic to bear on his enemy. Rimmer Dall surged upward with a roar, flailing with his gloved hand, the Shadowen magic scattering everywhere. Something in what Walker was doing to him was keeping Rimmer Dall separated from his corporeal body, his Shadowen self held just outside and beyond. Both parts struggled to reunite, but Walker was between them, blocking them from each other.

Par staggered backward and then came to his feet again. Walker's fingers closed into a fist, squeezing something within the Shadowen. Rimmer Dall thrashed and screamed, his rangy form surging upward and shuddering with fury. Shadowen fire burned downward into the floor, coring into the stone. Other Shadowen raced to give aid, but Rumor lunged between them, tearing and ripping.

'Use the Sword!' Walker Boh hissed at Par. 'Set it free!'

Par snatched up the blade and raced for the light. He reached it in seconds, unchallenged now, all eyes on the battle between the Druid and the First Seeker. He came up to it, this vast, pulsing mass with its scarlet-ribboned chains, and holding the Sword of Shannara in both hands, he laid it flat against the light.

Then he summoned its magic, willing it forth, praying it would come.

And come it did, rising up smoothly, easily, free of the constraints the wishsong's magic had imposed when his fears and doubts and Rimmer Dall's trickery had convinced him he was a Shadowen. It came swiftly, a white beacon that speared into the light before it, then raced back again to swallow Par whole. Par saw anew the truths of his life, the truths of his magic, of his Shannara and Shadowen heritage, and of his Elven ancestry. He breathed them in like the air that gave him life and did not flinch away.

Then he saw finally the truth of the light before him. He saw what the Shadowen had done, how they had used their magic to subvert the Four Lands. He saw the meaning behind the dreams of Allanon, and the reason for the summoning of the children of Shannara to the Hadeshorn. He saw what it was that he must do.

He drew back the magic of the Sword and dropped the blade to the cavern floor. Behind him, Rimmer Dall and Walker Boh still thrashed in a combat that seemed to have no end. The First Seeker was shrieking – not in pain at what was being done to him, but in fury at what Par was about to do. There were Shadowen closing from everywhere, fighting to get past Morgan Leah, back on his feet once more, and Rumor, who seemed indestructible. But it was too late for them. This moment belonged to Par and his friends and allies, to all those who had fought to bring it about, to the living and the dead, to the brave.

He summoned the magic of the wishsong one final time, brought all of it to bear, the whole of what burned within him, evolved out of his birthright into the monster that had nearly consumed him. He summoned it forth and shaped it once more into that shard of blue fire that had first appeared when he had fought to escape the Pit, that shard that seemed a piece of azure lightning come down from the sky. He raised it overhead and brought it down on the crimson cords of magic that bound the light, shattering them forever.

Par shuddered with the force of the blow and with what the effort took from him, a tearing, a rending, a draining away.

The light exploded in response, blazing forth into the cavern's darkest corners and from there upward into Southwatch. It chased the shadows and the gloom and turned what was black to white. It shrieked with glee at finding its freedom, and then it sought retribution for what had been done to it.

It took Rimmer Dall first, sucking out the First Seeker's life as if drawing smoke into its lungs. Rimmer Dall shuddered violently, collapsed in a scattering of ashes, and ceased to exist. The light went after the other Shadowen then, who were already fleeing in hopeless desperation, and swallowed them up one after the other. Finally it rose to consume Southwatch, racing up the black walls, into the pulsing obsidian stone. Par was dragged to his feet by Walker, who bent to snatch up the Sword of Shannara. Walker called to Morgan, and in seconds they were gathering the others as well, hauling them up, carrying those who could not stand. Rumor led the way as they surged toward a tunnel at the chamber's far end, racing to escape the cataclysm.

Overhead, Southwatch exploded into the morning sky in a geyser of fire and ash.

Stresa was the first to feel the tremors and hiss in warning at Wren. 'Elf Queen. Phfftt! Do you feel it? Hsst! Hsst! The earth moves!'

Wren stood slightly apart from Triss, the Elfstones clutched in her hand as she watched the coming of the Federation army, awaiting her confrontation with the Creepers. They had reached the mouth of the Valley of Rhenn, and with the front lines of the Elves and their allies less than three hundred yards away, the battle she dreaded was about to commence. Barsimmon Oridio, Padishar Creel, Chandos, and Axhind had dispersed to their various commands. Tiger Ty had gone to be with the Wing Riders. Home Guard surrounded the queen on all sides, but she felt impossibly alone.

She turned at the Splinterscat's words, then felt the tremors herself. 'Triss,' she whispered.

For the earth was shuddering more deeply with each series of quakes that passed through it, as if a beast coming awake to the rising of the sun, to the coming of the light. It shook itself from sleep, and its growl rose above the beating of the Federation drums and the marching of the soldiers' feet.

Wren caught her breath in dismay.

What was happening?

Then fire and smoke erupted far to the east and south, rising up against the sunlight in a wild conflagration, and the quaking turned to a desperate heaving. The men of the opposing armies paused in their confrontation and turned to look, eyes scanning the horizon, cries beginning to ring out. The fire and smoke grew into a cloud of black ash, and then suddenly there was a tremendous burst of white light that filled the sky with its brightness, pulsing and alive. It rose in a wild sweep, racing across the sun and back again, running with the wind and the clouds.

When it flew down into the earth again, the shudders began anew, rising and falling, filling the air with sound.

Then the light burst forth within the valley, spears of it breaking through the earth's crust, rising up through the terrified men. Wren gasped at its brightness and felt the Elfstones digging into the flesh of her palm as she gripped them tightly in response.

The light sped this way and that, yet not at random as she had first believed but with deadly intent. It caught the Creepers first, tore them asunder, and left them smoking and ruined and lifeless. It caught the Seekers next, enfolding them in shrouds of death, draining them of life, and leaving them in piles of smoking ash. It raced through the Federation army, weeding its ranks of Shadowen-kind, and in doing so stole away its purpose and courage, and the soldiers who remained turned and fled for their lives, throwing down their weapons, abandoning their fortifications and assault machines, giving up any hope but that of staying alive. Within seconds it was finished, the Creepers and the Shadowen destroyed, the soldiers of the Federation army in flight, the grasslands littered with the discards and leavings of battle. It happened so fast that the Elves, free-born, and Rock Trolls did not even have time to respond, too stunned to do anything but stare after and then to glance hurriedly through their own ranks to make certain that the light had not touched them.

On the bluff at the head of the valley where she had watched it all happen, Wren Elessedil exhaled slowly into the following hush. Triss stood next to her openmouthed. Stresa's breathing was a rasp at her boot. She swallowed against the dryness in her throat and then looked out across the Valley of Rhenn in astonishment as one final miracle came to pass.

All across the parched and barren plains, for as far as the eye could see, wildflowers were blooming in the sunlight.

36

'What was inside the light, Walker?' Coll asked. It was midmorning, and they were gathered in the shade of the trees on the slopes leading down from the Runne north of the ruins of Southwatch. Below, the Shadowen keep continued to steam and smoke and burn, its walls collapsed into rubble, the once-smooth black stone turned brittle and dull. Walker sat alone to one side, wrapped in the torn remnants of his dark robes. Par and Coll sat across from him. Morgan was leaning against the broad trunk of a red maple, chewing on a bit of grass and looking at his boots. Matty Roh was propped up next to him, her shoulder touching his. Damson lay sleeping a few yards off. They were battered and worn and covered with blood and dust, and Coll had broken an arm and ribs. But the tension had left their bodies and the wariness had faded from their eyes. They weren't running anymore, and they weren't afraid.

'It was magic,' Par said with quiet conviction.

They had fled the cellars of the Shadowen keep through the tunnel Walker had chosen, stone crumbling and falling in chunks all about them as they raced through the underground gloom with only the Druid fire to guide them. The tunnel twisted and wound, and it seemed that they would never get clear in time. They could hear the sounds of the keep's destruction behind them, feel the thrust of stale air and dust against their backs as the walls collapsed inward. They feared they would be trapped, but Walker seemed certain of the way, so they followed without question. At last the tunnel opened out through a cluster of brush onto a low hillside above the keep, and from there they scrambled upward into the shelter of the trees to watch the conflagration of fire and smoke that marked the keep's demise. Damson was unconscious again, and Walker labored over her intently, using the Druid magic, healing her as he had healed Par weeks earlier when the Valeman had been poisoned by the Werebeasts. Her injuries made her feverish, but Walker brought the fever down, cooling her so that she could sleep. While he worked, the others washed and bound themselves as best they could.

Now, the sunlight stretching toward the hills west, they sat looking back across the flats where Southwatch smoldered. Everywhere they looked, there were wildflowers, come into bloom with the collapse of the Shadowen keep and the return of the light to the earth. A profusion of color, the blossoms blanketed the whole of the land for as far as the eye could see, covering even those areas that had been sickened and ravaged. Their smell drifting lightly on the morning air seemed to signal a new beginning.

'Stolen magic,' Walker Boh amended.

What Par had been shown by the magic of the Sword of Shannara, Walker had been able to intuit with his Druid instincts. Walker's dark eyes were ringed in ash and dirt and his face was drawn, yet there was strength in his steady gaze. They had finished sharing their separate stories and were now considering the reasons behind everything that had happened to them.

Walker's face lifted. 'The light was the magic the Shadowen stole from the earth. It was how they gained their power. Elven magic in the time of faerie borrowed from the elements, most particularly from the earth, for the earth was its greatest source. When the Elves recovered that lost magic after Allanon's death, the Shadowen were the renegades among them

489

who sought to use it in ways for which it was not intended. Like the Skull Bearers and the Mord Wraiths before them, the Shadowen came to rely on the magic so heavily that eventually it subverted them. They became addicted to it, reliant on it for their survival. Eventually it was their sole reason for being. They stole it in small doses at first, and when the need grew stronger, when they wanted power enough to control the destiny of the races and the Four Lands, they built Southwatch to drain the magic off in massive amounts. They found a way to leach it from the core of the earth and chain what they had stolen beneath the keep. Southwatch, and the magic they gathered within, became the source of their power everywhere. But as they used it to propagate, to create things like the Creepers, to strengthen themselves, they weakened the earth from which the magic had been taken. The Four Lands began to sicken because the magic was no longer strong enough to keep them healthy.'

'The dreams of Allanon,' Par said.

'They would have come to pass in time. There was nothing to prevent it unless the magic was set free again.'

'And when it was, it destroyed its jailers.'

Walker shook his head. 'Not in the way you think. It did not deliberately destroy them. What happened was more basic. Once it was freed, it pulled back into itself the whole of what had been stolen. It took back the power that had been drained away. When it did, it left the Shadowen and their monsters bereft of the life that had sustained them. It left them as hollow as sea shells left to dry on the beach. The magic kept them alive. When it was taken away, they died.'

They were silent a moment, thinking it through. 'Was Southwatch a living thing, too?' Coll asked.

Walker nodded. 'Alive, but not in the sense that we are. It was an organism, a creature of the Shadowen that served to feed and protect them. It was the mother that nurtured them, a mother they had created out of the magic. They fed on what she gave to them.'

Matty Roh made a face and scuffed at the earth. 'Their sickness come back into themselves,' she murmured.

'I don't understand why there were so many different kinds of Shadowen,' Morgan said suddenly. 'Those at Southwatch, like Rimmer Dall and his Seekers, seemed in control of themselves. But what about those poor creatures in the Pit? What about the woodswoman and the giant we encountered on our way to Culhaven?'

'The magic affected them differently,' Par answered, glancing over. 'Some did better with it than others.'

'Some adapted,' Walker said. 'But many could not, though they tried. And some of those in the Pit were men who had been drained of their small magics by the Shadowen, the weak subverted by the strong. Remember how the Shadowen kept trying to come into you and become part of you? Like the woodswoman and the child on Toffer Ridge?'

Like Rimmer Dall, Par thought to himself but did not say so.

'They needed to feed to survive, and they fed where and when the need arose. They used up the humans around them as well as the earth that sustained them. If the magic was strong, the lure to steal it was stronger still. When the Shadowen had drained the magic away, it drove mad the creatures it had been drained from. Or in some cases, it drove the Shadowen mad to feed on it. It was a very destructive subversion. The Shadowen never understood. The power they sought was forbidden to them. The power that gives life to the earth and its creatures is too dangerous to tamper with.'

Rumor padded in from out of the shadows, singed and bloodied in a dozen places, patches of fur torn off in a dozen more. He seemed not to notice. His muzzle was wet from having drunk from a spring found somewhere back within the trees. His luminous eyes surveyed them briefly, then he wandered over to Walker, sat down, and began to lick himself clean.

Par picked at a wildflower growing near his feet. 'Rimmer

Dall wanted to drain the magic of the wishsong from me, didn't he?'

'He wanted more than the magic, Par.' Walker had shifted to a more comfortable position, and Rumor looked over to make certain he wasn't leaving. 'He wanted you as well. He wanted to become you. This is difficult to understand, but the Shadowen had discovered how to leave their bodies and survive as wraiths early on. The old magic let them do that; the earth magic gave them the power to be anything they wished. But they lacked identity that way, and they craved to be something more than smoke. So they used the bodies of humans, discarding them when they were ready to be someone or something new.'

He leaned forward slightly. 'But Rimmer Dall was First Seeker, the strongest of the Shadowen, and he hungered to be more than the others. He settled on being you, Par, because you gave him youth and power unlike that possessed by any other human. The wishsong was evolving; he knew that. More than that, he recognized the direction that evolution was taking. Your Elven blood was bringing the magic back around to what Brin Ohmsford had inherited from her father, the magic born of the Elfstones. Remember how she had struggled to keep it from destroying her? Rimmer Dall understood the nature of this magic. It was Elven, but it had its Shadowen side, too. If he could gain control of it, he could turn it to his own use. But this was not something he could do unless you helped him. The magic was too strong, too protective, to let you be subverted forcibly. He needed to trick you into helping him. It was what destroyed him in the end, his obsession with claiming you. He gave himself over to it, spending his time on finding a way to satisfy it, telling you that you were already a Shadowen, suggesting you were the very enemy you sought, letting you think you killed Coll and then bringing Coll back to life, chasing you about, harrying you into believing that without his help you would go mad.

'His cause was strengthened by his discovery that Allanon

492

had sent you in search of the Sword of Shannara. He knew of
your magic from Varfleet, but now he saw a way to make you
his ally against his most dangerous enemy. He needed to keep
close to you to make certain you did not discover the truth, and
your magic helped. It was Elven-spawned, and every time you
relied on it you told him where you were. It was not enough to
enable him to capture you, but it kept him close.'

'But he was wrong about the Sword of Shannara,' Par
insisted. 'He thought I was the only one who could use it,
and it was really meant for Coll.'

Walker shook his head. 'I don't know that it was meant
specifically for either of you. It seems that it was meant for
both. But it was necessary that Coll use it first if you were to be
saved from Rimmer Dall. You had to find a way to accept the
fact that even though your fears about the magic were true,
they were not determinative of your fate. Allanon was careful
not to reveal anything about Coll's role. He must have known
that it had to be kept secret if Coll was to help you.'

'Perhaps he knew that the Shadowen would discover the
charges,' Morgan offered. 'So he held one back.'

'What about the charges?' Par asked suddenly. 'What were
they meant to accomplish? We know why retrieving the Sword
of Shannara was important, but what about the others?'

Walker breathed deeply, looked away toward the plains for a
moment thinking, then turned back again. His knowledge and
his reasoning allowed him to divine more quickly than his
companions the truths behind what had transpired, and so
they were quick to look to him for an explanation. Foresight,
comprehension, perception, and deduction – Druid skills
bequeathed to him. Add to those the power of the magic
and the responsibility to use it wisely. He was beginning to
appreciate already the burden that Allanon had carried all
those years.

'The charges were given to accomplish more than simply
the destruction of the Shadowen,' he said, choosing his words
carefully. 'A combination of things was required if the Four

Lands was to survive. An understanding of who the Shadowen were and what they were about was necessary first and foremost, and the quests to carry out Allanon's charges provided that. More directly, there were the talismans that helped destroy them – the Sword of Shannara, the Elfstones, the wishsong, and Morgan's blade. And peripherally there were the magics that enabled us to recover those talismans.

'But the charges were given as well to sustain the Four Lands once the Shadowen were gone, to help keep the Shadowen or things like them from coming back. The Elves were returned to provide a balance that has been missing. The Elves are the healers of the land and her creatures, the caretakers needed to keep the magic safe and secure. When they fled, the Shadowen had no one to challenge their theft, no one who even realized what was happening. The Elves will work to prevent that from occuring again.

'And the Druids,' he said softly, 'will contribute to that balance as well. It was something I did not understand before, something I learned in becoming one of them. The Druids are the land's conscience. They do not simply manipulate and control. They seek out what troubles the land and her people, and they help to put it right again. It might seem sometimes as if they serve only their own purposes, but the misperception comes from fear of the power they wield. It remains a judgment for each of them, of course – for me, as well, I know – but the reason for their being comes from a need to serve.' He paused. 'I could not be one of them otherwise.'

'Once, you could not have been one of them in any case,' Par observed quietly.

Walker nodded and the hardness in his eyes softened. 'Once, Par, was a long time ago for all of us.'

Cogline would have agreed with that, the Valeman thought to himself. The old man would have recognized the truth in those words right away. Cogline had seen the passing of so many years, times gone out of memory and become legend, the disappearance of the Druids and their return, the transition from the old world to the new. Cogline had been the last of what once was, and he would have understood that the inevitability of change was the sole constant of life.

'So the black things are really gone,' Matty Roh said suddenly, as if needing confirmation, not looking at anyone as she spoke.

'The Shadowen are gone,' Walker Boh assured her. He paused, looking down. 'But the magic that sustained them remains. Do not forget that.'

Damson stirred then, and they went to see that she was all right. Overhead, the sunlight brightened through the early haze, and the air began to turn hot and sticky. On the flats below, the remains of Southwatch shimmered and steamed in the swelter, and after a time took on the appearance of a mirage.

Midday came and went as the company rested within the cool of the mountain trees. Damson woke from her slumber to eat and drink, then closed her eyes once more. She would heal quickly, Walker Boh observed. She would be well again soon.

They fell asleep after that, drifting off one by one, smelling wildflowers and fresh grasses, comforted by the forest silence. Exhaustion might have claimed them, but Par thought afterward it must have been something more. He dreamed that Walker spoke to each of them as they slept, telling them that they should remember what he had said about the magic, that they should remember its importance to the land. What part of the magic they kept with them – and here he spoke mostly to Par – they must ward carefully against misuse and neglect. Keep it safe for when it was needed; hold it in trust for when it must be used. He touched them each in some way that was not immediately recognizable, passing among them silently, soundlessly, leaving them rested and at peace. He changed in appearance as he went, looking at times like Walker and at other times like Allanon. He took from Coll the Sword of Shannara. So that it will not be lost again, he explained. Coll did not object, nor did anyone. The Sword did not really belong to them. The Sword belonged to the Four Lands.

Then Walker began to fade away like a shadow in sunlight. I must leave you now, he told them, for my healing requires the Druid Sleep.

When they awoke again it was late afternoon, the sky turning purple and crimson, the forest hushed and cool and still. Walker Boh was gone, and they knew without being told that he was not coming back to them.

Moments later Elven Wing Riders and their Rocs appeared out of the fading sunlight west bearing Wren and Padishar and the others who had fought at the Valley of Rhenn, and it was time for the explanations to begin again.

37

Time passed, and summer turned to autumn. The mid-year heat gave way grudgingly, the days cooling, becoming shorter and somehow more precious at the prospect of winter's coming. Wildflowers faded and leaves began to turn, and one set of colors replaced another. Birds flew south, and the winds out of the mountains grew cold. The light turned hazy and slow and seemed to drift out of the sky in deep, soft, silent layers that comforted like down.

Coll Ohmsford went home to Shady Vale to make certain Jaralan and Mirianna were safe and was surprised to discover that the Federation had lost interest weeks ago, abandoning the village and the elder Ohmsfords for more pressing concerns. The reunion was a joyful one, and Coll was quick to promise that he would not be traveling again for a long time.

Par Ohmsford and Damson Rhee journeyed north to Tyrsis and stayed long enough to determine that the Mole had indeed survived the Shadowen hunt to destroy him. Then they returned to Shady Vale to collect Coll. Par was already planning what they would do next. The three of them would open an inn somewhere north in one of the border cities of Callahorn where they would serve good food, provide a comfortable night's lodging, and on occasion entertain customers with stories and songs. Something had happened to the wishsong in the freeing of the land's magic at Southwatch. All it could

497

do now was what it had once done – create images. But that was enough for Par and Coll to tell the stories, just like before. Coll would resist leaving Shady Vale, of course. But Par thought he could talk him into it.

The Shadowen were gone from the cities of Callahorn, and there was a growing determination among the members of the population that the Federation occupiers should be gone as well. Almost immediately Padishar Creel began making plans for a free-born-instigated revolt that would drive the Southlanders from Callahorn for good. He told the men who aided him that his parents had once owned land in Callahorn. The Federation had imprisoned and then exiled them, and he had been given to an aunt to raise. He had never seen his parents, but he had heard that his father was commonly known as Baron Creel.

Morgan Leah kept his promise to Steff and went back into the Eastland to join the Dwarf resistance in its fight against the Federation. Matty Roh went with him, no longer wondering if she was making the right choice, no longer troubled by the ghost of Quickening. Morgan told her he wanted her to come. They would find Granny Elise and Auntie Jilt, and they would stay until the Dwarves were free again. Then they would return to the Highlands and he would show her his cabin in the hills. That was what he said, but she thought that maybe he was saying something more.

Wren Elessedil went back into the Westland as Queen of the Elves, mindful of her vow to see to it that the Elves resumed the old practice of going out into the Four Lands as healers. With Triss and Tiger Ty and now even Barsimmon Oridio backing her, she did not think the High Council would question her further. Her healers would come from among the Chosen. They would be caretakers not only of the Gardens of Life and the Ellcrys but of all the earth. They would not be accepted at first, but they would not give up. After all, it was not in the nature of Elves to quit.

The war with the Federation intensified for a while and then died away as the Southlanders began to withdraw back into their home country once more. Without the Shadowen to influence the Coalition Council, and with the defeat of their army at the Valley of Rhenn, interest in pursuing the war quickly began to fade. The uprisings in Callahorn and the Eastland led to growing dissatisfaction with the whole program of Southland expansion, and finally the Federation abandoned the outlying lands completely.

Time passed, and the seasons turned.

Paranor sat undisturbed through the fall and winter, rising up out of the shadowed forests that sheltered it, hemmed by the vast peaks of the Dragon's Teeth, a dark gathering of walls and parapets, battlements and towers. Now and again, travelers would pass by, but none dared enter the Druid's Keep. It was said by most to be haunted, a playground for the spirits, a crypt for the souls of Druids dead and gone. Some said a moor cat prowled within and sometimes without, as black as night, as big as a horse, and with eyes of fire. Some said the moor cat could speak like a man.

Within the Keep, Walker Boh slept the Druid Sleep undisturbed. Though his body rested, his spirit went forth often across the land, speeding on the wind to its far corners, riding the clouds and the backs of waves. Walker dreamed while he slept of things gone and of things to come, of what had been and of what should be. He dreamed of a new Druid Council, of a gathering together of the wisest men and women of the Races, of a pooling of knowledge that would let the Four Lands grow and prosper. He dreamed of peace. His dreams stretched farther than the journeys he embarked upon in spirit form, for there was no limit to what he could imagine.

Now and again, Allanon came to him. He was almost white now, a dark shade become a ghost, fading lines against the light. He spoke with Walker, but the words translated more as feelings than as thoughts. He was slipping farther and farther from the world of light and substance and deeper into the netherworld of afterlife. He seemed satisfied that he was leaving; he seemed at peace.

And sometimes, when Walker's heart was quiet and his mind at rest, Cogline would be there, too. The old man would draw close, his body a knotted collection of sticks, his hair wispy and tossed about, his features sharp and his eyes clear, and he would smile and nod. Yes, Walker, he would say. You have done well.

ARMAGEDDON'S CHILDREN

Terry Brooks

Armageddon's Children is the tale of the land that emerged from the *Great Wars* – which will eventually become one of the greatest worlds in modern fantasy. A fresh chapter in the legend is about to begin . . .

Fifty years from now, our world is unrecognisable. Pollution and warfare have poisoned the skies, the water and the soil. Pockets of society still exist, living in highly fortified strongholds, while those outside the walls roam the landscape – either predator or prey. But even these isolated compounds are not safe: armies of demons and once-men assault their defences, and inevitably, one by one, they succumb. Civilisation has fallen and anarchy is the only law.

Logan Tom and Angel Perez are the last two Knights to stand against the forces of chaos. These two extraordinary people have the ability to resist the dark tide, and to them will fall twin tasks: to find and protect a very old and a very new magic. They are humanity's last hope. Although the odds are stacked against them, Logan and Angel have the power to halt the destruction of the Old World. It will be up to others to usher in the New . . .

ARMAGEDDON'S CHILDREN

Terry Brooks

Armageddon's Children is the tale of the land that emerged from the Great Wars – which will eventually become one of the greatest worlds in modern fantasy. A fresh chapter in the legend is about to begin . . .

Fifty years from now, our world is unrecognisable. Pollution and warfare have poisoned the skies, the water and the soil. Pockets of society still exist, living in highly fortified strongholds, while those outside the walls roam the landscape – either predator or prey. But even these isolated compounds are not safe; armies of demons and once-men assault their defences, and inevitably, one by one, they succumb. Civilisation has fallen and anarchy is the only law.

Logan Tom and Angel Perez are the last two Knights to stand against the forces of chaos. These two extraordinary people have the ability to resist the dark tide, and to them will fall twin tasks: to find and protect a very old and a very new magic. They are humanity's last hope. Although the odds are stacked against them, Logan and Angel have the power to halt the destruction of the Old World. It will be up to others to usher in the New . . .

RUNNING WITH THE DEMON

Book One of The Word and the Void

Terry Brooks

It is the beginning of the hottest July in decades, and two men have come to Hopewell, Illinois. One is not human, a dark servant of the Void, who will use the anger and frustration of the community to achieve a terrible secret goal.

The other is John Ross, a Knight of the Word. While he sleeps, he lives in the hell the world will become if he fails to change its course on waking. John Ross has been given the ability to see the future. But does he have the power to change it?

At stake is the soul of a fourteen-year-old girl and the lives of the people of Hopewell. And that's just the beginning. This Fourth of July, while friends and families picnic in Sinnissippi Park and fireworks explode in celebration of freedom and independence, the fate of humanity itself will be decided . . .